dirty
IT UP

AMELIA BOND
ELIZABETH BROWN
ELIZABETH KELLY
AUBREY BONDURANT
RAMONA GRAY

Naughty Temptation

Amelia Bond

Chapter One

Kelsey

Returning to my hometown over the holidays was like taking a glimpse back in time to my childhood. I got to stay in my old room and partake in our Christmas traditions with my father. Best of all, I had absolutely no obligations when it came to school work or deadlines. Since this was my senior year at the University of Texas in Austin, I recognized that these days were coming to an end. Soon enough I'd have the responsibility of a job, bills, and everything else that came from adulting. But until then, I'd gladly enjoy one more winter break where I could spend my time in yoga pants and my school's sweatshirt, like every other American college girl.

I checked my phone as I made my way towards baggage claim in the Seattle airport. I was anxious to see my Dad. He'd be here to pick me up as always and tell me what he always did which was I was beautiful like my Mom. She'd died when I was three, but from the pictures, I had the same sandy brown hair and light green eyes as she did.

I walked past the security point of no return and out to the main terminal, where there were hordes of people greeting their loved ones coming in for the holiday. But there was no sign of my Pops. I glanced back at my phone screen. Not that he was much on texting, but he'd send the occasional one if he was running late or needed something. I always had to laugh, as he treated texting like he was writing a letter.

Dear Kelsey. This is Dad. I'm running late. Love, Dad.

It was no use explaining this stuff to him. My dad was just a dork like that. But no such text had come this time.

"Kelsey. Kelsey over here."

I turned at the voice calling out and saw the familiar face of our long-time neighbor and my father's best friend Jim.

"Hey, Jim. What are you doing here? Is my dad on a haul?"

My father was a truck driver who worked for Jim's trucking company. He often drove over the mountain pass to Eastern Washington, and sometimes he took extra gigs at the last minute. But I'd thought for sure he'd taken today off to pick me up. Plus, he always took Christmas Eve and Day off. It was tradition.

Jim looked uncomfortable with the question. My curiosity instantly morphed into fear. "He's okay, right?"

He swallowed hard. "Why don't we get your bag and talk in the car?"

He tried to turn to walk away, but I grabbed his arm. "Why don't you tell me now." I wasn't normally a brat in demanding my way, but his not answering my question with a resounding no, was starting to freak me out.

"Honey, your father had a heart attack this morning."

Blood rushed from my head as my chest pounded. "What? Is he - oh God, is he…?"

"He's in surgery. Double bypass." He glanced at his watch. "He should be out shortly. They said it would be about four hours."

Four hours? What could they be doing for four hours? "I need to see him."

"I'll take you straight there. I promise." He went on to explain my father had complained of chest pains that morning while in the office doing some paperwork.

After gathering my suitcase from the conveyer belt, which seemed to take an eternity, we walked out curbside. "Aren't you parked?" I asked, assuming we'd be heading for the garage.

"No, we figured it would be faster to have Scott pick us up here. Ah, there he is. We're in the red truck."

Scott was his son who was four years older than me. He'd been a senior while I was a freshman. Although he'd been homecoming king worthy back then, the man that stepped out of the truck made that boy look like chopped liver. We'd grown up next door to one another without a lot in common, except for the fact that our dads hung out all the time. He'd had a steady girlfriend all through high school, and had gone off to college by the time that I had started to notice boys were cute. But now, Scott Turner was all man. He had grown up, and as he got out of the truck I got to see how tall he'd gotten. He was definitely at least six-foot two, with broad muscular shoulders, and judging from the way he tossed my suitcase into the back of the truck with ease, some strong muscles.

"Hey, Kels," he greeted. His eyes were familiar, but soft, given the circumstances.

"Hey, Scott," I said, momentarily caught off guard. He looked too good in his hunter green Henley, with dark wash jeans and brown boots. Then I seemed to remember not only my brain, but the fact we were rushing to see my father in the hospital. Time to lust over the neighbor boy would certainly have to wait. I chalked up my physical reaction to the fact that I hadn't seen him in years. He'd been away on the East Coast getting his Master's Degree the last few years, and the last I'd heard was that he'd landed a job with Morgan Stanley.

We drove in silence on the way to Harbor View Hospital, which was a twenty-minute drive if traffic cooperated. Thankfully it did, even with the heavy fog settling in the area. Jim had updated me with what details he had. But I could scarcely listen to him. All I could think about was needing to see my dad.

❧ ❧

Finally, after what seemed like hours, but really was only twenty minutes, we arrived at the hospital. Jim took the lead in inquiring about my father. The receptionist said he was indeed out of surgery and in the ICU. We followed the nurse as she walked us to the elevator that led to the recovery room. It was eerily quiet when we went through the doors, with the beeping of machines and the quiet murmur of nurses at the desk the only noise.

My dad was my rock. He was a large man at six-foot tall, and probably had a good fifty extra pounds on him, but he'd never smoked, and seemed to eat somewhat healthy compared to some of the other truckers who were constantly shoveling down fast food. He'd always been strong, seeming bigger than life. So, to see him in a hospital bed, looking pale and weak was jarring. I stopped so suddenly, Scott ran straight into my back when I froze at the door. If I hadn't been so shocked, I may have appreciated his hands on my hips along with his broad chest pressed up against my back. Instead, all I could do was stare at my father looking lifeless in the bed. I wasn't even aware that Scott had moved to my side and put a comforting arm around my shoulders.

"Kels. He's gonna be all right," he whispered.

I blinked back the tears, finding my voice and meeting his eyes. "How do you know?"

"Because he's strong, and stubborn." He smiled a little, making me realize it wasn't just hard on me seeing him this way. It was difficult on anyone who knew my Dad and the big impression that he left with everyone that he came into contact.

"Can he hear me?" I approached the bed, trying not to let my emotions overwhelm me.

Jim answered from behind us. "The doctors said he was heavily sedated, but should be coming out of it soon. Go ahead, talk to him. Maybe it will help him to come around faster."

I took a deep breath and sat down on the single chair beside the bed trying to ignore all of the tubes coming out of the only family I'd had for most of my life. Reaching over, I touched his hand. "Pops, can you hear me? It's me Kelsey." I looked up to Jim and Scott as if they'd tell me whether or not he could understand.

"How about we give you some privacy. We'll just be outside," Jim offered.

I didn't want them to go, but asking them to stay felt like an imposition. Scott hesitated while his father went out of the door. His honey brown eyes focused on me. "You want me to stay?"

"I'm okay. Do you mind getting a doctor I can talk to?"

"Not at all. Let me go find someone."

Turning back towards my father once the door closed, I rubbed my fingers over his cold hand. The sounds of the machines helping him to breathe filled the space.

"I'm here. I flew in this morning and Jim picked me

up along with Scott."

I went on talking about classes and the foggy weather. All things he would've asked me in the car if he'd picked me up as planned. I felt like I was blabbering, since he couldn't answer back. I examined his face. When would he wake up?

"Daddy," I whispered. I hadn't used that word since I was a little girl, but now I was feeling the need. "Please wake up. We're supposed to hang the lights and decorate the tree, bake cookies and eat Thai food on Christmas, because we can't be bothered to make a turkey. Not trying to put a time frame on this, but I need you to be okay by Christmas Eve. Okay? Please?"

I hadn't realized Scott had stepped back in, this time with a man in a white coat who I hoped was the doctor.

"Are you Kelsey, the next of kin?" He was so matter of fact. What was it about *next of kin* that had the ability to send a shiver up your spine. It was so clinical and death like.

"I'm his daughter yes."

He narrowed his eyes, flicking a glance to Scott before asking me. "Are you of age?"

"Yes." I put my temper in check at his scrutiny. Now wasn't the time.

However, when he turned to Scott to ask the same question as if he was my guardian, I lost it. "What exactly do I need to be of age for? Smoking? Yes. I'm over eighteen. Drinking? Yes, I'm over twenty-one. Renting a car? I'm not quite twenty-five. But getting information from my father's doctor to find out what's going on with him? Absolutely I'm old enough."

He reddened. "Sorry, I just, well you look young."

I got that a lot, but right now I didn't have the patience for it. "I'm almost twenty-two. Can you please tell me what is going on with my dad?"

"Yes. Uh, the patient."

I cringed at his clinical use of the word, but listened as he went on to say he'd suffered a heart attack, that he had two blockages and they'd done the emergency bypass surgery. They expected he'd be waking up in the next half hour, but would need to stay in the ICU for at least the next five days. In other words, we'd be lucky to have him home in time for Christmas in a week's time.

"You want to go to the house?" Scott asked as soon as the doctor left.

I would have loved to take a shower, but I'd rather be here when my dad woke up. "Uh. No. But you don't have to wait. I can get an Uber or something."

He frowned. "I'll ask my dad if he wants to stay. Do you uh-want to get coffee in the meantime?"

I fought a yawn almost as if on cue. I could use the caffeine. "Coffee would be great." I walked with him towards the cafeteria, running into his father along the way. There was a strange look that passed between them. The kind that said they were keeping something from me.

"What's going on?"

"Nothing," Jim replied too quickly.

Scott leveled him with a look. "She deserves to know."

"Stay out of it son."

"Know what?" I asked.

Scott sighed. "Let's get coffee, then we'll talk."

His father seemed to relent. "You make sure you tell her what we discussed."

"Can someone please tell me something here." I was getting aggravated, being talked about as if I wasn't there was testing my patience again.

"I will. Come on, Kels." Scott led the way to the cafeteria.

Why did I have a feeling this wasn't going to be good?

Chapter Two

Scott

My immediate reaction upon seeing Kelsey Wegman was shock. The little girl from next door had turned into a real beauty. One who was unfortunately greeted with the worst kind of news. Like me, she only had her father. Our fathers were as close as brothers. The thought of losing either one of them was disconcerting. Now as we walked towards the cafeteria, I had to deliver a different kind of news. The kind that I knew in her position I'd want to know about, but wouldn't be happy to hear.

"Okay Scott, spill it. What's going on?"

At least she didn't beat around the bush. Her green eyes leveled with mine, a dusting of freckles across the bridge of her nose hinting still at her youth. "It's your father. He doesn't have medical insurance."

Her eyes rounded like saucers. "What do you mean? He works for your father's company, of course he has insurance."

I absolutely hated this. Because what I was about to say would break her heart. "He opted out. We didn't know until he was admitted this morning. He hasn't had insurance in three years."

"But why? Why would he do that?"

"I don't know. Do you have insurance?"

"Yeah, they have this school program because there's a hospital there. He told me I should sign up. Oh shit. It was three years ago. Why would he do that?"

"Probably to avoid the premiums, to save money."

"But why?"

I waited. Waited for it to sink in. It didn't take long. "For my tuition. Three years ago. The timing. Crap. Why didn't I see it? But he said he had a college fund for me."

"My dad and I were discussing it, and this is the part we want you to know. We'll pay for the hospital bills, whatever it takes."

She was already shaking her head. "That's very generous, but we couldn't possibly. I can um, I can see about getting a line of credit on the house."

I winced and knew the moment she saw it.

"What? What else?"

"There's already a second mortgage on it."

"But, but I thought it was close to being paid off." She stood up pacing. "This whole time he said that everything was covered. He kept going on about how proud he was for his little girl to be the first in his family to go to college. He said even with the out-of-state tuition that it wasn't a problem. He lied."

"I'm sorry. My dad didn't agree with me telling you this part, but I'd want to know if I were in your shoes."

She leveled me with a look. "Are you kidding? I definitely want to know. First things first, I'm withdrawing from school. Then I'll need to start working. Well, obviously I'll ask your father for a job. I mean I have my CDL and can drive my dad's routes for the next few weeks."

"Whoa, whoa, you can't withdraw. You're a semester away from graduating."

She shrugged. "This is more important. I can finish locally at a university this summer maybe."

"I can't let that happen, and you can't work for my dad."

"Why not?"

"Because I'm the one in charge of operations. I'm running the company right now." At least temporarily, as I'd agreed to try it for my dad's sake. Ultimately, I had no interest in taking over my father's business, but I knew it meant a lot to him to at least give it a go for a couple months, before I made a final decision.

"I thought you were living in New York?"

"I'm on hiatus. The trucking business is under my control for the moment." I wondered if she could see the regret in my eyes.

Her eyes simmered with temper. "You would seriously dump all of this on me and yet won't give me a job?"

Shit. I hadn't thought this through, because I knew in a heartbeat my father would have. "I don't want you to quit school. Like I said, my father and I will cover - "

She put her hands on her hips. Hips that I might add were in perfect proportion to her shapely thighs all encased in black yoga pants. "Would you take it? If the positions were reversed would you take the money? Would you go back to school knowing your father had mortgaged the house and gone without medical coverage, to be able to pay the tuition."

She had me there. "No. I wouldn't."

"Then let me drive my father's truck. I'll take his routes for the next couple of weeks. If I don't do something to help pay the bills, I'll go crazy."

I sighed. "He'll go crazy knowing that you're trying to work it off."

"Then we don't tell him. We just say I'm doing some routes for the holidays. I drove with my dad last summer, and the one before that. This would be no different, except I'd do the routes solo."

Yeah with the exception that she was now my responsibility, and I didn't like thinking of her out on the roads alone. Which was sexist I realized as there were plenty of female truck drivers. But just the thought of her, out on the road with all of those guys, made me tense with a strange protectiveness. They'd be all over her.

"I'm sorry. The answer is still no." Even as the words left my mouth, I knew I was in for a fight.

Chapter Three

Kelsey

"You know what? You're aren't the only trucking company in town." With that I spun on heel, about to walk away. Instead I felt my arm being tugged back.

"Wait. You can't just go and work for any company. There are some less than reputable ones out there."

I was aware of that, just as I was aware that his hand was still on my arm, and I was inches away from him. "Actually, I can. My dad still owns his truck, right?"

He ran a hand through his hair, drawing my attention to his sexy forearms. Somehow, I don't remember college boys having muscular forearms. You know the ones with veins visible and real man hair covering them.

"Yes. He still owns his truck."

"And it's in working condition, right?"

"It's older, but still gets the job done."

"Great. That means it could get the job done for anyone."

"Fine. I'll let you drive some routes on one condition."

I raised a brow almost afraid to ask what they'd be. "What?"

"I drive with you for the first couple of runs, to make sure that you can safely drive. It's been awhile since you've driven, and winter is challenging. After that, I'll make sure someone else is on your route at all times too, and no overnights."

"That sounds like an excessive number of conditions. This isn't my first time driving."

"Think of them as A, B, and C. And it's a take it or leave it kind of deal."

Not leaving me a lot of choice, as the scenario of trying to find another company hiring right before the holiday wasn't appealing, I took his hand in agreement. Ignoring the zing that came from the skin on skin touch and the warmth radiating through my body with it, we shook on it. "Fine. Deal."

"Let's go see your dad. Okay?"

I sighed. "You won't tell him that I know, right?"

He shook his head and motioned like a zipped lip with a key, making me laugh for the first time since he'd picked me up. "No, but my dad will want to. I'll convince him to wait though, until he's out of the hospital at least. He won't want to upset him right now."

I was relieved. "Good."

"Oh, hey, Scott. What are you doing here?" A female voice belonging to a very pretty blonde wearing scrubs came up behind us.

"Hey, Missy. I didn't know you worked here."

"Only over the winter break. Still in medical school at Stanford. Hoping after that to go out to the east coast to do a residency."

Missy Masterson. Scott's high school girlfriend. The homecoming queen to his king. The last thing I'd heard about Missy was that she was in medical school. She'd been a horrible mean girl in school to absolutely any girl she saw as a threat to her. Judging from the expression on her face as she turned towards me, not much had changed.

She thought I was the competition. That was hilarious.

"And you are?"

I didn't have time for this shit, and I wasn't about to get in a pissing match with Barbie in scrubs. I mean seriously, who looked that good in green scrubs? It was almost unfair. I swallowed. It had been less than a minute, but I didn't have time to spend taking a trip down memory lane. "I'm Kelsey. Uh, nice to meet you. I'm about to go see my dad though, so I have to go. See you later, Scott."

I didn't give either of them a chance to reply. Frankly I had more important priorities.

ॐ ✦

Back in my dad's room in the ICU, it took another hour for him to wake up. But to see his eyes focus on me was the greatest moment of relief that I had ever experienced. Thankfully they'd removed the breathing tube and he was now breathing on his own.

"Kelsey. You're here."

"I'm here, Dad." I lay down with my face on the bed next to him, feeling his hand stroke my hair. I tried unsuccessfully to hide the sobs.

"Don't cry sweetheart. My old ticker will live to see another day."

"It better. How's your throat? They said it may hurt from the tube you had in."

He swallowed hard. "It's fine."

Leave it to him not to be honest about how it was feeling. Always trying to protect me. Why didn't I see it sooner? "Liar," I chided softly. "I'll get you some ice chips and get the nurse in here to check on you."

I returned a short time later, but it was clear after a

few words that my dad was tired.

"How about you go home, honey, and come back in the morning. You must be exhausted with the trip."

The nurse piped in. "It would be better for him to get some rest too."

I hesitated, wanting to spend more time with him. Worried about being twenty miles away in case there were any complications. "Okay. I guess I'll see you in the morning."

The nurse seemed to read my mind, smiling kindly at me. "We'll call you if anything changes."

"Thanks."

I walked out, feeling exhaustion set in. It would be good to get a shower and grab a couple hours sleep. I hadn't eaten since early this morning and even then, it was only a Poptart. My stomach growled, clearly needing food. I figured my neighbors would be long gone by now, since it had been hours, but was surprised to see Scott in the waiting room.

"I drove my dad home, but figured I'd wait for you."

"You didn't have to."

"It's fine. It gave me a chance to catch up with Missy."

I bet. My eyes rolled before I could stop them, causing him to lift a brow.

"What's with the face? She said she was sorry to hear about your father."

I relented a little. People changed. Maybe she had. "Bad impression from high school. But maybe she's a nice person now. You guys planning to take a trip down memory lane?"

"We're having dinner tomorrow night. What do you mean about bad impression? She was a senior when you were a freshman. Everyone loved her."

I burst out laughing as we walked to the truck. "Uh no. Maybe you did. Most guys did, and maybe her clique of friends. But she was mean to every underclassman girl there was. One time she body checked my friend while she was just walking down the hall, because she thought she was checking you out. She made her drop her books and told her to keep her slutty eyes off of you."

He stopped in his tracks, looking astounded. "You're kidding."

"Nope. I'm not much on sugar coating things. Your ex-girlfriend was a real bitch in high school. Luckily, I only had one year of having to deal with her. And she had other slutty eyes to worry about, evidently."

"I'm at a complete loss. We dated for three years."

"Well I'm sure she was nice to you in all the very best ways." I laughed using my faux southern accent, as we continued to walk towards his truck.

On the twenty-minute drive home to Snoqualmie Falls, he spoke again. "You can skip a run tomorrow if you want to spend time with your father."

"How about I visit him in the morning, then go out on a run in the afternoon?"

"Okay. That's fine. We'll do a short one over to the east side."

"Sounds good. So, are you taking over your dad's business?"

"Maybe."

"Now there's a word that's loaded."

He glanced over while driving. "What do you mean?"

"I mean you worked in New York for the last few years. Now you're back home, and you *may be* taking over your dad's trucking business. Wait. Oh shit. Is he feeling okay?"

He was quick to reassure me. "Yes. Yes. His health is fine. Although not unlike your father, he probably wouldn't tell me if it wasn't. But uh, I needed a short break from New York."

Something told me he didn't reveal this tidbit to everyone. "I think I'd probably feel lost in the city. I love just knowing that I can drive to the mountains, ocean, or downtown, and it's all just right here. I like Texas and the big campus, but I've missed living close to home."

"Not owning a car there was weird, I missed driving."

"How long are you planning to be here then?"

"One month. Two tops. I've been back three weeks. But honestly, I'm not sure if running his company is what I want."

"Do you miss Wall Street?"

He shook his head. "Not really."

"I bet you looked good in a suit." Oops, hadn't meant to say that last part out loud.

He grinned. His trademark dimples still evident in his less boy, and definitely more manly face. "I doubt they'd go over well on the road."

"I don't know, Nell in dispatch might enjoy a change from the typical flannels and jeans." That woman had been around for forty years and was a fixture at the company.

He grinned. "As much as I love her, it wouldn't be worth the ration of shit from the guys."

"Probably not. So, you gonna start dating Missy again?"

He frowned. "Dinner, not a date, and what about you? College boyfriend?"

"Nope. Single. More fun that way." Considering I'd had one boyfriend in high school, I hadn't wanted the same sort of relationship to tie me down in college. Instead, I could be free to date who I wanted, and concentrate on school and football games. Go Longhorns.

"True. It was. Do me a favor and don't drop out of

college yet. Let's see how this week goes. At any rate, you have to go back to get your stuff anyhow."

I sighed deeply. "I don't know what to do."

"Think of it this way. You can help your dad a lot more with a degree, and you're a semester away. Get a college loan for it if you have to, but just don't drop out. It's tough to go back."

He was right on all accounts. "I'll have to think about it. Maybe I can get a loan."

Chapter Four

Scott

I'd felt terrible dropping Kelsey off at her house by herself. Of course, like a gentleman I'd offered to take her suitcase inside. But she'd waved me off, wheeling it to the front door and letting herself into the darkened house. It wasn't until I got inside of mine, that I realized she was probably starving. Telling myself it was only out of concern for her getting some dinner in her, I put some steaks on the grill and potatoes in the microwave.

After dishing up her plate, I left my dad some and went next door to knock. No answer. Pressing the doorbell, I couldn't hear anything. Thing was probably dead. Using the spare key, I opened the front door and called out. "Kelsey, it's Scott. You okay?"

Shit. What if she was crying. I could picture her sobbing in her bed. Putting the warm plate down on the kitchen counter, I went straight for her bedroom door which was slightly ajar. But instead of discovering her on her bed crying, she was in nothing but a towel, bopping to the music.

"Kelsey."

She turned quickly, eyes wide, gripping the only

thing she had around her. A towel not big enough to be called decent. "Jesus, Scott, you about gave me a heart attack." She covered her mouth quickly. "Oh my God, I can't believe I said that. I didn't mean to. That's horrible because my dad just had one."

I was already shaking my head. "It's okay, Kels. It's a figure of speech. A poorly timed one, but I knew what you meant. Uh, I brought you um - dinner. Thought you might uh - be hungry." Jesus, I was a twenty-five-year-old man who had in fact seen his share of women naked. Yet this one was wreaking havoc on both my senses not to mention my verbal prowess.

"That's really thoughtful. Give me a second to put on some clothes."

"Yep." I spun on heel, practically groaning at the fact she was naked under that scrap of terry cloth. I wasn't supposed to be lusting over my neighbor. My very young, still a college girl, father's best friend, who worked for the company that I may or may not take over some day's, daughter.

She came out in one-minute flat, dressed in a sweatshirt and shorts that did nothing for my thoughts about her, considering her legs were tan, toned and way too exposed for December. "Uh, won't you get cold?"

"Nope. I'm good. You want something to drink? I have water, or looks like Dad has some beer. Oh, wait, you only brought my plate. Sorry. It was nice of you to drop it off."

I should tell her to have a good night. Go home and eat dinner with my dad who was most likely watching Monday night football. "Um, let me grab mine. I'll be right back."

Her face lit up. "Okay. Sounds good."

When I returned she was waiting on me to dig into her food. "Eat up. It's not anything fancy, but meat and potatoes always hits the spot."

As she cut off her first piece of steak, I almost had to adjust myself under the table with the look of bliss that came over her face.

"This is amazing. I haven't had steak in forever."

"Glad you like it. I missed barbequing in New York."

She locked her eyes on mine across the table. "So, what happens if you decide you don't want to run your dad's business?"

"I don't know, to be honest. I thought about - " I stopped myself never having voiced my feelings out loud on this subject.

Of course, she wasn't about to let it drop. "Thought about what?"

"Starting my own firm. Doing investments for individuals, not corporations. Setting up trusts, estate planning and college funds." She sighed, and I realized my misstep. "Sorry, Kels, I didn't mean to remind you."

She smiled sadly. "Not your fault. Think of it this way, you could advise people like my father, how to invest and save for college instead of having to mortgage their house, or give up health insurance." She took one last bite before getting up from the table and putting the remainder in a container to save for later.

"What about you? What's after college?"

"That's easy. I want to be a teacher." I loved the way she was back to smiling with the thought.

"In Texas?"

"Nope. Probably back here. Somewhere close."

I found it curious she wanted to move back home, but held my tongue.

"Yeah. What grades?"

"Probably fourth. Old enough where I'm not wiping a butt, but young enough that they're not dicks."

I threw my head back and laughed. "You'd be the pretty teacher all the boys would want."

She blushed at my compliment.

"Uh, so I should get back home. I can drive you to see your dad tomorrow. Matter of fact you should put my number in your phone. Just in case."

She typed it in as I gave her the numbers. "I've got his car for rides. But I'll see you at the office tomorrow. Should I call you boss?"

A naughty thought popped in my head of bending her over my desk which was a big fat mayday. Abort mission. Leave and do not pass go.

I said goodnight and got the hell out of there.

Chapter Five

Kelsey

As nice as Scott had been yesterday, he was the complete opposite today as we were on the wet roads of Seattle, driving to the East side with him in the passenger seat. He gave new found meaning to the term 'back seat driver' by barking out directives on my driving.

"You need to go wider on that turn. Check your mirrors. Watch how you pump the brakes. If you wear them out before you hit the pass, you'll have a runaway truck."

I gritted my teeth. The bright spot of the morning had been seeing my father who was drinking chicken broth and sipping Sprite and, looking better than he had yesterday. He had a long recovery ahead, but at least his signs were better. He hadn't been thrilled with me driving his route today, until I'd mentioned Scott would be with me. That seemed to please him immensely. I tried to take the insult in stride. I was a girl, but I could drive a big truck. Hell, I'd grown up around one my whole life. Every summer I would go with my dad driving a semi-truck. He'd coached me through the nuances of driving but never once had my dad grumbled like Sir Barks-A-Lot.

"Jesus, Kelsey, watch your lane. You're over the line on my side."

Maybe it was the truck trying to get away from him too.

"I heard that."

"What?" I glanced over innocently not having realized I'd said the words under my breath.

"I'm only being hard on you because the road conditions aren't easy. Wet roads are dangerous. Snow around here is treacherous since nobody seems to know what to do in it, and the plows are all environmental and shit with rubber tips, which means they don't get the slush."

I smiled as my dad often complained of the same. Welcome to Seattle. Tree huggers paradise. "I'm aware." I wanted to say it had been months since I'd driven a semi, and to cut me a break. But, I didn't want to give excuses to support his criticism, even if I did find the set of his jaw sexy, I was more irritated with the way he kept commenting on my driving.

Once in Bellevue, I tried to park at the loading dock. For the record, it only took me two attempts. But Scott made it sound like a monumental error. I was fried, on the verge of hitching back home and trading in my driving credentials for a strippers' pole. The only problem with that was that I had terrible white girl rhythm, virtually no upper body strength, and it would most likely give my dad another heart attack.

Plus, it was cold outside, and I doubted I would get paid to be in a puffer jacket, twirling around. Which meant I needed to put on my big girl panties and get in the truck with Scott again. It didn't help that he smelled good. The critical devil really shouldn't sit near me wearing sexy smelling cologne that made me weak in the knees.

"Ready?"

"Yep," said lamb to the lion. Okay I was exaggerating and being a bit overdramatic. In my defense I was a twenty-one-year-old girl. It's what we did. And I'd almost started to believe I'd been too sensitive until he started barking again.

"Did you check your mirrors? Watch this side. You're cutting it close."

If his goal was to get me to quit before I started doing solo runs, he was making a very good case for it. But thankfully, traffic cooperated, and we were back at the truck yard before I decided I'd had enough of his criticism and jumped out on I-90, willing to take my chances with a tuck and roll into on-coming traffic.

"You planning to see your dad?" he asked, the minute we jumped down off the truck.

Back to nice guy? What the hell? "Yeah. I thought I'd have dinner with him. Although he's on a liquid diet and begging for me to sneak him contraband. I told him that's what got him into this mess. You uh, want to come?"

Because *nice guy Scott* was actually fun to be around. *Back seat driver - AKA boss man*, not so much.

He gripped the back of his neck with one hand, checking his watch with the other. "I can't. I have a thing tonight. Dinner."

"Right. With Missy."

His eyes studied mine. "Yeah. But we'll plan on doing this again tomorrow. You did well."

That was doing well in his eyes? Here's hoping I survived tomorrow.

෧ ෨

After my drive from hell with Scott, I went straight to

the hospital. My dad looked much better by the time I arrived. I'd brought some Miso soup for both of us, and he brightened up as if I'd just given him a chocolate sundae. I suppose it seemed exciting compared to the Jell-O or chicken broth he'd been eating.

"How was the drive with Scott today?"

"It was okay. He's quite verbal with suggestions."

"Good, good."

Clearly, he'd missed my sarcasm. Oh well, I didn't want my complaining to get back to Scott's dad anyway. It wasn't as though he was a total dick. Just while driving.

We visited for a couple hours which included a game of Go Fish, since I didn't know any other card games, and he seemed amused at my suggestion. The doctor came in, a different one this time, who thankfully didn't think I was too young to hear about my father's long-term plan. He indicated that Dad might not be able to come home until New Years. It was disappointing, but after the scare of losing him, I'd take any scenario that had him coming home at all.

I said goodbye with a promise to visit tomorrow after my drive. It was easier to get that out of the way first, then come in. Plus, I had promised him beef and barley soup for tomorrow.

Pulling up into my driveway, the first thing I noticed was that Scott's truck was not parked in his. It shouldn't bother me, but Missy had been everything that I wasn't. She was popular, rich and gorgeous. Oh yeah, and she was a bitch. The thought of Scott with someone as calculating as her left me cold. But then again, it wasn't my business. I told myself I didn't care.

Which is why checking out of my bedroom window for his truck every fifteen minutes was super annoying. Finally, at ten o'clock, I decided to turn in with visions of Scott staying the night at Missy's house. If he came to work in yesterday's clothes, I was kicking him out of the truck.

Chapter Six

Scott

Dinner with Missy had been weird. Of course, she'd looked the same as she had in high school. But she'd done nothing but go on and on about New York. How much she loved the city. How much she couldn't wait to escape back to the big city. It was a reminder that I had, and yet, here I was, back home.

I couldn't shake the thought that somehow returning here made me feel like I had failed. Forget that I never really liked New York. Everyone knew I'd left after high school. Now everyone was aware that I was back. They all assumed that the move was temporary, and I hadn't wanted to think about the possibility of anything else.

After dinner and an awkward goodbye, since Missy had invited me over to her place and I'd declined, I went to see George, Kelsey's dad in the hospital. He was awake, and I simply wanted to let him know that I was looking out for his little girl on the runs that she'd been doing. Thankfully, he thought it a great idea. I stayed an hour, then drove around to the west side of the city. It was a fantastic view to pull into the waterfront and see the illuminated city of Seattle. I'd missed it. So why couldn't I feel settled now that I was back here?

Waking up the next morning, I was anxious to get to work. I told myself it had nothing to do with seeing Kelsey and spending most of the day in her company. She'd been a trooper yesterday. I knew that I'd been hard on her, but I wanted to ensure that she'd be safe on the roads. Even if that meant I'd gone a bit overboard to make sure that I put on the boss's hat and not that of friend and neighbor. I especially didn't want to come off as the guy who was having a hard time getting her green eyes out of his head.

I practically growled when I saw her in the dispatch room with four men gathered around her. Three were her father's age, but one guy was in his twenties. And he was giving her an unmistakable look of appreciation. Then again, she was dressed in skinny jeans, which once again, were doing nothing to hide the shape of her ass or legs. I couldn't blame him, I appreciated the view too.

When I walked up, she was talking about her dad. My expression softened. Of course, everyone wanted to know about her father. He'd been driving at this company for forty years.

"You ready?" I asked, fighting the urge to put my hand on her back, and as if we were together. *Dangerous* should be stamped across her forehead to remind me.

"Yep. Let me get my backpack and coat."

I met her outside. Her father's truck was one of the older ones, which worried me if she were to get a run that took her over the pass. We needed to do one tomorrow, and with the holiday coming up, I couldn't keep driving with her. She'd have to start making some solo runs, so I could drive as well to alleviate the over flow. Perhaps I could talk her into taking one of my father's newer trucks.

"Tomorrow we'll run the pass. Thought we'd take my newer rig."

"Why?" She climbed into the cab and glanced over.

"Better heating. Newer. Safer."

"Yeah, but I like driving my dad's truck. It's comfortable. Plus, it reminds me of him, you know?"

I did know, and decided to drop it. It wasn't worth fighting about, especially since she wouldn't be taking any overnight routes if I could help it. I'd talk to Nell when I got back to ensure it.

"Okay. Just thought I'd offer."

We'd gotten onto the highway before she spoke again. "How was your dinner with Missy?"

"Fine." I didn't mention that Missy had sent me a text this morning, asking if I wanted to go to her holiday party on Friday night. I should say yes, as she'd indicated she really wanted a date, since she didn't know anyone at the hospital. So then why hadn't I responded to her yet?

"Hey, make sure you're signaling longer. Not everyone sees you." The routine of me pointing everything out to her had begun.

After driving a few more hours, I realized either I'd crossed the threshold of constructive criticism with Kelsey or she was biting her tongue. She was uncharacteristically quiet while we sat in gridlock on the way back from our run four hours later. There was nothing like the last five miles taking forty minutes with traffic.

"Everything okay with your dad today?"

"Yep. Fine. Oh, so uh, I have an awkward question for you."

It was adorable the way she was biting her lip. Like she was nervous. "Shoot."

"Is there a policy on dating people on the job? Like whether it's allowed."

Both of my brows shot sky high while my mouth formed into a grin. Was she about to ask me out? "Not that I'm aware of. Why?"

"Andrew asked me out for dinner on Friday."

Oh. That sneaky bastard. I knew he'd been looking at her a little bit too familiarly. "And you said yes?"

"Not yet. I told him I'd have to see about things with my dad first."

"There probably isn't a policy in the handbook, given that it was written in the eighties before women worked at the company, well except for Nell, but let's just say I don't think she's ever been asked out by the men." Most were afraid of the older, eccentric lady with a two-pack a day smoking habit, present company included. I'd seen her chew out a three-hundred-pound man for filling out his paperwork incorrectly a few too many times. No one screwed with Nell.

"Good."

"I didn't say it was okay though. What if you two have a falling out? Then there could be drama at work."

She laughed. "It's just dinner, and something to do while I'm home."

My phone buzzed. Taking it out, I sighed at Missy's name. She needed to RSVP if I was coming or not. I typed out that I would be there. Might be nice to wear one of my over-priced suits again for an evening.

"Fine. It doesn't matter."

She looked a little hurt with my half-ass reply. "Good. Glad we have that straight."

Chapter Seven

Kelsey

Could I help it if maybe I'd wanted him to be a little jealous? Remember, twenty-one-year-old girl here. Wanting to get the attention of the hot neighbor boy was a given. But he'd answered his text and hadn't thought twice about me going out with Andrew. Not that was the reason I would say yes. Andrew was cute and funny, and what was the harm in sharing pizza and talking about stuff with someone whose company you enjoyed? It wasn't as if I was looking for anything serious. Besides. Scott probably had plans with Missy. God, even thinking of her name elicited an eye roll. Maybe she'd changed now that she was studying to become a doctor and she had to look out for other people. Secretly, I sort of hoped not though, because it was easier to hate her if I didn't know she saved lives.

Arriving back in the yard, I filed my paperwork with Nell, gave her a wave, then texted Andrew that Friday would be great. Because God only knew that if I had texted while at a full stop in the truck, Scott would've had a conniption fit. I would definitely have been on the receiving end of a lecture about texting and driving, even if I had texted while stopped in gridlocked traffic, going nowhere. Grabbing my stuff, I headed out to pick up soup, then dropped in to see my Dad.

After a three-hour visit, I pulled into my driveway close to ten pm. Scott's truck was parked next door, not that I cared. Again, because, if I said it enough, I might even convince myself?

The house felt dark and lonely, the exact opposite of festive. But just the idea of decorating, not knowing if my father would be home for the holiday was depressing. On top of that, I had the pass run early in the morning with Scott. Hmm, were headphones legal while driving? The thought of jamming to my music and drowning out the asshole side of him sounded like bliss. It also would have my butt waiting tables, instead of driving, in no time flat.

I hummed, surveying the contents of the refrigerator. I needed to get to the store. Popping the top off one my dad's Pabst Blue ribbon cans, I whispered cheers to myself. Never knock the classic taste of PBR, because it tasted fan-freaking-tastic right about now.

The knock on the door surprised me, but not as much as Scott on the other side holding a casserole dish with two pot holders?

"I made chicken pot pie. Thought we could share?"

"Wow. Really? Yeah, come in." I was about to make a comment about Betty Crocker, but stopped. The man brought me dinner. This wasn't the time to make fun of hot men bearing food.

"Where did you learn to cook like this?"

"New York. My roommate was an amateur chef. I picked up some pointers. This really just shredded chicken, veggies and biscuits, the Pillsbury kind on top."

"Sounds amazing. You want a beer?"

"Sure. How's your dad today?"

"Better every time I see him. Not so happy about the

food or his new lower cholesterol diet, but hey, bypasses don't come cheap." I cringed at the word. "Um speaking of which, your dad isn't picking up the medical bills is he?"

Scott shrugged, taking a sip of the beer, I handed him. "Beats me. But let them deal with that between them. Your father doesn't know you know, at least not that I know of. Damn that was a lot of knows."

I chuckled. "It was. I applied for a student loan yesterday. Need my dad to co-sign though, so I'm sure that'll go over well."

"I think if you tell him it's that or you withdraw, he'll sign. But then he'll know you know. Shit, there go the knows again."

I laughed fully this time, making him do the same. "I know."

We each took a seat at the small dining room table after I brought over plates and forks along with a spatula for serving.

"Wow this smells divine. I only had soup with my dad tonight, so I was starving."

"Good."

It was amazing. Not that I'd turn down a homemade biscuit, but the flaky, buttery kind from Pillsbury on the top made it mouth-watering. "It's delicious." But hot, oh so hot. I slugged back the beer to cool off the fire from my mouth. Still worth it.

"Thank you." He paused while eating his. "Where you going with Andrew on Friday night?"

I shrugged. "Don't know yet. But since he asked me out, one would hope that he will have an idea. Nothing annoys me more than to go on a date, and the guy's first words are "so what do you want to do tonight?""

He laughed. "Fair enough. What's your ideal date?"

This. Dinner with just the two of us. Him cooking, us sharing our day. "I'm not sure. Guess I haven't had one yet. I'd like it to be good conversation though, so a movie isn't ideal."

"No, I don't suppose it would be."

"Are you going out with Missy again?" If he was asking about my dating life, fair was fair, and I had free license to be nosey about his love life too.

"Yeah. On Friday. She has a holiday party at work."

"Oh. That's nice." But internally cattily thinking, and I'll bet that she'll look even better than she did the other day, when I saw her in scrubs. I'll bet he'll wear a suit, the kind that would make me want to rip it right off of him, with a tie that I wish was wrapped—nope.

Down girl. Stop fantasizing. Missy is filet mignon. I am, well chicken pot pie, comfort food. How appropriate, given that I practically lived in leggings, or skinny jeans if the leggings were dirty, topped with sweatshirts and accessorized with fancy footwear that consisted of Uggs or flip flops.

"For the pass run tomorrow, are you ready? They're calling for rain I think."

"It's Seattle, so they're always calling for rain. It'll be good. Well, at least the driving part."

He smirked. "I'm hard on you because I care."

I about spit out my drink. "Okay, Dad."

His smirk quickly faded into a frown. "You're doing fine."

"Huh. A compliment about my driving? I'm going to start wearing a wiretap, so I can play these rare moments back."

"I'm not that bad."

I quirked a brow. "You've never been on the receiving end of your barking every twenty seconds."

"It's not that often."

"I timed them. You know, in between wanting to brake check you into the dashboard."

He laughed out loud. "Ouch. That's harsh."

I shrugged. It wasn't untrue. "Worried about your pretty face?"

He took another bite, studying me over the table. "You think I have a pretty face?"

Shit. Walked right into that one, and now I was turning pink, as I could feel the heat flood my face. "It's not ugly, you know if you're into handsome - " oh no, think fast, I was sinking down a slippery slope, "guys who make really nummy - " I did not just say nummy, next thing you know I'll be rhyming it with tummy. "Uh, dinners."

He busted out laughing. "You're adorable. All pink. Especially your ears."

I tried to fake indignation. "I pay you a compliment and you point out my pinkness?"

"It's cute. That's a compliment."

Cute. Like a bunny. Who has pink ears. Life goals right there for a hot guy to think that way about me.

"What? You don't like to be called cute?"

"It makes me sound like a fluffy rabbit or a toddler. Neither of which is how I want you to see me."

He took a pull on his beer, studying me over the top. Suddenly the vibe seemed to have changed. "How is it that you want me to see you?"

Time to put up or shut up, and for heaven's sake, don't say, better than a pot pie. "As a grown woman?" Damn. It had been good until the question mark.

"What makes you think that I don't."

Words lay thick on my tongue, unable to get past my lips, and suddenly I was looking at his lips.

"What are we doing, Kels?"

"I don't know about you, but I was about to hop on your lap and kiss you." Now would've been a good time to exercise a filter. But that was the problem with talking to a boy you've known your entire life. Comfort equaled saying what was actually on your mind.

Waiting was excruciating. It was only a matter of seconds, but with rejection hanging in the balance, if felt much longer. Until he scooted his chair back, with enough room to do as I'd suggested. Holy shit. This was happening.

I stood up on shaky legs, taking the two steps that separated us, and sitting on his legs. Like I would with Santa. Only let's just hope I wouldn't be having these same naughty thoughts with the bearded guy. Damn.

"Hi," I greeted, sounding breathless, as I put my hands up on his shoulders. Hopefully he didn't think I was out of shape from the two steps.

"Hi," he returned, inches from my lips.

"Probably a good thing we both ate pot pie and had beer." Now why? Why did I have to go and say something that unsexy?

"Yeah."

Unable to stand it a second longer, I shifted, moving within a breath of his lips. The smell of him tickled my nose. His chest rose and fell faster now, while his hand moved up under my hair. I moved first, or maybe he did. When you're talking millimeters, who knows? His lips were soft, especially his bottom one which was incredibly kissable. I sucked it between my lips, tentatively, tasting, exploring and taking my time, as if this couldn't be real. A groan reverberated from his chest when I did it a second time, then he groaned again when I slipped my tongue inside of his mouth. Suddenly I was shifted, and a kiss that had started out sweet, turned hot in an instant.

Chapter Eight

Scott

I needed to stop this. Resist the naughty temptation that was now on my lap. That was the last thought I had before tasting her lips. She'd been tentative at first, but then she'd slipped her tongue inside of my mouth and ignited something in me. I turned her body so her thighs were now straddling me, which was a hell of a lot sexier than sitting on my lap like I was Santa.

But it also meant that my hands, which had no choice in the matter, were down now on her ass. I took over the kiss, coaxing her tongue to dance with mine, then moved my lips, kissing down the column of her throat.

Knocking. Why did I hear knocking? Blood may be running south, but my brain was still somewhat functioning enough to recognize that there was an intrusion.

"I think someone is at your door?"

"What?" she asked in a dazed voice, clearly just as into this kiss as I was.

"Knocking. I hear knocking."

"Maybe they'll go away."

She captured my lips again, quieting any objection I

may have had. God, she was growing bolder, and I in turn, was growing harder.

"Kelsey, Scott, you in there?"

"Oh crap, it's my dad."

"Wh-what?"

I put my hands on her hips, lifting her up gently before adjusting myself. "It's my dad's voice. He's at the door."

The moment it sunk in, her eyes got big. "Right. Uh, you stay here." Her glance flicked down to my lap. "And um, let things, you know, get back to normal, while I'll get it."

"Kay." My father was just outside of the door and the erection still wasn't fading. Fuck. Time to bring out the big guns. Time to think of Grandma. Worked like a charm, albeit, a bit slower than it normally did. Standing up, I took a deep breath hearing them talk at the front door. Thinking it might look weird if I didn't join them, I walked over.

"Hey, Dad, what are you doing here?"

"Sorry to interrupt, but uh your old girlfriend is next door."

"What?"

"She said she'd dropped by to help you pick out your suit for Friday."

I was instantly irritated, but not as much as Kelsey who bid good night to the both of us without so much of a backward glance. "I'll let you go then. Thanks for bringing dinner over. See you both tomorrow."

The right thing to do would've been to tell my father I needed a few minutes. Talk to Kelsey. Apologize. Explain that I hadn't invited Missy over. Something. But I didn't because at the end of the day, I shouldn't be doing this. Not only could it jeopardize things at work, it could potentially blow up with our father's forty-year friendship. In all, I reasoned the interruption was for a good reason.

❧ ❧

Kelsey

I became a complete voyeur looking out of the window and over at Scott's house ten minutes after he left me to go to Missy. Although I wasn't a virgin, having been with both my high school boyfriend, and someone I dated in college briefly, I didn't have a lot of experience dealing with this type of emotion. Jealousy. I'd done the breaking up with my exes after things had fizzled. Any other time kissing a boy, I had never even remotely felt the way that I had with Scott's kiss. Probably because he most definitely wasn't a boy. Nope. He was all man. Except for the way he ran out of here.

Maybe it was the girl in me, hoping he would've followed me into the kitchen, instead of going next door. Maybe a woman would've taken it on the chin like a champ. So he'd kissed me, big deal.

Except it was a big deal, and that, in and of itself, was dangerous. We were neighbors, but most importantly I was leaving to go back to college, while he most likely was going to do anything to keep from settling back in town. He may not know it, but I could tell he was concerned what other people thought of him returning home after years in New York City. My future was here, that much I knew. I loved the Pacific Northwest. I missed it while I was away, and had every intention of moving back here once I was done with college.

The next morning, I woke up early. Going over the pass in a single day meant a way-too-early-to-bother-doing-anything-to-my-face-or-hair-kind-of-day.
Laziness. It really is its own artform. Plus, I didn't want to look like I was trying too hard for Scott. The route from Seattle to Yakima over the mountains normally

took three hours by truck, if traffic and the weather cooperated. So that meant at least six hours in his company, and that was only in the truck.

It didn't help that I was tired. I'd spied on Scott's house until Missy left, roughly about thirty minutes after he'd departed my house. Ample time to pick out a suit I guess, but maybe not enough time to have slept with him. Then I stayed awake in my bed for a while, waiting for the knock that didn't come, and the text that didn't buzz.

Which mean that this morning was bound to be awk-freaking-ward. I smiled at Nell. The men may be afraid of her, but I adored her. From her bee-hive to her horn-rimmed glasses and smoker's voice, it was all authentic and timeless.

"Hi, honey. I went by and saw your father last night. He's looking good. Tried to get me to smuggle in a cheeseburger though." She rolled her eyes. "I told him they'd probably send me to hospital jail for doing that. Anyways, how are you holding up?"

"Good. Good. Thanks for going by there. It keeps him in good spirits. I'll visit again tonight. They said he should be out of the ICU by then. I know he probably still won't be home for Christmas, but here's hoping."

"I'll send up a little prayer. Now then, you're going to Yakima today, right?"

"Yes ma'am. I need to wait for Scott though."

She glanced up at me. "Actually, he came by this morning, and said you were doing it solo."

I should be thrilled. Relieved. Overjoyed at the prospect of not having him bark at me over the entire pass. But instead, I felt rage. Yes rage, residual from last night, but now bordering on slightly homicidal. I was joking, but I was pissed. I managed a tight smile. "Thanks, Nell. Have a great day."

Walking directly towards Scott's office, I realized I

had never been in it before. I didn't bother to knock. Instead, I barged straight in and closed the door behind me. He immediately glanced up at the intrusion, looking way too good for five-o'clock in the morning.

"Why am I going solo today?"

"Because you're ready."

Liar. "You didn't seem to think so yesterday."

His jaw clenched. Well clench away. I was far from finished. "In fact, your opinion seems to have changed since last night, after you left me to go get a suit picked out for you by Missy."

"I'm not doing this here, Kelsey, and this only serves as a reminder of why last night was a mistake. I'm sorry. I got carried away, and it won't happen again."

A punch in the stomach would've felt better. He was right, my coming in here was crossing boundaries. But mostly hearing him call our kiss a monumental mistake hurt like hell.

"Okay then. I'd better get going."

I turned away, already fighting the tears.

"Kels. Wait."

I kept my back to him, not wanting him to see my face. "It's fine, Scott. Hell, if I'd known kissing would get me out of driving with you, I'd have done it sooner. See ya later."

I didn't break stride, fully intent on making it to the truck so I could have a proper cry. Now that would be a strange site, young woman crying while driving down I-5 in a semi-truck. I'd just about made to the cab when I heard Andrew's voice.

"Hey, Kelsey. We still on for tomorrow? I thought we could go see the new Thor movie."

I gave him my best smile. And heck, seeing Chris Hemsworth and not chatting sounded like a dream about now. "Sounds terrific. Um, I guess after work, okay? Tomorrow I only have a short round trip up north."

"Yep. See you then. Be careful on the pass today. They're expecting snow this evening."

"Good to know. Yeah. See you then."

I'd be back in six hours, beating the snow without a problem.

Chapter Nine

Kelsey

You know what they say about best laid plans, because wouldn't you know it, I blew a tire. As in one of the really big truck tires. I put my hands on my hips viewing the damage to the outside back tire of the cab. Thankfully I was at least, not yet on the freeway when I noticed the change in the ride. The problem, however wasn't that I didn't know how to change one. Even though doing it in a semi-truck wasn't easy. The problem was the fact that the tire weighed three hundred pounds. At least I had the right tools to get the old one off, and I had the EZ spare kit that allowed me to get it down without having to lift the tire. Hell, if I didn't have the upper body strength to make it as a stripper, I sure as hell wouldn't be able to lift a gigantic tire.

By the time I'd managed to free the old tread and get the tire down, it had been an hour. It took another one to get the damn thing on the truck. Thank God for YouTube which was very helpful in giving me tips. I could see Scott now, with a stop watch yelling at me to move faster. It was probably a good thing for his health that he wasn't with me.

I hoisted myself back into the cab, chugging down some water. Calling Nell on the radio, I let her know about my two-hour delay due to the flat. Well three if you counted the extra hour it had taken to unload because they couldn't get the forklift up and working.

"All right, honey. But let me check the weather. You may need to stay put. Snow is moving in."

Crap, and of course, I hadn't brought my overnight stuff. I was sure my dad probably had an emergency kit in the back, but who knows what was in it?

"Okay. I'm going to head on to the nearest rest stop at the start of the pass. Should be able to gauge it better there. It's about forty minutes away."

"Roger that. I'll let you know."

I was torn. Did I pull into the Walmart up ahead and get some things, just in case, or should I just try to hurry and make it home? I could almost hear my dad say better safe than sorry, and made the decision to pull into the store's parking lot. A half hour later-because everyone was stocking up for the first snow of the season, I was back in my truck with a case of water, food and a couple of blankets, but I had lost time.

Getting back on the road, I was driving when my cell phone rang. Glimpsing down at the number, I shook my head. It was Scott, and I smelled a trap. If I answered it while driving, he'd flip. So, I let it ring, again and again. But what if it was about my dad? Surely, he would use the radio if it was important. Since I only had ten more miles to go until I was going to pull over, I figured I'd call him back.

Turns out I didn't have to. "Kelsey, are you there?" Scott's voice blasted over the radio. The problem with using this method of communication, however, was that anyone on the wave length could hear you.

"I'm here. About ten miles away from the rest stop."

"Can you pick up your cell phone please."

I could practically hear his gritted teeth on the other end, and because I was a brat, I replied with, "No can do, boss man. I'm driving. But I'll call you just as soon as the vehicle is no longer in motion and I have it safely pulled to the side."

He was going to kill me. But it would be the sort of death that left me smiling in the end at least.

వ ఈ

Scott

I was going to kill her, right after I made sure that she was safe. Giving the go-ahead to Nell to have her hold at the rest stop, I let my dad know that I was on my way over the pass. He only raised a brow when I told him why.

I never should have let her go alone. At least she'd had a spare tire, but what if she'd blown more than one. Technically, I could've called our roadside assistance guys. They were great. However, the thought of her stranded on the side of the highway scared me. Then again, so did the idea of her driving in the blinding snow over the pass.

Loading up my pickup truck with chains and other emergency supplies, I started cursing at myself. If I hadn't kissed her, I would've gone with her as normal today. But no, I'd gone and bailed, because I didn't want to face the reality that I wouldn't have stopped last night if it hadn't been for my dad knocking on the door, or having Missy show up unexpectedly.

What was up with Missy dropping by out of the blue anyway? I don't remember her ever being so insecure, but that's what last night felt like. She'd called, but I hadn't answered the phone, so she just decided to pop over. This wasn't high school, and she wasn't my girlfriend anymore.

Then to make matters worse, I'd gone and hurt Kelsey this morning. It made me sick to my stomach to replay the look on her face before she'd spun around. I'd been beating myself up for it all day. Now this. I was worried about her being caught in the snow unprepared. That warred with wanting to give her a lecture on her little stunt on the radio. But like all things Kelsey, I was learning that even that was adorable.

Finally, my phone rang, and her voice came through. "Hello. You wanted me to call."

"Yes. I did." Smartass.

"Are you operating your mobile device with the hands-free option?"

I activated the blue tooth, fighting a grin at her prim and proper voice. "Yes. Where are you?"

"Pulled into the rest stop right before the pass with about a hundred other drivers. Nell told me to hold. Place is packed. Where are you?"

"Driving. Look, I feel bad, Kels. I never should've let you go alone. I feel responsible and - "

"Stop. Just stop."

"What?"

"I don't want to have this conversation over the phone, and you're not responsible for blowing my tire or for making me late because of the forklift. And you're certainly not responsible for the weather."

"Okay. We'll talk in person."

"All right. Drive safe."

"Yeah. Do me a favor and stay in the cab of your truck. Please. There are too many people there, and I don't want anything to happen to you."

"Sorry, but a girl has to pee, and it won't be in the truck. I'll make it quick. Talk to you later."

Shit. That meant she was getting out of the truck with all those other truckers around. Stepping on the gas I couldn't get there fast enough.

❧ ❧

It took two hours to get to the rest area, the last part of which had been through snow pelting down. My truck with snow tires had done well, and the traffic had cooperated. Dialing Kelsey's number, I waited for her to pick up. She hadn't been exaggerating. Every truck on the east side needing to get back was up here.

"Hello."

"Where are you?"

"At the rest stop. I feel like we've already had this conversation."

"I mean where in the parking lot."

"Uh, over to the right next to a Safeway truck. Why, where are you?"

"About to park in back of you. See you in a couple of minutes."

Chapter Ten

Kelsey

He was here? While my head tried to wrap around that fact, my girlie parts were already rejoicing. Down girls. Had I even shaved this morning? Why? Why did these thoughts have to pop in my head? I'd gone from amazed he was here to automatically sleeping with him. I was mad at him, not having sex. No wonder boys had a hard time figuring out a girl if I could go to such extremes in such a short space of time.

There was a knock on the truck door which made me smile. "Come in, it's open," I called out, laughing full out when his grumpy, yet still handsome face, poked in.

"You didn't even check to see who it was, and you should have had your doors locked."

"No, no, no. You don't get to come in and bark at me. You hung up the phone five seconds ago, of course it's you. And, I unlocked it in that moment." Maybe not the latter, but I'd meant to.

"I'm not barking. I'm just - I need to get some things out of the truck."

"Like what?"

"Blankets, food, drinks."

I pointed to the back. "Got it all, although I guess you might want to get some stuff for yourself." Wait was he staying in here with me or in his truck?

"I'll be back. Lock the doors until I am."

I gave him a mock salute enjoying messing with him. Once he returned, I had to ask the question burning in my mind. "Why are you here, Scott?"

He instantly appeared uncomfortable. "Because I was worried. You didn't leave for an overnight strip and I assumed you wouldn't have any supplies."

"I'm a big girl and smart enough to know that I needed to stop and get some things, just in case."

"You lost time stopping at the store."

Exasperation. Boss Man Scott was kind of hot, but he was also a real jerk. "Would you rather I be here without anything? Better safe than sorry. I thought it was your motto."

"Fine."

"No. Not fine. You underestimated me. Say it."

I don't know who was more surprised with my bossy tone, but that had nothing on the shock I felt when he said these words. "I did underestimate you, and for that, I'm sorry. However, I still didn't want you up here alone. I felt guilty that I was supposed to have gone with you today. But - "

"You wigged out," I supplied, too aware of how close we were sitting in the cab of the truck. As the snow fell around us, the windows started fogging with the heater on, it felt as though we were cocooned in our own little world.

"I didn't wig out."

"Yeah you did. It's why you cancelled out on riding with me today."

"I may have let it affect my - "

"Wigged out." Now I was just being bratty.

He smirked. "Maybe. It was wrong in either case."

"So, what now?"

"Friends?"

"With benefits?" Hey, my girly parts made me ask.

He groaned, looking quite pained. "You are not a 'friends with benefits' kind of girl, Kels."

I was mildly offended. Not that I'd ever done it before. But how hard can it be? Have sex with your hot friend. It really didn't seem to have a down side. "How do you know. I could have lots of friends with er - benefits." Crap that sounded slutty, didn't it?

His laughter filled the cab. I held my breath when his hand reached out, tucking a piece of hair behind my ear. "I don't want to have *the talk* after something happens, to say that I don't want to hurt you. You're going back to college and I'm - well I don't know what the hell I'm doing."

He'd used air quotes, so I did the same. "I don't want to have *the talk* either." I certainly had more pride than to beg for sex or give him all the reasons why everything would be fine afterwards. Instead I decided to focus on other matters.

"So, friend. What kind of snacks did you bring. I'll show you mine if you show me yours."

❧ ❦

It turned out that I had all the good stuff. "Wow, the reveal was kind of a letdown to be honest. Clearly I have the better end of the deal here."

He chuckled at my double entendre. "I was in a hurry, and beef jerky and protein bars are acceptable snacks."

"Not compared to cheese puffs and chocolate bars they aren't. Plus, what the hell are these, Scott?" I held up the hot pockets. "Where were you gonna find a microwave?"

"Some of the newer trucks have them. In my defense, I sort of did a grab and go."

"Man, a truck with a microwave sounds fancy. So, um, where are you sleeping?"

"I thought I'd sleep in here to keep you warm. Conserve heat. We can't keep the truck running all night long. I brought two cold weather sleeping bags."

Two huh?

The heater in this truck wasn't the best, and my hands were already freezing from being outside earlier and from having to change the tire. It seems like once I'd caught a chill, I had never really warmed up. But it was near thirty degrees outside and we could always start the rig back up if it got too cold in the cab. Or, maybe my friend could warm me up.

Chapter Eleven

Scott

As soon as we laid down, I knew we were in trouble. The space was tight, so we were close to one another. Although we'd blasted the heat before turning off the truck, I could tell after only a few minutes in, that Kelsey was already cold.

"You okay?"

"Yep. You?"

"Fine." I rolled over and tried not to think of her right next to me. I'd lied when I said I wanted to just be friends. Hell, my erection was telling me differently right now, for sure. But it's what I should've wanted. Because it was better for both of us. No truer words had been spoken about my not wanting to hurt her.

I dozed off, but woke up from the sound of unzipping.

"Sorry I have to dash out and go pee."

"No. You can't go out now."

She leveled me with a look, illuminated with her phone. "This isn't something you get to be bossy over. Non-negotiable, in fact. I'm going pee."

I cursed under my breath. "Fine I'll go with you."

"You don't have to."

"Like hell I don't." The last thing I would do is have her go outside at night, in the snow, with hundreds of men around, at a rest stop in the mountains.

We managed to get into our clothes and tromp through five inches of powder to the restrooms. Then tromp back. By the time we were in the truck, we had to fire it back up again to get the heat blasting. She was shivering.

I took her hands in mine. "Jesus you're ice cold."

"Yeah. Have been since changing the tire earlier. What I need is a long hot shower and soup to thaw me out."

"I don't have either one handy. Why don't you take your shoes off, since your feet probably got soaked since you are just wearing your tennis shoes, then go ahead and get into the sleeping bag."

She must be really cold not to have argued, I thought, blasting the heat and taking off my boots. I reached over and unzipped my sleeping bag first, then hers.

"Hey, what are you doing?"

"Zipping them together."

I was doing it because she was cold, and it made sense, not because I was actually looking forward to having her body pressed up against mine all night. Sweet torture is what it would be.

Turning off the truck again, I shimmied into my side of the sleeping bag, and shifted so that I could lay on my side, allowing my arm to go around her. I ran my hand over her upper body, rubbing some warmth into her. It was fine until she backed up, putting her amazing ass into the crotch of my sweat pants that I had worn for comfort.

There was nothing sweet about this torture. It was simply painful. "Are you warming up?" My voice sounded weird.

"Yep. Uh, should I ignore the uh - "

"Yes. Yes, you should." Think grandma. Think grandma. Oh sweet Jesus, she was shifting again.

"Could you stop that. Why are you moving?"

"Sorry, just trying to get comfortable. Here I'll flip over. That's better."

No, it was not. This was not better, because now I was just inches away from where I wanted to be sinking inside of her. Her lips were so close that despite it being dark, I could feel her breath. Even thoughts of grandma weren't going to help this situation.

"How long does it um last?"

"I don't know. Go to sleep." I hadn't meant to be snippy, but I was hanging by a thread trying unsuccessfully to remember why I couldn't kiss her.

"Remind me again why I let you in?" She flipped back over trying to scoot away from me as much as possible.

I reached around her and pulled her back firmly against me. Breathing in her scent, I realized I was fighting a lost battle.

"What are you? Oh - "

My hand had trailed down rubbing over her hip, ass and leg. "Turn around," I commanded gently.

She did as I asked. "Scott, what are we - "

I swallowed her words in a kiss. A kiss so hot, I was sure I'd combust with it. "I don't want to fight this anymore," I murmured trailing my lips down her neck.

"Thank God."

I pulled her into me, gripping her ass and sliding my tongue past her lips. Tasting, touching, wanting even more. She must've had the same thought because her hand reached for me sliding down my sweats to grip my length.

"Oh fuck. Cold, cold, cold."

"Sorry, sorry. I didn't think."

A shiver ran through my body at the freezing hand that had just gripped me. "Here. It's okay. Just a shock. Put them on my stomach to warm them up." We both started laughing, but then it was back to business when I captured her lips again.

I grunted when she put both hands against my skin, but slowly relaxed as the heat transferred and she explored up and down my chest under my shirt. As much as I'd love to get her naked, it wasn't exactly feasible with the limited space or with how cold it was. And, it wasn't as though I could see anything. But there was one thing I needed to be sure of first.

"Kels?"

"Mm."

I smiled at the way she got lost in the kiss. "You aren't a virgin, are you?"

"Not even close." She moved back, and I heard a slap.

"What are you doing?"

"Face palming for making myself sound slutty. You do that. You scramble my brain."

"I just didn't want… you know." Her first time to be in the back of a truck. It was bad enough that our first time was going to be in the back of a truck. But we'd have tomorrow to make up for it when I got her back to her house. No way I'd miss the chance to see her naked.

"I know, and I'm not. You know. Slutty. But it's not my first time either."

This time I laughed. "I'm well aware of your non-slutty reputation. I think your hands are warm now, by the way."

She smiled in the kiss. "Is that your way of saying you'd like me to resume my exploration before my ice-cold fingers shrank you two inches."

"Hey. Did not. Just shocked the senses. Ahh, yeah, like that." Her hand was curled around the base of my cock, sliding up and down.

I couldn't wait any longer to touch her, to feel her. My fingers slid past her waistband straight for her center. I practically growled with what greeted me. She was wet, soft and perfectly bare, with the exception of a strip down the middle. God, what I wouldn't give to get to dive in and taste her with my tongue.

Finding her clit, I circled it until she was writhing under the sensation, then I inserted a finger deep into her heat, sucking down the breath she drew in at the contact. "You feel so good."

"You too. I wish we had more room, and light."

"You and me both. I need to get the condom." Thank God, I had one in my wallet.

"Oh. It's good that you have one."

"I promise, I'm not slutty either."

"I'd be disappointed if bossy Scott hadn't shown up prepared."

"I didn't have the condom in there for you." Oh no.

"Pardon?"

"I didn't mean that the way it sounded. I meant, I didn't put it in there before I came up here, thinking we'd have sex. You know what, I'm just gonna stop talking now."

"Probably for the best. Although hearing you put your foot in your mouth is kind of adorable. Nice change of pace from when I do it."

I slipped on the condom in the dark, then snuggled back down with her noticing she was stripping out of her leggings and panties. Diving back into the kiss. I rolled her onto her back, sliding my hand down her flat stomach before fingering her most sensitive place. "I can't wait to see you, to taste you."

She shivered under my hand or with my words, maybe a little of both. Before long, her body went taut, and them she climaxed with the sexiest moan. There were girls who tried to do what they thought a guy wanted to hear during an orgasm, but Kelsey had just let her body feel, and the result was the single most sensual sound I'd ever heard.

Shifting so I was on top of her, I nudged her knees apart, seeking out that desperate relief I'd been craving with her. Moving forward an inch, it was my turn to groan. She was tight. But I didn't want to hurt her. I braced myself on my forearms, moving slowly, deeper inside.

"You okay?" I was hanging by a thread of control.

Then she broke it by gripping my ass and pulling me deep. A litany of curse words left my lips for the kind of sweet heaven I was experiencing. Moving now in a rhythm, I pistoned my hips into hers. Our sleeping bag slipped off, leaving me more room to move, to hold one hand on her shoulder and the other under her backside, to deliver the perfect drive home.

"Oh God, Scott. I - " a garble of words came out of her mouth while she shattered beneath me. But I wasn't done. I pulled out and settled her in front of me, her back to my front, taking her from behind. This position allowed me to play with her clit while I moved inside of her. Her response fueled my determination to make her come again.

"Tell me when you're almost there. I want to come with you. You want that?"

"Yes. I'm almost there. Scott. I can't."

Yes, she definitely could.

Chapter Twelve

Kelsey

Hi, my name is Kelsey Wegman and I'm addicted to sex with Scott. Because if that was what all the fuss was about, well holy shit. In the past, I'd had an orgasm a couple of times, but they were nothing like this. Those other orgasms did nothing that rocked my entire world, then quite literally, rocked it two more times.

We both lay there, panting for breath, oblivious to the fact we were now outside of the sleeping bag and in the cooler air. I winced when Scott pulled out, assuming he was taking care of the condom when he moved to the front of the cab.

I fumbled around in the dark for my clothes. As much as naked sleeping would be divine, common sense weighed in that it was too cold.

Is this the part where it got awkward? I refused. I was an adult. Who'd just had sex with a man instead of a boy, and wowsers, what a difference.

"So that was amazing." So much for not being awkward. I sounded like I'd just been to the carnival and taken a great ride. It was juvenile at best.

He chuckled. "It was. But next time we do it, I get to

see every inch of you."

Which meant reciprocation. My mouth formed a smile in the dark. "I'm liking that idea."

He wrapped me up in his arms spoon-like in an embrace, kissing the back of my neck. "Get some sleep, Kels."

ॐ ॐ

Waking up in the truck the next morning wasn't as weird as I would've thought, but it was hectic. Because every truck had learned the weather had cleared and was trying to get on the road. Myself included. Scott had left with a quick kiss, then left for his truck too. Business before the holiday was crazy, and he had a ton of things to get back to.

And although getting home and taking a nice long, hot shower would be nice, I had to return to the yard and pick up a new route for a pickup and drop off. At least this one was local. Then I wanted to stop by the hospital, and then I had my date.

Whoa. Shit. My date with Andrew. I'd almost forgotten. Obviously, I had to cancel. But wait, Scott had plans to go to Missy's holiday party. Was he still going to go, or was I being naïve in thinking that sex with Scott meant that we were now exclusive? See this is the sort of stuff I'd needed to think about before he'd left. But as it was, I had too much on my plate to dwell on it for the moment.

There was no sign of Scott when I returned to work, and Nell was quick to give me my next orders. "Here you go, sweetie. Running behind 'cause of all the snow. After this one, if you could take another, that'd be great."

I texted my dad and let him know that I would be by to see him later. I was head down in my phone when I turned the corner and ran smack into Andrew. We each started talking at once.

"About tonight - "

We both laughed. "Guessing you got double booked too," I asked.

"Yeah and now I have to go over the pass tonight. Raincheck?"

"Sure. Drive safe."

Whew. At least that had been easy. I was tempted to text Scott to see if he had a minute but then what? Ask if he still had plans? Find out he did and let it ruin my day. No thanks. I had trips to make and caffeine to find.

I finally pulled back into the yard at about seven o'clock that evening and had just turned the corner to drop off my paperwork on Nell's desk. I was completely exhausted, ready for a shower and pretty sure I looked as disheveled as I felt. Which is why the universe decided to put Missy in front of me, looking like glamour-time Barbie in her fire engine red dress with four-inch heels that I would kill myself in. Her hair was done, her makeup perfect and her smile insincere.

"Oh dear, rough day, sweetie?"

"Yeah. You could say that. What are you doing here?"

I already knew the answer, but maybe I was wondering why she was here instead of Scott picking her up. Was he trying to rub it in my face?

"Scott was running late, so I told him I'd meet him here. Had my roommate drop me off though so he can take me home later."

There it was, she was staking her claim. Then there he was, looking absolutely amazing in his black suit, as he came out of his office. "Sorry I'm ready – hey, Kelsey."

Guilt. It was etched all over his face. Missy didn't waste any time however, in focusing the attention back on herself. "Shall we go? We're already running late."

Either she didn't pick up on the tension, or she chose to ignore it. Either way though, she was about to get the man, so what did it matter. I tried to get a read on Scott's expression, but he only looked like he wanted to get out of here.

"Yeah. Have a good time." It was all I could manage before spinning around and practically sprinting out to the car. I would not cry. I would not cry. The stupid tears wouldn't listen though.

I parked in the lot next to the hospital and waited to collect myself before pasting on a smile, and visiting with my dad for the next hour, before he insisted I get home to get some rest. It was his fatherly way of telling me I looked like shit, too, I think.

But arriving to my darkened house that still had no real food in the refrigerator, no holiday lights of any kind on the house and nobody inside, set off a fresh round of tears. Scott's truck missing from his driveway wasn't exactly helping either. Pity party for one. Right here. Which is why I backed right out and went to 7-11. Because a proper pity party required cheese in a can that magically came out the top, crackers and mint chocolate chip ice-cream.

After my shower while I was half way through squirting the cheese directly in my mouth the knock came. I ignored it. It came again.

"Kels, open up. I know you're in there."

"Go away." Which sounded funny with a mouth full of processed cheese.

The sound of the key turning in the lock made me remember he had a spare key.

I stayed sitting in on the couch, the evidence of my pig out on the coffee table in front of me. I wanted to throw the can at him, but the fact that he looked stupid hot in his suit made me rethink ruining it with spray cheese.

"I don't want to talk to you."

"Too bad. Look, I know you're hurt."

I shook my head. "You don't know that."

He lips twitched, nodding towards the mess of junk food in front of me. "Okay."

"What are you doing here? Aren't you home early for your date?"

"I came over to apologize about tonight. I was so busy when I got back to the office, I completely forgot about my date with Missy. Then I felt bad having to cancel, but did try telling her I got delayed because of the weather. So instead she showed up there. She'd already added a plus one."

"And you happened to have a suit at the office?"

"Actually, yes because I'd had it dry-cleaned and picked it up yesterday before heading up the mountain to see you."

Where we'd had sex, but hadn't talked about what it meant. "We didn't exactly discuss this type of thing."

He sighed, taking a seat beside me. "Nope, we didn't. Matter of fact, I thought you'd be out with Andrew."

"He got stuck taking a load across the pass." Then it dawned on me why. "Oh my God, you stuck him with it."

He didn't even bother to deny it. "I simply told Nell that I thought he might be available. He didn't have to say yes."

"Mm hm. You and Missy looked like a couple tonight."

He rolled his eyes. "I'm finding out I prefer a girl in leggings and sweatshirts, who eats disgusting cheese stuff from a can, but still has the best ass I've ever seen."

"She's still beautiful."

"You're more beautifuller. College word."

I gave him a goofy grin. The kind that said you're not

off the hook yet, but saying things like that was really sweet.

"Nothing happened with Missy. Not tonight. Not the other night either."

"Really?"

"Really."

I believed him. "You look really good in that suit."

He smiled. "I was hoping it might be my ticket back into your good graces."

"It's kind of working. I was hurt to see you leave with her tonight. She seemed very intent of making you a couple again."

He gave a humorless laugh. "Yeah well if she knew I was contemplating not returning to Morgan Stanley I doubt she would be pursuing me so hard. I don't remember Missy being quite so driven in high school. Mostly, I think she just wants the image of the quintessential power couple, and to live in New York City."

"Why did you leave?"

There was a story there. One he wasn't telling me. Or maybe anyone. His eyes met mine. "Not now. It's heavy stuff and right now I want nothing more than to take you up to your bedroom, lay you down on the mattress and see you naked for the first time."

I had to hold myself back from sprinting up the stairs and tried to play it cool. "Yeah?"

He reached out, cupping my neck and bending his head down for a kiss. Wow, the man knew how to kiss.

"Let's get upstairs."

He didn't have to tell me twice.

Once we got to the bedroom, his gaze settled on me when I tugged the sweatshirt over my head. A heavy dose of lust was reflected in his eyes, giving me the confidence to continue removing first my T-shirt, and then my leggings. Standing in only my bra and thong, I heard a hiss of breath leave him.

"You're beautiful. Lay on the bed with your head propped on a pillow."

I watched while took off his jacket and loosened his tie. Then he toed off his shoes while I got settled. "What did you have in mind?"

My question was answered when he moved towards me hovering over the bed and hooking his thumbs in the sides of my thong, pulling it down, down. Oh God. I was completely exposed to him. But he wasn't done. Instead he reached up, pulling my bra straps down and undoing the clasp in the front, making it fall away. I shimmied out of it leaving me full naked for him.

"Your turn."

He shook his head grinning. "In a moment. But first I need to taste you."

I sucked in a breath never having had that done before. What can I say, high school boys got real intimidated when it came to giving oral. "I – ohhhhhh - " My words died when his face went straight into my center, inhaling deeply.

I found myself mesmerized watching from my vantage point as he spread my knees wide and ran his tongue up my inner thigh. Jumbled words mixed with curses, left my lips making him smile.

"I haven't even started yet."

My hands gripped the sheets. "I um, this is my first time doing this," I blurted out.

He looked surprised, then pleased. "You've never had anyone eat your pussy before?"

The crude words should've shocked me, but instead I found myself aroused that he'd talk this way. I shook my head watching as a grin spread across his face.

"You don't know how much that turns me on, and how incredibly sexy you are like this."

He made me feel that way. No reservations. No

hesitancy, only pure—holy mother of all things—his tongue licked the length of my slit. And instead of having cognitive thinking ability, I simply let myself concentrate on the feel. His lips. His tongue. Now, good Lord, his fingers, were exploring me gently until he seemed to have reached his breaking point with teasing and went full throttle with his assault.

My fingers tangled in his hair. My hips bucked without permission, completely operating on their own. I cried out with my orgasm, feeling as though I'd just run ten miles with the way I couldn't seem to catch my breath. But instead of coming down from the high, I was building again. The sensation so unbelievably overwhelming that I couldn't be held responsible for the incoherent words dropping from my lips. The second orgasm completely shattered me. But then, with the sight of him looking up at me, my arousal still evident on his face, and remaining in his suit, I was in sexy overload.

"I need you naked." Because if I was going to die tonight from pleasure, there was one last thing on my bucket list, and that was to see Scott Turner in all his naked glory, and when his clothes hit the floor, he did not disappoint.

"You're perfect." And he was with his muscular chest, strong arms and six pack abs. It only got better as I traveled south to see his impressive erection. How that had fit inside of me last night, I wasn't sure.

"Not so perfect, but I'm glad you think so."

I licked my lips. "You want me to return the favor?" I'd given a couple blow jobs in my limited sexual experience, but I don't remember ever quite craving them the way I did with Scott.

"Later definitely, but right now I need to be inside of you."

After quickly putting on a condom, he crawled up the length of me, dropping kisses over my stomach, then breasts, before traveling up to my neck. His hot breath in that sensitive spot below my ear gave me shivers. Then he was at my entrance pushing in, filling me slowly. Realizing I had free license to touch him, I ran my hands over his shoulders and down his back to his perfectly muscled ass, pulling him deeper.

"God, you did that last night too. It feels so good."

"Being able to see you tonight is so much better."

"Much."

His mouth met mine. Ceasing our conversation while pushing me to the brink again.

My legs began to shake, starting to build again. He was going for the triple crown again. And once he started groaning my name, grinding out his own climax, I went over the edge with him.

Chapter Thirteen

Scott

"Wow."

Her one-word expression summed up exactly how I felt too. "Yeah. Wow."

She propped up. "Is it always like that? The three orgasms? Because I have to say, you're, um, really good at that."

I chuckled, regrettably pulling out of her so I could dispose of the condom. "No, it's not always this way."

I could see her brain working overtime. "Is there anything more I should be doing?"

This time I went into full laughter, until I saw her adorable little frown. Pulling her into me on the bed, I kissed her gently, meeting her eyes so she knew I was sincere. "I'm not laughing at you. I'm only amused because your inexperience is a turn on not to mention if you were any better at it, I may not be able to walk again."

That seemed to soothe her as she relaxed in my arms. "When I got back tonight, I was upset, the house was so dark, my dad is still in the hospital, and you were out with Missy. This isn't the way I thought tonight would turn out. So, I guess this is my way of bringing up, the part of the talk where I say I don't think I'd do well with you dating other people."

"Kels, I don't know how long I'm going to be here. You're returning to school soon. But if you're asking if I'm going to see anyone else for the next couple of weeks aside from you, then the answer is no. If you think you're going to be going out with Andrew, the guy is going to find himself driving across the whole country, a lot."

She giggled before sighing. "Speaking of returning to school, I need to get my dad to sign the student loan."

"Good luck with that."

"Yep. I keep hoping he'll be home in three days for Christmas."

I squeezed her tight. "I hope so too. Everyday he's improving. And who's to say it has to be on that day. We could do it the day he gets home."

"That's true." She covered her yawn. "Are you spending the night?"

"Do you want me to?"

"Mm hm."

Then she was out, leaving me to listen to her soft rhythmic breathing. I started to really think about what it would be like, not to have this beautiful girl in my life a week from now.

&ç ç&

"Do you want to do a run with me today?"

She crinkled her nose, putting on yet another pair of black yoga pants. I swear the girl has twelve pairs. "On a Sunday?"

We'd just woken up and taken a shower together, and oh what a fucking amazing one it had been, lifting her up and having her against the tiled wall. "Yeah. Got one to do to the east side. Won't take but a few hours."

"Sure. Are you driving?"

"Yes. Definitely." Not that she wasn't a good driver, but I didn't want to ruin this good mood we had between us by barking at her today.

We took separate cars to the office, so that she could leave to go see her dad afterwards. It was the perfect opportunity for the surprise that I had planned, considering that I had texted my dad, and we had a mission for tonight. I knew the holidays would be rough for her this year with her dad being in the hospital, so I planned to bring a bit of holiday cheer at least to the house.

We pulled onto the freeway, which unfortunately was a parking lot going southbound. I frowned, but funny enough, when I glanced over, Kelsey was grinning.

"What has you smiling?"

"I was replaying our shower from this morning."

Christ. I was getting hard because now I was as well. "Oh yeah?"

"Yep. Matter of fact, it got me thinking."

I grinned. "About what?"

She took off her seatbelt and scooted over to me, her hand going right to my ever-growing erection.

"Kels, I'm driving." Actually, I was virtually parked, but still. The fact that she wasn't buckled in was bothering me. "You don't have a seatbelt on."

She removed her hand and quickly fastened the middle belt around her. "Now where was I. Oh, so I was thinking about putting my mouth on you."

"Right now?" My voice sounded like a pre-pubescent teenager and I was torn between helping her unzip my jeans and responsible driving. Glancing around I could see no other trucks within viewing distance.

"Yes. Right now. That is if you think you can keep your eyes on the road?"

Traffic had started to move a little. "This isn't a good idea." Even to my own ears, it was a weak excuse, because the truth was, I couldn't wait to feel her mouth on me.

"That wasn't a no." Her deft fingers unbuckled my belt before unsnapping and pulling down my zipper. I shifted so she could pull the jeans down.

And wouldn't you know we were starting to move again. I missed a gear while shifting, hearing the grind of them, before getting the right one. All because her hand was around my shaft.

"Uh, uh, watch your shifting. Don't want to go and lose a transmission because you aren't paying attention."

Sassy girl. This was payback for all the things I'd barked at her. Holy shit her tongue swirled my tip. I applied the brake a bit too much.

"Do we need to talk about proper braking. Ease into it."

"Fuuuuuuck," I muttered, feeling her mouth ease down the length of me, taking me to the back of her throat.

"Kels. Traffic is speeding up."

"Guess I'd better do it faster then. Eyes on the road. Check your mirrors and try not to crash."

If I wasn't having my cock sucked by the most amazing pair of lips on the planet, I might have laughed. But as it was, all I could do was grip the steering wheel and try to fight the urge to throw my head back and close my eyes with sheer pleasure.

"No, no, not the balls." Never would I think those words would come from my mouth, but if she, oh good Lord, she was. She was cupping them, then licking. I was going to die. Death by blow job, then a fiery crash off the side of I-5.

I took a hand, and put it on top of her head, groaning at the fact she was now bobbing with an enthusiasm I had to say I was a big fan of.

"Ah, ah, both hands on the wheel, Mister."

Probably a good thing I did. "Kels, I'm going to - you might want to - "

Nope, my girl swallowed it down as if it was her absolute honor to do it. Then she popped up, wiped her lips and grinned.

I had sweat on my forehead, my hands ached from my death grip on the steering wheel and my entire world had been rocked.

"You okay?"

"Give me a minute." Deep breaths. Deep breaths. "I um, wow."

She laughed, doing me the favor of tucking me back inside my pants. "That does seem to be our word lately. Good job on the driving, although you should know, distracted driving can be quite dangerous."

"You enjoyed that little payback didn't you."

She sipped on her water before smirking. "Immensely. Play your cards right and you may get another one on the return."

I wasn't sure I'd survive it, but what a way to go.

Chapter Fourteen

Kelsey

After our return trip, which hadn't nearly been as fun as the one there, simply because it was raining, and Scott had been insistent over no blowjob. Unfortunately, I hadn't been able to talk him into my favorite new road activity.

After returning to the office, I went to see my dad. I brought him some dinner, thankful that he was now on solid foods, and we played some cards. He was trying to teach me Gin Rummy, as I think the Go Fish wasn't doing it for him anymore. But the positively best news so far, was to see him up and walking now without assistance. He wasn't about to win any marathons, but at least he could get around. All of it progress.

I arrived home, but instead of the usual dark, depressing house to greet me it was all done up in Christmas lights. The ones my father usually hung from the roof were up, the different colors on the bushes. The best decorations were the lit-up candy canes outlining the sidewalk. I hadn't realized how much I'd missed it all until now. I got out of the car and approached the house with tears welling up. No doubt Scott was behind this.

The front door opened revealing both him and his dad. "You like it?" he asked.

"I absolutely love it." I was hard-pressed not to go up and throw my arms around him just to let him know how much.

"We should've thought to do it sooner," his dad said, giving me a hug.

"I think this is the right time now that I know my father is doing better. He was up walking without assistance tonight. Not saying that he can come home for Christmas yet, but it's looking better."

"Great news."

"Well I'm gonna get on up to the hospital to see him. You two kids can decorate the tree. See you both later."

Huh. Now I was alone with Scott, and once he shut the door behind his Dad, we were both naked in a matter of seconds.

あ め

After one round of sex where we christened my father's couch and I made a mental note to wipe it down later, we got around to actually decorating the tree. I told Scott about the special ornaments, pointing out that some of them had been my mother's, as we took them out of the boxes. I hadn't realized how much I'd needed this until now, and the fact Scott had been so incredibly thoughtful to do this for me made it all that much more special. We lay on the couch after, with only the soft glow from the tree illuminating the room.

With his arms wrapped around me, a wave of emotion and affection for this man washed over me. I'd told myself not to get too attached, but I was falling hard and fast.

"I left New York because my roommate who was

also my co-worker at Morgan Stanley killed himself."

I stopped breathing, absorbing Scott's whispered words full of vulnerability. "Oh God. What made him do it?"

"He'd been working fourteen-hour days. We all had. It was stressful and chaotic. Then he messed up on a serious account. I mean I knew he'd gotten reprimanded, but I didn't think he'd take it that hard. We were friends and I didn't see it. Returned home one night and there he was."

"You're the one who found him?"

"Yep. I cut him down, but it was too late."

My heart absolutely broke that his friend had thought there was no other solution. But it also hurt for Scott who'd found him and was still dealing with wondering what he could've done.

"I'm so sorry, Scott."

"Yeah. Me too."

"You quit your job after?"

"No. Took leave. Given the circumstances, they were more than happy to grant me a few weeks. My dad had been after me to spend some time back here. Told me if I learned the business I may want to take it over some day. Frankly I just needed the break."

I turned over to face him, grasping his face between my hands, kissing him gently.

"He was a good guy. It makes me not want to go back there."

"But you don't want to take over your dad's business either?"

He shook his head. "I respect the hell out of it, and out of him for starting it, but no."

"What if you do as you hinted at before. Start your own business with investments. Work with people instead of companies. I'm sure there's a lot of need around here."

"My career is there. I can't give that up."

"Yes, you can. If it's not making you happy."

He kissed me lightly. "It's so simple for you. You've always wanted to be a teacher and live here."

I stiffened at the unintentional dig. "Guess I'm sort of a simple girl. I want to do what makes me happy without worrying about what other people think."

He sat up, running his hands through his hair. "Yeah, you say that."

"What does that mean?"

"It means you don't know the pressure. I have my father disappointed if I don't do the trucking business and take over. But I waste my master's degree if I don't stick with New York."

"Why would you be wasting it if you start your own business instead?"

"There's no way I can move home."

It finally sank in what he was saying. "Because doing that means you failed."

He nodded as if he couldn't even verbalize his admission.

"If you choose to leave New York and Wall Street, you aren't failing at anything."

"That's not the way it works."

"Yes, it is, if you don't base your opinions on the Missy's of the world. Am I a failure for going to college in Texas, then coming back here to work and live?"

"No of course not."

"Why not? I mean if your logic is that anyone who—"

"Because nobody had those expectations of you," he nearly shouted before wincing. "I'm sorry, I didn't mean it that way."

I swallowed hard past the lump quickly forming in my throat. "Yes, you did. After all, I wasn't homecoming king, captain of the football team, or slated to be part of a power couple who could take some big city by storm. I'm just a simple girl who's too lazy some days to put on real pants or shoes, who wears pony tails and drives big trucks. I'm chicken pot pie."

"What?"

I fought my tears. "I'm chicken pot pie while you're looking for steak in some fancy city."

"Kels, that's not true." He reached for me, but I stepped away.

"I'm really sorry about your friend, Scott. But I think you may be missing the point of doing something that makes you happy instead of being so wrapped up in a job, that you'd get to that point. I think you were miserable in New York, and you may not like running your father's business, I get that, but it makes me sad that you think that being here, being with me, is failure."

"That's not what I said."

"No, but it's what I heard. I think you should probably go."

The very last thing I would've expected was for tonight to end the way it did. But I didn't need to feel *less than* because I didn't want to be a lawyer, doctor or do investments in some big city. But mainly I asked him to leave because I didn't want to take a chance in making this about me. To say, "choose me", when he was telling me in black and white he wasn't capable of doing it.

He dropped his hand and put on his shoes, his face looking resigned. "I'm sorry."

"Me too."

Chapter Fifteen

Kelsey

He didn't call. Not that I'd expected him to, but damn it hurt when he didn't. Logical Kelsey knew we'd gone into this knowing it was short term. But optimistic Kelsey, that stupid girl, was hopelessly in love with him. I was way past falling. Yeah, I'd fallen all right.

The next day was Christmas Eve and I got up bright and early - well at least early since it was foggy and dark, as were most holidays around the Seattle area, and drove to the hospital.

"Hey, Dad."

"Hi, honey. Merry Christmas Eve. I have some good news."

My eyes got big. "Yeah?"

"Yeah, I'm getting out of this place, but not until the twenty-seventh. Sorry. Tried to make Christmas, but the doctor wasn't budging."

"But that's terrific. We can do Thai food then."

"Sure will. Hey what's that in your hand."

Oh crap. Maybe now wasn't the time. "Um, we can talk about it later."

"I think we can do it now."

My dad always knew when I hesitated I didn't really want to talk about something. But I didn't want to have a scenario where he was on the verge of coming home only to have another heart attack.

"Hand it over, honey."

I did, watching his face as he read it.

"This is a student loan form."

"Yeah. It needs your signature."

"You don't need it. I'm paying for it."

Time to get real. "Dad I know about the insurance, or lack thereof. I also know about the second mortgage."

He cursed a litany while turning red. My eyes flicked to the machines hoping that I wasn't sending him into cardiac arrest.

"Stop eyeing the machine. I'm fine. Just pissed that Jim told you."

"He didn't. At least not directly. But, you should've told me."

"You're the first in our family to go to college, there's no way that I'm letting you pay for it."

Time to be firm. "Well you either co-sign that loan or I withdraw from school."

We were in a stare down. "You're so stubborn."

"Right back at you pops. Now what'll it be? I, for one, think that a little student loan debt will make me more appreciative of my educational opportunity."

His lips twitched with the hint of a smile.

We both turned when the door opened, revealing Scott who seemed to have eyes only for me. "Hey, Kels. Uh, I didn't know you would be here. I can come back."

For a guy that didn't want to make our relationship obvious to our dads he was doing a bang-up job of doing the opposite. My father's raised brow confirmed it.

"It's actually good timing. My dad has a few things to think about, and I have to get to the office to do a short run. I'll be back this evening pops."

I kissed him on the cheek and left without meeting Scott's eyes. Love did that to you. Made you just want to run away and hide. Why did people willingly do it again?

It was a short drive to the office, but when I came in, Nell was in a flutter.

"What's going on?"

"Judd called out with the flu. He has an over the pass run and back. Everyone else is off or already on one."

"I'll take it."

"You sure, honey? It's to Spokane. No way you're getting back tonight."

Spokane was clear on the other side of Eastern Washington. But the appeal to take a drive on the open road rather than face Scott, or to sit at home waiting for him, was just too much to pass up.

"Yeah. No snow being called for, right?"

She checked. "Nope. None."

Good because I needed to be back by tomorrow to see my dad.

"I'll take it then. Merry Christmas, Nell."

"Merry Christmas, sweetie."

Chapter Sixteen

Scott

I'd handled that terribly, and judging from her father's face, he wasn't about to let it go unremarked upon. But he surprised me by going a different direction with his conversation.

"My daughter is stubborn. Just like I am."

"She is that."

"But she also wears her heart on her sleeve like her mother used to."

Shit. Luckily, he didn't wait for me to respond, but his question was worse.

"Did you tell her about the insurance and house?"

"Yes, Sir. The insurance. She figured out the house part when she wanted to take a loan against it. She deserved to know."

"Guess I can't blame you." He held out the paper. "She gave me an ultimatum. I'm to sign her loan document or she withdraws from school. Even I know better than to call her bluff."

I couldn't help but chuckle. "Yes, Sir. I wouldn't." My stomach was still sick over last night. She wasn't wrong in what she'd said, about my perceptions clouding my decisions over moving home, but she was wrong about my perception of her. She was anything but simple, and the thought of losing her was weighing heavy on me.

"Parenting is a funny thing."

"How's that?" Although I was anxious to chase after Kelsey, without much to say, I didn't know what to do. So, I took a seat instead. Perhaps wisdom could be gained.

"Because we're always trying to do what we think is best for our kids. Sometimes we get it wrong. Sometimes we don't. But it doesn't matter in the end, as long as our kids are happy."

I got the feeling he wasn't only speaking of Kelsey. "How do you define that. Happiness?" Because I'd been asking myself that question all night. What made me happy. Aside from Kelsey's sweet face appearing over and over, I wasn't sure what else.

He seemed to mull over the question, looking up with the door opened and my father came in. They exchanged a slight nod as if they had a secret code for 'we're in parenting mode here'.

"How do I define happiness. Well, no offense to your father or trucking, but it definitely wasn't a job or a place that I lived. It was always about the people in my life. My wife. My daughter. My best friend. Hell, even my co-workers. A job is something that pays the bills and allows us to afford to make memories whether it's vacation, paying for college, or simply Christmas gifts. But in the end, it's the spending time with the people who love you that should truly make you happy."

"I'd agree," my dad offered.

"But you love your business." Not that he'd put it first, but it was clear the trucking company was his baby over the years.

He clapped a hand on my shoulder. "I love what it's

provided in my life. That it's not only sustained my family, but all of those others who've worked for me. But you have to understand, I'll always love you more. I know you don't want to take over the business son. But it's okay. You need to follow your own dreams."

I swallowed hard. "I tried. I was miserable in New York." It was the first time I'd said it out loud. Because my roommate's death was symbolic over letting a job make you so unbelievably miserable, that you ended it all. I didn't want that life.

"I know. Why do you think I asked you to come home?"

"To see if I'd take over the business."

Both men grinned that kind of smile that made me feel as if they were in on a secret I wasn't privy to.

"More because I could hear it in your voice. You were burning out. Then when you told me about your co-worker, I thought I'd offer it up, to get you home, to get you some space, some perspective. Hell, if you'd wanted to take over the business, great. But mostly I just needed to ensure you were okay."

"I am. But if I don't go back, I'll feel like a failure, like I let the job beat me."

My father shook his head. "Takes a stronger man to change his course when it's not up to his expectation. Nothing beat you in New York. You simply don't want that life. Better to know then ever wonder."

Well, while we were here, I might as well get it out. "I want to start my own business. Still in doing financial advising, but more along the lines of estates, wills, college funds. That type of thing."

"I imagine Seattle would be a good as place as any. Unless you want to go somewhere else?"

Kelsey came to mind. I thought about taking her out on proper dates, decorating the tree come Christmas time, and spending our nights together. Now that was happiness.

"I don't think I do, but I need to go find Kelsey."

Now that this was all off my chest, I was desperate to find her.

Her father grabbed his buzzing phone. "Speak of the devil. Just got a text she's heading to Spokane. Said she'd be back tomorrow to bring me contraband food if I sign this damn letter. Now that's just cruel. Blackmail."

My dad chuckled. "Smart girl."

"I've gotta go. By the way, Dad, I love you, but consider this my two weeks' notice."

Chapter Seventeen

Kelsey

The drive was clearing my mind, but it was also making me miss Scott, even his stupid barking orders. I could almost hear him telling me to stop day dreaming and concentrate on the road.

At least the five-hour drive had been uneventful, with very little traffic and only a pocket of rain. I picked up the trailer, then headed back West stopping at a busy truck-stop outside of the city. There were dozens of trucks, probably all on their last routes before the holiday. But the best part was the diner. I walked in, smiling at the assortment of pies in the glass case. When was the last time I'd had homemade pie?

"Woo-wee, you lost, sweetheart?"

I looked over to see a young guy dressed in camo pants and a black sweatshirt checking me out.

"Uh no I'm not lost."

"You drivin' with your boyfriend."

Really? I wasn't in the mood. "Nope. Driving my own truck."

I asked for a menu from the hostess hoping to grab a couple things to go. The place was crowded, and a few men had focused their attention on the jackass hitting on me since he couldn't seem to keep his voice down.

"No way. Sweet thing like you driving a truck? Pfft, I don't believe it."

"Believe what you want."

"You know, you want to get warm tonight, I'm the Lowe's truck outside."

If ever there was a lamer pickup line. "No thanks." I was aware we had an audience now and just wanted him to go away.

"It's your loss, cause' I'll give you a ride you'll never forget."

I slapped down the menu, looking the asshole in the face. "Seriously? This is how you think it's appropriate to talk to a woman? Yes. I drive a truck. Matter of fact it's my father's truck since he's in the hospital over Christmas just having survived a massive heart attack. But please, sexually harass me some more. I'm sure it would make your momma real proud to know she raised such a man with such manners."

He simply gaped. Gape. Now there was a word.

The man closest to him at the counter swatted him with his hand. "Get on outta here, Mike, before I kick your dumb-ass."

The dumb-ass known as Mike turned on his heel and left with big splotches of red showing on his face. I took a deep breath, turning back to my thoughts of pie.

"How about you have a seat here, girlie."

I was about to go full on attack on the guy, before I realized it was the old man who'd shooed him away.

"No thanks. I'll just eat in the truck."

He patted the stool. "Come on, I'm buying. The chili is excellent, and it's Christmas Eve. Don't let that shit for brains spoil it."

I smiled at his description. What the hell. It beat being lonely in the truck.

Sitting on the stool, I let the waitress fill my coffee cup and ordered the chili along with blueberry pie.

"I'm Kelsey by the way."

He took my offered hand. "Curt. Nice to meet you."

I dug into the pie first, because that was the best part about being an adult. Having dessert first.

"That true about your dad in the hospital, and you driving his truck?"

"Afraid so. He's going to be okay though. He just won't be home for Christmas."

"Christmas is about being together, no matter where you are. Just my opinion though."

"You're right. It's just been a rough week, I guess." I thought of Scott and tried to hold back the tears. Nobody wanted a girl crying in her chili at a truck stop.

"Don't you go crying now. Can't go tearing that dipshit a new one, then sit down and cry. And, we're all men here, you'd clear the place out."

I started laughing at the vision of doing just that. "Wouldn't want that."

"You know how to change a tire on your truck?"

"Sure do, did it a couple days ago, in fact."

"Good girl. Great. Looks like you may have to tell off another one."

I turned to see Scott standing in back of me. "Tell off who? You had to tell someone off?"

Curt raised both brows. "Boyfriend?"

"Nope. Boss unfortunately."

He slid me his card. "You ever need a new one, you let me know. You have a Merry Christmas, Kelsey. I hope your dad has a speedy recovery."

He threw down a couple twenties, nodding to the waitress while he vacated his seat. "Hers is on me."

"Thanks, Curt. Merry Christmas to you too."

Scott took his seat next to me. "You know him?"

"Just met him."

"Who did you tell off?"

"Some guy who offered me a ride, and not the kind on the road."

I glanced over to see his jaw clench.

"What are you doing here? Did you have a route?"

"No. Heard you were taking this trip."

Okay. Part of me was thrilled he was here, the other part wanted to shake him until he told me why.

"Gave my two weeks' notice to my dad."

"Guess you'll be returning to New York then?"

The waitress took that moment to come in and ask for an order.

"Do you have chicken pot pie?" Scott asked.

"Sure do, hun. Also have beef."

"Chicken would be great. Thanks."

I fought my smile when he turned towards me. "Is that some sort of statement?"

"Absolutely. Turns out I've found myself falling for pot pie lately."

"That really sounds weird."

He chuckled, taking my chin in his hand. "Then how about simply. I'm falling for you, and I'm sorry about last night. You're anything but simple, Kels. You're so much more."

I sucked in a breath at the intensity of both his words and his eyes. "But what about New York?"

"I'm traveling to get my stuff next week. Then I was thinking I'd visit my girlfriend down in Texas a few times until she moves back, all while hopefully starting my business."

I wasn't sure what to focus on first. My brain was working overtime. "In Seattle?"

"Yep."

"And I'm the girlfriend?"

He dropped his lips to mine for a quick kiss. "I sure as hell hope so."

"But what about - "

"I was miserable in New York. Mostly because I didn't want to give up. Then my roommate. He - let's just say that was hard. But it should've taught me a lesson. No job is worth being that depressed over. I want to be happy. I want to try to do it with my own business, probably not in our town, but maybe closer to Seattle."

"I want to teach in Seattle schools. But what about the long-distance thing?"

"It's five months. You'll come home for spring break, I'll go down there some weekends. We can make it work."

"You sound really committed to this."

"That's because I am. By the way, I think tomorrow we should tell our dads. Then we'll plan on getting Thai food when your dad comes home on the twenty-seventh and celebrate Christmas then? Would that be okay?"

I nodded thinking Christmas really was about spending it with those you loved.

"One question though. Would you still wear suits? I mean even if it's just in the bedroom?"

He smiled. "Every night if you wanted, naughty girl."

"Every night, huh?"

He leaned in, whispering in my ear. "All the nights I can get."

"Well in that case you'd better get your pot pie to go."

Epilogue

Scott

My girl loved Christmas time and this year I was hell bent on making the season extra special. Because unlike the last holiday, her father was healthy, and we were all celebrating together by having dinner at her fully decorated house.

I was doing most of the cooking and couldn't wait until I gave her my Christmas present later.

In addition to her graduating college and starting her student teaching, we'd moved in together in an apartment in North Seattle six months ago. It was thirty minutes to our home town and close to both of our offices.

Yes. I'd started my business, and I couldn't be happier. I not only felt like I'd found my niche, but I'd also made peace with making the decision to return here. Of course, Kelsey made that decision a no-brainer.

Speak of the devil. Arms came around me as I stood at the sink.

"Hi. Can I help with anything?"

"You sure you're willing to take orders from me?"

She scoffed. "Please. After the ones you used to give

me while driving, this will be easy."

I smiled, remembering those days. "Challenge accepted. Now get to work on peeling those potatoes."

"On it. Hey, are you making chicken pot pie?" She asked eyeing the shredded chicken in the casserole dish.

"Maybe. Mind your business."

She laughed. "One would think it's become your favorite."

I leaned over, whispering in her ear. "I could eat it every day."

She swatted me. "Behave. Our dads are in the other room."

"Sitting on the sofa that we once - "

She was grinning. "No, no. no. You're bad."

"You like it."

I think the first week we'd moved in together, we'd christened every available surface.

"I do."

"Do me a favor and reach into my front pocket?"

"Perv. I'm not doing that. At least not until later."

I chuckled. I wasn't sure when this evening I'd have a chance to do it, but suddenly I couldn't wait any longer. "It's your Christmas gift."

"Oh yeah? I can open it now?"

She slid the box out of my pocket, gasping at the shape it, most likely guessing what it meant. She undid the bow slowly, then opened the lid.

I bent down on one knee.

"Kels, will you do me the honor of being my forever? I love you madly, and I want to be the reason you say wow every day. Will you be my wife?"

Her eyes were wide. "A thousand times yes. I love you too."

I stood up, enveloping her in a hug and giving her a kiss.

"Hey now you two. Keep the PDA away from the

food," my dad called out as he walked in with Mr. Wegman.

Kelsey flashed her left hand for them to see. But instead of congratulating us like normal dads, they high-fived. As if they'd known it all along.

Kels and I shared a look, then burst out laughing. Evidently, they'd known all along that happiness was right next door.

About the Author

Amelia Bond writes hot, sweet romance with unforgettable heroes and strong heroines. When she's not writing, she enjoys being a #girlboss, playing with her kids, and strong martinis. She lives on the West Coast.

If you would like more information about Amelia, please visit her at:

https://ameliabondbooks.wixsite.com/bond

Indecent Holiday

Elizabeth Brown

Chapter One

Lily

"Do we have the red Tupperware case?" my mom asked, scanning the trunk of our silver Subaru one last time. "The one with all the beads?"

I glanced at my watch. "Mom, I told you, I got everything. Relax. It's inside the box with the felt." We were headed up to our cabin in Tahoe for our annual Christmas vacation, and being late made me itchy.

Not that I had any reason to be in a hurry.

I was pretty sure this week, unlike our normal vacations, was going to be hell on earth. See, I love the holidays—like, triple-o *looove* them. Fourth of July, Halloween; hell, I even celebrate National Donut Day (June first, by the way) because, well, *donuts*. But my favorite of them all has to be Christmas. Because during the six-ish weeks between Thanksgiving and New Year's, the world is, inarguably and scientifically, a better place.

Evidence?

Sparkly lights go up on any surface that will hold a nail.

You have an excuse to indulge in wonderful things

that don't even make sense, like peppermint hot chocolate and rum balls.

People throw parties that involve wearing awesomely gaudy sweaters, and yet somehow, the glow of candlelight makes everyone look great.

And...there is a magical thing called snow that softens all the hard edges of the world.

I loved every last bit of it.

But what did I love about the holidays most of all?

Well, up until two days ago, it would have been going to our family cabin in Lake Tahoe. Built by my grandfather back in the fifties, the A-frame cottage is the epitome of relaxed mountain cool. It's all soaring beams and knotty pine and huge windows that look out to an unobstructed view of pine trees and snow-dappled mountains.

Christmas perfection.

We'd go up there every year and play board games and sit by the fire and wait for it to snow. Even after my dad left us, Mom and I still made the pilgrimage. The first year without him, when I was in sixth grade, I thought it would feel lonely and weird. And it did, to some extent, but my mom did a hell of a job distracting us. I was always super into art, so she brought craft supplies and made all my favorite foods, and we started new traditions, like making ornaments and eating crab spaghetti on Christmas Day.

I know, it sounds gross. But don't knock it till you try it. I mean, think about it: is it that much different than putting mint in your hot chocolate?

Anyway, what I'm getting at is...the cabin was my special place. A place I went during my most favorite time of year. A place we'd worked hard to pull together and turn into something that was just for us.

And it was about to be invaded.

"You okay, baby?"

I leaned my head against the window. We were almost to the cabin, and the glass was already ice-cold, despite the warm air from the car's heater. I checked my iPhone.

35 degrees.

Almost snow weather.

"You seem distant."

"I'm fine, Mom." I sat up and pulled my long, dark hair into a ponytail.

"I'm so excited all of us finally get a chance to spend some time together. Lance is really a good guy, once you get to know him."

"I do know him, Mom. You've been dating for almost a year."

A smile crept up on her lips, and her gold charm bracelet jingled as she turned onto our street. The bracelet was a gift from Lance for her birthday a month ago. That's when she'd revealed he'd be coming with us to the cabin for the holidays. To my sacred space, during my most favorite time.

It was strange enough to have another man step into the role my father used to have. That alone would have been enough to adjust to. Only it wasn't just him. His son was coming too.

Rhys Conner.

Irreverent tease.

Cocky jerk.

And the boy who'd stolen my heart in high school.

I'd made a concentrated effort to forget about him after graduation. Our hometown of Mill Valley, California, was small, so that meant holing up at home and avoiding all downtown areas where I might run into him. Then we both left for college in separate cities, and well, I moved on.

Or at least I thought I had. Until one night a year ago,

when my mom proclaimed she had a date.

"I think you might know him, actually. Lance, Lance Conner? I think he had a son in your grade?"

I felt a warm, soul-melting heat clench inside of me and then drain slowly out. "Rhys?"

She glanced up from the vanity. "Yes! Rhys, that's it. Did you know him?"

Did I know him?

Of course I knew him. Rhys Conner sat next to me in art class senior year. He was tall and good-looking in the kind of way where you couldn't stop gazing at him. He had dark hair and eyes and that bad-boy aura that made all the girls crush on him. But it wasn't just that. His smile, it was almost devilish. Wicked. And those cheekbones could cut glass.

Knowing he'd be here with Lance made me feel torn. I wasn't crazy about Lance, but in the end, I just wanted my mom to be happy. She'd been so angry and sad after my dad left that she hadn't come out of her room for two weeks. I couldn't blame her. He was an architect and had run off with one of his building engineers, some woman named Vicki. He never even said goodbye or anything - he just packed up his things and left on a Tuesday. He never reached out, but then again, I don't know what I'd have said if he did. How can you abandon your wife and kid?

I threw my energy into helping my mom move on. I wanted her to be happy; really, I did. So when she started dating Lance, I just shut my mouth and didn't say anything. I figured the likelihood of things working out with them was low. But now, a year into it, I couldn't hide from Rhys anymore. We were spending a week together after not seeing each other for almost four years.

In high school, I'd sat next to him at our table in art class, keeping almost silent for the first week. He barely noticed me, busy making a name for himself within the hierarchy of the room. At first, he concentrated his attention on a girl at the table next to ours, Bree Henderson. Bree was who Rhys should have wanted. She had pale ivory skin, strawberry blond hair, and was one of the most beautiful girls in our grade. Since she was captain of the dance team, I'm pretty sure she was taking art as an elective to keep up her GPA, not because she was actually really into it. I, on the other hand, needed to do well because I was trying to get into Henning College of the Arts, which was super competitive.

I managed to stay under Rhys' radar for almost a month, despite sitting right next to him. During that time, we covered drawing, which he was surprisingly good at. Now, we were moving onto a unit about collage.

I liked collage. We were using magazines to find photos, and it was soothing to spend time searching for just the right color for your project.

I was working on a mosaic of a large butterfly, with the wings made up of pictures of lakes and trees and nature.

"Butterflies?"

I looked up, Rhys' honeyed voice interrupting my concentration. Both his arms were crossed as he leaned into my personal space. He smelled different than I expected, kind of like soap.

I rolled my eyes and frowned at his observation. "Yup."

"Hmm. Surprising."

I turned to him.

His face was close, his eyebrow slightly lifted, one corner of his mouth tucked up like it was poised to curl into a smile but…didn't.

"Why?" I ask, sticking to single words.

He leaned back on his stool. "I wouldn't have thought you'd choose butterflies, that's all," he said with a shrug.

My skin prickled as heat travelled from my face to my toes. I wasn't immune to him.

Just like every other girl.

I shrugged, mimicking his movement. "What's wrong with liking butterflies?"

His lips graduated into a smirk. "A little cliché, don't you think?"

I frowned at the jab. "More like classic. Butterflies have been symbols for growth and new beginnings since, like, Roman times."

"Is that why you like them?"

His eyes fell onto my lips, and I could barely hear him. "Huh?"

"Huh. I bet you have a tattoo of one, don't you? Where is it? Your ankle? No...your parents probably would see it. On your lower back?"

I rolled my eyes. "I'm seventeen."

"So?"

I just looked at him.

"No? Nothing? That's too bad." He glanced off into the distance for a second and then locked eyes with me, lowering his voice. "You know, I've got a guy."

"I'm not getting a tattoo."

"Aw, come on, Hayes. You afraid it would hurt?

"No."

He lowered his voice further. "Chicken?"

His whisper had a seductive edge, and it made me feel all kinds of things.

Tingly things.

"I'm not chicken. I just don't want anything that much."

He tilted his head at me.

"You know, like, forever. You should only get a

tattoo if it's something you want forever."

Keeping his eyes locked with mine, he sat back and pushed up his sleeve. On his exposed forearm, an intricate script spelled out a woman's name.

"Who's that, a one-night stand from summer camp?" I immediately regretted my sarcasm. I had to admit, it was a beautiful tattoo. The script was simple, delicate but strong. And his forearm wasn't bad, either. Tan, with a light dusting of dark hair and a few veins wrapping the musculature in the sexiest way.

Did I just say sexiest?

I looked away, and he rolled the sleeve back down.

The bell rang, signaling the end of class. He put away his collage of black-and-white photos and threw his backpack on.

"See you tomorrow, Hayes."

When we got to the cabin, I learned something new. Things were more severe than I'd thought: Mom had given Lance a key.

"He wanted to come up early and turn the heat on for us. I figured why not. I told him how much you hate waking up early," she explained. "You're not mad, are you? I thought it was sweet for him to offer."

I held back a sigh. "No, it's fine." I didn't care that Lance had a key. I cared that Rhys had shown up before me. Because I knew that shifted the power dynamics between us.

And I needed to retain all the power I could during this trip. I needed to stay strong.

We dragged our suitcases up the front steps, but before my mom put her key in the lock, the door swung open.

Lance was standing tall, grinning widely, dressed in jeans and what looked like a brand-new, red flannel shirt.

"New shirt, Lance?" I asked as he ushered us in and we exchanged hellos.

"How'd you know?" he asked, beaming.

"Tag's still on it." I pointed at the XL sticker on the front.

He laughed and pulled it off. "Oh, ha, whoops. Thanks, Lily."

They started to chitchat about the drive up, but my mind went elsewhere. I was distracted, scanning the cabin for evidence of Rhys. When I didn't see any bags or anything, I started to wonder if maybe he hadn't come. It was a possibility I hadn't considered: maybe he'd opted out.

The thought hit me in a way that was strange and unexpected. An ache almost. Was I disappointed?

"Rhys is in the bedroom," Lance offered, breaking me out of my haze.

I looked up at him.

"Oh, uh, hun," my mom cut in, "I know there's a trundle bed, but maybe they want, you know, their privacy. Since they're both adults."

Lance rubbed the back of his neck. "Of course. Right. Lily, I can tell Rhys to take the loft."

"No, no, it's cool." I turned to hide my flaming face. "I'll take the loft. No big deal."

I grabbed my bag and headed upstairs, going left when I'd normally go right. Truth? I was a little miffed that Rhys went ahead and claimed the bedroom. I mean, it was our cabin. But then again, maybe I'd luck out and he'd end up staying behind that closed door all week.

I threw my stuff into the guest dresser and put my toiletry bag on top, but I still needed to make up the loft bed.

And the linens were kept in the bedroom.

I paused in front of the mirror before heading to see Rhys, fluffing my hair to the best of my ability and using some lip gloss from my toiletry bag. This was so strange. It'd been almost four years since I'd seen him, and my stomach was doing flips. I told myself it was nerves, not excitement. I couldn't be excited to see Rhys. After all, I'd changed a lot since high school, and he probably had too.

The door to my bedroom was closed, so I paused outside and debated what to do. Part of me wanted to just barge in. After all, it was my room, not his. But on the other hand, I wasn't really keen on catching him with his dick in his hand.

Or worse.

I took a deep breath and went with a quick knock.

No response.

I knocked again and waited a few seconds. Still nothing, so I tried the knob.

It twisted, so I slowly pushed the door ajar, averting my eyes and reaching out with my voice. "Rhys? Are you in there?"

Still nothing.

I pushed the door open a little more. There he was, sitting on my bed, headphones on and his back to me, sorting clothes in his suitcase. My breath stopped in my throat as I took him in. It'd been years, yet somehow he still felt so familiar.

I felt my stomach twist.

"Rhys," I said again before I heard the muffled music and realized he probably couldn't hear me. I took a few steps forward and tapped him lightly on his shoulder, holding my breath.

His shoulders twisted in my direction, his navy T-shirt stretching over the broad expanse of his back. He'd grown, that was for sure. His shoulders had broadened, his muscles developed. Where before he'd been athletic, now he was dense and strong.

As he turned, his face tilted up, and his eyes

connected with mine.

Almost immediately, my cheeks felt like they were on fire.

He was sexy as hell.

It took only a split second before his eyes registered me. As he did, the corners of his mouth ticked up in cool amusement. "Well, well, well," he said, slowly removing his headphones and leaving them around his neck. "Liliana Hayes."

The way my name slowly rolled off his tongue made me feel tight and bubbly. He was the same, yet different. His grin still taunted me, and his voice was clever and thick. It quickly seeped through my skin and grabbed hold of me inside.

It was shocking and unnerving, but familiar and warm at the same time.

In an instant, I fell right back down the rabbit hole of him.

It was so… confusing.

I steadied myself as he examined me up and down. His eyes penetrated me, like he knew my shape, even under my jeans and sweater.

"I need sheets," I said, trying to explain my presence, even though it was my freaking room.

Rhys cocked one eyebrow in confusion.

"For my bed."

His eyes twinkled. "Yes, that's generally how they work."

I pushed out a huff and tried to explain. "The closet." I nodded toward the corner. "That's where we keep them."

He angled his head and sparkled his eyes at me. "Don't let me get in your way, Hayes."

I paused and then retrieved the sheets while Rhys went back to sorting his clothes.

"Thanks." I passed him again, but then stopped and

hovered between him and the door. "Don't you think we should talk about it?"

He got up and put some clothes in the dresser without looking at me. "Talk about what, Hayes?"

I stared up at the ceiling and swallowed. Ugh. He wasn't making this easy. "I don't know. Your dad, my mom? I mean, it's strange, right?"

Rhys turned and leaned back on the dresser, crossing his arms. "You look good. You still doing the art thing?"

I held the sheets in front of my chest. "Yeah. I'm in my senior year at Henning. Graphic design major."

He nodded. "That's awesome. You were always super talented."

I scoffed. "Hardly. Trust me, I'm nothing without Photoshop. You're the one who was super talented."

He untangled his arms and gripped the dresser behind him, looking up at the ceiling. "Eh."

I shook my head in disbelief. "Oh, my God, shut up. You had so much talent. Remember that charcoal drawing? The one of the magnolia blossom?"

He lowered his face. "You remember that?"

"It was insane! Seriously, do you still have it? Because, hand to God, I'll buy it. Right this second."

He threw back his head and chuckled. "Yeah, right. My dad made me toss all that stuff as soon as I brought it home from school."

"What?" I exclaimed. "No!"

"'Fraid so. Said the shit was clutter."

How anyone could have said Rhys' artwork was clutter was beyond me. "Mom said you were in school in Chicago. Are you at the School of the Art Institute?"

He laughed. "You must be kidding. There's no way Lance Conner's son would be an artist. I'm at the University of Chicago for business."

I blinked at him. "Business? Seriously?" That didn't fit him at all. Not the Rhys I knew, at least.

He scowled. "I didn't have a choice. It was that, or he was going to cut me off."

Huh. For some reason, it really surprised me that Rhys had given in to that threat.

"I was eighteen," he offered as an explanation.

I guessed that made sense, thinking back to that time. God, high school felt like so long ago.

"Lily?" my mom's voice travelled up from the stairs. "Are you up there?"

Rhys and I locked eyes for half a second, and I felt a wave of panic before I realized we weren't doing anything wrong.

I pulled the door open. "Yeah, Mom. I'm just talking to Rhys."

She finished her ascent and came into the room. "Hi, Rhys, honey," my mom said, looking past me. "We're so glad you could make it."

"Me too, Mrs. Hayes."

"Please, call me Gail, Rhys."

His lips parted into a grin as he glanced at me. "Of course. Gail. Thank you again for having us."

He was being so...cordial. It gave me flashbacks to how he'd been with our art teacher. He'd also had her wrapped around his finger.

"You settling in all right, Rhys? Do you need blankets or anything?"

"No, Gail. Lily was just showing me where the extra blankets were, actually, but thank you."

My mom rubbed her hands together, and I silently prayed she couldn't see my cheeks flushing. Rhys made me crazy the way he'd just seeped back into my life, like it was no big deal. "Well, then. Listen, your father and I were thinking it might be nice to go and get a tree today while it's still clear outside. What do you think? You guys want to come?"

"That sounds like fun, Mrs. Hayes. We'll be right

down."

"Excellent," my mom said, without even glancing at me. "Well, we'll see you in a minute, then."

I waited until my mom had gone and then whipped my head around to Rhys. "What the hell was that?"

His grin had vanished. "What?"

"You were… You were being so..." I paused. "Nice."

"I'm a nice guy. You know, you never told me your mom was so hot, Lily."

"Oh, my God," I yell-whispered. "Do not ever say that again."

"What, that your mom is hot? She is."

"Rhys, wait, I need to be clear about something."

"Clear about what?" he asked, not so innocently.

I took half a step back and realized I was pinned against the wall. I closed my eyes as I took a hit of his scent. The soapy smell instantly took me back, and I had to use all my might to keep my knees from wobbling. Rhys was only inches away from me, and my body was helpless against him. I was like a junkie who'd been abstinent for years but then realized: all that strength I thought I had? All the power I'd felt in moving on?

It was fake. Not real.

The truth? College had pulled me from Mill Valley. It hadn't been my willpower or mental resolve.

I'd been saved because I left. Because leaving is what you do when you're eighteen.

I'd be lying if I said I hadn't thought about him during that first semester at Henning. Truth was, he was all I'd thought about.

"Lily." He put his hands on the curve of my hips and angled his face toward mine and I. Could. Hardly. Breathe.

"Are you still scared of me?"

I swallowed, my heart thumping in my chest. Was I? Maybe. Maybe not. He felt dangerous. Or maybe that was just me. Around him, I felt like gasoline.

I knew one spark would ignite me.

And possibly incinerate me.

But how good would it feel to burn at the hands of Rhys Conner? Even now, he'd barely touched me, and I felt like my insides were combusting.

My mind was flooded. I should have stopped. Slowed down. Pushed him away. Taken a moment to think.

But I didn't.

"Rhys," I whispered, need thickly wrapping itself around my vocal chords so I could barely speak. I felt like I was going to pass out.

His eyes, heavy and hooded, searched my face, landing on my lips.

My nerve endings tingled all the way down to my toes, and I closed my eyes, unable to look at him. It was too much, too many sensations, too much want, too much everything.

I felt him bend his lips to my ear. "You're staring at me like you want me to kiss you, Liliana," he taunted quietly.

My lips parted to respond, but I couldn't make a sound. Only Rhys Conner had ever managed to make me feel so wobbly with desire.

"I'm not sure if it's such a good idea. Good ol' Mom and Dad might not approve."

I felt a twist deep in my stomach. He was feigning disapproval? That was hilarious, since he was the one even suggesting it. The sheer ridiculousness of it gave me strength to respond.

"What happened to the Rhys Conner I knew who never cared about what other people thought?" I looked up to see how my comment landed.

He grinned. "Touché, Hayes."

"Lily?" my mom's voice rang out. "You guys coming?"

"Shit," I said.

Rhys gave me a hard look. "Let them go. Let's stay here."

For a moment, I absolutely was on board. Until I got hold of my senses. I couldn't do this.

Not again.

"Lily?" My mom's voice called up the stairs.

"Come on," I said finally. "We have to go."

Rhys rolled his eyes.

"It's tradition."

He sighed. "Okay, fine. Just...stall them for five minutes, okay?"

I quirked my head at him, and he gestured to his pants, where a very clear hard-on was holding court. Shit. He was turned on? Like, for real? By me?

I tried to play it cool. "Oh. Right. Gotcha. No problem."

I pretended to have lost my jacket. By the time I piled into Lance's Lexus SUV, Rhys was ready. On the way to the tree farm, my mom played Peter, Paul, and Mary on the stereo, and Rhys just stared out the window, ignoring me.

Talk about hot and cold.

Chapter Two

Lily

Seeing Rhys again didn't just bring back feelings. It brought back a flood of memories, of people and faces I hadn't thought about in years. I hadn't expected that. I'd been eager to move on from high school, and I guess Rhys wasn't the only person I'd fallen out of touch with over the years.

My friend Kinsey was a good example. Sure, we probably became friends because we were in four of the same classes during freshman year, and we both liked our French fries with mayo instead of ketchup. Beyond that, we didn't have much in common. Kinsey had goals of becoming a doctor, whereas I was an art student who wanted to become a graphic designer. While Kinsey was the very definition of boy-crazy, I was deemed the…asexual one.

Or at least that's what she called it, since I never seemed to crush on anyone.

"Come on, Lily, you have got to admit he's hot," Kinsey crowed at me as we shared an order of fries during lunch on the quad. *"Did you see him during gym? Have you ever seen abs like that on a guy our*

age?"

I just shook my head. Another day, another Kinsey crush. This time it was on Bryce Cherubini, some football douche. Kinsey had been asking my opinion a little more than usual lately, because her goals had recently changed. It was the first week of senior year, and she'd decided she wanted to lose her virginity before graduating. That meant no more waffling around, stalking guys on Facebook, and hanging out around their lockers. Nope, Kinsey was on a mission.

"Yeah, abs," I agreed, only half paying attention.

"I definitely want it - Hey, Lily, are you listening?"

I felt a tap on my shoulder. "Huh? Sorry, what?"

"What's up with you? You've seemed distracted lately."

I shook my head, giving up my gaze. "Sorry. No. I'm fine. Why?"

She followed my line of sight and settled on Rhys, who was sitting alone reading at the other end of the quad. "Uh-huh. Right. Is that the new guy?"

I snorted. "Yeah. I think he's from San Francisco or something," I mumbled, immediately feeling stupid for knowing that much about him.

"A city boy, eh? He's cute."

"Is he?" I deadpanned as I felt my ears start to burn.

Kinsey laughed. "Oh, shit, does Lily finally have a crush on someone?"

"What? No. Absolutely not. He's actually kind of an asshole. He's in my art class sixth period."

"You're turning red, Lily!"

"No, I'm not. I'm serious. He's in my art class sixth period and just flirts with Bree and Tabitha the whole time."

"And does this make you jealous? Because you like him?"

"I don't like him, Kinsey. End of story."

She didn't look convinced. "Okay, okay, if you say so. But Lily, just to remind you, we are going to college next year."

I crinkled my forehead at her. "And?"

"And I'm just saying, you may want to consider not being the only one who still has her v-card intact."

I groaned. Kinsey knew full well I had yet to kiss a boy, let alone go all the way. And as much as I hated to admit it, something deep in my gut told me she was right in suggesting Rhys. Because even though I didn't like him, I felt attracted to him. The way he moved, the sound of his voice - it reached way down somewhere deep inside me and captivated me.

Kinsey was too close to the truth; I had to get the spotlight off me. "Kinsey, please." I offered up a distraction. "What about Bryce? Abs, remember?"

Her face lit up as my diversion worked. "Yes! So, like I was saying, I think he works at the hardware store downtown..."

Chapter Three

Lily

Present Day

The next morning, the sunlight pushed in past the flimsy curtains, summoning me awake before I was ready. I'd shut myself in the loft after dinner, afraid of what would happen if I spent more time around Rhys. That almost-kiss yesterday had been a problem.

A huge problem.

Because up to this point, I'd been able to deny things. Things like the way his smile made all my nerve endings jump to attention. Things like the way I used to drive the long way home from the grocery store, hoping that maybe I'd see him outside his house.

Things like how I used to stay up late senior year, hanging out at the coffeehouse, hoping to run into him. I've always been more of a morning person, but Rhys had me approaching midnight back in the day.

And years later, here I was, still up late because of him.

Thinking about him.

I took a deep breath and threw off my covers. I was

not doing this again. I was a grown-up now. Rhys Conner did not own my life. Maybe if I was clever and developed chronic bronchitis, I could avoid seeing him at future family functions. Hell, maybe I could even move abroad after graduation and avoid him for the rest of my life. In any case, I could come up with that plan soon enough. For now, I just had to get through this week.

I normally walked around the cabin in what I'd slept in, just a tank and shorts, but in order to survive in a house with Rhys, I needed armor. I put on my sweatpants, some thick socks, and my oversized burgundy Henning hoodie. I even debated brushing my teeth, thinking morning breath might serve as a deterrent to keep me from talking to him, but my sense of decorum won out.

As I wandered downstairs, a familiar scent hit my senses. I only allowed myself to be excited about it once I saw Rhys wasn't around.

"Is that what I think it is?" I asked carefully.

"Cinnamon rolls!" My mom beamed. "Extra icing, just for you."

"Oh, hell, yeah." I sidled up to the table as Mom served me up a plate. "You know, you are my favorite mom. I don't think I tell you that enough." I picked up one of the gooey, cinnamon-scented buns.

"It's a good thing she makes them only on special occasions," Lance added. "Those are a heart attack waiting to happen."

My mom rolled her eyes as Lance kissed her on the cheek.

"Tree looks good," I said as I took a big bite, ignoring Lance's comments.

My mom smiled. "Lance insisted on putting it up last night."

"No sense in buying a tree and letting it go to waste."

"I still wonder if it's too big?" My mom tilted her head.

"That's what she said," I muttered under my breath.

"What, dear?"

"Nothing, uh, just wondering if we have coffee?"

"Over on the counter. Just brewed a fresh pot," Lance offered.

My mom raised her eyebrows. "How much coffee are you drinking these days?"

I rolled my eyes as I got up to get a mug. She was always on my case about drinking too much coffee, but I wasn't going to stop anytime soon since it was my most favorite beverage in the whole wide world. "Mom, I finished growing a long time ago. Relax."

She grumbled, but only for a second before changing the subject. "I was thinking maybe we could decorate the tree today. What do you think, Lily? Maybe make some hot cider?"

"You know, honey," Lance interrupted, turning to my mom. "Before you do that, I think there's something under the tree."

"What?"

"Over there, under the tree. Do you see it?"

My mom glanced at me.

I took a long sip of coffee and shrugged.

She got up and walked over to the tree. Sure enough, a red envelope was sitting under it.

"Lance," my mom admonished. "What is this?"

'It' was a gift certificate to The Spa at the Lake Tahoe Hyatt.

"Consider it an early Christmas gift. I also have reservations at the restaurant and a suite booked."

My mom's mouth gaped. "Lance, this - this is too much."

"Too bad. It's not optional," he teased.

"What's not optional?"

Our heads collectively swiveled towards the stairs where Rhys had appeared, looking all sexy in a T-shirt and pajama pants, with his dark, wavy hair poking out in different directions.

"I'm taking Gail to the Hyatt as an early Christmas present. I trust that's all right with you?"

Rhys shrugged dismissively. "Whatever."

"Well, then," Lance continued, unfazed by Rhys' rudeness. "Pack a bag, darling. They're expecting us."

I went back to the loft and tried to read, but a few minutes later, there was a knock at the door. I sat up and ran my hands over my hair before answering. "Yes?"

The door opened a bit, and my mom stuck her head in. "Hey, honey, mind if I come in?"

I wasn't sure if I was relieved or disappointed. In any case, I scooted toward the edge of the bed and nodded.

She came in and sat down next to me. "I just wanted to apologize. We came up here to spend time as a family. I'm going to tell Lance we can go another time."

I frowned at her. "Mom, no. Come on, I appreciate that, but it's fine. Really."

"No, no, I got caught up."

"Don't be ridiculous. He planned this big romantic getaway for you; you have to go."

"I know, but it's not worth it if you are going to be mad at me."

I let out a sigh. "I'm not mad, Mom. Trust me."

She brushed a lock of hair out of my face. "Are you sure? You left the kitchen pretty quickly."

Yeah, cause Rhys showed up.

She paused. "Is it Rhys?"

My heart stopped. I'd always secretly suspected moms could read minds. Why was she suggesting Rhys? Had she noticed something?

She continued. "I know you two aren't really used to

being around each other yet, but the whole point of inviting him was so that you guys could get to know each other. However, I don't have to go, if you aren't comfortable."

Not comfortable? Being uncomfortable had nothing to do with it. Being uncomfortable barely covered the gamut of emotions I felt around Rhys, which in turn fed my feelings of guilt. "No, Mom, it's fine, really. Please, go on the trip. Lance obviously put a lot of thought into planning it."

My mom hugged me. "Thanks, baby. I appreciate your understanding."

"So," I said carefully. "You really think he's getting close?"

"To a proposal?"

I tried not to gag. "Yeah."

My mom attempted to hide her grin and failed. "I think maybe. He was trying to be all sneaky the other day and was asking my ring size."

Wow. This really was serious. I'd been able to stay in denial about it up to a point, but a ring meant business. If she and Lance got married, that would mean Rhys would be my stepbrother.

That was too weird.

"What's that face, baby?"

I let out a sigh and leaned my head against her shoulder. "Nothing. I just want you to be happy, Mom. Really. I'm glad you found Lance."

My mom smiled and put her arm around me. "Thanks. I have to admit, it's nice having a man around. I think I'd forgotten how nice. Plus, you never had a sibling, and I always felt guilty about that. It could be nice for you to have Rhys around."

I almost snorted. *Right. That's it. Nice.*

"Well, I should get packing." She got up and brushed some invisible lint off her jeans. "There's food in the fridge, and you have your credit card if you need anything at all, but don't try to drive if it's snowing, okay? Just order pizza or something."

"Yes, Mom. Go." I got up to walk her out.

"And don't forget to lock the back door at night."

"Mom?"

"Yes, hun?"

"Go! Have fun. And stop worrying. We'll be fine."

I shut the door. Now, if I could only follow my own advice. I was going to be alone in the cabin with Rhys Conner for twenty-four hours.

What could possibly go wrong?

I immediately decided I had two options. Option one: I could hole up in the loft. But somehow that felt like retreating, almost like letting Rhys win by showing him he'd gotten to me.

So I went with option two and decided to stake my claim to the living room. I arranged the crafting supplies on our giant wooden coffee table, made myself a mug of hot chocolate with extra marshmallows, popped *The Holiday* into the DVD player, and got comfortable on the rug, feeling confident that the girlie-fest would keep Rhys at bay.

As I opened the Tupperware organizers, I felt little taps of nostalgia. When I was younger, Mom and I did simple things, like make green and red felt hearts and reindeer made out of wine corks. But once I'd gotten older, the techniques had evolved. Little brass cross-stitch rings with wreaths and angels and Christmas trees made from ribbons. The one rule was that we made them during our time up at the cabin. One year in particular was the year of glitter. Martha Stewart had just come out with a line of designer glitter at the craft stores, and mom and I may have gone a little bananas. We coated everything we could get our hands on in it: little fake trees, plastic snowflakes, those cheesy resin Santa's they sell at the dollar store. Everything got a coat of finely milled, iridescent glitter. And just like snow, it seemed to make everything better.

This year, we'd bought out the bead section of the craft store, which was perfect because beading was detail-oriented, and I needed a complicated project to distract me from thinking about kissing Rhys.

Which, yes, I still was. But we're not going to talk about that or the fact that my clit was still throbbing even though it was more than fifteen hours later.

So, yes, back to the beading. Mom had prepared a bunch of stuffed, felted rounds so that we could decorate the surface with colored embroidery floss and beads of all shapes and sizes. It sounds kind of strange, but theoretically, we'd end up with a bunch of super cool, bohemian-chic ornaments.

Trust me, there was a Pinterest page that had inspired her. It looked better than it sounds.

I wondered absently if my mom had thought about Lance while she'd planned this. Lance didn't strike me as a bohemian-chic type of guy. In fact, if I was to characterize him as an ornament, I'd say he was more of a glass ball. The plain, clear kind that most people fill up with stuff like feathers or ribbon. But Lance's would be empty. Nothing really wrong with it, just...simple.

And also very different from what we were making.

Rhys, on the other hand, might be into these things. He'd always been good at art, even though he'd tried to play it off like the class was lame. And he was pretty good with color and detail-oriented projects.

Annnd, there I was, thinking about him again.

I forced an exhale, located my needle, and set about planning my first design. Rather than try to do a figure or anything representational, I decided to do the first few as studies in red. Red was my favorite color, holidays or not, because it was just so festive. Red felt alive and vibrant, like happiness.

I mindlessly went to work, running my needle through the felt, adding beads in a rhythmic motion.

I was in the zone. That perfect, happy, numb zone only crafting can create. Kate and Cameron had just switched homes on the screen, and my cocoa had cooled to the perfect temperature.

Then Rhys had to show up.

His steps were loud and forceful as he came down the stairs and beelined for the kitchen, nary a hello or good morning. Cupboards started to open and then slam shut. Over and over and over.

I swear to God, I think he's doing it on purpose to annoy me.

"Do you need something?" I finally yelled over.

"Is there more coffee somewhere?"

"Pantry, middle shelf."

The slamming stopped. I heard the pantry door creak open and then slam shut.

My shoulders tensed. "Can you be a little quieter? I'm trying to watch a movie."

Rhys didn't respond, so I tried to ignore him and went back to my beadwork.

A few minutes later, I smelled coffee. Out of the corner of my eye, I saw Rhys glance out the front window.

"They gone?"

I hit pause on the remote and bit my lip before answering. "Yeah, they left almost an hour ago."

Rhys looked mildly amused. Happy, even. His eyes seemed slightly brighter.

"Awesome," he said and headed back upstairs. A few seconds later, he re-emerged with a joint tucked between his lips.

"You can't smoke in here."

"Relax, sweetheart. I'm going out on the porch. You want to join me?"

I looked back down at my needlework. "I don't smoke."

"It's weed."

"No, thank you."

"You sure?"

"It's bad for you."

"Life is bad for you." He lit the joint and went out on the deck.

Rhys Conner was bad for me. I just knew it. I debated going out to the porch and making him talk about whatever it was that had happened yesterday, but that felt like giving in. No; I decided I would stay put just where I was and stop thinking about it.

But I couldn't just stop thinking about it.

Rhys was like those cream-filled dessert cakes made with partially hydrogenated oil. I knew he was bad for me, but he tasted so, so good. Last night felt aggressive, almost like he was on the offense, trying to strike before I could signal one way or another. But at the end of the day, he was still the guy I'd had a crush on for years. The guy who made my stomach flip even when he was being an ass.

I went back to the movie and tried to distract myself with the mindless needlework. It worked for a while, but after half an hour or so, he came back inside. I pretended to ignore him, keeping my eyes on the beading. I'd managed to finish one ornament and was on to the next.

I prayed he'd go back to his room. *Please, just leave me alone. Just go.*

No such luck. Rhys went to the kitchen, and a few seconds later, I heard him pour himself a mug of coffee. I felt his eyes on me. Sure enough, when I snuck a peek out of the corner of my eye, I saw him leaning against the kitchen island, staring at me.

I looked back down, feeling sick and delirious just from being around him. But it wasn't a bad feeling - more like all-encompassing. Flooded. Like I was under the surface in a warm saltwater sea. I knew I needed to come up for air, but at the same time, being underwater felt so...good.

I could drown in Rhys Conner if I let myself. And I wasn't going to let myself.

He stood there, watching for what felt like a long time.

I debated saying anything. If I reacted, he'd know he was getting to me. But if I didn't, he might assume he could just be a weirdo and I'd take it. Rhys Conner was as unpredictable as a winter storm. If I left any part of me exposed, he'd find it and sear into me like frostbite.

I wasn't going to let that happen again. I gathered my thoughts, but just as I was about to speak, he beat me to it.

"What are you doing?"

I didn't look up, trying my best to seem uninterested. "Making ornaments."

He took another sip of coffee. "Right. I can see that, but why? Why not just buy them?"

"Because it's fun."

"It is?"

I shrugged. "My mom and I make them every year."

"You make ornaments every year?"

"It's a tradition."

"There you go with tradition again. Why do you care so much about tradition?"

I put my hands down and looked up at him. He was gorgeous, of course. His dark waves were arranged in a perfectly disheveled way, and even though they were slightly red from the weed, his eyes were sharp and penetrating.

"I don't know. I just...I just like it. It feels festive

and...stuff." I felt stupid and tongue-tied.

Rhys ambled over in that quietly confident way of his and sat down on the floor not three feet from me. He was wearing dark jeans and a black T-shirt that showed off his arms, which were muscular and smooth and looked more like a man's arms than a boy's. That's the thing about being my age: being twenty-one meant nothing. Some guys were still boys. In fact, most were, at least mentally. The rare few seemed like men yet, and Rhys Conner was definitely ahead of the curve physically. Then again, he'd always been. I think that's part of the reason he'd always been so cocky, so confident.

Mentally, he still had a way to go.

"How do I do this?"

I snapped back to the present. Rhys was picking through my beads.

He wanted to make an ornament? This was weird. So weird it made my tongue catch in my throat. I didn't know what to say.

So, I showed him.

"And you take the needle and hold the felt like this." I demonstrated on my own felt round.

Rhys watched my fingers carefully, and I tried not to blush. His face quieted when he was concentrating, any aggression dropping away.

"Then what?" he asked, his needle halfway through the felt.

I got up on my knees so I could get a little closer to him. "Then you take a bead and thread it like this." I chose a bead and held it so he could slip the needle through. As he did, his fingertip grazed mine in the softest way, and my breathing stopped. We barely touched each other, but that small part of me blazed with prickly heat that spread from the tip of my finger all the way down to my toes, making me dizzy and nervous all at the same time.

I sat back down and watched as Rhys worked his fabric with the needle. His motions were slow and deliberate as he moved the thread up and down and occasionally reached for a bead.

I debated bringing up yesterday. I could, I reasoned, bring it up to let him know I wasn't interested. But that felt sort of lame. I mean, I still wasn't sure if he'd been serious or just messing with me. Sure, there was the erection, but didn't guys get those all the time? I felt completely confused. I decided to point the conversation in another direction.

"So...did you have any traditions growing up?" I asked, keeping the subject neutral.

"No," he paused. "Not in a long time."

"But you used to."

He chose a purple bead from the table. "With my mom, yeah."

Five years ago

"Do you have any indigo?"

I picked up a small metal tube and tossed it across the table. It was finals week. The teacher had left the art room open after school hours so we could finish our final projects before the holidays. The project was to paint an abstract portrait of someone important to you, and I'd been having trouble. Picking someone you admire was a hard topic for kids who had barely experienced life.

I mean, Mikey Chang and Tony Lacosta both picked Beyoncé, for Christ's sake, and I'm pretty sure it was just because they wanted to stare at a picture of her boobs for three weeks while pretending to paint.

I settled on my mom. A little cliché, but at least it felt honest. I had a hard time getting started, though, and went through several sketches and a couple canvases before finally finding an idea I liked. Hence, I was behind. And with winter break only a few days away, I had to get this project done.

Rhys was behind too, but not because he'd been procrastinating. His canvas kept evolving. At first, it had been a sea of dark red, but he'd been gradually layering shades of blue over it, so there was almost this translucent purple quality to it. It was sad and somber but, at the same time, actually really beautiful.

The hours clicked by, the Beatles playing in the background on the art room stereo. Several students had come and finished their work, but by seven o'clock, Rhys and I were the only two left.

"That's really good," I said. "I love the way the colors are layered."

"Thanks." He unscrewed the cap and squeezed a drop of dark blue gel onto his Plexiglas palette.

"Who is it?" I asked, finally. We'd both been working on our projects for weeks but hadn't actually told each other who they were of. "I mean, you don't have to tell me if you don't want to. It's cool - "

"Nah," he interrupted. "It's okay." He put his brush down and rolled his neck. "It's my mom."

I tilted my head at the painting. It didn't feel like a mom to me. It felt painful and complex.

"She died when I was ten," he offered. "Overdose."

I was shocked. First that he'd also lost a parent, but then that he'd volunteer such a detail. An overdose? Like, drugs? I wasn't sheltered. I knew people died of drug overdoses all the time, but still, I'd never actually known anyone who had. And his mother? I couldn't even fathom it. "I'm - I'm sorry, Rhys." My response felt wholly inadequate.

He shrugged, staring at the painting. I saw a sadness in his eyes but also something else. Anger, like the red in the painting.

"Can I ask what happened?" I said carefully. "I mean, you don't have to tell me - Never mind."

He took a deep breath and let it out slowly. "I need a fucking cigarette." He got up and patted his pockets. He looked back at me. "You coming, Hayes?"

I didn't smoke, but somehow Rhys inviting me to go outside with him made my insides scream with anticipation. I felt like I was being invited into something private, secret.

Leave it to me to flub it.

"You can't smoke on campus." I felt like an absolute dork as soon as the words left my mouth.

"It's after hours. No one's here. Relax, Liliana," he returned, unconcerned, his haughty voice grating over my name. No one called me Liliana except my mom and only when I was in trouble. Normally, I hated it. But not now. Not when Rhys said it.

When Rhys said it, I felt electricity shoot through my skin.

Rhys cocked an eyebrow at me.

I hesitated but only for a second. Grabbing my hoodie, I followed him, my heart whooshing rapidly in my chest.

Outside, he led us up past the gym to the concrete planter that overlooked the football field. The football lights weren't on, but the campus was lit with those dim kind of lights that tinge orange at night.

He went around the front of the planter and used his arms to push himself up to a sitting position on the edge, his legs hanging over the side. The movement was so fluid, so confident and easy. I examined the distance between the top edge of the planter and the ground, trying to figure out how I could get up there.

"You coming?" He looked back at me and patted the concrete spot next to him.

I carefully stepped through the top of the planter, around the hedge, and lowered myself to the rough concrete edge.

He pulled out a pack of cigarettes and stuck one in his mouth. Then he offered the pack to me.

"No, thanks."

He chuckled, cupping the cigarette with his hands and flicking a lighter. "Liliana Hayes," he said slowly, exhaling a cloud of smoke, "Good girl till the end."

I'd never liked being around smokers; hated it, in fact. But I liked being near Rhys. And his smoking was different, sexy even. We sat there in silence, just looking out at the empty football field, our vision occasionally punctuated by a cone of smoke that would quickly disappear into the dark.

I didn't know what we were. We weren't friends. We didn't hang out; hell, we never even talked outside of class. A few days ago, I'd come to the after-school hours to work on my project, but he was packing up as I arrived. I'd be lying if I said I came today hoping he wouldn't be there. I hoped he would. Practically prayed for it, in fact. I'd even worn my black jeans and Converse, thinking in some vain way that maybe he'd think I was cool.

I wasn't cool. I was just normal, and nobody liked normal.

Normal was boring.

Yet, somehow, here I was. Norm-core Liliana Hayes, hanging out with Rhys Conner as he silently smoked in the dark.

I felt tingly all over and wondered if I should make conversation. But what do people talk about? I was more of a listener type. Rhys didn't seem uncomfortable with the silence, though, so I let it hang for a little while longer.

"It wasn't coke or anything," he said suddenly, still

staring out at the field.

"What?"

He took one last drag of his cigarette and tossed the butt down to the ground.

"The overdose. It wasn't cocaine or heroin if that's what you were picturing."

"Oh. Right. I wasn't - "

"That's normally what people assume when they hear how she died, but they don't fucking know."

He wasn't angry, exactly, although his words carried an acerbic edge to them.

"Can I ask what happened?" I was careful not to make my tone demanding.

Rhys leaned back on his hands and looked up at the sky. The nearby city lights made it impossible to see all but a few stars. The moon was behind us, halfway through its cycle.

"She was in a car accident when I was little. I had a reading delay when I was younger, and she was on her way to pick me up from my tutor when some idiot in a semi blew through a red light. She broke an arm and a leg and fractured her spine."

I gasped.

"She was lucky though. They said if the fracture had gone a millimeter deeper, she would have been paralyzed."

"Jesus, Rhys. That's crazy."

"Anyway, she was in rehab for, like, over a year, and they put her on some pretty heavy painkillers. She supposedly weaned off them. We didn't know she was still using. She seemed...normal, I guess."

"People can be good at hiding things."

He snorted. "Yeah. I guess so. Still, I don't see how you cannot know your wife is a drug addict..." he trailed off. "Anyway, one day she OD'd. Dad found her in their bedroom when he got home from work."

I was horrified.

"I'm so sorry, Rhys. That sounds…terrible." We sat in silence for a beat.

"I know it was tough for my mom. But that…it must have been devastating for your dad," I said, struggling to find words.

Rhys snorted and looked off to the side. "Yeah, well, don't waste your time worrying too much about him."

I quirked my head at him.

"All right, that's enough story time for today." He jumped down off the planter and offered his hand to me. "Come on. You don't want to get in trouble for smoking on campus."

I made a face at him as he helped me down. "What? But I didn't - "

His eyes lowered to mine. "I'm just kidding, Hayes. God, learn to take a joke, would you? Come on, let's go clean up."

After graduation, I was pretty sure I'd never see Rhys again, but my attraction to him was unrivaled. I'd hung out with a few different guys in college, but none of them had made my stomach flip and my heart seize like he did. Maybe that's why I was still a virgin. Maybe deep down I wanted that feeling he gave me. Maybe I needed it. It was a measuring stick I hadn't even realized I'd been using. And now, here we were, years later, and my mom was dating his dad.

Fate had a twisted sense of humor.

"So," I said carefully, keeping my eyes on my ornament. "What's Chicago like?"

He shrugged. "It's okay. School is boring, but the city is cool. Lots of galleries and museums."

I stopped beading for a second and looked up at him. "I still think you should be doing art."

"Yeah, well, we don't always get what we want, right?"

My eyes caught his, and my heart slowed. "You, uh, have a girlfriend out there?"

He chuckled. "Nope." He grabbed another bead.

I felt his eyes study me for a long minute, and I could barely look up at him.

Finally, he shifted and spoke. "You really aren't going to admit it, are you?"

I frowned. "Admit what?"

He shifted again. "Did you like me, Liliana?"

"What?" My voice dripped with incredulity while my heart clenched in my chest.

"Did. You. Like. Me?" He paused. "In high school. You did, didn't you?"

I felt my skin blister as my body admitted what my mouth couldn't. "Rhys, I - " I flamed up inside. This wasn't happening. He was making this so weird! What was I supposed to do? Say yes? It was so long ago. And now the way he was looking at me - if I said yes, what would that even mean? Would it just be something for him to gloat over? Because this was Rhys Conner we were talking about.

I kept my eyes on my project as he continued.

"Why didn't you say something?"

Why didn't I say something? Wasn't it obvious? My face started to heat with something else, an anger I'd buried a long time ago. The question actually made me sort of mad, as if he were oblivious. I knew he couldn't be that stupid. "I don't know, Rhys. Maybe because I was seventeen. Maybe because you left."

He stilled. "That wasn't because of you."

I shrugged. "Sure seemed like it."

He exhaled and stared up at the ceiling. "Hayes, I swear. Would you please just believe me that I wouldn't have done that if - ugh. Never mind."

We both went silent.

"I was seventeen," he said, throwing my defense back at me. Then after a long pause, he added, "I'm sorry. That was shitty."

Wow. He actually apologized. Out of all the things I'd expected to come out of his mouth, that was the last. I dropped my hands, needle still between my fingers. "I thought you hated me."

Rhys ignored me and stood up from the coffee table. "All right. I need some air. I'm going for a walk. You wanna come?"

I hesitated. If I went, what was I agreeing to? No, I needed time to process what he'd just said. I mean he basically just confessed he'd had a crush on me all those years and knew that I liked him. No. This was way too much info and made what happened last night all the more confusing. I needed some alone time.

"I think I'll stay here. I have a lot of ornaments to make."

His eyes squinted a bit, but he nodded. "Have it your way." He tossed me the ornament he'd been working on, grabbed his jacket, and headed out the door.

After he was gone, I looked down at the ornament and gasped. He'd edged the felt in red and white beads and across the center, in blocky and somewhat misshapen letters, was my name with something stitched right below it. It was crude, but I could definitely tell what it was.

A purple butterfly.

Just liked the collage I'd made in school.

He remembered that?

Rhys Conner was a mystery. Now more than ever.

Chapter Four

Lily

Four Years Ago

"Lily, Earth to Lily."

Hearing my name snapped me back to attention. Kinsey was standing next to me, staring at me with a concerned look on her face.

"Sorry," I said. "What were you saying?"

She frowned. "Are you okay? You've been really distracted lately."

I knew she was right. I had been distracted. The school year was drawing to a close, and I had one thing on my mind.

You guessed it. Rhys Conner.

Things had gotten strange between us since that night at the football field. Any time someone else was around, he ignored me. But when we were alone, sometimes we'd get into these long conversations about art and music. At the same time, we'd steer clear of certain topics. Like, we never talked about the future or graduation or our families. I sometimes thought it was my fault; I could be pretty closed off. But then again, some days he was the *one who shut down completely.*

I found it all very confusing.

"Rhys, did I say something wrong?" I asked one day, close to the end of spring semester.

He pushed back from the table and looked at me. "What? No. Look, I've just got some stuff on my mind, okay?"

Rumor had it that Rhys was headed to Chicago for school.

"You know you can talk to me, right?"

He snorted.

"Whatever," I said, getting up and putting my artwork away. "You act all tough, but everyone needs someone to talk to. But go ahead, be a dick."

And I left.

It was a few days later that he stopped showing up at school. Even Kinsey noticed.

"Do you know what happened?" she asked one day during lunch. "It's only a week until graduation."

I shrugged, secretly worried and totally confused.

Kinsey lowered her voice. "I heard he got in a fight with his dad, and he shipped him away."

I'd gotten the sense he and his dad didn't get along, so it wasn't completely unbelievable. Except for the fact that Rhys took no bullshit from anyone.

"I doubt that," I replied. "I'm sure he's just cutting or something. I mean, it's senior year."

Only, Rhys didn't come back to school. Not even for graduation.

I walked the stage and accepted my diploma, the whole time wondering if he was somewhere in the back of the crowd.

Even though I knew he wasn't.

Present Day

Rhys didn't get back until after dark. I had to admit, once the light started to wane, I grew nervous. Tahoe wasn't like Mill Valley. There were, like, bears and shit. Sure, they were probably hibernating this time of year but still...

I tried to distract myself by making dinner even though I was barely hungry. My mom and I had gotten provisions on the way up, so I figured I shouldn't let them go to waste. I set a pot of water on the stove and proceeded to boil noodles for lasagna. It was my mom's family's recipe and involved making everything, even the tomato sauce, from scratch. The recipe took almost three hours, but I swear to God, this shit was so worth it.

I located a bottle of red wine in a cupboard and poured myself a glass while it cooked.

The wine helped my shoulders relax. I'd been insanely tense since Rhys had dropped this huge bomb on me. I could still barely process it. He liked me. He liked me, and he knew I liked him. Well, maybe he didn't know for sure, but he had a strong inkling. So what the fuck went wrong? Why did he take off without saying goodbye four years ago? And, more importantly, were his feelings only in the past tense?

"Fuck," I cursed as I accidentally spilled béchamel sauce on my shirt. Between the wine and the distracting thoughts, I guess I should've been paying a little more attention to the things in front of me that involved hot liquids and live flames.

I finished putting the lasagna together and then went upstairs to change. And yes, I'm ashamed to admit I took a little longer picking out what to wear, knowing Rhys would be back soon. I didn't want it to seem like I was trying too hard, though. He already had me on defense. I ended up going with a fitted, burgundy plaid shirt. It was cabin-appropriate, and leaving the top two buttons undone felt cute but not like I was trying too hard.

Ugh, Hayes, you are the worst, I scolded myself as I fluffed my hair and added a fresh coat of mascara.

Back downstairs, I started up a new movie while the lasagna cooled on the stove. Rhys still wasn't back. I started to wonder if I should get his number from my mom and text him. But knowing Mom, she wouldn't just give it to me; she'd want to know what was going on, and it'd become this whole big thing and...yeah.

I wasn't going to do that.

So I cut myself a corner piece of lasagna, poured myself another glass of red wine, and was just settling in at the table when the front door opened.

I took another big gulp of wine, already feeling warm from the purple liquid. I really wasn't used to drinking despite being almost done with college—probably because I didn't have many friends at Henning. Well, that and because I'd managed to get into a school whose only organized sport was Ultimate Frisbee and whose campus brochure proudly boasted that they'd hosted absolutely no Greek life since its founding in 1889. Don't get me wrong; weed and other mind-altering substances were plentiful, but on a Saturday night, I was more likely to be found in the computer lab than at a party.

"You cooked me dinner, Hayes," Rhys stated confidently, striding into the kitchen. His cheeks were rosy from the cold, and the cool smell of night and smoke trailed behind him. "You shouldn't have."

"It's lasagna." I tried to stop my eyes from travelling to his hips. I'd always been attracted to that part of him. The way his jeans hung on him, the confidence that exuded from that area. Once in art class, he'd reached for some charcoal off a high shelf and his shirt had hitched up, granting me a glimpse of his abs. They'd been lean but strong. Nothing obnoxious like an eight-pack but taught and muscular, with a nice V leading below his belt.

As he helped himself to a plate, I watched his back and the way it tapered from his broad shoulders downward to his hips When he turned, I looked away before he could catch me checking him out.

He eyed my glass as he sidled up to the table. "Wine?"

My throat stuck, stunned that Rhys knew when my birthday was. "I don't think Mom will miss it."

He laughed. "Guess you're not as much of a good girl as I thought." He got up, grabbed a glass, and poured himself some. "Didn't realize there was any alcohol in this place. You were holding out on me. We could have been having so much more fun today."

I swallowed, trying to decipher what he meant. One glass already down, my assumptions skewed dirty. I had to admit, getting drunk with Rhys was tempting. With my inhibitions reduced, I could finally admit that I wanted him. Dick or not, he was still Rhys Conner, the boy I'd had a crush on for years. I wanted his hands on my body, I wanted to feel him pressed up against my skin, his excitement hard against me as he took me and didn't apologize.

That's what I wanted.

I felt my skin burn with desire and wondered if he could tell how I felt. I didn't dare say anything though. That would be stupid. There was a lot you could blame on wine, but confessions of unrequited love definitely weren't one of them.

We ate in silence. When Rhys finished, he sat back and eyed me.

"That lasagna was really good."

"Thanks."

"Did you follow a recipe or something?"

I shook my head. "Nah. My mom taught me how to make it."

"Ah."

A long pause developed, so I changed the subject. "So, your dad seems nice."

Rhys snorted.

"What?"

He glanced up at me and took another swig of wine. "Have you spent any time with the guy? Like real, extended time?"

"Well, no, not really. I've been away at school. But my mom likes him."

Rhys mumbled something and rubbed his thumb against his glass.

"What was that?"

"Nothing. Never mind."

We were quiet for another minute while we sipped our wine.

"Where did you go?" I asked.

Rhys looked out the window. "Just for a walk."

"You were gone for a long time."

His eyes grabbed mine. "You miss me, Hayes?"

I looked down at my plate. "It's just a long time to be gone, that's all."

He stared at me for a moment, and it made me feel nervous, like I didn't know what was coming next.

"I went down to the lake. That's it."

"You went down to the lake for seven hours?"

He shrugged.

I wasn't going to pry him for more info. He'd shared what he was willing share, and I wasn't going to beg. "Here, give me your plate." I got up and took the dishes to the sink. I was a little more wobbly on my feet than I anticipated.

Rhys got up and leaned against the counter next to me as I rinsed the plates. I felt his eyes burning into me as I went through the motions of rinsing and drying the dishes.

"Why are you looking at me like that?" I finally asked.

"Like what?"

Like you've been lost at sea and I'm the shore. I placed the last plate on the drying rack and looked up at him.

His dark eyes slammed right into me, hard and fast.

"I was thinking, Liliana. At the lake. That's what I was doing."

I swallowed as he stepped into me. "About what?"

He took his hand and ran the back of it along my jaw. I shivered.

"You."

I closed my eyes. This wasn't happening, was it? Holy shit.

"I want to kiss you, Lily," he whispered as he bent against the side of my head.

My eyes still closed, I nodded ever so slightly. I felt his hand slip along the nape of my neck as he tilted my face up toward his. I didn't dare open my eyes. A moment later, I felt the soft pressure of his lips as they connected with mine.

Holy shit, I was kissing Rhys Conner.

He tasted like leather and berries from the wine and faintly like cigarettes. It was naughty and forbidden and, if I was being honest, completely delicious. He pulled me into him, enveloping me, taking me until I grew so light-headed I had to stop and pull back.

"Whoa," I said, panting, our foreheads still touching.

He just grinned and went in again. I felt his erection hard against his jeans as he trailed his hand down toward my waistband and then under my flannel shirt.

Rhys was feeling me up!

My breasts were so sensitive that when he cupped them I felt a shock trace deep into my core.

"You okay?" he teased when I shook.

"Mmmhmm." I nodded. "Don't stop."

We made out for a few more minutes, and I grew wet and heavy with need as I felt his hardness grow against me. He must have noticed me pressing against it, because he reached down, undid my jeans, and slipped his hand inside.

"Oh, God," I breathed as he gently brushed against my nub.

"You like that?"

"Uh-huh."

"Lily," he rasped. "How many glasses of wine have you had?" He pulled his lips back an inch.

I blinked and swallowed, drunk off desire. "What? Why?"

His eyes grew dark. "Because I want to fuck you right now, but if you've had too much to drink, then I'd be taking advantage of you."

My mouth grew dry as Rhys Conner sucked the air right out of my lungs. I wanted it, wanted him so much it hurt. And he was basically telling me that right here, right now, he wanted me too.

"I'm not drunk," I confirmed with all the strength I could muster.

His grin stretched from cheek to cheek. "Excellent. Because we have twelve hours until our parents get back, and I intend to use every single one of them. Don't even think about sleep, Liliana, because you aren't going to get any."

Rhys hoisted me up onto the kitchen counter and rubbed me harder as he kissed my neck. "Do you still have those red shorts you used to wear?" he whispered into my ear.

"The striped ones? Maybe. I'd have to look," I panted. I was so wet, already climbing with need.

"I can't tell you how many times I beat off thinking about you in those shorts, Hayes."

He what? Oh Jesus. I was barely holding on.

He grunted and started to peel my jeans off me.

I followed suit and tore off my flannel shirt. I was almost naked on the counter, in nothing but my panties and bra. Of course, all the underwear I'd brought was holiday themed because, well, that's how I roll. And because I hadn't planned on getting undressed by my ex-crush during this trip.

Rhys examined me quietly, his eyes serious and dark.

"Sorry about the underwear," I said finally, gesturing toward the candy cane print. "It's all I brought."

His eyes ticked up to meet mine, and I felt heat in his voice. "Lemme guess...tradition?"

I pushed down a smile. "Maybe."

He pulled me up off the counter like I weighed nothing at all and carried me down the hall.

"Where are we going?" I asked, even though I knew.

"I've waited years for this, Liliana. I'm doing this fucking right."

He took me to his room and laid me down on the bed. I should have felt self-conscious; I wasn't accustomed to getting naked in front of random guys. But then again, Rhys wasn't a random guy. No one else in my twenty-plus years on this earth had ever made me feel like he did. Lying there on the bed, I felt confident, I felt sexy, I felt desired.

It was heady. Powerful.

Rhys lowered the lights so they were dim, but we could still see each other. Then, he watched me, his gaze hard and steadfast as he pulled off his shirt.

Holy-Mother-of-Moses. His chest was so firm and smooth, rippling abs leading down toward that perfect V I remembered.

His belt clanged as he unbuckled it and then undid his zipper. His erection was already evident through his jeans; I'd felt it earlier, and I was growing even wetter as

I saw his interest. I wanted to see him, taste him, touch him in every way I could.

He slowly removed his pants and boxers to reveal his cock, thick and heavy, defying gravity as it angled skyward.

I wanted it. I wanted all of it so badly. My hand trailed down to my sex; I felt desperate to relieve the tension building inside of me. I needed to come.

Rhys knelt over me on the bed and pinned my hands to my sides. "Uh-uh, dirty girl. You don't get to come until I tell you. You hear me?"

I let out a little moan.

"That's right. That's what you get for making me wait all those years. But don't worry, I'm not going to make you wait long. You want to come, Liliana?"

I whimpered.

"I'm going to make you come all... night... long," he said, his cock bouncing against my swollen clit. "God damn, you're so fucking beautiful, you know that?" he whispered.

I angled my hips, trying to get some more of that amazing feeling. I was beyond ready and desperate for relief. If he didn't make me come soon, I felt like my head would explode.

His fingers found my panties and slipped inside. As he ran his fingers over my channel, he murmured appreciatively. "Wet already, Liliana?"

I pushed my hand against his face, pressing him away, and he responded by pressing my clit with his thumb and thrusting a finger inside me.

A shiver rippled through me, and a second later I rocked against the pressure.

"Good, sweetheart?"

I nodded appreciatively.

"Good. I'm gonna take my time with you, but you stay with me, okay?"

I nodded again.

He pulled off my panties and unhooked my bra. "You always had the best fucking tits in the entire school." He dipped down to take my nipple in his mouth. "Did you know that?"

"You're just saying that because they're the tits in your face," I joked.

He stopped and looked up at me. "No, I'm serious. You should have heard the guys in the locker room. You and Araceli Mendez."

Ara - who? I couldn't process what he was talking about. Sensation was taking over. He played with my breasts until they were so sensitized I thought I could come just from him touching them.

"I'm gonna fuck these titties later," he rasped, his eyes drunk with lust. "But first I want to taste you."

He lifted off me and picked up my legs by the ankles, spreading me.

I couldn't look up, knowing I was on full view to him without even darkness to conceal anything. I squeezed my eyes shut. I'd never let a boy anywhere near there before, and my heart was beating so fast I thought I might pass out. But it was exciting and intoxicating, the way I felt, and despite everything, I trusted him.

He lowered his mouth to me, and I felt a surge of electricity rip through me, emanating from my most sensitive parts.

"Fuck Liliana," he groaned. "You're so fucking sweet."

He licked and ate at me, teasing me in the very best way as I felt my sex pulse and grasp for the relief I knew was almost within my reach. I built and built, twisting and tensing so much that I almost saw stars and then -

I heard a car door slam outside.

I almost didn't pay mind to it until I remembered there weren't any neighbors close by.

Shit.

"Rhys, Rhys," I pleaded, pushing his head out from between my legs.

He looked confused, still in a daze similar to mine.

"Rhys, I think someone's outside."

He rolled his eyes. "No one's there." He pulled my legs back apart.

I snapped them back together. "I'm serious. I heard a car."

Less than a beat later, we heard the front door open downstairs. "Lily? Rhys? Are you home?"

Rhys' eyes widened. "Shit!" he whispered. "What the fuck are they doing home? I thought you said they were spending the night."

"They said they were," I hissed. "Hurry, put your clothes on."

I jumped into my underwear and looked around the room. "Shit, shit, shit!"

"What?"

"My clothes - they're in the kitchen!"

"Don't you have any clothes up here?"

"I do, but they're all the way in the loft. What if they see me?"

Rhys rubbed the back of his neck. "I'll go downstairs, distract them. Then you go and get dressed and come down."

"What if they come upstairs anyway?"

"Then I'll tackle them. I don't know, Lily. Geez, do you have a better idea?"

"Okay, fuck. Hurry. You have to make sure they don't come up here."

As Rhys threw on a shirt, I noticed some scars on his back I hadn't seen before. Thick and pale, the marks spread out in an uneven pattern from his shoulder blades down.

I gasped. "Rhys."

He glanced over at me and ran his hands through his hair, ignoring my reaction. "You gonna blow it for us, Hayes?"

I fell silent and watched as he checked the hall and then left.

I got up after him and pressed my ear to the door, my heart thumping. A few seconds later, I heard him start talking to them downstairs. I darted down the hall and into the spare room.

I gathered myself as quickly as I could and dressed in jeans and a sweater. With blue balls the size of Texas, I padded downstairs to find my mom sitting at the dinner table as Rhys made tea.

I tried to play it cool as I scanned the room for my discarded clothing.

"Hey, Mom. What's going on? I thought you guys were staying at the Hyatt."

My mom looked up. "Oh, hey, honey. I was just telling Rhys, we had a little change of plans."

I looked at her quizzically, not daring to glance toward Rhys. *Where the hell were my clothes?* Shit. I was starting to get worried.

"Seems there was a little mix-up with the hotel. They booked the spa day and dinner just fine, but I guess they managed to lose our reservation for the room."

"What do you mean, lose your reservation?" I asked, only half present.

Rhys brought over a teapot and a couple cups. "Lily, you want tea?"

"Uh, sure, thanks." I tried not to blush as I remembered that not five minutes ago he'd been complimenting my tits.

"You okay, honey? You look a little flushed. You aren't getting sick, are you?"

"Nah, Mom, I'm fine. I just had a little of your wine. Sorry, I should have told you. So, the hotel? What happened?"

She shrugged. "I honestly don't know. I think it's just one of those freak things. And unfortunately, since it was the holidays, they couldn't move us to another room. They did offer to put us up at the Marriott, but Lance had a fit and stormed out."

"Whoa." I ventured to look at Rhys, who was listening as he leaned against the counter.

"He's still a bit ticked off, so he's driving it off," my mom said matter-of-factly. "It's fine. I told him he can come home once he's calmed down."

Rhys chortled. "Yeah, good luck with that."

My mom turned to him. "He'll be fine; he just needs some time."

Rhys didn't say anything but locked eyes with me.

That night, I lay awake in my room, unable to sleep. I couldn't sleep because I couldn't stop thinking about Rhys. I mean, what was I planning to do? Sleep with him and then what? We weren't relationship material. No way.

Rhys had gone up to his room before we had a chance to talk about things, so now I was more confused than ever. I was still a virgin, so I didn't really have any experience with one night stands. I guess I could sleep with Rhys, and then...we could go our separate ways. That could work, right? No one would need to know, but I could die knowing I'd scratched that itch.

I picked up my phone. I didn't have his number, so I opened up Facebook and searched his name. When it came up, I was surprised to see he'd changed his profile picture to a photo of Lake Tahoe.

I guess he really did go for a long walk.

My finger hovered over the profile as I debated what to do. Messaging felt really forward. Almost like a booty call or something. Was I really doing this? If I messaged him, what would I even say? 'Hi'? 'Hi' seemed too perky. Maybe 'Hey'? 'Hey' was more casual, right?

I started to blush even though I was the only one in the room. This was ridiculous. I wasn't going to message Rhys. Yes, he was hot, and yes, I wanted him, but I wasn't going to do it like this. Besides, what did I think would happen? This was crazy. My hormones were working overtime and making me behave illogically.

I put my phone back on my nightstand just as there was a soft knock on my door.

My stomach flipped.

I sat there frozen for what felt like forever, but then the knock came again.

I got up and slowly made my way to the door where I heard Rhys hiss, "Hayes, you in there? Open up."

My heart seized up as I gripped the metal door handle and turned.

I opened the door only a few inches. "What are you doing?" I mouthed.

"Hey." He pushed past me easily, tossing my missing jeans and shirt on the bed. "Thought you might want your clothes back."

I glanced down the hallway to make sure no one had seen him and then carefully shut the door so it didn't make a sound. "Oh, thank God. Where were they?"

"I hid them in a cabinet when your mom wasn't looking."

"Wow," I said, relieved. "Thanks."

"Can't have her thinking her daughter was about to fuck someone in the kitchen," he teased, stepping into me, pinning me up against the wall, and pulling my mouth into his.

I let myself enjoy the sensation for exactly ten seconds as my body rocketed back to life. When we both pulled away for air, I gasped. "What are you doing?"

He reached down for his belt and unhooked it.

"Finishing where we left off."

"Rhys."

His dark eyes met mine, and I felt a heady wash of dizziness take over me.

"Are you sure this is a good idea?"

His mouth spread into a wicked smile. "No, Liliana. I think it's very, very bad. But that's what I like about it."

"My mom is downstairs."

"So we'll have to be quiet."

He picked me up and took me over the bed. As he removed his clothes, I did the same, and we watched each other silently as we disrobed. Once he was naked and I was just in my bra and panties, he gripped his dick and gave it a few slow pumps.

"God fucking damn, Liliana. This? You right here? Fucking perfection."

I held his eyes and let my hand travel down inside my panties.

His eyes narrowed. He knew I was defying him on purpose.

He took a knee to the bed and crawled over me, taking my hand and wrapping his fingers around it. "You like that, sweetheart?" he said, pressing our hands against my clit.

The relief was still so far away, but the pressure felt exquisite. "Shh. You have to be quiet. Maybe we should move to the bedroom?"

"Stop worrying. They're in for the night." He continued to rub me with my fingers. "You like it like that? You like feeling how wet you are?"

I quietly moaned an affirmative.

"It's time for you to explore, Liliana." And with that, he removed our hands and started to tug down my panties until he'd pulled them off completely.

I clapped my knees together, nervous about what was to come.

"Uh-uh, baby girl." He smoothed his hands up my calves and then gently eased the knees apart so I was on view to him. "That's it. Let me see you."

I squeezed my eyes shut, too embarrassed to look at him.

He noticed. "Look at me, Liliana," he commanded.

I did as he asked.

He locked eyes with me. "You have a beautiful pussy. Don't be ashamed of it."

I swallowed and nodded.

He climbed to the side of me. "Give me your hand."

He locked his hand around mine again and slowly dragged it down my thigh and around my hips before dipping in between my legs.

"So wet," he observed appreciatively. "You wet for me?"

I nodded feverishly. I was splayed open but caring less and less. I needed to come.

His fingers held mine in place as he used them to trace the fleshy area surrounding my entrance.

"You feel that?" he asked. "You're so soft. I can't wait to get my cock in there. I bet it feels just like fucking heaven."

I closed my eyes again, anxious about this being my first time. "Rhys," I said nervously. "I should tell you…"

I felt him slow. "Yes, Liliana?"

"I, uh, see, I'm, uh, a virgin. I mean, it's not a big deal, but I just wanted you to know."

For a moment, neither of us moved. But then Rhys let out a chuckle. "I know, Hayes."

I twisted to face him. "You do?"

He shrugged. "Well, I wasn't one hundred percent, but let's just say I was pretty sure."

"Oh," I said, uncertain what to make of that. "Okay."

"Don't worry, I'll go slow."

I nodded.

He resumed the control he had of my hand and singled out one finger. Together with his, he angled it toward my entrance, and slowly they slipped inside.

"Does that feel okay?" he asked, looking down at me.

I nodded, biting my lip. "Yeah."

"You're really fucking tight, Liliana," he said with a rasp to his voice.

"Is that bad?"

He chuckled again. "No, sweetheart, it's good. Can't wait to feel you wrapped around my dick."

He fucked me with our fingers a little more, moving in and out, slowly building a rhythm until my hips started to move with him. Then he took it all away and sat back on his heels to sheathe himself with a condom.

"I want to go down on you, but I can't wait any more," he grunted, coming back on top of me as he spread my legs and coated his erection with my wetness. "God damn, Liliana, promise me I can have this all night because I already know once isn't going to be enough."

I wrapped my arms around his muscular shoulders as he found my hips and angled himself into me.

"Are you ready? I can go slow," he offered.

I shook my head. "I need it, Rhys. Please."

His eyes burned, and the smallest of smiles darkened his face. Then he bent down and bit my neck as he thrust into me, jolting me with a fullness I never knew existed.

I felt a burn and tightness and sucked in a breath.

"Are you okay?" Rhys gritted out.

"Yes," I replied as the pain dissipated into a deep throb. I rolled my hips just a bit to let him know I was ready, and I felt him smile against my neck.

Rhys gripped my hips as he rolled into me, creating a sweet rhythm that let us build together. We grew, tightening more and more until we burst into an explosion of pleasure that radiated from every cell of my body.

I didn't know it could be that good.

After we gathered our breath, we lay splayed out on my bed, completely spent and exhausted.

"So that's sex," I said finally.

Rhys rolled over onto his side and brushed a piece of hair out of my face. "What did you think?"

I tried to tamp down a smile. "Not bad."

"Not bad?" Rhys scoffed. "Seriously?"

I laughed quietly. "Alright, alright...it was pretty good, actually."

He cocked an eyebrow at me. "Pretty good?"

I squeezed my eyes shut, unable to wipe a stupid grin off my face. "I - I see what all the fuss is about, okay?" I paused. "Do you think we were too loud?"

He trailed his fingers over my hip and to my stomach. "Fuck it. Who cares? You're fucking amazing, you know that?"

"Rhys," I started as I felt his erection grow hard against my pelvis.

"Mmm?" He dipped his head to my thighs, kissing them softly.

"Never mind."

Chapter Five

Lily

I woke up with Rhys the next morning. Every time I tried to send him back to his room, he'd roll over and pulled me back into him. I was pretty sure his kind of stamina wasn't normal, but I wasn't going to question it. I was enjoying things too much.

When the sun started to get strong, I finally looked over and checked the time. *Shit!* It was after ten. I scrambled to get up and started throwing on my clothes.

Rhys rolled over, his luscious naked body covered only halfway by a sheet. He rubbed his face and grinned at me. "Fuck and run, Hayes? Tsk, tsk. That's poor manners."

"It's after ten," I hissed. "What if my mom comes up looking for me?"

He shrugged. "So, what? It's not like we're related. Besides, I think your mom would approve. I caught her checking me out the other day."

I stopped mid-button. "Oh my God, please take that back."

He sat up and shrugged. "Hey, it's cool. It's a compliment."

I held my hands up over my ears. "Oh my God, I cannot believe I slept with you."

He got up and came over to me, wrapped one hand around my hips, and trailed one back around my ass. "Relax. Your mom may be a MILF, but only because she reminds me of you."

I frowned at him. "Sweet, Rhys. Real sweet."

He looked down at me. "You sore, baby girl?"

I pressed my lips together. "Only a little," I lied. Truth? Hell, yeah, I was. Rhys and I had gone at it for hours last night. I felt like I'd done a marathon yoga class inside and outside my vagina. He didn't just take my v-card; he'd torn it to shreds.

"I - we have to go downstairs," I managed to say as he squeezed my ass. I could already feel him hard against me.

"They can wait. I want you again."

"Rhys," I said, completely awash in sensation. I was floating on a cloud of arousal, drunk and lost in pleasure. He controlled me completely.

"I'll be gentle, I promise. Just say yes."

I swallowed. "Okay."

After Rhys and I finished, we went downstairs ten minutes apart to avoid arousing suspicion.

Mom and Lance were in the kitchen, cooking up a storm.

"Hey," I said, trying to seem nonchalant as I entered the kitchen and bee-lined for the coffee.

"Oh, there you are, honey. I wasn't sure if maybe you'd gone out."

I faked a yawn. "Oh, no. Just, you know, slept in."

My mom looked at me. "You sure you're feeling all right? Your cheeks are still rosy like yesterday."

I almost choked on my coffee. "Yeah, Mom, I'm fine. I just couldn't sleep last night, so I overslept is all."

"Oh, okay. If you say so. But let me know if you start to feel nauseous. The flu is going around this time of year."

"Are you guys making what I think you're making?" I asked, changing the subject. Lance was mincing carrots and onions while my mom was browning some ground meat in a large pan.

My mom grinned. "I promised Lance I'd teach him how to make Bolognese sauce."

"Your mother's Bolognese is the evidence that there is a God," Lance added. "I knew as soon as I tasted it, I was going to marry her."

My mom gave Lance a little bump with her hip. "Hmm... So then, maybe I shouldn't teach you the recipe?"

"Don't you even say that," he teased back. Before I knew it, they were going in for a kiss.

I groaned and shielded my eyes. "All right, you two, that's enough. Is there any breakfast?"

"Leftover pancakes are on the table," my mom said, only half paying attention.

I settled in and had just drowned them with syrup and butter when Rhys sauntered down the stairs.

"Smells good," he said. "What's that, Gail?"

"Ground pork and onions for Bolognese. My grandmother's recipe," my mom replied.

Rhys nodded and went for coffee. "I didn't realize you guys were Italian." He pulled up a chair at the opposite end of the kitchen table.

"One hundred percent," my mom boasted proudly. "My grandparents moved here when they were in their twenties. Liliana's only half, though. Her father was a mutt from northern Europe."

Rhys turned to me. "Is that right?"

I felt my face burn with the attention.

"You are half Irish and half Portuguese, right, Rhys?"

He swallowed a sip of coffee. "Yes, ma'am. My mother's family was Portuguese."

"I've seen photos of her. Beautiful woman."

"Thank you."

"So, what are you two doing today? Lance and I were thinking about heading to town for lunch and a little window shopping. Would you two want to come?"

"Oh, that sounds - "

I felt a kick under the table.

"Actually, Lily and I were thinking about going for a hike. Take advantage of the nice weather."

I shot him a look, worried this would seem too out-of-the-ordinary.

"That is, if you guys don't mind," he continued, unfazed. "It's just so beautiful up here."

"Of course, of course. You two do what you want. I'm glad you're enjoying it. Usually it's snowed in this time of year, and I was actually feeling a little bad it's been so nice. Don't you worry about us. Lance and I will just have a couples' lunch, won't we, honey?" She kissed him on the cheek.

I nodded. "Sounds good. All right, I should go upstairs and take a shower."

I headed upstairs and sat on my bed, waiting, hoping that Rhys would figure out a way to follow.

Sure enough, two minutes later, he let himself in.

"What was that?" I hissed, getting up and putting my hands on my hips.

Rhys stalked toward me, his eyes dark and hooded. "What was what?"

I groaned. "You totally just said we were going to hang out."

His lips spread into a calm and deliberate smile. "We are, Hayes. How many days until Christmas again?"

I swallowed, my heart beating out of its chest. He was only inches away but hadn't put so much as a hand on me. And I wanted that hand. I wanted both of them to touch me, feel me, take me. I wanted it so badly that my core throbbed.

"Four," I whispered.

"That's right. That means we have four more days to fuck each other's lights out, and I intend to take full advantage of every opportunity we have. Are you with me, Hayes?"

My brain felt fuzzy, like I was drunk, but I knew there was only one answer.

"Yes," I whispered.

The corners of his mouth ticked up, showing his dimples. "Fuck, yeah. Grab your hiking shoes, sweetheart." He turned to leave. "I'll meet you downstairs in ten."

Wait. What?

"Wait. You really want to go hiking? I thought..." I trailed off.

He turned back. "You trust me?"

My mouth hung open in confusion. "Well, yeah, but -"

"Then put on your fucking shoes and meet me downstairs."

He slipped out without another word.

I changed into a green plaid flannel and my puffer jacket, and threw on my hiking shoes.

Downstairs, Mom and Lance were still in the kitchen, so I said goodbye and joined Rhys on the front porch.

"So we're seriously going for a hike?" I eyed his backpack. "Like, for real?"

He didn't say anything and instead just nodded ahead, indicating I should follow him.

We walked down the street in silence and then headed up another street, toward the mountains. The homes were thinning out even more by now. Before long, we were at the end of a cul-de-sac.

"Okay, now what?" I asked as we approached the end of the street.

"This way." He indicated a gravel road that went uphill. Cold winter sunlight filtered through the pines, illuminating the narrow gray trail as we twisted through the woods.

"You know, I understand it's winter, but it's still bear country up here," I cautioned after we'd been walking for close to half an hour. We had to be a couple of miles from the cabin by now.

Rhys just looked back at me and smiled. "We're almost there."

A few minutes later, we rounded another bend in the road. In front of us was a small clapboard cabin that couldn't have been bigger than a trailer.

"What?" I turned to Rhys. "What is this?"

"Relax," he said, striding up to the front door.

"Rhys, wait. What if someone's in there?"

He ignored me and untwisted a piece of thick wire that was serving as a makeshift lock.

"Rhys, this is breaking and entering," I hissed, my eyes darting everywhere all at once.

"No one's been here for a long time, Hayes. Chill."

A second later, Rhys swung the door open for me. "Check it out."

I glared at him for a moment and then entered gingerly.

"What - what is this place?" I looked around. It was small, probably less than ten feet by ten feet, with a cast-iron stove and small sink on one side, and a tiny wooden table with two chairs in one corner. Along the far wall was a small bed, if you could call it that. More like a wooden platform with a thin mattress.

"I think it's a hunting cabin," he said, unpacking his bag. "Coffee?"

Coffee? I couldn't think about coffee right now. We

were in someone else's *property*. "Hunting cabin?" I repeated.

He went over to the cupboard above the sink and located a kettle, afterward filling it with some bottled water from his bag. "Yeah, you know, it's like an outpost that people keep while they're hunting."

I suddenly noticed a set of antlers above the table. "Oh." But certainly, this place wasn't abandoned. It was small, sure, but it was kept up. "What if the owners show up?"

Rhys shrugged. "It's not hunting season. Besides, it's the holidays. Trust me, Hayes. We're safe." He took some wood from next to the cast-iron stove, shoved it inside, and lit some of the smaller pieces with his lighter.

"How did you ever find it? I've never been up here."

"Yesterday. After going to the lake, I went exploring." He got up and walked over to me. "It's peaceful, isn't it?"

I nodded, looking around at the small space. Upon a second look, I decided he was right; it seemed like no one had been there in a while. There was a very thin layer of dust coating the small table.

He continued. "You are incredibly hard to read, Liliana. Anyone ever tell you that?"

I turned back to him and tilted my head. "What?"

He reached up and cupped my jaw with his hand. "I should take you to Vegas. You'd be great at poker."

I felt all fluttery and warm inside. I'd spent years wondering what Rhys was thinking, wondering if he'd ever even considered me anything at all, so to hear he was just as perplexed by me was definitely a surprise.

And of course, I blushed.

He ran his thumb over my lips. "God, you are so fucking innocent. I've always liked that about you."

There he went again. Just lobbing big old statements out there. What did he mean, always *liked that about me*? What the heck was that about?

Rhys walked over to the bed and slowly removed his jacket and shirt. I got a glimpse of the scars on his back again. In the daylight from the window, they were more obvious than when we'd been rolling around in the dim light of the cabin.

"Rhys."

He glanced back at me, his eyes soft, but when he caught me slack-jawed, he turned so his back was hidden.

"Rhys, what happened?" I asked quietly.

He came over and tilted my chin up so our lips could connect, silencing me.

"Hey, wait," I said pushing back against him. "Rhys, please. Your back… I just need to know."

Rhys looked out the window, his jaw tightening. "Lily, do you really want to do this now?"

I nodded. I'd known him for so long, yet so much of him was cut off, guarded.

"It was a long time ago."

"Rhys," I said carefully. "It was Lance, wasn't it?"

He deliberated for a moment before responding with a sigh. "I told you he's an asshole. Do you really want to waste our time talking about him?"

"Rhys, I care about you. Plus, he's probably gonna marry my mom. Why didn't you tell me?"

He frowned. "It's not my place."

"That's bullshit."

"What was I supposed to say? 'Hey, Ms. Hayes, nice to meet you. Oh, and just so you know, this guy likes to take a belt to kids'?"

"Yes!"

"Bullshit."

We both went silent for a moment. "I can see why you really hate him."

He sighed. "Hate doesn't even begin to cover it."

I reached my hand up to his face, and he flinched as if I'd shocked him. "I'm sorry. I didn't mean to ruin the moment."

He recovered, taking my hand off his face and kissing it. "It's not your fault. But can we please not talk about that asshole anymore, okay? I don't like to waste time thinking about him. Plus, it's been almost eight hours since I've had you, and that's way too fucking long."

I glanced at the small bed. It was barely two feet wide. "Rhys, you don't seriously think - "

Rhys smirked. "Watch me."

As he undid his belt buckle, I could already see the hard outline of him against his jeans and any soreness I had evaporated, replaced with a need to show this man tenderness and love.

As he removed his pants, I watched the hard planes of his chest rising and falling, his eyes fixed with desire. I'm sure the cabin was freezing, but my skin was hot.

After trailing his hands to my waist, he made quick work of removing my shoes and jeans until I was standing in front of him in nothing but my green-and-red plaid underwear. I watched with rapt attention as he examined me, my eyes glued to the hard, broad lines of his body and the smooth, tan skin which was occasionally punctuated by dark tattoos.

In an offering, I pressed myself against him. He caressed my breasts and fondled the flimsy bra that held them in place until they grew swollen and heavy, and my nipples were hard against the fabric. He was so sexy, so masculine, yet so vulnerable. I couldn't wait any longer. I dipped my hand between my legs and rubbed, searching out that heady high I knew was near. He'd barely even touched me, and I was desperate to come.

He took a hand and wrapped it around his length. "Goddamn, Liliana, you are so fucking sexy. I feel like

I'm gonna fucking come just from watching you finger yourself."

I simply whimpered, bending forward from the pressure building between my legs.

He stepped into me, pulling my hand away from me and placing it on his cock. "I want to come with you," he grunted, whispering into my ear as he kissed and started to bite my neck.

I murmured an affirmative.

"You sure you aren't too sore?"

"I'm sure," I panted, desperate for that feeling of fullness.

He reached down past my ass and pulled me up, my legs wrapping around him as he walked me to the table.

Setting me down, he spread my legs wide and pulled me to the edge. The height was perfect for him to enter me, so I knew at once he was going to fuck me on the table.

He produced a condom—from where, I don't know—and as he put it on, he gave his cock a few extra pumps while looking at my pussy.

"You wet for me, baby girl?" he rasped, his voice rough with lust.

"Uh-huh," I confirmed, intoxicated with need. I scooted to the edge of the table and spread my legs a little wider. "Please."

He gave me a wicked grin, holding me with one hand and guiding himself into me with the other.

I felt him at my entrance and then a second later as he pushed in.

"So...fucking...tight," he groaned as he paused and let me adjust to him.

I didn't know what to say, so I just wrapped my arms around his back and held on as he started rolling against my clit in a way that I was pretty sure was going to make my head explode.

He held off coming until I'd come multiple times and was barely holding on anymore, my head swimming, carried away with too many orgasms to count. When he finally came, his chest vibrated with a groan so deep I was sure all the nearby animals scattered.

"So...fucking...good," he whispered, pulling off me, his eyes looking drugged. "Goddamn, baby girl, I fucking love your pussy."

We stayed up at the hunting cabin for the rest of the day, alternating between fucking and napping and drinking coffee. It was so awesome knowing there was no one out there for miles and that we could just be us. Whatever that was.

Rhys turned over and brushed a stray lock of hair off my face. "How much do you think this cabin costs?"

I made a face at him. "What do you mean? Like the real estate?"

"Yeah. You come up here a lot. How much do cabins cost?"

"Well, Lake Tahoe is pretty expensive, but most of those cabins are real cabins, not shacks." I smirked at him. "But the land is probably a pretty penny."

Rhys nodded.

"Why, this your dream house or something?"

"I don't know. Maybe. I've always wanted a place that's all mine."

"What do you mean?"

"You know, a place where you can feel, I dunno, like you can be yourself. Like you don't have to walk on eggshells and shit."

I stilled. "Is that how you feel at home?"

"All I've ever wanted was my own place. I thought college would be like that, but my dad is still footing the bill, so it's like he's omnipresent."

"Nice vocab word, college boy. Okay, say you lived

here. Wouldn't you get bored? What would you do all day?"

He glanced up and caught my eye. "You."

I shook my head at him. "Be serious."

"I'd do whatever I want. Smoke. Read. Draw."

I smiled.

"What's that look, Hayes?"

I paused. "Nothing, I just - I'm glad you still want to draw, Rhys."

He scoffed and got up to put the kettle on top of the stove.

"No, seriously. You were always so good."

His eyes met mine and then darted away. "Yeah, well, like my dad says...we all have to grow up sometime, right?"

Rhys and I spent the next few days at the hunting cabin. We'd always leave our place separately, to avoid arousing suspicion. Rhys would say he was going for a hike, and then I'd leave a few minutes later, saying I was going to take a walk down to the lake. Then, we'd meet up at the cabin.

Everything was easy up there. College and families and all that pressure and drama ceased to exist. In our little shack, it was just me and Rhys and the silence of the mountains. All the insecurities I'd felt sort of fell away, and we were left with just...each other.

"Did you know you have a mole on your back?" Rhys asked languidly as we waited for a pot of coffee to brew on the woodstove. "Right here," he said, lightly touching just under my shoulder blade.

I glanced behind me at him. "It's not a mole, it's a birthmark," I clarified. "My mom used to joke that she was worried it meant I'd become a racecar driver."

"Wait. What?"

"The birthmark. Look at it upside down."

I felt his body shift against mine. "Holy shit. It's a fucking racecar."

I smiled and let my head lie back down. I was enjoying this. Things with Rhys were so easy, so natural.

I think, in the back of our minds, we both knew the arrangement was only temporary. But that didn't stop us from enjoying ourselves. We made the bed up with a few extra quilts we smuggled in, and we'd spend the better part of the day fucking each other until our limbs turned to jelly and we fell asleep together.

Normally, I think it'd be obvious to most people that something was up, but Mom was so enamored with Lance that I think I could have said I was off to join a travelling circus, and she barely would have said anything.

The days silently counted down, and as they passed, I tried to ignore the growing pit in my stomach. The truth was, this was the first time in my life I didn't want Christmas to come. Because Christmas marked the last day of our holiday and, more significantly, the end of my time with Rhys.

It made me nervous, knowing the end was near. I felt desperate to cling to my independence, certain we weren't ever going to be anything beyond the walls of the hunting cabin. I had to save myself from disappointment.

But truth?

I was falling for him.

It didn't make any sense. Rhys and I were opposites in every way. I was a rule-follower, he was a rule-breaker. I cared about family and tradition, and he spurned them both. I was careful, and he was reckless.

I was wood, and he was fire, and my lust for him threatened to consume me at every turn.

"What are you thinking about?" Rhys whispered in my ear as we lay together naked in the hunting cabin. It was two days until Christmas, which meant our hours were dwindling. I'd put up a pine branch in the shack yesterday and decorated it with a few stolen ornaments from the house. That, combined with the quilts and the cozy woodstove and Rhys' warm skin, made the thought of leaving almost unbearable. Yet, another day was winding down. The light outside the window was starting to wane, and I knew we'd need to head back soon.

I swallowed. "I'm going to miss this."

He looked down and grinned at me. I loved his smile. He didn't smile a lot, so every time he did it, I felt like I was seeing a shooting star.

"You know, this doesn't have to be the end."

I grew nervous. "Rhys."

"Lily."

I didn't respond. What he was suggesting… It felt reckless.

"Lily," he said again. "Why are you doing this?"

I shifted my body so my back was against him. "Doing what?"

"You're literally turning away from me."

"Rhys," I sighed, able to talk now that I wasn't facing him. "I…I think I need some time to think."

My words hung in silence for a while. When he didn't respond, I finally spoke up. "We should head back. It's getting dark."

"Lily."

I sat up and looked over at him expectantly, and he slowly sat up.

"Okay. Let's go."

We dressed without saying anything, twisted the wire to lock the cabin door, and headed back to the house in silence. As we walked, I stared up at the sky. The winter sky was so clear, and as the sun set, stars started to appear.

"Pomanders," Rhys said, breaking the silence.

I looked up at him, my head tilted.

He left out a deep breath. "You asked what Christmas traditions I had growing up. My mom used to buy cloves, and we'd decorate oranges with them. Even now, the scent totally reminds me of sitting at the kitchen table with her."

I met his eyes. "I love that."

"It was harder than it looks, you know," he said. "You have to use a lot of cloves. It takes a while."

I just grinned up at him, incredibly pleased he was sharing something so personal. "I didn't say anything."

He wrapped his arm around me and pulled me in. "All right, Hayes, that's enough. Pomanders are totally a respectable craft. You can stop looking at me like that."

Chapter Six

Lily

After dinner with Lance and Mom, I went on a quick trip to the grocery store. I had some special items to pick up.

Yep, you guessed it - oranges and cloves.

I felt guilty about how the afternoon had gone, so I hoped making pomanders could make it up to him. Thankfully, I scored the last tin of cloves on the shelf. I also picked up some instant coffee and toilet paper, so we could replace what we'd used at the hunting cabin.

On the way home, it started to snow. Nothing heavy, just a light sprinkling. When I was little, I used to call it fairy snow. The kind that catches in the breeze and dances on its way to the ground, like powdered sugar or dandelion seeds.

It was perfect weather to put together pomanders. I would make hot cider, and we could set a fire and put on Bing Crosby's Christmas album. Rhys would love it, and hopefully, it would erase the awkwardness I'd caused.

I parked the car. As I went to the trunk to get the groceries, I heard shouting coming from the house. At first I thought maybe Mom and Lance were watching an action movie, but as I grew closer, I could tell it wasn't the television. I made my way up the front steps, one at a time, holding the paper bag close, the scent of oranges and cloves mingling with the smell of snow. My heart picked up as I recognized the voices of Mom, Lance, and Rhys.

I opened the front door and followed the noise toward the living room. Lance was standing in the middle of the room with Rhys, both looking angry and red faced. The Christmas tree, at an awkward diagonal to the ground, had fallen behind them. Ornaments were scattered all over the floor, and the curtain had been pulled halfway down with it.

Lance looked so angry. His face was twisted and sweating with a vein protruding from his forehead. Half a second later, his palm connected with the side of Rhys' head.

"Look! See what you did? You fucking idiot!" Lance shouted.

"Honey, stop," my mom shrieked.

Rhys just stood there, holding his ground, his face red.

"This is all your fucking fault. You've ruined everything!"

"What is going on?" I said, dropping the bag of groceries. "Rhys?!"

His eyes found me, and for a second, time slowed down. His eyes were watery and red. He made his way toward me but didn't stop, pushing past me and pounding up the stairs.

"What the fuck, Mom?" I screamed again. "You're just going to let him hit Rhys?"

Lance blinked, almost like he was coming out of a trance, and he turned to my mom. "I'm sorry, I just... I was so mad he ruined the tree."

My mom simply looked at him, flabbergasted.

"Lance, Rhys never even touched the tree. It probably fell over because we didn't tighten the base enough."

I turned and started toward the stairs just as Rhys clambered down with his backpack and coat on.

Alarm came over me. "Rhys, what are you doing?"

He gazed at me with a somber look. "I have to go. I'm sorry, Lily. I have to go."

"Rhys," my voice caught in my throat, but he pushed past me and left.

I turned back to the disaster scene in the living room. "Mom - "

"Lily, can you please give us a minute?"

"Mom, Rhys just left! He doesn't have a car, I don't - "

"Liliana. I need a moment with Lance, please. Alone."

I turned and stared coolly at Lance as I tried to decide whether I should go after Rhys in the car or stay with my mom. It was an impossible decision, but at least Rhys couldn't get far on foot. "I'm not leaving you alone with him."

"Sweetheart. I am a grown woman. Go upstairs."

"No. I'm staying here," I said, crossing my arms.

"Liliana. Upstairs," my mom repeated firmly before softening her voice. "Please."

I glanced at the two of them for another beat and then retreated toward the stairs. "I will be right up here, and if you so much as breathe on her wrong, I'm calling the police," I said to Lance.

I went upstairs, and while keeping an ear to the door, I sent Rhys a message through Facebook.

Me: Are you okay?

I waited a few minutes, but he didn't respond.

Me: What happened?

Still no response.

Me: Please tell me where you are. I can come pick

you up.

I lay back on my bed and closed my eyes. What the heck had just happened? I knew what I'd seen. Rhys was right to hate Lance. He was a monster. He hadn't grown or changed. He was the same monster who'd hurt a child.

I tried messaging Rhys again. I wanted him to know that this wasn't normal, that we weren't going to turn a blind eye. I cracked open my door just in time to hear the front door slam and a car start up in the driveway.

I crept down the stairs and peered around the corner. My mom was sitting in the living room next to the toppled tree with her back to me.

"Mom?"

Her hands went to her face, and she blew her nose before turning toward me. "I'm here, honey. Sorry, I'm a little bit of a mess."

"Did he touch you?" I asked immediately, my temper flaring. "I'll fucking kill him."

My mom chuckled through the tears. "No, no, nothing like that. I - I threw him out."

I blinked at her, surprised.

"What? You didn't think I had it in me?" she joked through the tears.

I shook my head. "No, Mom, that's not it - I just....wow. Good."

She nodded. "I've seen his temper flare a bit here and there, but it was always with stupid things, like getting a parking ticket. But to see him hit his own son... No, there are just certain things I can't forgive."

I put my arm around my mom. "I'm sorry, Mom."

"I'm not. I won't have a man like that around you."

"I know you loved him."

She blew her nose again. "Did you find Rhys?"

I pressed my lips together and checked my phone again. "No. I was going to drive and look for him."

"I'll go with you. Come on, it's cold out there. Let's go get him."

We ended up driving around for three hours that night, but we couldn't find him. We even stopped at the police station, but they suggested we wait to file a report since it had only been a few hours.

The next morning, I woke up to a Facebook message.

Rhys: I'm fine. I took the bus and I'm staying with my aunt until I figure out what to do. I'll be in touch.

I didn't know that was going to be the last time I heard from him.

Chapter Seven

Lily

Two Years Later – New York City

I did not see Rhys again after that night two years ago. I'd tried messaging him through Facebook a few times, but never heard back. I was devastated, of course, but at the same time, it wasn't like we were dating. We'd traded orgasms in the woods, I reasoned. That was it.

I tried to tell myself it was partly my fault. I'd told Rhys we couldn't be together, so when it came time for him to leave, he left. I was certain he wasn't ruminating over it like I was. Hell, I probably dodged a bullet, I eventually decided.

Once I'd moved past the ice-cream phase, I focused my energy on school. Graduation came soon after, and then I threw myself into my job search. At least I had control of that part of my life.

Eventually, I'd created a life that was free of Rhys Conner, once and for all. It wasn't easy, but I became proud of myself for moving on. So proud that I would do almost anything to maintain the distance I'd created.

So when other people from my high school started

tagging him online, I got rid of Facebook.

When I first heard his name on television, I changed the channel.

But despite my efforts, I knew Rhys had done well for himself. I surmised that he must have abandoned school after the incident with Lance because Rhys ended up becoming a working artist.

Successful. Respected.

He'd allowed himself to become what he was destined to be.

I wasn't going to be that girl who dragged him back to what he'd worked so hard to escape.

I closed my laptop and lined up the pens on my desk. Almost everyone had emptied out for Thanksgiving week, and I was one of only three left out of an office of thirty. Most were headed to places like Ohio and Nebraska, to eat turkey, relax, and watch football with loved ones.

Me, however, I was staying put. Not long after the blowup with Rhys and Mom's subsequent breakup with Lance, she'd sold the cabin and so ended our holiday trips.

Still, I wasn't bummed. New York was my new home base, and it took on a new kind of magic during the holidays - I was looking forward to absorbing every bit I could. The city seemed to come alive with a special kind of sparkle during the season, and by staying in town, I could do whatever I wanted. Wander through Central Park with a pumpkin spice latte. Battle the Macy's Thanksgiving Day Parade crowds to scope out the store windows on Fifth Avenue. It would be fun.

No, scratch that. It would be *great*.

I'd moved to NYC having gotten a graphic design position not too long after graduating from Henning. I worked for an avant-garde arts and culture magazine called *Butterknife*, thanks to a referral from my mom's brother who knew the editor. Honestly, I don't think I would have gotten the job otherwise - the magazine was way cooler than I was. But somehow I'd fooled them and managed to work my way up from an assistant to the senior layout designer. It was a pretty sweet gig.

The light outside started to wane as I set my out-of-office message and took my plant to the break room to give it one last drink before I left for the long weekend.

As I came back, I noticed a figure standing near the reception area. His back was to me as he checked out the large Shepard Fairey painting that dominated the space. The receptionist had left yesterday, so I headed toward him.

"Hey there, can I help you?" I asked carefully. After all, the day before Thanksgiving was a strange time for an appointment.

His throat cleared, and my brain recognized the tone a split second before he turned around.

Rhys.

His eyes were the first to register me, dilating and darkening with surprise. Then his head tilted, and the corners of his mouth ticked up in amusement.

Rhys Conner, ever in control.

In control of himself, but also in control of me. With that one look, I felt my heart crash through the floor.

He was here. In New York. In my office.

I felt paralyzed. Not because he was famous or successful, but because even now, I felt drawn to him. Connected. He held the room like it was just the two of us. His focus felt singular. Special. His confidence and the primal nature of the way he looked at me still sent shivers down my spine.

He looked good. Really good. Gone were any traces of the boy who'd teased and tortured me. His face had a scruff to it, which was a good look for him. He wore black leather work boots, dark jeans, and a navy snorkel jacket.

"What are you doing here?" I asked, sounding more rude than I meant to.

Rhys tucked his hands into his pockets and glanced behind me. "I'm supposed to meet with Dan."

Dan? Dan, like, editor Dan?

"Is he expecting you?" I propped my plant against my hip.

Rhys rolled his tongue around inside his mouth in a way that made his cheekbones emphasize and his lips pucker. Then he locked eyes with me and nodded.

I blushed from my scalp to my toes as I remembered what it felt like to have that tongue and those lips on me. I'd dated a little here and there since moving to the city, but no one - *no one* - had ever kissed me like Rhys Conner.

I felt my insides claw inside of me. It was as if my body remembered him on a cellular level.

Seeing him felt like the first drop of whiskey after years of sobriety.

Dangerous. Terrifying.

Exciting.

"Rhys. Hey, man, I thought I heard someone out here!" Dan's voice came booming behind me. "Sorry, I forgot to mention our receptionist is out for the holiday, but I see Lily here was able to greet you."

Rhys and Dan shook hands, but Rhys kept his gaze on me.

"Lily," Dan continued. "This is Rhys Conner. He's going to be our cover story for April. That is, if I can convince him. For some reason, he rejected me when we saw each other at the Andrea Rosen opening last month. But I think he's just playing hard to get, don't you?"

I blinked back to earth at the question. "What, sorry?"

"You okay?"

"Sorry, yeah. I just spaced out for a sex. I mean, sec!" I blushed fiercely and then turned back to Rhys. "You're going to be in the magazine?"

Dan turned back to him, and Rhys shrugged.

Dan continued for him. "I'm gonna say yes until this guy actually gives me a hard no. We've been trying to get him to agree to an article for months now, but ever since Rhys was named one of the top ten artists to watch by *ArtWeek*. But lately his shows have been selling out within minutes, and now he's *very* hard to get in touch with."

Rhys had an expression on his face I'd never seen before. It took me a second to realize he actually looked slightly embarrassed.

Rhys Conner, embarrassed? Wow. This was new.

"Well," Dan said when I didn't respond. "Shall we go back to my office, man?"

Rhys nodded.

When he passed within a foot of me on the way to Dan's office, it was all I could do not to reach out and touch him as my skin flamed.

I didn't know what to do next. I wanted to stay, but to what end? Rhys and I had ended a long time ago. I was shocked at how I was reacting. It was like no time had passed.

I sat at my desk for at least ten minutes, weighing the possibilities in my mind, and finally decided to leave. This was overwhelming, seeing him after so many years of trying to forget. Trying to forget how he'd left that night.

I'd never been one for fate.

I powered down my computer, grabbed my purse and coat, and left.

Chapter Eight

Rhys

You never know what are going to be the most important moments of your life.

Most people think those moments are when you are achieving something, like winning a gold medal or graduating college or some shit.

I would argue the opposite.

The most important moments in your life are the ones where you commit.

Commit to the training.

Commit to work.

Commit to the realization that you just left the best thing that ever happened to you sitting back in an office without taking advantage of the fact that the universe - yes, I said the fucking universe - was pushing you two together with the equivalent of giant flashing neon signs.

I'd fucked up with Lily before. And I'd be lying if I said I hadn't replayed that night in my head a thousand times.

Because leaving Lily?

It killed me.

She messaged me through Facebook a few times, and

I spent hours composing messages back, only to delete the words. I knew I was in love with her; hell, maybe I even knew it in high school. But I'd been a stupid kid back then. And somehow, deep down, I'd known I wasn't ready.

You can hate me for it. I hated me for it.

I'm not claiming excuses.

So back to commitment. Over the years, I'd learned that once I put my head to something, I was a pretty stubborn motherfucker. And a few poor life choices notwithstanding, I thought things had generally worked out. I was a fucking working artist - who gets to do that? Luck had nothing to do with it. I worked twelve hours a day most of the time. I was as focused as any douchebag on Wall Street and earned just as much. It was a hustle. But like I said: I was stubborn and committed.

If there was one theme to my adult life, it was that I get what I want.

And right now? Right now I knew exactly what I wanted, beyond a shadow of a doubt:

Liliana Hayes.

Dan had taken a seat opposite me and began talking excitedly about the cover story he was pushing. You'd think I'd be right there with him; hell, this was *Butterknife*. If you'd told me when I was eighteen that I'd eventually be on the cover of the most influential arts and culture rag, I would have flicked my cigarette at you and called you a dumbass.

My point: something huge would have been required to distract me at this point.

I stood up. "Hey, uh, you guys got a bathroom?" My abruptness probably made it look like I was about to shit my pants, but I didn't care.

Dan blinked at me. "Oh, uh, sure. Just down the hall to the right."

I bee-lined out of his office and made a left, heading

back to Lily's desk, determined to set things right.
It was empty.

Chapter Nine

Lily

"Wait. So let me get this right. Rhys just showed up at your work, and you...left?" My roommate, Jen, clarified this with a slightly offensive level of disbelief. She was a paralegal in Lower Manhattan. We'd gotten paired up a few years ago when she ran an ad on craigslist for a roommate to share her apartment on the Lower East Side. She was as outgoing as I was introverted, but somehow, we still managed to become fast friends.

I ignored her as I raided the fridge for some leftover sauvignon blanc.

"The same Rhys that you've loved since you were, like, five."

I frowned at her. "I didn't know him when I was five."

"Okay, five, seventeen, whatever."

"I told you, it's not like we dated or anything."

"Oh, come on, what is dating anyway? From what you told me, the timing was just shit."

I sighed to myself. *Is that what it was?*

"Whatever. I still think you should reach out to him.

After all, this guy is the standard you hold all other guys to."

I paused as my expression soured. "I do not."

"Oh, yeah? What about Phillip?"

"Dude," I said, unscrewing an already open bottle of wine and giving it a sniff test. "I tried with him. We went on three dates, but come on. You know Staten Island is just way too fucking far."

"And Carlos?"

"That's not fair. He smelled like old lady. I kept sneezing."

Jen crossed her arms and leaned against the counter. "And what about the banker? Marcus, right? He took you to Madison Square Garden to see Ed-fucking-Sheeran for your first date. That was freaking cute, and expensive, Lily. But remind me...how long did that last again?"

I looked away and took a slug of wine right from the bottle.

"Oh, that's right, you ghosted him after that, and then he showed up here, and I had to lie and tell him you'd moved while you hid in the bathroom."

I opened my mouth to object when there was a knock at the door.

Jen's eyes widened. "Oh, shit, it's the ghost of Marcus past! He's come to exact his revenge!"

I rolled my eyes at her. "Relax, spaz," I said, feeling the effect of my wine. "It's probably just UPS. I ordered a few things off Amazon."

"Anything for me?"

"Ha ha," I said, opening the door, fully expecting a brown-clad delivery man.

Instead, I got Rhys Conner.

Chapter Ten

Lily

I blinked several times, still in disbelief. Honestly, I'm surprised I didn't drop my wine bottle. Rhys Conner was standing just outside my door.

The door of my apartment.

In New York City.

How the hell did he find me?

"How…?" I started, unable to finish the sentence. I don't know what it was, but somehow his presence decimated me, like any semblance of coherent thought rushed out of my brain. I could no longer think, only feel.

And feel I did.

His cheeks were rosy from the cold, his dark wavy hair curling out from the edges of his beanie. He squinted at me, his pupils dark in the low light, and fuck me if those eyes didn't burn.

Jen slid over next to me in the doorway. "Well, hello there. Can we help you?" she asked, her tone confident and somewhat flirtatious.

Clearly, she didn't realize that the subject of our discussion was right in front of us. I'd never so much as shown her a picture of him, probably in a lame attempt to keep him from dominating my thoughts.

"Jen, this is - this is Rhys," I said softly.

Her head jerked back oh-so-slightly. "Wait. What?"

Rhys stepped forward and removed a hand from his jacket pocket, extending it to Jen. "Rhys Conner. Liliana and I are old friends. I got your address from Dan. I promised him you wouldn't mind." He paused, and his eyes connected with mine again. "I hope I'm not wrong."

I felt warmth rush from my head to my toes, and I swallowed. "It's...fine."

Jen crossed her arms and grinned like a fool. "Well, well, well. It's so great to finally meet you, *Rhys*. Listen, I was just heading out, so you two hang out, relax." She turned to me. "I'm staying with Chris tonight, so I won't be back."

I flushed for a second time at her obvious implications, unable to look back at Rhys even though I could feel his eyes on me, prickling my skin.

"Jen," I said sternly, summoning all my strength. "Could I see you in the kitchen for a second?"

I had to poke her because she wouldn't stop staring at him.

"What? Sorry, yes, yes, of course." She turned toward Rhys. "You. Don't you go anywhere."

We scurried away and lowered our voices.

"Holy shit, Lily. I take it all back. If that is Rhys, then I can fucking see why you're so fucked up. That man is the finest thing I have ever seen. Seriously, if we had guys like that in our high school, I would have had perfect attendance."

"Jen," I yell-whispered. "You are not helping! What am I supposed to do?"

She cupped my face with her hands. "Oh, sweet, sweet Lily. You really don't know, do you?"

I blinked at her face, immobilized.

"You take that fine specimen of a man, and you fuck the living daylights out of him." She pulled me closer. "You take him to your bed and ride the shit out of him until your pussy is fucking gone, you hear me? Because it is your duty, as a member of the female species, to not let a man like that go to waste. Do you hear me?"

"I - "

"I said, do you hear me, Liliana Hayes? A man you have loved since you were seventeen has *tracked you to your apartment*. I guarantee you he is here to make amends. And involved in those amends will be a giant amount of orgasms. So let him fucking *make amends*. Don't make me handcuff both of you to the bed."

I shot her a look. Jen wasn't kidding. She really did have handcuffs.

"Or, if that's what he's into, I'm happy to lend them," she said with a smirk.

I took a deep breath. "That won't be necessary," I said, buying a moment to think. "I guess we can just talk. It's been a long time."

Jen's lips drew into a bow. "Yes, talk. Perfect. Talking is a great prelude to sex. Awesome. Good call. In the meantime, I will be at Chris'." She turned and started to leave the kitchen.

I grabbed her arm to stop her. "Wait. Are you sure you don't - you know - want to...stay?"

Jen chuckled. "Sorry, babe. You're cute, but you know my rule: threesomes only with dudes."

"Well, Rhys," Jen said as we re-entered the front hall. "Like I said, it was super nice to meet you." Without changing out of her yoga pants and sweatshirt, Jen grabbed her coat and shoved her feet into her boots.

As she did, my trepidation grew. She was leaving me alone with Rhys. It's not that I didn't trust him; it's that I didn't trust myself.

As she freed her hair from the neck of her coat, she turned to Rhys. "You guys have fun tonight," she said, making her implication crystal clear.

"It was nice to meet you, Jen," Rhys said politely. *Too politely.*

Ugh, he was totally going along with it!

And yet his words, however banal, made my stomach somersault.

We watched Jen disappear down the hall, and then he turned to me. He was still standing in the doorway, his hands tucked into his coat pockets.

"Well, can I come in?"

Chapter Eleven

Lily

Rhys Conner was in my apartment.

Repeat: Rhys Conner was in my apartment.

I wasn't a teenager anymore; I shouldn't have been panicking about having a boy in my apartment.

But this wasn't any boy. This was Rhys.

And he was in my apartment.

Did I say that already?

I felt melty and hot, and my brain had this *fog* around it that was making everything feel slow and fuzzy.

"Do you want something to drink?" I finally asked, heading toward the kitchen. It was a vain attempt to put some distance between us. Despite Jen's urging, I still wasn't sure what I wanted to happen.

"Sure, if you're having something." Rhys stayed in the living room, looking around. "Nice place. Got an early start on Christmas, I see?" He nodded toward the fake mini Christmas tree on the table and then at the white fairy lights I'd strung around the room.

I brought over the wine along with two glasses. "You know me."

His eyes met mine as he took his glass. "I always

loved that about you."

I blushed. Hard.

"I like that you celebrate shit. That you put in the effort. It's pretty awesome." He spoke softly as he took a step closer to the tiny tree.

I smiled at the floor, unsure what to say to that.

"You kept it."

I looked up. He was fingering one of the ornaments. A purple piece of felt with my name stitched on it.

I felt my heart clench.

"It's one of my favorites," I said quietly.

His back was to me, but I swear I could see him smile as he ran his thumb over the front.

"How's the cabin?" He turned back to me.

I took another sip of wine before answering. "I wouldn't know, actually. Mom ended up selling it a while back."

Rhys raised his eyebrows at me. "No. You're serious?"

I nodded. "'Fraid so. I assume you heard she and Lance broke up."

Rhys took another drink of wine and walked over to the windows. Our apartment looked out toward a small park across the street. "I heard."

I bobbed my head. "It was for the best." Then I paused. "Rhys, I know it sounds weird, but Mom actually felt grateful for that night."

Rhys scoffed, still staring outside.

"No, really. She was horrified by how he treated you. She said in some way she felt lucky that she got to see his true colors before they got engaged. But she also felt really guilty after you left." I hesitated for a moment, trying to gauge his reaction. "We both did."

Rhys finally turned to me, a look of incredulity on his face. "There's nothing for either of you to have felt guilty about. The guy was an asshole. That was on him."

I pressed my lips together. "I heard he passed away. I'm sorry."

Rhys sucked in a breath. "Yeah, well, I'm not. He was a dick until the end."

"You spoke with him?"

"He got pancreatic cancer. My uncle called and somehow convinced me that if I didn't come see him, I'd regret it. So I ditched an opening to go visit him."

"And?"

"And he was a jerk. The guy wouldn't even look at me." Rhys let out a rough sigh. "Hell, I don't know why I thought being on the edge of death might make him suddenly not be an asshole. Turns out, that situation just brings out your true colors. He used the time to tell me how worthless I was, that I was a mistake, and that he'd tried to get my mom to have an abortion."

My mouth fell open. "Jesus."

"It's funny; in a way, I guess it did provide closure, though. Made me one hundred percent sure I'd done the right thing in cutting him out of my life."

I stared at my shoes with no idea how to respond.

"How is your mom?" Rhys took a few steps back toward me.

I looked up, glad for the reprieve. "What? Oh, she's…she's good, actually. It took her a while to get back to dating after everything, but she met this really good guy, Hank. He's retired and has a boat, and they just sail around most of the time. They're down in Mexico right now."

His eyes softened. "That's good. Your mom is sweet. She deserves a good guy."

We stared at our wine glasses in silence for a moment. I wasn't sure how to ask Rhys about us. After all, what would I even be asking? I guess at the core of it, I wanted to know if I'd meant anything to him, if Tahoe had meant anything. But that felt so…shallow.

And even then, if he said yes? Then what? Did I want to know because it would be some sort of permission to kiss him again?

If I wanted to kiss him again, what did our past matter?

"So," I said finally. "Are you seeing anyone?"

I swear the corners of his mouth ticked up ever so slightly.

"No one important," he replied, his eyes sparkling as he took another step toward me, closing the distance between us.

I rolled my eyes and groaned. "Oh my God, typical Rhys Conner, ladies and gentlemen."

He tilted his head at me. "What do you mean?"

"No one important? Once a dog, always a dog."

He put his glass down on the coffee table and slid his hands down around my waist. "Hmm, is someone jealous?"

"You wish." I hoped my sass would counteract the pink flush on my cheeks. "So, you have tons of floozies flocking toward you now that you're all successful, huh?"

He simply shrugged.

"Oh my God, he doesn't even try to deny it," I teased, my voice uncontrollably breathy.

His eyes settled into mine, liquefying my insides. "Okay, okay, there are no *floozies*, as you so eloquently put it." He chuckled. "You've always been sassier than you look, you know that?"

"Rhys," I warned as he closed any distance remaining between us, pressing right against me. "What are you doing?"

His eyes moved down to my lips. "God damn, I've missed you."

I swallowed, my chest heavy with need as the wine buzzed in my head. It'd been years, but my body remembered exactly where we'd left off.

"Rhys," I breathed, "I...I can't do this again."

Tilting my chin up with his fingers, he locked eyes with me.

"Do what?"

I hesitated, my blood running fast and hot. "This. Us. I just can't."

"Why, Lily?"

"Because it isn't going to end well."

He stared at me. "How could you know that?"

"Please," I begged, pulling away from him. "You have no idea how hard this is for me."

His forehead scrunched. "No, Lily, this is ridiculous. I finally find you for the first time in years, and you want to dismiss me? Just like that? No. I won't accept that. Something keeps pushing you and me together. I, for one, want to explore that."

His words sounded so good, so true, I almost allowed myself to believe them. But deep down, I couldn't let myself to be overtaken again. It had been so much work to get myself back together after he'd left - both times. I couldn't give up my peace of mind.

"Rhys, you left me. You always leave me. Why would I think this would be any different?"

"Lily." He took a deep breath.

I looked at the floor.

"Look - I made mistakes, okay? We both did."

I stared at him, my head tilting back. "We both did?"

"You told me that day at the cabin that we couldn't be together. You basically ended us before we could even begin. How do you think that felt?"

I went silent. He was right.

"Probably not...not good."

He sighed. "It's okay. I understood. You weren't ready."

There was an awkward silence for a moment until he

spoke again.

"You know, I tried to find you."

I looked up. "What?"

He crossed his arms and looked off behind me. "That summer. I finally got myself set up. It was a shit-show that year, with me leaving school, and I just had to take care of all that crap. But I looked for you online."

I pressed my mouth into a line. "I deleted my Facebook profile."

"Yeah, you did." He uncrossed his arms and ran his hands over his face. "I figured you were avoiding me."

"I wasn't avoiding you." *Okay, maybe I was avoiding him.*

"It's okay. I get it."

We were silent again as Rhys stared at me.

I stared back at the ground.

"You know I even called Henning once?"

I looked up. "You called my college?"

"They wouldn't give me your info. Said it was a student privacy issue."

I still couldn't believe it. Rhys had tried to track me down. This was new information. Not that it changed anything. Simply him being here brought all these feelings up, new and old. It was overwhelming, and I was having a hard time processing it all.

"Rhys," I said quietly but firmly. "I need you to leave."

His face turned stony. "Lily."

I went over to the door and slowly pulled it open.

He didn't move. "No. I'm not leaving."

"Please - don't make this harder than it is. I can't - I can't think with you here."

"What do you need to think about? It's me, Lily."

"Exactly! And you're overwhelming. I get flooded around you, Rhys. Please. I just…I just need some time alone, okay?"

"That's bullshit."

"Rhys."

"Lily."

"Please."

Rhys came and stood with me at the door. "Fine. Fine. I'll go now, but I'm not giving up on you, Liliana. This is not going to be the end of us."

He left.

As soon as he'd turned down the hall, I locked the door, slumped to the ground, and cried.

Chapter Twelve

Lily

I stayed on the floor by the door that entire night. Every time something creaked in the hallway, my whole body would hear it, and I'd seize, thinking maybe, just maybe, he'd come back. I spent the night only dimly sleeping as I vacillated between emotions. Half of me was proud that I'd held my ground, kept my pride, and told him to leave. The other half felt sick, wondering if this meant I'd never see him again. I mean, I'd kicked him out, right? The boy I'd loved since I was seventeen had come to my apartment, and I'd basically told him to fuck off.

I woke up with the cool winter sun streaming through the living room window the next morning.

Shit. It was Thanksgiving.

I pressed my hands against the hardwood floor and slowly pressed myself up. My neck and hips hurt from lying on the ground all night, and it took me a moment to get up.

I made my way to the kitchen and set about making myself some coffee. As it brewed in the French press, I searched the living room for my phone, finally finding it between the couch cushions.

My breathing paused as I flipped it over. I told myself I was just looking for the time, but the truth? I was hoping he'd texted me. I know, it was crazy. I'd basically kicked him out, and he didn't know my number, but still, I hoped.

Nothing.

It was eleven thirty, later than I'd realized. I was supposed to be at Jen's boyfriend's apartment at five for a Friendsgiving dinner. But I'd already picked up the wine I was supposed to bring, so I had a few hours to kill. I flicked on the television and settled on a marathon of the *Home Alone* movies.

"How appropriate," I muttered to myself as I sipped on my coffee and flipped open my laptop.

As the movie streamed in the background, I pulled up Instagram. I spent a few minutes scrolling through pictures of pumpkin pies and the requisite *"I'm flying home"* shots out of airplane windows until I gave in and typed Rhys' name into the search bar.

I started to feel my neck turn red as soon as I saw his name, and the heat flared even more when I clicked on it.

I'm not sure what I was expecting. Rhys had never been big into social media, so it shouldn't have surprised me that his last post was a month ago. His photos were mostly candid shots of gallery openings or pics of paintings in progress. I took a few moments to look them over. They were really amazing; his talent had definitely developed over the years.

Clicking through, I paused. There, amidst the hipsters and artwork, was a photo of a butterfly, yellow and black, resting on a railing. The shot was candid and uncaptioned.

Strange.

I kept scrolling. A minute later, another one. This

time, the butterfly was orange and brown, and it perched next to a paper cup of coffee on an outdoor table.

I started scrolling faster. The pattern wasn't obvious, but it was there. Every few months, there'd be an uncaptioned photo of a butterfly. It was the only type of photo that wasn't work related. Each one solicited a myriad of responses, all of the female variety.

Ohh, so pretty!

Nice pic, Rhys! We should hang out soon!

Missed you at the Gansevoort last week ☹

After the fifteenth shot, I sat back. Was I reading too much into this? But it was weird, right? A guy posting shots of butterflies? That couldn't be a coincidence.

As I sat there contemplating, there was a rustle at the door. I shut my laptop and tossed it next to me on the couch. A key clanged against the lock a few times, probably waking up the entire floor.

"Hello? It's me," Jen called out before opening the door all the way.

"It's fine, Jen," I deadpanned. "He's not here."

She threw open the door and marched in, smiling from ear to ear. "Dang, Lily, you did a *wham bam thank you ma'am* on Thanksgiving?"

I frowned. "Not quite. What are you doing here? I thought I was supposed to meet you at Chris' place?"

"I came back to get my outfit. Now stop avoiding the question. Well? How was it? Oh my God, you have to tell me everything." She pushed me to the side and dropped down next to me on the couch.

I let my head flop backward. "There's nothing to tell."

Jen sat up straight. "Uh-huh. No way. You do not get to pull that meek shit on me. I have heard about this boy since I met you. I need details."

I shrugged. "There are no details. I sent him home."

Jen stared at me. "I don't understand."

"I told him I couldn't do this again. And then I sent him home."

"Wait. Hold up." Jen got off the couch. "I'm not following. Rhys comes over, seeks you out, and then what?"

"Jen, don't make me go over this. We talked, and I told him I didn't want to get together. Now, I really don't want to talk about it. Can we just finish this movie and get ready for dinner?"

My roommate sighed but nodded. "Okay. Sure. Whatever you need, babe."

Whatever I needed.

If I only knew what that was.

Chapter Thirteen

Lily

Thanksgiving was fine. I spent most of it in a self-inflicted turkey coma on the sofa watching the game. For most of the following weekend, I stayed in bed watching old episodes of *Gilmore Girls* and basically avoiding reality. When I finally went back to work on Monday, the routine was a distracting relief. Things were getting back to normal.

That is, until I got home on Tuesday evening. Because I couldn't actually *get* home, as there was a wall of boxes blocking entry to my apartment.

"Mrs. Joblowski?" I called out.

Wiry movers wearing back-braces swiftly encircled me, carrying furniture and huge boxes with preternatural ease.

What was going on? Mrs. Joblowski had lived in her unit across the hall since the eighties and was one of the oldest tenants in the building. I started to get worried.

"Mrs. Joblowski?" I called again. As I approached her door, a painter in coveralls pushed past me.

That's strange.

I crossed the threshold of the apartment, and as I

slowly made my way inside, I gasped. All of her pink and green furniture was gone, replaced with a modern sofa and dining table that looked like it was straight out of Design Within Reach. The floral wallpaper had been stripped, and the walls of the small space had been painted a dark gray, which I had to admit was pretty sexy.

What the hell?

"Excuse me." I stopped one of the movers. "Have you seen Mrs. Joblowski?"

He tilted his head at me. "Who?"

"Never mind." I started to get worried. Had she died, and no one told us? She was pretty old.

"She's upstairs," a voice came from behind me.

I spun around.

Rhys.

I blinked at him. "Wait. Rhys? What are you doing here? What's going on? Where's Mrs. Joblowski?"

"I told you," he said, stepping toward me. "She's upstairs."

"I don't understand."

He tucked his hands into his pockets and looked up at the ceiling. "She moved. She's in the top floor apartment now."

I frowned at him. "What? That makes no sense. She's on rent-control; there's no way she could afford that one."

He lolled his tongue around inside his mouth in that way that made his cheekbones stand out. "Let's just say she got a deal."

It all started to click into place.

The move.

The masculine furnishings.

Rhys fucking *being here*.

I couldn't believe it.

"Rhys, you didn't. Tell me you didn't."

The corners of his mouth ticked up. "Hey, neighbor."

My eyebrows flew up. "Oh my God, are you serious? You're moving in across the hall from me? Why? What would compel you to do such a thing?"

He shrugged. "I liked the building."

I pressed my hands against my forehead. "You can't do this. Didn't you hear me the other day? I said no, Rhys."

He stepped into me. "You said you were mad because I'd abandoned you, Lily. And you were right. I fucked up, big time. But I'm not making that mistake again. And I don't care how long it takes for me to convince you of that. I'm here, and I'm not leaving this time."

I blinked at him, still completely in shock that he'd moved in across the hall from me. "This is insane," I hissed, keeping my voice low as a mover walked by. "I'm not going to change my mind just because you're my neighbor."

Rhys only smiled and crossed his arms. "We'll see."

Chapter Fourteen

Lily

The inquisition started the next morning.

I peeked out the peephole of my apartment with Jen behind me, breathing down my neck.

"Is he there? Can you see any light through the crack in the floor?" she whispered.

I pulled my head back and sighed. "I can't see anything."

"I still can't believe he moved in across the hall. It's like one of those romance movies." Her voice had a dreamy quality to it, which made my face sour.

"Or one of those psycho-killer ones where he collects women in his basement. Should I be worried? I should be, shouldn't I?"

Jen shook her head. "Nope. I'm really good at reading people and I definitely didn't get psycho-killer vibes off him. Plus, silly, apartments don't have basements."

I looked out the peephole again. "I can't wait any more. I have to go, I'm gonna be late for work."

I slowly removed the chain from the lock, trying to stay as silent as possible. Then I turned the doorknob and slowly opened the door, nodding goodbye to Jen. I took three careful, quiet steps out into the hallway.

No sooner was I free from the doorway than Jen slammed the door behind me, creating an echo all the way down the hall.

I froze mid step, my shoulders pinched up around my ears.

Fuck! There's no way he didn't hear that.

I started to rush down the hall, past his door.

But sure enough, less than a second later, his door flew open. He was dressed in his work boots and parka, holding two paper cups of coffee.

"Morning, Lily." He spoke like it was totally normal and no big deal for him to be there. "Got you a cup of coffee. Holiday Blend, your favorite."

I eyed the paper cup skeptically.

"Relax. It's good, I promise." He thrust it toward me. "You headed to the office?"

I took the cup. "Yeah. And I'm late, so I really should get going."

"Perfect. I'm supposed to meet with Dan at ten. We can share a cab."

Nine hours later…

Jen practically assaulted me when I got home, wanting to know what happened.

"So, tell me what happened! Did you guys make out in the elevator?"

I made a face. "Are you serious? I'm a little offended that you aren't more worried that I might have a stalker."

Jen blew raspberry. "Girl, I told you, he's not a stalker. You've known this guy forever. I think it's cute that he brought you coffee. He knows it's your favorite!"

"It was morning. Everyone drinks coffee in the morning. Thanks for the door-slam by the way." I frowned.

She shrugged. "Just trying to do my part. You know, since it's the holidays and all. Hey, wouldn't it be cool if you guys got together in time for New Year's? Then you could kiss him when the ball drops."

"Jen."

"Yes."

"Please stop."

"Okay, but if I end up being right, you have to make me your lasagna."

Rhys continued to scare me with coffee each morning, even when he wasn't headed to my office. As much as I hate to admit it, after a while I started to expect and even enjoy them. Rhys was hard to hate. He wasn't aggressive. Just...sweet.

Not that I was falling for him or anything.

Ugh. I was so confused.

"So where's your studio, anyway?" I finally asked as we rode the elevator down to the lobby one day.

"Over in West Chelsea."

"Oooh," I teased. "Fancy."

He glanced down and shook his head. "It helps to be near the galleries. The VIP's like being able to come to the studio to experience a 'real-life artist'." He made air quotes with his fingers as we exited toward the street.

We paused out on the sidewalk, coffees in hand. It had been an unseasonably warm holiday so far with no snow in sight. Still, the air was crisp and cool, and the light of the morning was bright.

"Rhys, I am really proud of you. I don't know if I've told you that. You've made something for yourself."

He looked down at his cup and then locked his eyes with me. "Thanks. That means a lot."

We stood in comfortable silence as pedestrians swirled around us.

"You gonna be home tonight?" he asked finally.

"Yeah, why?"

He offered a small smile and started to take a step backward, in the direction of his studio. "No reason. Have a great day at work, Liliana."

Then he turned and left.

Chapter Fifteen

Lily

When I arrived back at my apartment, Rhys was waiting in the hall, playing with his phone.

Only, he wasn't alone.

Next to him was something seven feet tall, bushy, and green.

"Oh my God," I gasped. "What have you done?"

"There she is," he said, putting away his phone and grinning right at me. "You like?"

"Are you serious?"

"Yes, ma'am."

I blinked at him. "It's a Christmas tree."

He nodded slowly.

"You got us a Christmas tree."

"Not just any Christmas tree. It's a Balsam Fir. The guy said it had the most Christmas-y scent," he informed me proudly.

I walked over to it, leaned close, and breathed in.

"Good?"

"So good," I said dreamily before popping back into reality. "Wait. This is crazy. You seriously got us a tree?"

"Well, I saw you only had that small one, and I was walking down Delancey Street, and there was a tree lot, so, yeah. I figured it was a safe impulse buy. You like it?"

A smile spread over my face. "I love it. But it's huge. Are you sure it will fit?"

He tilted his head and grinned at me until I realized what I'd just said.

"Perv," I said, socking him gently on his arm.

"Shall we get it inside?"

A few minutes later, I'd cleared a space by the window, and Rhys had carried it into position.

"Wow. That looks so great." I inhaled deeply. "I haven't had a real tree in years. It smells so good."

"My pleasure."

We stood next to each other for a minute, just admiring how nice it looked.

"Well, I should get going." He stuck his hands in his jeans pockets.

"You, uh, you don't have to," I said. "I think I have some wine if you want."

Rhys' eyes met mine, and he scratched the back of his head. "I wish I could, but I'm meeting someone at the studio."

"Oh, okay," I said brightly, trying to mask any disappointment.

"I would change it, but they're in from London and flying out tomorrow."

I shook my head. "No, no, it's totally cool. I just wanted to say thanks for the tree. Really, it's all good."

I walked him to the door.

"Raincheck?"

My stomach fluttered. "Sure, totally. Another time. Have fun at the studio."

"Night, Liliana."

I closed the door and went directly to the fridge for

that aforementioned glass of wine.

And then I started arguing internally. First, I scolded myself.

Seriously, Lily? Wine? What were you thinking?

Then, I responded.

He brought me a tree. What else was I supposed to do? If a plumber comes over, you offer them water, right? It's simply the nice thing to do. That's all I was doing. He brought a tree, I offered wine. Emily Post would be proud.

And then the counter-argument:

Wine is not water, and Rhys Conner is not a delivery man, Liliana Hayes. You know better.

Chapter Sixteen

Lily

I treated myself to a cab after work. Everything with Rhys was so mentally exhausting that I couldn't face the hustle of the subway. The traffic to the Lower East Side was pretty gnarly, even though it still hadn't snowed. By the time I got home, it was dark. I checked my phone, half hoping to have gotten a message from Rhys. I hadn't heard from him since he'd brought the tree over a few days ago.

I slunk against the wall of the elevator as it made its way up to my floor, too tired even to stand. As the doors parted, I held my breath. Maybe, somehow, Rhys would be waiting for me in the hallway with Chinese takeout and those gorgeous cheekbones. But as I turned the corner, my heart sank.

The hallway was empty.

My shoulders slumped as I poked around in my purse for my key. "I really need to clean out my bag," I muttered to myself as I found a half-wrapped candy cane I'd forgotten a few days before. Finally, I found my key and went for the door.

And stopped.

My apartment door was ajar.

Why was my apartment open?

The hairs on my neck started to stand up, and I whipped my head around to make sure no one was behind me.

"Hello?" I called out through the crack in the door, feigning a deep voice. No answer. I took out my phone and dialed Jen.

No answer.

"Shit," I said under my breath. I tiptoed over to Rhys' door and hesitated before knocking, softly, so as not to disturb the burglar-slash-killer inside my apartment. "Come on, be home," I whispered. "Come on, come on," I urged, hoping he'd hear me.

No one came to the door.

Could Jen simply have left the door open by mistake? She was sometimes scatterbrained like that.

I glanced up and down the hall and finally decided to peek inside, reasoning that if things went south, I could always make a run for the stairs.

I moved carefully, stepping around the squeaky floorboard, and slowly pushed the door open just enough so I could poke my head in.

I gasped.

The whole apartment, every corner, was…glowing. The entire place had been filled with small white twinkle lights, and white paper snowflakes hung from every surface. Everything glimmered and sparkled and…I was stunned into silence.

Then my eyes caught on the figure by the tree.

"Rhys?"

He whipped around, but once he saw it was me, his face softened. "Hey."

I opened and closed my mouth a few times. "How - how did you get in?"

"Jen let me borrow her key."

Jen. Of course. I surveyed the decorations. "Did you do this?"

He nodded, looking bashful.

Bashful was not a normal look for Rhys Conner.

"They're… it's beautiful."

He reached out to rub the back of his neck. "Thanks."

"How…how'd you even…" I trailed off. It had to have taken days to make this many snowflakes. It was incredible.

He shrugged. "I took a few days off. You always say it's not Christmas without snow, right? Do you like it?"

"It's amazing."

He smiled. "You're amazing."

I glanced back at him and then down at the floor. "Rhys."

"Lily, wait. Before you say anything, there's something I need to say. Can you come sit down?"

He gestured to the sofa, and I took a seat.

"Lily." He pushed his hands into his pockets and sat down on the coffee table opposite me. "I came here because I needed to talk."

I swallowed. "Rhys."

"I can't do this anymore."

I pulled back. *Wait. What?* That was not what I was expecting him to say.

"I need to be honest. Can I be honest with you?"

I nodded slowly, not sure where this was going.

"I love you. I've loved you since our senior year. Maybe I was too young to realize it, but the important thing is that I realize it now."

He paused, letting his words echo and reverberate in my head.

My mind was swimming. What was he saying? I knew I should say something, but the words just weren't coming.

"Do you - do you have anything to say?" he asked

finally.

He looked so gorgeous in the low light, the shape of his strong jaw casting shadows and his eyes deep and reflective.

A pit of anxiety started to take hold in my stomach. He loved me? What did that mean? "Rhys," I said, struggling to piece together my feelings. "Thank you. Really. That's so sweet." I turned and gestured to the room. "Really."

He locked eyes with me for a long minute, and I fought to stay afloat in his gaze, his pupils threatening to consume all of me. Could I do this? Could I let myself get lost in him?

"What is it?"

"What?"

"That look… do you hate it? I can take it down. Just say the word." He searched my face.

"No, it's amazing. It's just…I'm scared, Rhys."

He held his distance and nodded. "Okay."

"This really is amazing." I gestured to the room.

"Sure," he said, but something in his voice had shifted.

Rhys got up. "I should go."

I stayed sitting as he paused yet again, waiting for me to acknowledge him.

So I gave the smallest of nods.

And then he left.

A few hours later, I was still on the couch in my work clothes when Jen got home.

"Whoa, holy-jingle-bells, what the hell do we have here?"

I didn't respond as she took off her coat.

"What the hell happened here? Did a paper shredder and a snowman have an orgy?"

"Rhys did it," I said quietly, still staring at the tree.

"Damn, seriously? Ah, so that's why he wanted the key. Well, I guess you've said he's pretty skilled with his hands." I heard her open the fridge and pour herself a glass of wine. "You want a drink?"

"No. Thanks."

"So, where is he? Tell me he didn't just drop a snowflake bomb and leave."

"I - I don't know."

"What do you mean you don't know?" She came over and sat next to me. "Hey, are you okay? You look pale."

I pressed my lips together as my emotions balled up inside my throat and shook my head. "I think...I think he just broke up with me."

Jen tilted her head at me. "What are you talking about? Broke up? No offense, but you guys weren't even together. What happened?"

"I don't know! One minute, he's practically a stalker and I can't get away from him, and the next he's over here with, with this." I gestured toward the room full of decorations. "And then all of a sudden it's like something switched."

"That does seem strange. So he just came over, jizzed snowflakes everywhere, and took off?"

I went silent.

"Lily? What are you not telling me? Oh shit, did you guys sleep together again?"

My head snapped up. "What? No! Nothing like that."

"Not even oral?"

"Jen." I frowned at her and then looked back at the tree. "He...he said he loved me."

"Oh, Lord." Jen took another swig of her wine.

"What?"

"Rhys Conner told you he's in love with you."

I nodded.

"And you did what, exactly?"

"What do you mean, what did I do?"

"I mean tell me exactly what you did. Rhys told you he loved you, and you said…what?"

I sputtered. "I…I don't get what you mean. He told me, and… I dunno… I listened."

Jen sat back and groaned. "Dude. Seriously?"

"What was I supposed to do? Tell him I loved him back? This is Rhys we're talking about."

"Exactly! The man you've loved since you were seventeen!"

"No," I said holding up my hands. "I don't love him. Not anymore."

Jen examined me. "Oh my Lily. My sweet, sweet, little Lily. You just don't get it, do you, babe?"

I stole the wine from her. "What?"

"Do I need to spell it out for you? Look, I love you babe, but you have some major abandonment issues. Like, Harvard-research-study level. I mean, I get it, your Dad left you guys, and now you think Rhys is the same guy because he ran off in Tahoe. But you're forgetting something huge. He was, like, twenty years old."

"Twenty years old is still an adult," I shot back.

"Yeah, but he's a guy. We all know guys mature way slower. Whatever. All I'm saying is that I think you're doing, uh, what's that word? Transference? I think you are doing some of that. Cut the guy some slack. You think he wants to be living in a shitty six-hundred-square-foot apartment in the Lower East Side? He's a fucking successful artist. He's only here because of you. He brings you coffee every morning and bought you a fucking Christmas tree."

"Yeah, but - "

"No but. You do realize a Christmas tree is like the Lily-equivalent of a thousand red roses? So, come on, girl, and I say this as a friend, but you need to wake the fuck up!"

I frowned. "But I don't like him that way anymore."

Jen stood up. "Okay, hang on. I'm gonna need another glass of wine for this discussion."

She went over to the kitchen and a minute later settled back into the armchair opposite me.

"Okay, repeat after me," she said, sitting cross-legged facing me. "I, Liliana Hayes..."

"I'm not doing this, Jen."

"Just say it. I, Liliana Hayes."

I sighed. "I, Liliana Hayes."

"Have been and still am madly in love with Rhys Conner and his big dick."

"Jen!"

"Say it, and tell me how it feels."

I frowned. "I'm not saying it because it's not true."

"I thought you said his dick was huge?"

"I didn't mean - argh! Jen. Be serious. I don't know what to do."

She sat back. "Well, I think it's pretty simple." She took a sip of wine. "You need to figure out how you feel. That's all he's waiting for! I mean, this boy is clearly in love with you. You told him that him running off fucked you up, and he's been busting his ass trying to make up for it."

I went silent.

"You know I'm right. It might take you a little while to realize that, but I know you, Lily."

I sat back and stared at the tree. The tree Rhys had bought down on Delancey and carried three blocks. Not because he loved Christmas. He bought it because *I* loved Christmas.

Jen was right. It was the Lily-equivalent of a thousand red roses. How had I not seen that?

I'd been so worried Rhys hadn't changed that I never stopped to consider that I was the one who'd stayed the same. The hang-ups that used to haunt my dreams were now present in my waking life and were threatening to ruin the best thing that had ever happened to me.

I looked back at Jen. "Shit, I think you're right."

"Oh, thank fucking God," she said, taking another sip of wine.

"I have to go see him." I got up.

"Well, lucky for you, he's right across the hall."

Across the hall.

"I - I…. Do I look okay?" I smoothed the front of my work shirt and pants.

"Yes, but hang on." Jen jumped up and rifled through her purse before pulling out a red lipstick. "Here, purse your lips."

I pressed them together.

Jen dabbed the lipstick on ever-so-slightly and then stood back and smiled. "Perfect."

I turned to the mirror by the front door and smoothed my hair with my hands. "Okay, I'm going."

Jen swatted my ass. "Go get him, babe!"

I nodded and exited to the hall, careful to close the door behind me. The last thing I needed was my roommate listening in on a conversation that had my heart pounding through my chest. I still didn't know how I'd start. Should I apologize first or just run in and tell him how I felt? Either way, the weight of everything was starting to feel heavy on my chest. *I'd basically rejected him.* I couldn't see how he'd take it any other way. But I was ready to eat crow, if required.

I made my way across the hall, stepping carefully and quietly over the worn wood floors toward his door. The apartment number still sported the two dried flowers Mrs. J had glued there years ago.

I knocked softly and then listened for movement on the other side of the door. I imagined the look of surprise on his face, maybe at first spoiled by confusion, but he'd come around.

He had to.

I knocked a little louder, my stomach feeling like lead. *Maybe he's in the bathroom*, I reasoned.

When he still didn't come, I crouched down on the floor and looked through the gap under the door.

No light came through. He was gone.

Chapter Seventeen

Rhys

I ended up staying at my studio until late. Painting had always helped me clear my head, and with Lily rejecting me, well, let's just say I needed some hardcore art therapy.

I blasted some heavy metal, which I used to do when my dad would get to me. Only this time, it didn't really help. Truth was, this was a different kind of hurt. I loved Lily. I knew that somewhere deep down, she loved me too. But I'd fucked up and caused her to bury those feelings.

It fucking killed me.

I found myself staring at my canvas for long periods of time, simply thinking about her, seeing her in the colors, the swirl of red and white paint reminding me of the shorts she used to wear.

Late into the night, I finally glanced at the clock. It was half past four. I decided wearily that my bed would be a better place to crash than the hard floor of my studio, so I went out into the cold, dumped myself in an Uber, and headed back.

I let myself into my apartment, took off my shoes, and got myself a beer from the fridge. On the way to the bedroom, I rolled my neck, trying to loosen the tightness that had accumulated over the evening. It hadn't been an easy night, and I was looking forward to falling into bed.

I took one last slug of the beer, put it down on my bedside table, and then peeled off my clothes. I'd gotten paint on my new jeans, but I was too exhausted to give a fuck. They came off, along with my shirt, until I was only in my boxer briefs.

I had just sat down on the edge of the bed when a voice called out.

"Rhys?" the sleepy voice asked.

I jumped up and turned on the bedside lamp. "Lily? What are you doing here?"

She slowly sat up. "What time is it?"

"It's late." My eyes raked over her. She was still dressed in her work clothes, the top few buttons of her shirt undone so that her bra was exposed. I was so confused - What was she doing in my bed?

"You left," she said, her voice still throaty from sleep.

"I did," I agreed carefully. I was trying to piece together why the woman who'd rejected me eight hours earlier was now in my bed. "How did you get in here?"

"You aren't the only one skilled at B&E."

"B&E?" She was so cute when she was half asleep. Her face was more relaxed, her voice rough but unguarded.

"Breaking and entering. Robbing lingo."

"Ah, got it." I examined her. Was she drunk? I didn't think so.

"You were gone a long time. Where did you go?" she asked, slowly propping herself up.

"The studio."

"Oh. Okay."

Her ease of appeasement amused me. "Why?"

"I was worried you were with some hussy," she admitted, offering a small smile.

"No hussy," I assured her. A moment passed in silence before I asked again, "Lily, what are you doing here?"

Her eyes darted up to meet mine, glowing in the low light. "I fucked up, Rhys."

I tilted my head.

"Hang on." She unbuttoned her shirt. "There's something I want to show you."

My heart started to pound. Lily was undressing in my bed. This felt like such a turn of events, I needed to understand what was happening "Lily, wait."

She ignored me and shrugged off her shirt, twisting to show me the back of her shoulder, which was covered in gauze.

"What is this?" I glanced between the bandage and her.

"Conner," she said. "Just take a fucking look."

I went slowly and carefully removed the pad.

"Do you recognize it?" She turned back to me expectantly.

"Lily," I said, almost inaudibly.

She reached over to the other nightstand and gave me the ornament I'd made for her all those years ago in Lake Tahoe. She'd taken the butterfly I'd stitched and gotten a small tattoo of it on her shoulder blade.

I looked at the ornament and then back at the tattoo. "When did you do this?"

"Tonight. After you left, I came looking for you. When you weren't here, I made Jen take me out. She knew a guy."

I was quiet for a few minutes, simply taking in the beauty of her pale shoulder and the red ink. She had something I'd created put on her skin forever.

"Say something, would you?" she finally said.

"It's… amazing. You know tattoos are permanent, right?"

She rolled her eyes and laughed as she pulled her shirt back up. "Yeah, thanks. I think I know how they work."

"Why did you do it?"

She reached out and touched the side of my face. "Because I love you, Rhys."

She loved me? I felt my heart fly out of my chest but at the same time the pain of caution. "Wait, Lily. Are you sure? You just woke up."

"This isn't a sleep-induced confession, Rhys. I've loved you for a long time. I'm sorry I didn't say it back."

I almost couldn't believe my ears. Lily loved me?

"Rhys," she asked carefully. "Can you kiss me now?"

I pulled her in, and as we connected, I found my home. Instantly, I was transported to the safest place I'd ever been. I'd missed this place. With Lily, nothing could hurt me.

I slid one hand down around her hips, her eyes darkening as I cupped her face with the other. My touch caused her to shiver in that good way I'd almost forgotten about. I wanted to go slow and savor every moment of this, but Lily grew impatient and pressed her lips to mine.

Soft and firm and warm. I hesitated for just a second and then grinned against her mouth.

"Hayes," I whispered. "So forward. I like it."

"Shut the fuck up," she teased back as we kissed.

I reached down and helped her take off her pants. Then she finished unbuttoning her shirt for me.

"Wow. I'd almost forgot."

She looked down at her boobs and blushed.

Candy cane bra.

She shrugged. "You know me."

"Tradition. I fucking love it."

I pulled out her tits so they were resting on top of the cups and gently squeezed her nipples, causing her to shudder with delight.

"Are you on birth control?" I grunted, my throat hoarse as I rubbed the outline of my erection with one hand. "I'm clean. I was tested last month and haven't been with anyone since, I promise. I want to feel you."

She nodded. "Yes. Me, too."

The idea of feeling her without anything between us did me in.

We were both wet and drunk with lust and couldn't wait anymore. She moved her hand toward the apex of her thighs, looking for relief.

I cocked an eyebrow. "Uh-uh. Not yet, sweetheart."

She frowned at me.

I stepped toward her and pulled off my boxers in one clean movement.

Her knees instantly fell back together, only to have me push them apart again.

"No, I like you like this," I said, holding her feet apart. "I want to look at you."

I took a step back, our naked bodies glistening in the low light. I knew Lily was looking at my new tattoos.

Her eyes widened. "Are you kidding me?"

I raised my eyebrows in confusion. "What?"

She pointed at my chest. "That!"

I grinned and shrugged. "It's a butterfly."

"You - you got one too?"

I cupped her jaw, and tilted her forehead against mine. "Babe, I got it a long time ago."

Lily

I still couldn't believe Rhys had gotten a tattoo also. I

needed to process this. Unfortunately, I was fairly distracted at the moment.

I'd forgotten how good he'd felt. How good *we'd* felt.

He kneeled onto the bed and pushed my knees wider, dipping his dick between my legs and running it up and down my channel, coating himself in my wetness and then using it to give himself a few more pumps as he stared at me.

I pressed my lips together and tried to clench my thighs.

"Mmm. Princess doesn't like that?"

He looked so content, so confident. Meanwhile, over here, I could barely hold it together.

He just winked and then backed up. He pulled me by my hips to the edge of the bed.

"Rhys?" I asked, confused for a moment, but then I realized what he was doing. Oh, God. "Rhys, uh, you don't have to - "

It was his turn to scowl up at me. I swear to God, somehow having Rhys Conner scowl at you from between your thighs - I didn't expect it to be, but it was one of the sexiest things I'd ever seen.

I lay back as he hooked my legs over his shoulders and started devouring me with long, slow licks. He was finding sensitive areas I didn't even know I had and abusing that power in the most delicious way. When my clit was so swollen I thought I would burst, he added a finger and then two inside me and started sucking on it.

I exploded.

"Oh my God." My thighs clamped down on his head, preventing him from moving as a current pulsed through me like an electric shock.

It took me a moment for the energy to die down and for me to loosen my grip on him. Once I did, he climbed up next to me.

"Holy shit, Rhys," I panted. "What the fuck?"

He grinned. "Not bad?"

I blinked, still trying to find my words. "Yeah, not fucking bad. Jesus."

He trailed his fingers over my stomach and massaged one of my breasts. "You are so fucking beautiful, you know that?"

I turned to him. "You are not so bad yourself. I mean seriously, what the fuck, Rhys? Are you, like, working out or something?"

"Something like that." He grinned and reached down to pump his erection. "And you, princess, you make me so fucking hard."

"Oh, yeah?"

He shook his head. "You don't know what's coming for you."

I grinned. "Bring it."

"You sure you're ready for it?"

His eyes darkened, and he crawled up, kneeling before me on the bed. He paused, and then in one fell swoop, he flipped me over and pulled my hips back to his, so that my ass was pressed against his erection.

Fuck. Rhys had always been good in bed, but it was clear he'd learned a few things over the years.

He circled my ass with his hands, squeezing me, and then leaned forward and pulled my hair off to the side, his lips close to my neck. "God damn, I've fucking missed this."

I felt his length push between my legs, finding my entrance from behind. It felt easy and familiar but at the same time exciting and new. We were strangers but old friends, two people who had known each other as intimately as two people could, but then parted and found separate lives.

He fucked me slowly at first, taking his time as he filled me, and hitting that sweet, sweet spot deep inside me. Rhys had owned my body from the moment I first saw him, and now back together, we melded completely. He was a caring and impassioned lover, taking what he needed but in a way that made me feel necessary and protected.

He took me to the brink and back, teasing me at first so that I was begging for release. When he finally gave me what I whimpered for, it didn't end there. Over and over I came, so quickly it almost felt like it was against my will. He'd let me recover, but only for a moment until he brought me back again. It was like surfing an unending wave. His control, and his control of my body, was other-worldly.

"Rhys," I stammered, my body and mind both weak after coming again. "What about you?"

I felt his hands tighten around my hips as he spoke. "Are you ready?"

I nodded. I wanted him. I needed it.

He pulled out and flipped me over on the bed so I was staring up at him. He stalked over on his knees, spreading my legs, my swollen cunt between us.

"Are you sure? Can you take more?"

I nodded, my breath shallow. I needed him to come inside me. I wanted to feel the rush of him filling me up.

He crawled over me, finding his place between my thighs and angled to my entrance. I raised my legs, trying to create more of that sweet pressure.

"Look at me, princess. I want to come inside you."

"Me too," I panted, desperate for him.

"Are you ready?"

I nodded, and he plunged into me. The sensation caused my mouth to gape, but we maintained eye contact even as he bucked and rolled against me, pulling me along with him.

And then I was lost, the sensation overtaking me as I entered into freefall. Heat erupted as he pistoned inside me, lubricating us from the inside out. I felt all his muscles tense and then release as we collapsed together.

After the fog passed, he pulled off and fell onto the bed with me.

"Wow."

"Wow is right," I agreed.

"Was it like that in Tahoe?"

"It was amazing in Tahoe, but I think that might have topped it."

He let out a long sigh. "You're fucking amazing, princess."

Chapter Eighteen

Rhys

Six Months Later

It'd been about six months since Lily and I got back together, and it was easily the best six months of my life. Work was still on fire, but now instead of going out to parties or back to an empty studio each night, I came home to the most amazing woman I'd ever known. Lily challenged me and made me laugh, held me accountable, and took care of me.

I was never letting her go again.

I gave up the dinky apartment in her building because we'd basically been living at my studio since we got back together. It took weeks of hounding her, but when she finally told me she wasn't renewing her lease with Jen? Best day of my fucking life.

The one catch? She wanted us to pick out a place together. Lily said that when a girl moves into a guy's place, the relationship is unequal. At first, I scoffed. I mean, the closet had more of her clothes than mine, and my fridge was full of shit like chai tea and capers.

When I pointed this out to her, she took her index

finger and poked me in the chest.

"See?" she said.

"Hey, ow. Watch those nails, princess," I teased. "What? What did I do?"

She huffed. "You said my fridge. This is exactly what I meant. This will always be your place. We have to find a new apartment that's ours."

"Babe, I told you. I need a place that has studio space."

"This is New York. Aren't there tons of studios?"

"Not that easy, babe. It took me four months to find this place."

"I can wait."

I eyed her. Her lips got extra pouty when she argued, which was super-hot. I really wanted to kiss her and take her back to the bedroom. Hell, fuck apartments. New York was full of them, right?

I stepped into her and wrapped my hands around her waist. "Okay. We'll get a new apartment."

She blinked at me. "What?"

"If it's that important to you, we'll find something else. All I care about is that we're together."

Her face lit up. "Really?"

I nodded. "Really. Just...can we please make sure it's not in a lame area? And nothing that requires crossing a bridge. I can't do that shit."

She squeezed me tightly. "Don't worry. I'll find the perfect place."

Four months and almost thirty showings later, things weren't looking good. It's not that Lily wasn't trying, it's just…well, inventory wasn't great. I was secretly sort of okay with it because then I got to stay in my place and still get Lily. But I could tell the search was wearing on her.

Then one night, Lily texted me with excitement.

Lily: I found it!

Me: Yeah?

Lily: Yep! It's perfect! We can see it tonight. Meet me at home at 7?

I was skeptical, especially since this wasn't the first *perfect* place, but I had to show I was at least willing to try, even though I was secretly hoping she'd tire of looking and realize we had a really good fucking place in my building.

Seven rolled around, and Lily got home from work. I could tell she was pumped.

"You ready?" she asked upon entering.

I'd just finished some emails and closed my laptop. "Yep. All set."

As we made our way to the elevator, I asked her about where we were headed. "So, is it far? Should I call an Uber?"

She looked at me and grinned. "No, I don't think we need that. It's not far. I think we can walk."

I squinted at her. "You sure? It's, like, forty degrees out. You'll freeze."

She only shrugged as we got in the elevator. I pressed 'G' for ground floor, and we rode the elevator down. Once the sliding door opened to the lobby, Lily held me back.

"Hang on." She hit the button for the top floor.

"Babe," I said, confused. "What are you doing? Did you forget something?"

"Just wait."

I looked at her, perplexed. Why were we going back up?

A few moments later, the elevator dinged, and we exited to the landing. There was a single door on the floor, and it was open.

Lily took my hand and pulled me with her.

"What are you doing?" I was hesitant to enter

someone else's space.

"Lily," a familiar voice called. "Is that you?"

Footsteps made their way toward us as we crossed the threshold.

"Lily, Rhys, good to see you." It was our real estate agent. What was she doing in our building?

I turned to Lily. "What's going on?"

She grinned. "I think this is the place."

I blinked at her. "This place is for sale?"

"It's going on the market tomorrow," the agent interrupted. "No one's seen it yet, but the sellers are highly motivated. It's slightly bigger than your unit, and this one has a larger living area and access to a roof deck because it's on the top floor."

I scanned the space. It was almost identical - the same wood floors, huge windows, and soaring ceilings that had made me fall in love with my place. Plenty of space to create art and still live a life with Lily. It would be almost effortless to move here.

"How much?" I asked reluctantly. I knew Manhattan real estate. The words *rooftop* and *deck* always came with dollar signs attached.

The realtor smiled and glanced at Lily. "It's actually highly negotiable. The owners are leaving the country and want to off-load it. I'm confident you'd actually be able to come out ahead if you purchased it and then listed your property."

"Isn't that amazing, babe?" Lily asked.

"I'll give you guys some time alone to look around while I make a phone call," the realtor said, slipping out the front door.

I walked around the open-plan space and rubbed the back of my neck. Lily came up behind me and slipped under my arm.

"Well, what do you think?"

"I - I don't know what to say. It's perfect."

Lily squealed. "It is, isn't it? I mean, it's the same place, same location, except...except it'd be ours. Come on and look at the deck."

I followed Lily as, once again, she dragged me by the hand. The roof deck was accessed via a door off the living area. Outside, it was freezing, but the noise of the city was dampened from the snow and the height.

"It's so peaceful," she said, folding her arms in to warm herself. "I know how much having your own place matters to you, and I realized I didn't want to take that away. So I thought maybe this could be a good, you know, compromise."

I wrapped an arm around her. "Babe, it's perfect. You're a freaking genius."

"Oh, oh, but I saved the best part for last. Look." She pointed off to the distance. "You see that? It's Rockefeller Center. And you know what?"

"What?"

"The agent said you can see the tip of the tree during the holidays. Can you believe that?"

My girl and her fascination with Christmas. I pulled her in and kissed her on her head. "It's perfect. Let's take it."

Epilogue

Rhys

Later, in December...

"Is the blindfold really necessary?" Lily asked as I helped her onto the private helicopter. She was already bundled up in a puffer jacket and a red wool scarf and hat. The only part of her face that was still visible was a narrow strip around her cute mouth.

Loved that mouth.

But back to the blindfold. She already knew we were somewhere on the West Coast, since I couldn't get her past the airport gate without her seeing we were headed for San Francisco. But I wanted everything else to be a surprise, hence the extra measure.

"What if I get airsick?" she yelled as we settled into the seats, and I strapped her in. "You don't want to make your girl sick on Christmas Eve, Rhys."

"Just let me know, and I'll get you a bag. Don't worry. We won't be airborne for long."

Lily frowned the way she usually does when she's annoyed at me, in the way that means she's only sort of annoyed, but not really. Trust me, I know. She's been doing it since we were in school, and I'd had more than a few chances to see that face over the last year.

If I was being honest, I was probably the one who would need the airsickness bag because helicopters secretly freaked me out. But it was a risk I was willing to take because the end result would be worth it. I'd planned this whole trip to a T, and the helicopter was absolutely necessary.

Less than an hour later, we touched down in the middle of a field. The chopper blades spun down as I helped her off our ride and into a meadow. It had snowed recently. About an inch of white gilded the forest and mountains around us.

"It's cold," Lily remarked, crossing her arms to conserve warmth. "Where are we?"

"Just wait." I led her through the meadow and toward the trees.

We walked for about ten minutes, until the sound of the helicopter had been replaced by the sounds of nature.

"Is this some weird Christmas present? Because you're not getting off the hook; I still want that set of bath bombs from Lush."

"You'll get your bathtub things, don't worry," I teased, continuing to lead her carefully down the trail.

As we broke through the trees, our destination lay in front of us. I could finally remove the blindfold.

"Okay, we're here." I took the cloth off her eyes.

Lily's eyes took a moment to adjust to the late-afternoon light, but after a second, she gasped.

"The hunting cabin?"

I nodded.

She alternated between looking at me and looking back at the shack we'd both loved.

"I can't believe you helicoptered us up to our shack. You're crazy! Where did you even land? Wait. I'm so confused."

"There's a meadow not too far from here. I turned it into a landing pad."

She pulled her neck back. "Wait. What? How - ?"

"I bought it, Lily. For us. The land was up for sale, and we had a little profit from the studio, so…"

She blinked at me. "How did you even know - ?"

"I've had a realtor watching the listing for a few years now. The family decided to sell a couple months ago."

She grinned. "You are insane. You know that?"

I shrugged.

Her eyes sparkled. "Can we go inside?"

I nodded. "I don't see why not."

A light snow started up again as I trailed behind her toward the door. She untwisted the wire lock. Once she went inside, she gasped. I'd had someone come out earlier that day and decorate it with Christmas lights and tinsel and those type of paper snowflakes she loved so much. It practically glowed.

"Oh my God, did you do this?" she squealed.

"Maybe." It made me happy to see her this excited.

"This is so cool, Rhys." Lily ran her fingers over the small table and chairs and then spun in the center of the small room. "So we can come here whenever?"

"Yep. Although we might want to expand. Add a real bathroom and an actual lock or something."

Lily laughed. "I don't know; I kind of love it like it is. This is such a special place, you know?"

I pulled her into me. "I can't tell you how relieved I am to hear that, because I actually brought you here to ask you something. Something important."

Her face tilted.

I reached into my pocket as I dropped to my knee. "Liliana. You mean more to me than anyone I've ever known. You challenge me to be a better person and do it with more warmth and humor than I thought was humanly possible. You are both beautiful and talented, and your collection of holiday-themed underwear is unmatched. Lily, what I'm trying to say is, I want you to be my tradition. Will you marry me?"

I opened the small box to reveal the diamond ring I'd designed myself. It had a large center diamond flanked by smaller diamonds all around so it formed a -

"A snowflake! I love it. Oh, my God, I love it so much!"

A wave of relief passed through me. "So is that a...?"

"Yes, of course I'll marry you, dummy! I love you!"

Relief and unmatched joy flowed through me.

She said yes.

It was the best moment of my life, and it was Christmas.

About the Author

Elizabeth Brown writes contemporary and erotic romance. When she's not reading or writing, she likes to eat tacos, watch makeup videos on YouTube, and dream about Charlie Hunnam. She lives in California with her husband, who incidentally, is not at all jealous of that last hobby.

If you would like more information about Elizabeth, please visit her at:

https://readelizabethbrown.wixsite.com/books

Books by Elizabeth Brown

The Off-Limits Series
The Lessons
The Rules
The Mistakes

The Determined Trilogy
Determined
Determined to Love
Determined to Win

Sordid Games

Elizabeth Kelly

Chapter One

Daisy

"Laid off? But you were just hired six months ago."

"Yeah, I know." I collapsed on the couch with a harsh sigh and rubbed at my temples.

Frannie plopped down on the other end of the couch and grabbed my legs, pulling them into her lap before beginning to rub my feet. "I'm sorry, Daisy."

I groaned in pleasure and rested my head against the back of the couch as Frannie continued to rub my feet. I had only been roommates with the tiny, blonde woman for five months, but we were already best friends.

"Me too, Frannie. I really liked this job, you know? My patients were great, my boss was great, my coworkers were…"

I trailed off and Frannie grinned at me. "Great?"

"Mostly," I said.

"There are other rehab facilities in the city, you'll find something," Frannie said.

"Yeah, but not this close to Christmas," I said as the front door slammed. Moments later Frannie's boyfriend, Owen, sauntered into the room.

"Hey, sexy ladies, what's happening?"

He sat in the armchair across from us and winked at Frannie. She jumped up and hurried across the room to sit in his lap. They kissed deeply and when Owen's hand began to inch up toward Frannie's boob, I said, "Keep it in your pants, buddy."

Owen laughed as Frannie blushed and gave me an apologetic look. "Sorry, sweetie."

"I can't help it. My lady is hot," Owen said as he gave Frannie an appreciative look.

Despite my current jaded attitude toward love and men, I had to admit, it was kind of cute how crazy Owen and Frannie were for each other. Owen was good looking with his shaggy blond hair, blue eyes and lean body, but I liked my men tall and big with dark hair. Nothing made me hotter than a strong jaw with the perfect amount of stubble. Of course, even if Owen had been Mr. Tall, Dark and Handsome, he was definitely not my type. His laid-back and easy-going nature was perfect for Frannie, but it left me cold.

"Why so sad looking, D?" Owen suddenly asked.

"She lost her job," Frannie said.

"Blows," Owen replied. "Sorry, dude."

"Thanks, Owen," I said.

"So, are you going to start looking for a job right away?" Frannie asked.

"No, I'll wait until January," I said as I picked at a thread on my jeans. "It's like a week before Christmas. No one will be hiring over the holidays."

"So, now that you're not working, you have zero plans for the holidays," Frannie said.

I threw one of the couch pillows at her. "Way to make me sound like a complete loser, Frannie."

She didn't reply. She was staring at Owen and he cocked an eyebrow at her. "What, babe?"

She pressed a kiss against his mouth before sliding off his lap and joining me on the couch again. "Daisy, why don't you come with me to my parents' place for Christmas?"

I shook my head. "That's very sweet, but I'm not intruding on your family time."

"Sweetie, I want you to come. Now that you and Dick have broken up, you'll be all alone at Christmas."

"One, his name was Richard not Dick, and two, I've been alone at Christmas before. It's no big deal. I'll order Chinese food and do a Netflix marathon," I said.

"Or, you could come home with me and enjoy a traditional Christmas dinner, open presents with my family on Christmas morning and participate in all the holiday festivities around town. You might even meet someone."

Frannie wiggled her eyebrows at me and I rolled my eyes. "I've taken a vow of celibacy, remember? I have no interest in meeting *someone*."

"Can you even be a nun if you've already had sex?" Owen said.

"A vow of celibacy doesn't automatically make you a nun, Owen," I replied as Frannie giggled.

"Fair enough," Owen said. "Hell, not even nuns are celibate anyway. I knew this chick once who was a nun and she like, banged two different guys at the same party."

"Oh my God," Frannie said, "that was a Halloween party, baby, and she was in a nun costume."

Owen squinted at her. "You sure?"

"Positive," Frannie replied.

"Fuck," Owen said, "I gotta cut back on the weed."

Both Frannie and I laughed, and Owen gave us a cheerful grin before pulling out his cell phone. He studied the screen as Frannie took my hands and squeezed them. "Seriously, sweetie. I think you should come with me. My parents have an extra room in the basement. Say you'll come with me…please?"

I studied her silently, noting the way her gaze didn't quite meet mine. "What's going on, Frannie?"

"Nothing," she said as she darted a quick look at Owen. "Nothing's going on."

"Don't lie to me," I said. "Why are you suddenly so anxious for me to spend Christmas with you and your family?"

Frannie took a deep breath. "Okay, so, don't freak out but, I need to ask you a really big favour."

"What?" I said.

"Now that you're not working and have no plans for the holidays, I want you to come home with me and pretend to be my girlfriend."

I blinked at her. "I – what?"

"Babe, that's brilliant," Owen said.

I gave him a look of confusion as Frannie said, "I want you to tell my family that you're my girlfriend and we're in a relationship."

"I know I swore off men, but I'm not switching teams. I'm practicing celibacy not lesbianism," I said. "And spoiler alert – you're not a lesbian either."

"Damn straight," Owen said without looking up from his phone. He held his fist up and bumped the air as Frannie gave me a pleading look.

"Please, Daisy. Just help me out, okay?"

"No," I said. "No, definitely not. Why would your parents believe that we were lesbians? You've been dating Owen for a year."

"Well, they don't exactly know about Owen," Frannie said.

I blinked at her. "What? How can they not?"

"It's kind of a long story," Frannie said.

"You just asked me to tell your family I'm your lesbian lover, I think you can sum up the long story for me," I said.

Frannie blew a lock of her blonde hair out of her

face. "Okay, you know that Owen and I grew up in the same town, right?"

"Yes. Your families live next to each other."

"Right. So, years ago, my dad and Owen's dad were like stupid big rivals at their high school. They were both really popular, and they were both on the basketball team and they, like totally hated each others' guts. They were constantly trying to outdo each other, and everything was one big competition between them. My mom said that even though he hated public speaking, my dad still joined the debate team just because Owen's dad did. Anyway, they still hate each other and growing up, I wasn't allowed to be friends with Owen or his sister even though they lived right next door to us."

"Are you kidding me?" I said. "It's been like thirty years. They can't still be enemies over stupid high school shit."

"Dude, you don't know our dads," Owen said solemnly. "They're both stubborn as hell."

"Anyway, I barely even talked to Owen when we were kids. I didn't even know he'd moved away from Darville until I bumped into him here," Frannie said. "We started talking and I realized that he was really a pretty cool guy and then we…"

She trailed off and Owen said, "Then we started boning."

"Owen!"

"What? It's true, babe. You can't keep your hands off this." He lifted his shirt and rubbed his admittedly impressive looking six pack.

Frannie rolled her eyes. "Anyway, Owen is going home for Christmas too and we thought we were going to tell them then. But Owen's dad wants this historical home torn down to make room for new town houses. So, the Darville Historical Society got involved in saving and restoring it."

"What does that have to do with anything?" I said.

"My dad is the president of the Darville Historical Society," Frannie said.

"Oh," I replied.

"Dude, my dad like, hates history and stuff," Owen said before staring at his cell phone again.

"We can't tell them right now, Daisy," Frannie said. "It'll make everything worse."

"Okay, fine, I get that," I said. "But I don't understand why you need me to pretend to be your girlfriend. Just pretend to be single."

"Yeah, see, my parents really want grandchildren," Frannie said. "Now that they think I've been single for over a year, my mom and my grandma have already made it clear that they're going to try and set me up with half the damn town over Christmas. We've got a lot of single guys in Darville, Daisy. I don't want to spend my entire holiday fending them off!"

"What about your brother?" I said.

"Dude, she can't pretend to date her brother. That's disgusting," Owen said.

"Shut up, Owen," I said. "Your brother is older than you, right? You said he's flying in for Christmas too. Maybe you can convince your mom and grandma to try and set him up instead."

Frannie shook her head. "It won't work. My brother is immune to Mom's guilt trips about not giving her grandkids."

"You can't spend the rest of your life pretending to be a lesbian," I said. "Sooner or later, you and Owen will get married and then what?"

"We're going to tell them once the holidays are over and this stupid historical house thing is done. When things are a bit calmer, and our fathers only hate each other the usual amount, then we'll tell them."

"But they'll think you're a lesbian!" I nearly

shouted.

"I'll tell them I'm bisexual," Frannie said. "We are going to tell them. Just not right now."

"I don't think I can pretend to be a lesbian," I said. "I love you, Frannie, but I'm not, I mean…"

I trailed off and Owen said, "You don't give her a lady boner, babe."

"Owen!" Frannie said before turning toward me again. "Sweetie, my parents are super conservative. Honestly, it's going to freak them out when I tell them we're dating. They probably won't let us sleep in the same bedroom together. At the most, we'll have to do a bit of handholding, maybe kiss once or twice."

"If there's tongue, make sure you get a picture," Owen said.

"No tongue," Frannie said firmly. "Only a quick, close-mouthed kiss once or twice to sell the relationship."

"You should still get a picture," Owen said.

"Please, Daisy," Frannie said.

I hesitated and Owen glanced up from his cell phone. "Babe, if Daisy really doesn't want to do it, we shouldn't make her."

Frannie gave him a look of frustration. "Baby, if my parents believe I'm a lesbian for a few months and then I tell them that I'm dating you, it'll work in our favour. They'll probably be so relieved I'm not a lesbian, that they'll be happy we're dating."

"You'd do that to your own family?" I said.

"It's a good lesson for them," Frannie said.

"Wait," Owen said. "Dude, are you telling me that your parents will only think I'm good enough for you because I got a penis instead of a vagina?"

"Possibly," Frannie said.

Owen considered that for a moment before grinning. "Harsh, but fair."

"Frannie, I don't know," I said.

"C'mon," Frannie pleaded, "I don't like the idea of you spending Christmas all alone, and I really need your help with this. Please, Oopsie?"

I could feel myself caving when she said her nickname for me. Shortly after we had become roommates, Frannie and I had gone out to a bar together. Long story short, we drank too much and I bit the pavement outside the bar, falling flat on my face. When Frannie had rolled me onto my back, asking frantically if I was hurt, I had grinned and mumbled, "Oopsie-Daisy".

She'd burst into laughter before falling down next to me. We had giggled hysterically until the bouncer had came out, picked us both up and pushed us into a cab. That night cemented our friendship.

"Fine, I'll do it," I said, "but you seriously owe me for this, Frannie."

Frannie squealed and threw her arms around me. She hugged me before kissing my cheek. "Thank you, Daisy. You have no idea how much you're helping us."

Chapter Two

Daisy

"Why are we stopping at a motel? I thought we were staying with your parents?" I stared out the windshield at the glowing neon sign of the motel.

"Well," Frannie said as I shut the car off, "technically we're not supposed to be at my parents until tomorrow."

"Then why did we leave today?" I asked. There was a knock on my window and I screamed and jumped, banging the top of my head against the top of the car. "Ouch! Goddammit, Owen!"

"Sorry, dude," Owen said cheerfully as Frannie climbed out of the car and ran around to my side. She hugged Owen before kissing him

"I missed you, baby."

"Missed you too, babe," Owen said before kissing her again.

"It's been two days since you saw him last," I said as I climbed out of the car.

"It's been hell without you," Frannie said solemnly. "I hate being apart from you."

"Well, get used to it," I said a bit irritably. "You're a lesbian starting now, for the next week, remember?"

"Starting tomorrow," Owen said. "Pop the trunk and I'll get your bags."

"Wait? You're staying here tonight too?" I asked.

He nodded as Frannie popped the trunk and said, "I booked a couple of rooms at the motel for tonight. I thought maybe once we were settled, I could slip over to Owen's room and we'd have one last night of - "

"Boning," Owen said as he walked over to us carrying both my suitcase and Frannie's.

"So, I'm supposed to hang out in the motel room by myself all night?" I said. "Way to treat your pretend lesbian lover, Frannie."

"I'm sorry, sweetie, but this is my last night with Owen!"

"For a week," I said. "You seriously can't go a week without having sex with him?"

"I'm really good at boning," Owen said.

"I just want one more night with my baby," Frannie said. "There's a bar not far from here. You can go have a drink, maybe meet someone."

"Won't your parents wonder where you are?" I asked Owen.

"Nah, I told them I was gonna chill with my bros tonight," Owen replied as he shifted the suitcases in his hands.

"What happens when someone sees you with Owen?" I said to Frannie. "The lesbian lover story will be blown before it even starts."

"No one is going to see us," Frannie said. "The motel is a good ten miles outside of town and besides, technically I'm staying in your room with you."

"You just made out with Owen in the parking lot," I said. "He's carrying our suitcases for God's sake!"

"I'm a gentleman," Owen said.

"No one saw us making out," Frannie said. "One last night, Daisy. Go to the bar, have a drink and relax.

Enjoy your alone time, okay? Starting tomorrow, we'll be smothered by my family."

"You didn't mention the smothering when you talked me into this crazy idea," I muttered.

"Maybe smothering isn't the right word, more like really intense mothering," Frannie said.

"Fantastic," I said. I grabbed my suitcase from Owen and, walking carefully on the snow-covered ground, started toward the lobby of the motel.

ও ৬

Wes

I wanted her the moment I saw her. I'd been sitting in the bar for nearly two hours, nursing my beer and people watching when she'd walked in, shrugged out of her thick jacket and sat down at the long, curved bar. I didn't recognize her but that wasn't surprising. The bar was outside of town and I wondered briefly if I had chosen this one because I was deliberately avoiding old friends.

Of course, if the woman sitting at the bar and sipping a glass of wine had lived in Darville when I was growing up, I may never have left. She was wearing skinny jeans with a dark red long-sleeved shirt that hugged her breasts. Despite how slender she was, she had to be a C cup, maybe a D. They looked firm and perky through her shirt and I was suddenly itching to touch them. Her light brown hair brushed against her shoulders and I wondered if it was as soft as it looked.

She lifted her wine glass and took a drink. Her back was to me so I couldn't see her face, but I remembered it easily enough from her short walk to the bar. Pale skin, cute little button nose, perfect pink lips and gorgeous blue eyes. I studied her hand as she drummed her fingers restlessly against the gleaming wood of the bar.

She had long fingers and I wondered idly what they would look like wrapped around my dick.

For a moment, I was tempted to stand up from my table in the corner, cross the bar and ease onto the stool beside her. It'd been a while since I'd gotten laid and the woman was hitting all of my buttons. Hell, I had half a stiffy just from staring at the back of her damn head. Before I could even try and hit on her, another man sat down next to her. A weird little trickle of possessiveness went down my back and I shook it off. What the hell was wrong with me? I didn't even know the woman. I forced myself to look at the TV mounted in the far corner. I wasn't here to get laid. I was here to spend time with my family at Christmas.

Of course, that didn't stop me from glancing over at the woman every five minutes for the next half-hour. I couldn't hear what the guy sitting next to her was saying but it was obvious she was blowing him off. He either didn't get it, or didn't want to take the hint. I watched with growing irritation as he continued to hit on her. She wasn't mine, I didn't even know her damn name, but I was instantly angry when the guy dropped his arm around her shoulders and pulled her up against him. When she tried to pull away and he refused to let her, I was on my feet and headed toward them without a second thought.

Daisy

I was starting to regret coming to the bar. I should have stayed in my motel room and watched *The Bachelor* instead. The guy sitting next to me for the last half hour was an asshole who was totally ignoring my 'fuck off' signals. I took another big gulp of my wine and waved at the bartender for the bill. She ignored me as she flirted with a big lumberjack looking fellow at the far end of the bar. I sighed and rubbed at my forehead.

"So, what did you say your name was again, hot thing?"

I rolled my eyes and tried not to wince. The guy sitting beside me was good looking enough but he was already halfway plastered, and his breath could have knocked over a dragon.

"I didn't," I said. "Listen, you're not picking up on my very obvious body language, so I'm going to straight up tell you that I'm not interested in you. Go away."

The man didn't blink an eye and I made a soft squeak of surprise when he dropped one heavy arm around my shoulders and yanked me closer. "C'mon, don't be like that."

"Let me go," I said before trying to pull away.

He held me tighter, his arm a band of steel around me and fear trickled down my spine. I shook it off. I was in a public place and there were plenty of people around.

"Let me go before I kick you in the nuts," I said.

"I hate women with smart mouths, you know that?" He was slurring his words a little and I couldn't help cringing when his fingers dug into my arm. "And you seem to have a real smart mouth, don't ya?"

"Fuck you," I said. "Let go of me now or - "

"Sorry I'm late, honey. I got caught up at work."

I turned my head toward the low raspy voice coming from my left side. The man of my goddamn dreams was standing next to me and it was all I could do to keep my mouth from dropping open. I stared up at him as he leaned against the bar and cocked one eyebrow at me. His eyes were the colour of dark chocolate and he had a perfect nose and perfect lips and a faint indent in his chin that I suddenly wanted to touch. With my tongue. Dark stubble covered his square jaw and my nipples beaded into hard points. How would it feel to have that stubble rubbing against them? Me and my nipples wanted to find out. Immediately.

He was well over six feet with broad shoulders and a narrow waist and what I was sure would be a perfect damn ass clad in stupidly tight jeans. I stared briefly at his package, my cheeks reddening when I lifted my gaze to his and there was amusement in his eyes.

My lust-fogged brain finally clued in that he was speaking and I stuttered, "W-what?"

"I asked who your new friend was." He stared around me and gave the man a tight grin. "You might want to take your hand off my woman."

I heard the audible click of his throat as the drunk man swallowed, and the heavy weight of his arm disappeared. I didn't object when my dream man put his arm around my waist. In fact, I leaned forward and eagerly tilted my head up toward him. I wanted this utterly perfect stranger to kiss me.

He didn't disappoint. His head dipped down, and I closed my eyes as his warm, firm lips brushed against mine. I returned his kiss with an embarrassing amount of enthusiasm. I parted my lips and made a soft whimper of pleasure when he briefly dipped his tongue between them to touch mine. The whimper turned into a moan of disappointment when he lifted his head.

He stared pointedly at the man sitting on the other side of me. "You should go now."

The man stumbled away and some of my common sense returned when the stranger let go of my waist and sat on the stool next to me. I stared at my almost empty glass of wine and tried to control my runaway heartbeat. What the hell was happening to me? Pretend lesbian relationship aside, I was done with men for at least the next ten years. Celibacy. Celibacy was what I both wanted and needed.

"You okay?"

His deep voice made butterflies flicker to life in my stomach. Hell, butterflies? I had a goddamn gymnastic team practicing their tumbling routine in there.

"Yes, thank you," I said. "I appreciate the help."

He shrugged. "You seemed to have it under control but sometimes the pretend boyfriend routine is easier and cleaner than the kick them in the balls route. No one likes to see a grown man burst into tears and vomit simultaneously."

I laughed. "I suppose not. I'm Daisy, by the way."

"Wes." He held out his big hand and I hesitated briefly before shaking it. Immediately the gymnasts in my stomach broke out into synchronized cartwheeling. Shit, I was in trouble if just the touch of his hand made me want to drag him back to my motel room.

I realized I was still holding his hand and dropped it with a muttered apology. He smiled at me and waved at the bartender who immediately came over.

"Well, hey, Sugar. What can I get you?" She purred.

"I'll take whatever you have on tap and whatever the lady would like."

"I'll have another glass of wine, please," I said.

She nodded and hurried away as I smiled at Wes. "Thank you."

"You're welcome." He smiled again at me before saying, "So, in the interest of not getting my ass kicked – do you have a boyfriend?"

I shook my head. "No. Do you have a girlfriend?"

"Would you be surprised to know I'm single?" He asked with a flirty grin.

"Shocked, actually."

"Is it because of my good looks or my charming personality?"

"Probably a little of both."

"Good to know," he said as the bartender returned with our drinks. He took a drink of beer as I sipped at my new glass of wine.

"Do you live around here?" I asked.

"Used to," he said. "I'm home for the holidays. How about you?"

"No. I came here with a friend," I replied.

There was a bit of awkward silence and I tried frantically to think of something witty to say. Oh God, why did I have to suck so hard at flirting? And why the hell did Wes have to smell so good? It was short-circuiting my ability to think straight.

I took another sip of wine.

You've got this, Daisy. It's just a beautiful guy who you have no interest in sleeping with because you've taken a vow of celibacy. You don't need to flirt with him. Just say something cool for God's sake.

I took a deep breath and said, "So, uh, what's a nice guy like you doing in a place like this?"

He laughed and I did a face plant into the palm of my hand.

"Isn't that supposed to be my line?" He teased.

"Sorry," I said. "I have no idea why I said that. I can't sleep with you - I've taken a vow of celibacy."

Wes choked on his swallow of beer and with my face flaming red, I pounded him on the back as he coughed repeatedly.

"Shit! I'm sorry! I don't know why I told you that – forget I said it!" I said. I smacked him on the back again and gave him an anxious look as he wiped his hand across his mouth. "Are you okay?"

"Yeah, thanks," he said.

"Good, I'm really sorry."

"It's fine," he replied.

I waited a beat and said, "Is there any chance you'll forget the celibacy thing?"

"Not a chance," he said.

My groan of dismay made him grin before he leaned

a little closer. "So, any particular reason you've taken a vow of celibacy?"

"Six months ago, my boyfriend and I broke up. It was amicable enough, we just wanted different things, you know?"

Wes nodded and took another drink of beer.

"I decided to try online dating."

"Uh oh," Wes said.

I laughed. "Yeah. I went on first dates with five different men over a period of six weeks. All of them were terrible and the third and fifth one bordered on complete disasters."

"How disastrous?" Wes asked.

"The third one told me he was a musician."

"You don't look like someone who dates musicians," Wes said.

I shrugged. "He wasn't a musician, really. Unless you think playing gigs at the local senior's home for free makes a thirty-year-old man a musician?"

He roared laughter and I flushed with pleasure at the sound of it.

"Wow, he told you this on the first date?"

"Oh no," I said, "Our date was at the senior's home. He thought I would enjoy watching the way he 'worked a crowd'."

"You're joking."

"I wish I was," I said. "But to be fair, some of those seniors really got into it. An old lady at the front threw underwear at him."

Wes nearly howled with laughter as I said, "Mind you, they belonged to the guy sitting next to her, but I overheard him telling the nurse she threw farther than him."

"Holy shit," Wes said as he wiped at his eyes. "I can't believe that's a true story."

"It is," I said. "The fifth one was worse."

"It can't be."

"He brought his mom on the date."

"Do you live in a sitcom?" Wes asked. "Is that what's happening?"

I laughed. "Trust me, there was no laugh track for this date."

"What did you do?" Wes asked.

I shrugged. "I had dinner with him and his mom. At the end of the date, he walked me to my car. His mom stood at their car and shouted across the parking lot not to kiss me. That she could tell I had the sex disease."

Wes' mouth dropped open and I laughed and said, "I can assure you that she was wrong. I don't have the sex disease."

Wes laughed again. "That's crazy."

"Yeah, now you know why I took a vow of celibacy. Five online dates in six weeks were more than enough to convince me that celibacy was the way to go."

"Fair enough," he said.

"What about you? Why are you single?" I took another sip of wine and tried to look like I wasn't about five minutes away from sticking my hand down his deliciously tight jeans.

"The cliché of being too busy with my career, I suppose," he said. "I've dated off and on the last few years but nothing serious."

"What do you do for a living?"

"Engineer."

"My dad was an engineer," I said.

"Is he still one?"

"He and my mom passed away a few years ago. Rainy night, bad brakes on their car," I said.

He reached out and squeezed my hand. "I'm sorry."

"Thank you. It's still hard, especially around their birthdays and the holidays but I've done lots of grief counseling and have a few really good support groups that I belong to." I smiled at him. He held my hand a moment longer and I shivered all over when he rubbed his thumb over the palm of my hand before letting go.

"What do you do for a living?" He asked.

"Rehabilitation therapist," I replied.

"Do you like it?"

"I do," I said. "I like helping people. Do you like your job?" I asked.

"Yes. I work for a smaller company and we have good clients."

"That's great," I said. I studied the stubble that surrounded his mouth and wondered how it would feel against my inner thighs.

"Shit."

I jerked at Wes' low mutter and said, "What's wrong?"

"I'm sorry. I need to go," he said as he pulled out his wallet and placed some bills on the bar.

Disappointment coursed through me. "Oh, yeah. Of course. Okay. It was nice to meet you."

I held out my hand and Wes stared at it for a moment before stepping closer. He ignored my hand and cupped my face, staring intently at me as his thumb rubbed across my cheekbone.

"Let me make something perfectly clear, Daisy. I don't want to leave. You're beautiful and sexy as hell, but if I stay any longer I'll do something stupid."

"Like what?" I whispered.

"Like telling you that I want to fuck you until you forget all about your goddamn vow of celibacy."

I shivered all over and stared wide-eyed at him as he studied my mouth. For a moment, I thought he was going to kiss me but instead he lifted my hand to his mouth and pressed a kiss against my knuckles. The scrape of his stubble sent a new wave of lust through my body and I swallowed heavily as he gave me a look of regret.

"Instead, for once in my life I'm going to do the right thing. It was a pleasure to meet you, Daisy."

He kissed my knuckles again and I watched in numb disbelief as he walked out of the bar.

ঌ ঌ

Wes

"You fucking idiot," I muttered to myself as I unlocked the truck. "You're lucky she didn't slap you across the face when you said you wanted to fuck her."

I yanked the door open and then froze when I heard my name called. I turned around. Daisy was hurrying toward me.

"Wes, wait a minute, I – shit!"

Her feet slipped on the icy pavement and she pinwheeled her arms madly as I lunged forward. My own feet slipped out from under me as I grabbed her around the waist and we fell to the ground with a heavy thud. I twisted as we fell and cushioned Daisy's body with my own. Her soft and curvy body felt way too good on top of mine, even with most of it hidden by a thick winter jacket. I stayed on the ground, holding her tightly against me despite the coldness of the pavement under me.

"Wes! Oh my God, are you okay?"

She tried to scramble off of me and I held her a little tighter as I stared at her mouth. I had kissed that mouth, felt the softness of her lips and tasted the sweetness of her tongue. My cock hardened in my jeans and without thinking I shifted her against me so her pussy was pressed up against it.

Her eyes widened and she licked at her bottom lip. I groaned and cupped the back of her head, pulling her down until her lips met mine. I immediately took control of the kiss, threading my fingers through her soft hair as I angled my mouth over hers and thrust my tongue into her mouth. She sucked at it and I groaned again and rubbed my dick against her.

Her sweet little moan set my blood on fire, but I pulled her head back and stared at her swollen mouth with regret before easing her off of me and climbing to my feet. I took her hands and helped her stand.

"Sorry," I muttered. "I shouldn't have done that. Are you okay?"

"I'm fine," she said. "Are you? You were the one who actually hit the ground. Did you smack your head?"

"No," I said.

She stared at me and I cleared my throat before stepping back. "I gotta go."

I reached for the door of my truck, hesitating when she said, "Wes, wait!"

Sighing, I turned around. She was closer than I thought, so close I could smell her perfume and feel the brush of her winter jacket against my abdomen. "Daisy, I - "

"What if I want that too?" She interrupted.

"Want what?" I asked in confusion.

Her cheeks turned pink, but she took a deep breath and said, "What if I want to be fucked into forgetting about my vow of celibacy?"

My dick reacted to her words, growing so goddamn hard that I was certain an imprint of my zipper would be on it. I ignored my urge to yank her into my arms and instead said, "I'm staying at my mom and dad's house."

What the fuck?

Her mouth dropped open and it was my turn to blush when she started to giggle.

"Shit," I said. "I meant that fucking a woman in my childhood bedroom with my parents down the hall isn't exactly dignified for a thirty-two-year-old man."

She laughed again. "Lucky for you, I have a motel room. It's nothing special but..."

She trailed off and gave me an uncertain look. I slid my arm around her waist and pulled her nice and close, letting her feel the hardness of my dick. I bent my head and nuzzled her throat liking the way she moaned and lifted her head to give me better access. "Are you sure this is what you want?"

"Yes," she said. "But, Wes, I – don't take this the wrong way but I'm not, um, looking for anything more than tonight. Okay?"

I lifted my head and kissed the tip of her nose. "Okay."

"Are you sure?" She said anxiously. "You understand that I don't want anything but sex?"

I couldn't help but laugh. "Yes, I'm sure and yes I understand you only want sex."

She blushed again. "Sorry, I sound like I'm totally full of myself. I'm not assuming you want anything more than sex with me, it's just – I've never done anything like this before so I'm not really sure how the, uh, rules, work."

"I haven't done this before either, but I don't think there's a set of rules to follow for a one-night stand," I said.

"Right," she said, "of course. So, uh, did you want to follow me back to the motel?"

I nodded immediately. "Yes, I do."

Chapter Three

Daisy

I was nervous. I didn't want to be, I wanted to look sexy and confident but the way my hand shook when I tried to insert the card key into the lock, didn't exactly scream confidence. Wes' big hand covered mine and he helped me insert the card into the slot. The red light turned green and I opened the door before stepping out of the cold air and into the room. As I fumbled for the light, I had a sudden dismaying thought. What if Frannie was here? What if she had finished with Owen and was sleeping in the second double bed?

She won't be. She's spending the night with Owen and you know that, you goober. Relax for God's sake. Just because you're about to get naked and have sex with the perfect man doesn't mean you have to act like a complete idiot.

I took a deep breath. My inner voice was right. Besides, maybe Wes was good looking and funny and smart. Maybe the little dimple that showed up in his right cheek every time he smiled at me made me nearly drip with anticipation. But he wasn't perfect. No one was.

He looks perfect.

He looked perfect, but he wasn't. He probably had, I don't know, a small dick. I seized on that thought almost desperately. Yes, he probably had a small dick and was terrible in bed. He probably sucked at sex and it would be awkward and weird and my first one-night stand would be a complete bust.

"Daisy?"

I realized we were still standing in the doorway in the dark and I hurriedly found the switch and flipped it on. Both double beds were empty and I took a deep breath before turning to smile at Wes. "Sorry."

He studied me carefully. The door was still open and coldness was creeping into the room.

"Are you going to shut the door?" I asked as I crossed my arms nervously over my torso.

"If you've changed your mind, I can leave," he said.

I blinked at him. "I – I haven't changed my mind. Have you?"

"No, but you look nervous."

"I am nervous," I admitted.

"Don't be," he said as he shut the door and locked it before taking off his boots. I kicked mine off and held my hand out for his jacket. He handed it to me and I tossed them onto Frannie's bed.

"Easy for you to say," I said. "You're really handsome and have the perfect body so…"

I studied the cheap carpet under my feet. What was wrong with me? I usually had more self-confidence than this in bed. Of course, I hadn't been with anyone but Richard in the last two and a half years. Richard was used to the scar on my tummy from my appendectomy, my weirdly long toes, and the –

I suddenly froze and gave Wes a look of panic. "Oh shit."

"What?" He was reaching for me and he stopped

immediately. "What's wrong?"

"I haven't shaved."

He laughed. "I haven't shaved either."

"You don't understand," I said. "I haven't shaved in *weeks*. We're at Sasquatch levels of hair."

"I really don't care if your legs aren't shaved, Daisy. I swear," Wes said. He reached down and adjusted the obvious bulge at the front of his jeans. "Let me show you how much I don't care."

"It's, uh, not just my legs," I said before glancing at my crotch. "I haven't exactly kept up with my, uh, waxing routine since I've been single."

Wes followed my gaze to my crotch and I turned bright red. "You know what? Let's turn the lights off."

"Are you kidding me?" Wes said teasingly. "You can't tell me something like that and then expect me not to look."

"No way," I said. "I want the lights off and both of us under the covers."

Wes grabbed my hand before I could shut off the lights and said, "Sorry, darlin', but that's not happening." He pulled me into his arms and kissed me until I was clinging to him and panting. He kissed his way to my ear and sucked on my earlobe. "I want to see every inch of your tight little body tonight."

"Oh God," I moaned. "I – I could have a quick shower first. My razor is like right in my bag, give me ten minutes and – aah!"

Wes picked me up and carried me to the bed, dropping me onto it before stripping off his shirt. I sucked in my breath and stared hungrily at his broad chest and wide shoulders. A layer of dark hair covered his upper chest and arrowed down in a thin line below his belly button. Unsurprisingly, he had a six pack and I licked my lips and rose up on my elbows as he reached for the button on his jeans.

"Crap! I don't have a condom!" I said as he flicked open the button. He grinned at me and reached into his back pocket for his wallet before bringing out the foil package and placing it on the nightstand.

"Thank God," I muttered as he stood gracefully on one foot and removed his sock before switching legs and removing the other.

He hesitated at the zipper and I waved my hand at him. "Hey, no stopping now. You're just getting to the really good part."

He laughed and with one agile movement, pushed his jeans and briefs down his legs and stepped out of them. I stared at the biggest, hardest dick I'd ever seen and tried not to drool.

"Oh no."

"Not the reaction I like to hear when I take off my pants."

I shook my head. "You really do have the perfect body."

"I don't."

"You do. I told myself that you probably had a small dick, but you don't. You really, really don't."

He gave me an arrogant little grin. "No, I really, really don't."

"Your self-confidence is not at all annoying or – oh!"

Wes had grabbed my feet and he quickly peeled my socks off before tossing them on the floor. "Your turn, Daisy."

I took a deep breath and sat up before reaching for the hem of my shirt. "Okay, but try and remember that I wasn't expecting to sleep with someone tonight so no judgement for my mismatched underwear. Okay?"

"If it helps, I'm not planning on you wearing it long enough for me to notice it doesn't match," Wes said. He was still standing next to the bed without a lick of clothing or shame. When I glanced at his dick, he reached down and rubbed it.

Watching his rough hand rub his own dick made me drip into my panties and I quickly stripped off my shirt before unbuttoning and unzipping my jeans. Wes released his cock and reached for my jeans, helping me tug the tight material down my legs.

He added them to the growing pile of clothes on the floor before reaching for my calf. I tried to pull my legs away and with a sexy little growl, he cupped both my calves and pulled me closer. He rubbed his hands over my hairy shins as I closed my eyes and tried not to die of embarrassment. "I told you - Sasquatch levels."

"I like it," he said with a little grin before lying on his side on the bed beside me. He traced his finger over the front clasp of my bra. "May I?"

"Yes, please."

He unclasped it and pulled back the cups. When he inhaled sharply, I glanced at his face and blushed at the look of pure lust on his face.

"Wes, I - "

"So beautiful," he growled before cupping my left breast. He teased the nipple with his thumb, making a noise of approval when it hardened. He tugged on it before kneading my breast. I arched into his touch and he kissed me softly on the mouth.

"Beautiful and perfect," he whispered against my lips before bending his head and sucking my nipple into his mouth.

I moaned and arched again, clutching at his head as he teased and toyed with both of my nipples until I was panting and shamelessly begging. He lifted his head and grinned at me. "Do you have any fucking idea how hot you are, Daisy?"

I tugged his head up until I could kiss him. We kissed repeatedly, our tongues flicking and tasting and licking. I reached down and wrapped my fingers around his cock, marveling at the hard steel covered with velvet soft skin. I rubbed him lightly, smiling when he groaned and thrust into my hand.

"Fuck, that feels so good," he moaned.

I crowded closer, rubbing my nipples against the rough hair on his chest before licking and nibbling at his thick neck. He tasted delicious and I bit him on the collarbone. He jerked against me and I squeezed his dick before rubbing hard.

"Oh fuck," he muttered before pulling my hand away and pushing me onto my back.

"Hey," I said with a small pout. "I wasn't done yet."

"It's my turn," he said.

The tone of his voice brought fresh wetness to the crotch of my panties and I shivered against him as he reached for the waistband of my panties. "Hips up, flower girl."

"Let's shut the lights off first."

"No," he said. "You're worrying for nothing, darlin'. I prefer the natural look, I promise."

"It's definitely natural," I muttered. I closed my eyes and lifted my hips. Wes pulled my underwear off and dropped them on the floor. There was silence and I opened one eye.

"Wes? Are you horrified into silence or – oh my God!"

Wes pushed my knees apart and bent his head. He pressed a kiss against the curls at the top of my pussy as his fingers stroked my wet pussy lips. "So wet," he said appreciatively.

I tried not to hump his hand like a horny dog as he kissed the scar on my stomach. "What's this from?"

"App-appendectomy – oh my God, oh fuck…"

Wes had slid one thick finger into me and I couldn't stop my hips from thrusting up. He laid down next to me again and propped his head up in his free hand as he grinned at me. "I love your greedy little pussy, darlin'."

I blushed bright red, but his words made me squeeze around his finger. He groaned and brushed his mouth against mine. "I can't wait to feel you squeeze like that around my dick."

"Me either," I moaned. "Grab that condom."

He shook his head. "Not yet, little flower. I want to watch you come all over my fingers first."

I immediately tensed. "So, uh, don't take this personally because this is my issue, not yours, but it's really difficult to make me come. I usually need to, uh, do it myself."

He studied me silently and I said, "I'm sorry. I swear it isn't you."

"Don't apologize," he said. "You have nothing to apologize for but," he leaned down and kissed me as he pressed his thumb against my clit, "would you let me try?"

I gave him a cautious look. "I don't want you to be upset with me when it doesn't work."

"I won't be upset."

"You say that now but when it doesn't work…"

Anxiety replaced the lust in my belly.

A flicker of anger crossed his face. "Did your ex get upset?"

"Sometimes," I said.

He rubbed my clit with his thumb before kissing and nuzzling my neck. "I promise I won't get upset, Daisy. In fact, why don't you show me how you like to be touched?"

He pulled his finger from my pussy and reached for my hand, guiding it to my clit. "Show me," he whispered.

I rubbed at my clit as he watched. He was watching me with such intensity that I felt a little self-conscious. I wasn't sure I would come even by my own hand, but when he bent his head to my breast and sucked on my nipple, a new wave of lust rolled through me. I moaned softly and concentrated on touching my clit while his warm mouth worked my nipple into a hard bud.

When Wes pushed two thick fingers back into my throbbing pussy, my eyes popped open and I cried out with surprise and pleasure. He had released my nipple and was staring at my hand between my legs. I ground my pussy against his hand, my fingers rubbing my clit frantically.

"Good girl," he said in a low voice. "Rub your pretty little clit for me while I fuck you with my fingers."

The rough need in his voice, the firm thrust of his fingers sent my lust spiraling out of control. Panting and moaning, I rubbed at my clit as he watched closely. I made a sharp cry, gave my clit one final hard, little pinch and my orgasm burst inside of me in a sweet and almost overwhelming flood of pleasure. I shook wildly, my pussy clenching and unclenching around Wes' fingers as he bent his head again and kissed one hard nipple.

"So beautiful," he murmured.

I lay on the bed in a daze as he slowly eased his fingers out of me and then sat up. He grabbed the condom and quickly rolled it onto his cock before lying on his back beside me.

"Wes, that – that was really good," I breathed.

He grinned at me. "I'm glad. Climb on top of me, Daisy."

My legs felt like wet noodles, but I did what he asked. I straddled him, grabbed the base of his cock and guided it in. He groaned loudly but stayed perfectly still as I slowly sank onto his thick length.

"Good?" He asked.

I nodded. Wes was bigger than I was used to, but his thickness felt amazing as I stretched around him. "Yeah, so good."

I braced my hands on his broad chest and did a few experimental bounces. He groaned, and his fingers dug into my hips as he stared hungrily at my breasts. "Your tits are amazing."

I grinned at him. "Thank you."

"Touch them," he demanded.

I cupped both of them, pulling on my nipples as Wes watched. I gasped when he grabbed my ass and made two hard thrusts. He groaned again. "Fuck, you're so goddamn tight."

Bracing my hands on his chest again, I met each of his strokes, using my knees for balance as I rose up and down. Wes' low groans of pleasure and his hard hands cupping and squeezing my ass made my swollen clit throb. I was reaching to touch it again – multiple orgasms weren't my thing, but Wes had me so hot, I figured it was worth a try – when Wes let go of my ass with his right hand and moved it to my pussy. He caressed my swollen and wet lips before rubbing my clit with the pads of his fingers.

I moaned encouragingly and dug my fingers into his chest as I rode him with hard, long strokes. I loved the roughness of Wes' fingers, they were so different from my soft skin, but he was touching me too gently. I needed a firmer touch, needed him to move a little to the left…

Without thinking, I grabbed his hand and moved it slightly before pressing hard on his hand and moving his fingers in firm circles against my clit. It felt incredible and I cried out happily before rocking back and forth against his hand as I continued to move his fingers the way I wanted.

"Does that feel good, darlin'?" Wes panted.

I froze against him and then yanked my hand away from his. Richard had always hated it when I grabbed his hand, said it made him feel useless and incompetent.

I gave Wes a nervous look as I perched completely still on top of him. "I'm sorry. I shouldn't have done that. You're doing a great job at touching me, really."

He laughed and I moaned a little when it made his cock rub against my inner walls. "It's not that I don't appreciate the pep talk, but can we get back to the fucking? You do whatever feels good and makes you come all over my cock."

"I – are you sure?" I whispered.

An almost painful look of need flickered across his face and he gave my clit a rough pinch that made me squeal with pleasure and clench around his dick.

"Fuck! Yes, I'm sure!" He muttered.

I pressed my hand over his again and moved his fingers against my clit. His left hand was still cupping my ass and I leaned back a little into his grip before letting my head fall back. I wanted to come again, wanted it desperately, and I closed my eyes and concentrated. Vaguely I was aware of the way Wes pushed in and out of me with slow, rhythmic strokes, as I manipulated his fingers against my clit. The feel of his hard cock filling me up, the roughness of his fingers against that throbbing bundle of nerves made me nearly weak with desire.

When Wes squeezed my clit between his fingers and gave it a sharp tug, my orgasm hit me as hard as a runaway train. I screamed, my back bowing and my nails digging into Wes' chest and wrist as I was consumed by the overwhelming intensity of my orgasm. I'd never had such a powerful orgasm before and my pussy squeezed Wes' cock in a vice grip.

He made a low moan and then muttered a curse under his breath before shaking free of my grip and grabbing my hips with both of his hands. He pumped rapidly as I rode him like a boneless rag doll. His back arched and he groaned loudly. My legs shaking, I collapsed on his chest, clinging to him as he thrust hard and came inside of me. His warm breath stirred my hair and I listened to the rapid thump of his heart beneath my ear.

"Fuck," he rumbled, "I've never lost control like that."

"Hmm," I said. I was suddenly exhausted. I nuzzled his neck and whimpered in complaint when he eased me off of him.

"Shh, flower girl," he said in a low voice. "Let me get rid of this."

I curled on my side and watched sleepily as he disposed of the condom before pulling out the covers from under me. He pulled them up over both of us and spooned me before kissing me on the back of the shoulder.

"Should I leave?"

"Nuh-uh," I said before yawning. "Do you need to call your mom and ask her if you can have a sleepover at a friend's house?"

His laughter made his chest vibrate against my back and I twitched when he gave me a playful slap on the butt. "Smart ass. Go to sleep, flower girl."

"Yeah, kay," I mumbled. "It was really good, Wes."

"It really was," he whispered before kissing my shoulder again.

࿐ ࿐

"Daisy, wake up. C'mon, we gotta go."

I muttered a curse and pushed at the hand that was poking me in the forehead. "Stop it."

"It's time to wake up."

I opened my eyes and stared blearily at Frannie. "What?"

"We have to go," she said as she sat on the other double bed. "I told my mom we were leaving the city early this morning and would be at her place by ten and it's nine-thirty."

I suddenly sat up, clutching the blankets to my naked chest and staring wild-eyed behind me. The bed was empty and there was no sign of Wes or his clothing. I breathed a sigh of relief as Frannie gave me a curious look.

"What?"

"Nothing," I said.

"You looked weird for a minute there."

"You look weird."

"Shut up."

"You shut up."

"Hey, Daisy?"

"Yeah?"

"Why are you naked?"

I blinked at Frannie before clearing my throat. "Uh, I was really hot last night. Plus, I always, um, sleep in the nude."

"Sure you do," Frannie said as she collapsed on her back and stared up at the ceiling. "I guess as your girlfriend, I should know that."

"You really should." I sat up, keeping the bed covers wrapped around me, and ran a hand through my hair. "I need a shower."

"Why do you have just-been-fucked hair?" Frannie asked suddenly.

"I don't," I said.

"Yes, you do."

"No, I don't."

"Yes, you do."

"Shut up."

"You shut up."

"Grab my robe out of my suitcase, would you?" I said in exasperation as Frannie grinned at me.

"Listen, honey, I'm all for you getting laid but try not

to forget that you're pretending to be my girlfriend okay? You can't be fucking random guys all week."

"I won't!" I said as Frannie dug through my suitcase and pulled out my robe. "It was a one-time thing. Besides, it's your fault. You were the one who told me to go to the bar and have a drink."

Frannie laughed and handed me my robe before kissing me on the forehead. "I'll take the blame for it. Honestly, I'm glad you found someone to have a little fun with. We've lived together for nearly six months and you haven't had sex once. I'm surprised things haven't dried up down there."

I glared at her and she giggled before kissing my forehead again. "Seriously though, good for you. Now, get your butt in that shower so we can go to my parents' house and pretend to be lesbians."

෨ ෬

Frannie's childhood home was a cute little two-story with grey brick and dark blue trim and shutters. As I pulled into the driveway and shut the car off, Frannie said, "Dad's truck isn't here. I thought mom said he was finished work already."

We climbed out of the car and Frannie stared at the house to our right. It was a similar looking two-story as well but covered with cream coloured siding and the trim and shutters were a cheery red. A large oak tree grew between the houses and Frannie grinned at me.

"When we were kids, dad and Owen's dad got into a fight over that tree. It's smack dab in the middle of both our properties and they almost came to blows over who it actually belonged to."

"Sounds like a fun memory," I said as I grabbed my suitcase from the trunk. Frannie laughed and grabbed her own suitcase before slamming the trunk lid shut.

"That's Owen's bedroom right there. It's right across from mine."

She stared up at the window on the second floor with a look of longing on her face. I nudged her with my elbow. "Hey, try not to be so obvious, would you?"

She sighed. "You're right. I just miss him so much already."

"It's been what? An hour since you saw him?" I said as we headed up the sidewalk toward the front door.

"Yeah, but we only had time for sex once this morning," Frannie said in a low voice.

I rolled my eyes. A mental image of riding Wes flickered through my head and a shameful amount of liquid immediately dampened the crotch of my panties. I shifted my suitcase to my other hand. I had to admit that I was a little upset he had left without waking me up and saying goodbye, but I had been the one who told him it was only sex last night. Still, waking me up would have been the polite thing to do.

Are you mad that he didn't wake you up to say goodbye or mad that he didn't wake you up to have sex again?

I ignored my inner voice and followed Frannie as she opened the front door and stepped into the narrow hallway. She dropped her suitcase with a loud thump and shouted, "Mom? We're here!"

A slender, blonde woman stepped into the hallway and made a loud squeal of happiness. "Oh, Frannie!" She hugged Frannie before kissing her on the cheek. "I'm so glad you're home."

"Me too, Mom," Frannie said. We hung up our jackets and took off our boots. Frannie indicated for me to follow them as her mom took her hand and tugged her down the hallway to the kitchen. The kitchen was small and tidy with a little nook at the end of it. A heavy-set man with an iPad in his hand, and an older woman with short white hair were sitting at the table that was placed in the nook and Frannie hurried over to hug both of them.

"Hi, Dad. I didn't see your truck out front so I thought you weren't here."

"Your brother has it," Frannie's mom said as she grabbed mugs from the cupboard. "I asked him to run to Phil's Buy and Save for me."

"It's good to see you Frannie-pants." Her father had a deep voice and he hugged Frannie before sitting back down. "How was the drive?"

"Fine," Frannie said. "The roads weren't bad. Hi, Grandma."

"Francine, you look so cute today," the older woman said as Frannie bent and kissed her cheek. "You're in love. Who's the lucky boy?"

Frannie jerked all over before giving her grandmother a guilty look. "Grandma, I'm not in love."

"Of course you are," her grandmother said. "I can see it on your face."

Frannie's mom laughed. "Mother Francine, hush now." She turned toward me. "You must be Daisy."

"I am," I said. "It's nice to meet you, Mrs. McKinley."

I held out my hand and squeaked in surprise when Frannie's mother gave me a tight hug.

"Oh, please, call me Patricia or mom," she said. "We aren't formal around here."

"Uh, sure, okay," I said as Frannie stepped toward me and put her arm around my waist. I tried to look natural as Frannie took a deep breath.

"Mom, Dad, I have something to tell you. Daisy and I aren't just roommates. We're, um, dating."

There was complete silence and I gripped Frannie's hand when it slid into mine. She cleared her throat and said, "I'm a - a lesbian."

"You're a what?" Her father said.

"She's a lesbian," Frannie's grandmother said. "It means she likes to have sex with other women, Gregory."

"I know what it means, Mom!" Her father replied as his face went red.

Frannie clutched my hand in a death grip before staring at her mother. Patricia bit her bottom lip as tears slid down her cheeks.

"Mom, please don't cry," Frannie pleaded. "Don't be upset okay? I know this is a shock but - "

"Upset?" Her mother said. "Honey, I'm not upset. I'm crying because I – I'm so happy!"

Frannie gave me a bewildered look as her mother threw her arms around both of us and hugged us hard. "I was so worried that you were all alone in that horrible city but you aren't! You're in love! Oh, honey. I'm so happy for you both! And honestly, I always suspected that you were a lesbian."

Frannie gaped at her and I bit the inside of my cheek to stop the laughter from spilling out.

"You – you suspected that I was a lesbian?"

Patricia nodded. "Of course I did, dear." She kissed both of us on the cheeks and stepped back before wiping the tears away. "Gregory, say something to your daughter."

Frannie's father was already scrolling through his iPad again. He looked up and said, "Happy for you, honey. Hey, did you hear that I'm the head of the historical society of Darville now?"

"Yes, Dad," Frannie said. "We already talked about it."

"Right, right," he said distractedly as Frannie's grandmother stood up with a grunt and walked slowly toward us. She took both of our hands and squeezed them.

"I knew you were in love, Francine," she said with a grin. "You can't hide that from your grandma."

"I – I guess not," Frannie said with a quick look at me.

"Now, Daisy do you want kids?" Her grandmother asked.

"Grandma!" Frannie said. "It's a little soon to be talking kids."

"It isn't," Patricia said as she added coffee in neat little scoops to the filter in the coffee machine. "As lesbians, it won't be as simple to get pregnant. You'll need to decide if you want to do sperm donation or adoption and if adoption, are you adopting a baby or an older child and are you adopting locally or internationally. There are lots of decisions to make, not to mention are you going to get married here at home or - "

"Mom!" Frannie said. "Stop talking about marriage and kids. You're freaking Daisy out."

"I'm sorry, Daisy," Patricia said with a warm smile. "Sometimes I do get a little enthusiastic about my kids."

"Uh, that's okay," I said.

There was an awkward silence and Frannie said, "So, we'll just take my suitcase to my room and Daisy's downstairs to the basement. We'll be right back."

"Downstairs?" Patricia said. "Honey, don't be silly. Daisy can stay in your room with you."

"Oh, um, that's fine," Frannie said. "I told Daisy that we would have to, um, have separate bedrooms and she's fine with it. Aren't you, Daisy?"

"Yes," I said. "It's not a problem."

"Oh please," Patricia said. "You act as though everyone in this house are old fuddy-duddies. We're perfectly fine with you sleeping in the same bed together. But do remember that both your father and I are light sleepers so if you're going to have sex, keep the

_ ”

"Mom!" Frannie said as her face turned bright red.

Patricia shrugged. "No need to be embarrassed, sweetie. Sex is perfectly natural."

Before Frannie could reply, we heard the front door slam and a deep voice said, "Mom? I'm back."

The blood drained from my face at the sound of the familiar voice and my entire body stiffened as I tightened my grip on Frannie's hand. She winced and tried to pull her hand away. "Daisy, ouch!"

"I got the lemon pepper, but Phil says they've never heard of tarragon. I'm not shocked. Honestly, I'm surprised they have spices beyond salt and pepper."

I stood frozen to the spot as Wes, my one-night stand with the perfect goddamn body, walked into the kitchen.

Chapter Four

Wes

"Hey, Wes!" My sister said.

I barely noticed Frannie. All the breath had been sucked from my body and I stared dumbfounded at Daisy. What the fuck was she doing standing in my mother's kitchen? And why the fuck was she holding my sister's hand?

Before I could say anything, Daisy dropped Frannie's hand and stepped toward me. She held her hand out and said, "Hi, I'm Daisy! You must be Frannie's brother. I'm Daisy! It's nice to meet you! I'm Daisy! I'm Frannie's, um, roommate."

I stared at her hand for a moment before shifting the bag of groceries to my left. I took her hand and was immediately thrust into the memory of Daisy riding me, of her nails digging into my wrist – hell, I still had the marks from her nails on my chest and wrist – and the way her perfect tits had tasted.

"Don't be so shy, Daisy," my mother said. "Wes isn't a prude. Daisy is Frannie's girlfriend, honey."

My hand squeezed Daisy's compulsively. Girlfriend? Daisy was Frannie's girlfriend? I decided I had misheard my mother. "Girlfriend," I said in a weird voice that didn't sound at all like my normal one. "Meaning, you're her friend and you're a girl."

"No, dearest," my grandmother said from her spot at the table. "It means that Daisy is Frannie's lesbian lover. They're having sex."

"Grandma!" Frannie said as my mouth dropped open. Daisy yanked her hand free of mine as Frannie joined us and slipped her arm around Daisy's waist. She hesitated and then pressed a brief kiss against Daisy's mouth.

Hot and unpleasant jealousy immediately tingled down my spine. I placed the groceries on the floor and took a step back. What the fuck was going on?

"Wes, are you okay?" Frannie said. "You look kind of pale."

"I'm fine," I said hoarsely. I stared at Daisy. She was as pale as I was, and she gave me a worried look before glancing at Frannie and then shaking her head very slightly. It was more than obvious that she wanted me to keep my mouth shut.

"How – how long have you been dating?" I asked.

"Uh, only a few months," Frannie said.

I stared at Daisy as she gave me a bright look of desperation. After a moment, I said, "Nice to meet you."

Relief flooded her face. "It's nice to meet you too."

I bent and picked up the grocery bags as Frannie grabbed Daisy's hand. "We'll grab our suitcases and put them in my room. Be right back."

She dragged Daisy out of the room and I set the grocery bags on the counter. "Since when did Frannie become a lesbian?"

"Oh, I always suspected," my mother said as she began to empty the bags. "I'm happy for her. Very happy. You know, it doesn't matter to me or your father who you date." She gave me a meaningful look. "We'll love you no matter your life choices."

"I'm not gay, Mom," I said.

"I know, honey," she said before pinching my cheek affectionately. "I just want you to know that we love you no matter what. Unless you never get married and give me grandchildren. That will get you kicked out of the will. Okay?"

She smiled sweetly at me and I nodded. "Yep, got it."

"Good. Now, you still haven't told me where you were last night."

I cleared my throat. Somehow telling my mother that I was screwing my sister's lying, cheating girlfriend didn't seem like a smart thing to say. As anger burned in my belly, I said, "I caught up with some old friends and ended up crashing on their couch."

"Isn't that lovely," my mother said.

"Yeah. I'm going to go have a shower." I kissed my mother's cheek and left the kitchen, climbing the steps two at a time. I paused in front of my sister's room and raised my hand to knock before changing my mind. My shock at seeing Daisy had turned to anger. She had seemed sweet last night and the sex had been the best of my life, but any lingering affection for her or regret I'd felt this morning from leaving without saying goodbye had disappeared. She was lying and cheating on my baby sister. I would find out what kind of game she was playing and then give her the choice to tell my sister what she had done or I would.

Daisy

I slipped outside into the cold night air and took a few deep breaths. It was almost nine and I had a headache and felt nearly sick to my stomach from the tension between Wes and me. Not that Frannie or the rest of her family had seemed to notice. We had gone shopping with Patricia and Frannie's grandmother for a few hours in the afternoon before returning to the house. I had tried to avoid Wes as best I could, but the house was small and every time I turned around he was there. Staring at me with those dark eyes. They were cold and angry without a single hint of the warmth that was there last night. I shivered delicately and zipped up my jacket before walking around to the side of the house and leaning against the freezing cold brick.

I had told Frannie that I needed to grab something from my car but really, I just needed a moment to myself. Or, more accurately, a moment away from Wes and his barely contained rage with me. Fuck, I had really screwed things up. What were the odds that my one-night stand would be with Frannie's brother?

I rubbed at my temples and tried to think past the headache. Okay, I could fix this. I needed to get Wes alone and give him a condensed version of the truth. He didn't need to know that Frannie was dating Owen. I would just tell him that Frannie was trying to avoid being set up and that –

"Thinking of escaping into the night?"

I made a breathless squeal and jerked against the brick before staring wide-eyed at Wes. "Oh my God, you scared me! Don't sneak up on a person like that."

"Sorry."

"No, you're not," I said.

"No, I'm really not," he said in a voice that was colder than the brick I was leaning against.

"Wes, listen, I know you're wondering what's going on and I – oh, God!"

Moving quickly, Wes stepped in front of me and rested his hands on the wall on either side of my head. His body brushed up against mine and even through our jackets, my body remembered the heat of his. I was shamefully aroused instantly. My hips pressed instinctively against him and I blushed when he jerked his pelvis away from mine and said, "Are you fucking kidding me, right now?"

"I'm sorry," I said. "I can explain."

"Can you?" He growled. "He lowered his face until it was only inches from mine. "That's good, because I'd really like an explanation for why last night I was balls deep in a woman who turns out to be my baby sister's lesbian lover."

"I'm not a lesbian," I said quickly.

"No? So, you're a cheating bisexual instead of a cheating lesbian?"

"I'm not a cheater or bisexual or - "

"What kind of game are you playing? Is your name even Daisy?"

"What? Of course it is! Wes, I know you're angry but listen for - "

"Does my sister know that you're a damn cheater?"

"Shut up!" I suddenly snapped at him.

He blinked in surprise at my sudden burst of anger as I glared up at him. "Shut your big, stupid mouth and let me explain before you make a complete ass of yourself."

"Fine. Explain yourself."

I took a deep breath and said, "I'm your sister's roommate. Frannie has been dating a man for the last year that she doesn't think your family will approve of. She knows your mom and grandmother were going to try and set her up with someone during the Christmas holidays, so she begged me to pretend to be her lesbian lover so that they would leave her alone. Against my better judgement, I agreed. I'm not a lesbian or bisexual. I am playing a part for your sister because she's very important to me and I love her. Like a sister."

I took another deep breath and stared up at Wes. He

wouldn't believe me. Why would he? It was a crazy, stupid story and –

"Who's the guy?"

"I'm sorry?" I stared at him in shock.

"Who's the guy she's dating?" He asked.

"I – I don't know," I lied.

He studied me closely before pressing his body against mine. This time he didn't move away when my pelvis pushed against his. "You're a terrible liar, flower girl."

I bit my bottom lip as my gaze flickered to Owen's bedroom window. "I don't know."

"So, you're telling me that your roommates with my sister and have never once seen or met the guy she's dating?" He breathed into my ear.

"Y-yes," I said unsteadily.

He stepped back and raised his eyebrows. "Tell me, Daisy."

My eyes flickered to Owen's bedroom window again and I cursed inwardly when Wes followed my gaze.

"Owen?" He said. "Frannie is dating Owen Brenner?"

"You can't say anything," I said frantically. "You can't tell your parents. Frannie will kill me if you do."

He rubbed his big hand through his hair before glancing at Owen's bedroom again. "What the hell does she see in that guy?"

"He's a good guy," I said.

"Doesn't he work at a Best Buy?"

"He's a manager there," I replied defensively. "Listen, I know you have this family feud thing going on, but you can't say anything, okay?"

He stared blankly at me. "Say anything? Are you kidding me? I'll take this goddamn secret to my grave. If Dad finds out that Frannie is dating Owen Brenner, he'll have a fucking heart attack."

He rubbed at his own temples before shaking his head. "Fucking hell. What is Frannie thinking?"

"She loves him," I said. "She loves him and they're good together. He's a great guy and he treats her really well."

Wes didn't reply and I gave him a few seconds before I said, "So, uh what do we do about the other thing?"

"What other thing?"

"What do you mean 'what other thing'?" I said. "I slept with my best friend/fake lesbian lover's brother!"

Wes shrugged. "You didn't know who I was."

"Damn straight I didn't!" I glared at him. "That's entirely your fault, by the way."

He gave me a look of confusion. "What?"

"I'm friends with Frannie on Facebook and Instagram and Twitter. I know all of her friends and family on there, but I have never once seen you on her friend feed or even a picture of you!"

He shrugged. "I'm not on social media and I hate having my picture taken."

"Not on social media? Who the hell isn't on social media?" I sputtered.

"You can't tell me my sister has never mentioned me by name," Wes said.

"I – I – maybe she did," I stammered. "I really don't remember. But if she had, there's more than one Wes in the world!"

He grinned and I scowled at him. "If you had a goddamn Facebook account, none of this would have happened. I would have known exactly who you were the minute you waltzed up to me at that bar and started flirting with me. It would have been a hard no, buddy!"

"Flirting with you? I think what you're trying to say is when I came up and saved your cute ass from that drunk guy," Wes said.

"I had it all under control," I said. "Until you came along with your perfect body and your perfect mouth and your – your giant perfect dick!"

Wes burst into laughter and after a moment, I started to giggle too. I buried my face in my hands and said, "I'm sorry. I don't really think it's your fault."

"Nothing has changed," Wes said. "We were two people who agreed to have one fun night together. It's a little awkward now but we're both adults. We can handle a little awkwardness for a week, right?"

"Yeah," I said as I dropped my hands. They were turning ice cold, I was shivering madly and I could barely feel the tip of my nose. I needed to go back inside but instead I said, "You didn't say goodbye this morning."

"I should have."

"Why didn't you?" I asked. When he didn't reply, I said, "Was it – was it because I wasn't that great in bed?"

He immediately shook his head and I couldn't stop my low moan when he put his arm around my waist and drew me into his embrace. He kissed the tip of my cold nose and said, "I didn't wake you up because I didn't have another condom."

"What?" I ignored my instinct to burrow against his warm body.

"I didn't have another condom," he repeated patiently, "and if I had woken you up to say goodbye, I would have kissed you. If I had kissed you, then I would have touched you. If I had touched you, then I would have fucked you."

I blushed bright red and stared at the snow on the ground. "Oh."

He pulled me closer and nuzzled my neck. "I had an amazing time last night, Daisy. I know you have a vow of celibacy going on but I want to make you break that vow repeatedly."

I shivered all over, this time from need instead of cold, before pulling away. "I – I can't, Wes. I'm pretending to be your sister's girlfriend, remember?"

He sighed and nodded. "Yeah, I remember."

"We'd better go back inside."

"You go first," he said.

"You won't say anything about Owen, will you?" I said.

He shook his head. "No, I won't."

Wes

"Mom, we'll be fine. We have snow in the city." Frannie's voice held a note of impatience. "Besides, we're only going to the mall and it's like a twenty-minute drive."

I wandered into the kitchen, my gaze automatically dropping to Daisy's ass. She was bent over the dishwasher, putting her plate in the bottom rack and I could feel my dick twitching. I quickly looked away from her ass. Jesus, I needed to get some control.

"I don't know why you have to go today," Mom said. "It's snowing like crazy and the roads will be slippery."

"We'll be fine," Frannie said as Daisy straightened and turned around. She gave me a tentative smile as Frannie grabbed her jacket from the back of the chair. "Daisy has a waxing appointment."

This time my gaze dropped to Daisy's crotch before I could stop it. She cleared her throat and I forced myself to look at her. She was blushing brightly and I really wanted to grin at her. It was strange to me why she had made the waxing appointment. Last night, she had made it perfectly clear that we couldn't have sex again. So, why the sudden waxing appointment?

I wondered if I could convince her not to wax her sweet little pussy. It was her body and none of my business what she did with it, but I wasn't lying when I told her I preferred the natural look. I scowled inwardly at the thought of her soft curls being ripped out with hot wax before I reminded myself that it didn't matter anyway. I wouldn't be seeing her pussy again, whether it was natural or waxed bare.

"Why don't you let Wes drive you in Dad's truck?" Mom said. "Honey, do you mind? I would feel so much better about the girls' being out in this weather if you drove them."

I took a quick look at Frannie. She shook her head and gave me a pointed look. I grinned at her and said, "Sure, I don't mind at all."

"No," Frannie said with another pointed look at me. "Daisy is perfectly happy to drive in this weather and we don't need my big brother tagging along with us. Isn't that right, Daisy?"

Daisy hesitated and Frannie elbowed her in the side. "Isn't that right?"

"Um, yes. I'm fine with driving." She chewed on her bottom lip and despite having just met her, I knew she was lying.

"I'll drive," I said as Frannie gave me a death glare and Daisy gave me a look of gratitude.

"You can't hang out with us," Frannie snapped. "We have," she hesitated, "girl stuff to do."

"Yeah, yeah," I said. "I'll do my own thing and you can text me when you're ready to go home."

"Perfect!" Mom said. "I feel so much better about this plan."

She followed us out of the kitchen and into the hallway, chatting happily as we pulled on our boots and our coats. "Daisy, honey, you don't have a scarf."

"I forgot it," Daisy said.

"I'll crochet you one tonight," Mom said. "You'll need one for when we get the Christmas tree."

"You don't have to do that, Patricia," Daisy protested. I grinned to myself. Daisy didn't know it yet, but she was fighting a losing battle.

"Of course I do! You're part of our family now, sweetheart," Mom said. "What's your favourite colour?"

"Oh, uh, I like red," Daisy said.

"Fantastic! I picked up the softest red yarn the other day!" Mom said. "It'll make a perfect scarf for you. Now," she kissed Frannie's cheek, then Daisy's and finally mine, "be careful out there, you three, and be home for dinner please."

"Yes, Mom," Frannie said as she glanced at her cell phone. "Wes, let's go for God's sake. I don't want to be late for…"

She gave Daisy a sudden blank look.

"My appointment," Daisy said quickly.

"Right. Her appointment." Frannie took Daisy's hand and dragged her out of the house.

I followed them to the truck. The snow was falling heavily and I studied the flakes that were caught in Daisy's eyelashes as Frannie opened the passenger door. "Daisy, get in."

"What? No, I want the outside," Daisy said with a nervous look at me.

"No way," Frannie said. "I hate sitting in the middle. Get in, Daisy."

She sighed. "Fine."

Dad's truck was old and loud and had a bench seat. The thought of Daisy sitting next to me made me nearly as giddy as a goddamn school girl. As I watched her struggle to climb into the truck, I brushed past Frannie and put my hands around Daisy's waist. She made an adorable little squeak as I lifted her into the truck.

"Uh, thank you, Wes," she said.

"No problem." I boosted Frannie into the truck and slammed the passenger door shut before crossing to the driver's side. I leaned in, started the truck and grabbed the snow brush before turning the heat on high and shutting the door. I cleared off the windshield and hood of snow then climbed into the truck.

"Ready?" I asked.

Daisy nodded. Frannie was texting on her phone and she made an impatient gesture with her hand. "God, yes. Drive on, Jeeves."

I rolled my eyes and pulled out of the driveway and onto the street. Daisy's leg was pressed against mine and it was taking all of my willpower not to put my hand on her thigh. She was wearing yoga pants and they clung to her firm thighs. Christ, yoga pants had never turned me on so much before. I ignored my hardening dick and concentrated on driving. The roads weren't actually that great and it was slow going. By the time we reached the mall parking lot, Frannie was nearly shaking with impatience.

"Finally!" She muttered as I parked and shut the truck off. Her phone rang and she glanced at it, a happy little smile crossing her face. "Um, this is a private call. Give me a minute."

She opened the door and slid out of the truck, slamming the door behind her. She wandered away, speaking into her cell phone as I turned to Daisy. "That was Owen, wasn't it?"

Daisy nodded. "Yeah, that was his ring. She's meeting him here for a few hours."

"Do you have a waxing appointment?" I asked.

"Yes." She blushed brightly and stared at the back of Frannie's head. "Thank you for driving us. It makes me a little anxious to drive in bad weather."

"You're welcome," I said. I glanced around the

parking lot. There was no one walking by and Frannie wasn't looking at us.

I placed my hand on Daisy's thigh, rubbing it firmly as she gave me a startled look. "Wh-what are you doing?"

"What are you getting waxed?" I asked as I slipped my fingers between her legs and rubbed her inner thigh.

Her soft little moan made my dick harden. I pulled on her thigh, pleased when she immediately widened her legs. I let my hand inch up a little higher. "What are you getting waxed, flower girl?"

"You know what," she whispered. "Wes, your sister is right there."

"She's not looking," I said. "Are you sure you want to wax your sweet little pussy?"

"I – I should."

"I don't think you should." I cupped her pussy through her pants. "I like it just the way it is."

She moaned again. Her cheeks were bright red and she was biting compulsively at her bottom lip but she widened her thighs even more. "I usually wax it."

"That's too bad," I said. "But if you insist on waxing, then you need to let me touch those soft little curls of yours one last time."

"What? No, we can't," she said as I pressed rhythmically against her pussy. "Your sister is right there and we're in the middle of the mall parking lot."

"There's no one around and Frannie's busy with Owen," I said. "Lift your jacket up for me, darlin'."

I continued to stare out the windshield, watching for others as Daisy hesitated. "Wes, I shouldn't."

"Yes, you should," I said. "Do it, Daisy. I want to touch your pussy."

She moaned and lifted the bottom of her jacket to reveal the waistband of her pants. Moving quickly, I slipped my hand inside her pants and panties and cupped her pussy. She gasped, her thighs clenching around my hand. "Your hand is cold!"

I grinned and stroked her pussy lips. She was wet already and my dick pressed painfully against my jeans. "You're so warm, darlin'. Warm and wet just for me, isn't that right?"

"Yes," she whispered as she undulated against my hand. She latched onto my arm, staring desperately out the windshield as I rubbed her clit until it swelled against my fingers. I slid my fingers down her slit and pushed one into her tight entrance. She squealed and then clapped her hand over her mouth before lowering it back to my arm.

"Oh God, Wes!"

I moved my hand again, tugging on her soft curls before stroking her clit. She moaned and then said, "Harder."

I didn't reply and she blushed and gave me a quick look. "Sorry."

"Don't be sorry. Tell me what you want. What you need," I said as I rubbed her clit with rougher strokes.

"Oh, oh God," she whispered. "Smaller circles and a little more pressure and…oh, yes, like that."

She was panting now, her hips rising and falling as bright colour infused her cheeks. Fuck, she was so beautiful, it made me ache. I rubbed hard and fast in small, tight circles against her clit and smiled with satisfaction when she stiffened against my hand and made a low, drawn-out moan. Fresh wetness flooded my fingers as she collapsed against the back of the seat and stared wide-eyed at me.

"Holy crap," she said.

I laughed and she blushed again. "I – that's never happened before."

I gave her a curious look. "What's never happened before?"

"I've never – oh!"

I had suddenly yanked my hand out of her pants and shoved it into my jacket pocket. Frannie was back and reaching for the door. As she opened it, Daisy pulled her jacket down over her crotch and gave Frannie a bright smile.

"Hi!"

"Hey," Frannie said before frowning at her. "What's wrong?"

"Nothing's wrong," Daisy said.

"Do you feel okay? Your face is really red."

"I feel fine. Ready to go?"

"Yes," Frannie gave her a doubtful look. "You sure you're okay?"

"Of course," Daisy said. She slid across the seat and out of the truck. I stayed where I was, praying like hell that Frannie didn't notice the very obvious bulge at the front of my pants.

Frannie turned toward me. "Are you going into the mall?"

I shrugged. "Not sure, Frannie-pants."

"Don't call me that, Wesley!" She said with a small grin. "Thanks for the ride, big brother. I'll text you when we're finished, okay?"

"Yep. Bye, Frannie, bye, Daisy."

"Bye, Wes," Daisy said.

Chapter Five

Daisy

I wiped the steam from the bathroom mirror and smoothed my wet hair back from my face. Today had been another stressful day of pretending to be in love with Frannie while trying not to think about how ridiculously attracted I was to Wes. Of course, letting him finger me to an orgasm in the truck this morning probably didn't help me ignore my attraction to him.

I sighed and quickly threw on my pajamas before hanging my towel on the rack. I decided it was much harder to be a pretend lesbian when you wanted to hump the leg of your pretend girlfriend's brother every time you got within ten feet of him. I smoothed cream onto my freshly-waxed legs and combed my hair before gathering my toiletry bag and dirty clothes. It was just after eleven and I was ready for bed. Frannie's dad had made the entire family play Monopoly with him after dinner and the damn game had gone on for nearly four hours. Wes and Frannie had engaged in sibling trash talking that made me laugh before Wes kicked all of our butts and won the game. I had to admit that I found his competitive spirit a teeny bit attractive. I opened the bathroom door and stepped out into the hallway. Hopefully I would sleep and not lie awake and think about Wes naked and –

"I like your pajamas."

I jumped about a foot and squinted at Wes in the dim hallway. He was leaning against the wall with his arms crossed over his broad chest and - oh sweet Jesus have mercy - he was wearing only a pair of sleep pants that were barely hanging onto his hips.

I swallowed hard and clutched my toiletry bag and clothes against my braless chest with one hand as I tugged self-consciously at my shorts with the other. "What are you doing here?"

"Waiting to use the washroom?" He arched his eyebrow at me and I cleared my throat.

"Right, of course. Sorry I took so long."

"That's fine," he said.

He stayed where he was, and my nipples hardened when he gave my body a slow, hungry look.

"Wes," I whispered, "don't look at me like that."

"Like what, little flower?" He said in his low and raspy voice.

"You know like what," I said shakily. "I – goodnight, Wes."

"Good night, Daisy."

I slipped by him, making sure to leave lots of room between our bodies and slipped inside Frannie's bedroom. "I am so ready for bed, Fran – oh my God, Frannie!"

Owen and Frannie sat up on the bed as I glared at them. "What the hell!"

"Keep your voice down!" Frannie said in a loud whisper.

"What are you doing here, Owen?" I said in a low voice.

"Dude, I miss my lady," Owen said.

"You saw her this morning."

"Yeah, but I couldn't like, touch her or anything."

I rolled my eyes. "Are you being serious right now? How did you even get in here?"

He grinned at me and pointed to the window. "I totally used the tree to go from my bedroom to my lady's bedroom."

Frannie giggled and kissed his cheek. "You're so smart, baby."

"Well, sorry to break up your little love nest but I'm tired and I want to go to sleep," I said.

"Daisy," Frannie gave me a look that would melt butter. "We really miss each other. I just want a little time with my baby."

"What my lady is trying to say is we want to bone," Owen said cheerfully.

"No!" I said. "No way, Frannie! I am not staying in here while you two bang like bunnies! That's disgusting!"

"You don't have to stay," Frannie said.

"But I'm cool with it if you do," Owen said.

I glared at him as Frannie smacked him on the chest. "Behave, baby."

"Go to his room!" I said in a fierce little whisper.

"I can't climb across that tree!" Frannie said. "Besides, we have the extra room in the basement, remember? Mom and Dad usually get up at seven. As long as you come back upstairs to my room before seven, they'll never know you slept down there."

"Frannie, no! You guys can wait until we get back home."

"Dude, no!" Owen said. "I can't. I've already got a wicked case of blue balls."

"Ugh," I said.

"Please Oopsie-Daisy," Frannie said. "It's really stressful for me being around my family. I need to relieve it somehow!"

"Have you thought about a long, hot shower?" I snapped.

"It's not my fault," Frannie said. "I didn't think my mom would be cool with us sharing a room, you know?"

"Frannie…" I trailed off as she gave me another pleading look.

"Please, honey," she said.

"Fine! But if you get caught screwing Owen, I'll play the jilted lover card with your family. Do you understand?"

"I do. We won't get caught," Frannie said happily. "Thank you so much, Daisy. You're the best."

"Yeah," I muttered as I dropped my clothes and toiletry bag into my suitcase. "Good night."

"Good night." Frannie was already lying back on the bed next to Owen and I slipped out of the room quickly, forcing myself not to slam the door.

I groaned inwardly. Wes was walking into his bedroom and he gave me a curious look. "What's wrong?"

"Nothing," I said.

"Tell the truth, please."

I sighed and crossed my arms over my chest before whispering, "Turns out that Owen is like a damn monkey and crawled across the tree to your sister's room, because they can't go more than forty-eight hours without having sex. Now I'm banished to the basement so your sister can get lucky."

"Gross," Wes said.

"Yeah. Anyway, good night."

"The bed in the basement is really uncomfortable. Mine is much more comfortable."

"That's sweet of you to offer to give up your bed," I said tartly, "but I've slept in uncomfortable beds before."

He grinned at me as I pushed past him and started

toward the staircase. "Hey, Daisy?"

"Yeah?"

"My parents are really light sleepers. What excuse are you going to give them for sleeping in the basement?"

"I'll be quiet. They'll never know."

"They'll hear you. See that floorboard with the knot in it? The minute you cross over it, my mom will wake up and she'll be out of her bedroom to find out what's wrong."

"You're only saying that to try and get me into your bed."

"Nope, I'm telling you what I've learned from years of trying to sneak out of the house as a teenager. You're going to get caught."

"I'm better at sneaking out than you."

He grinned. "Good luck then, flower girl."

I stuck my tongue out at him and his grin widened before he ducked into his bedroom and shut the door.

I took a deep breath and walked quietly down the hallway. I stepped over the floorboard that Wes had pointed out and paused, holding my breath and listening intently. There was nothing and I snorted to myself before moving to the top of the staircase. Wes was full of crap, just like I knew –

"Daisy! Sweetheart, what's wrong?"

I groaned and turned around to smile at Patricia. "Uh, nothing."

A door further down opened and Frannie's grandmother stuck her head out. "What's going on?"

"There's something wrong with Daisy," Patricia said.

She hurried out of her room as Gregory hollered from inside their room, "What's wrong with Daisy?"

"There's nothing wrong," I said quickly. "I was, uh, getting a drink of water."

"Oh sweetie, I have bottles of water right here in this

closet." Patricia opened the linen closet door.

"What's wrong?" Gregory hollered again.

"She's thirsty!" Frannie's grandmother shouted back.

"Get her some water from the closet!" Gregory yelled.

"I am, love!" Patricia said.

She pulled out a bottle of water and handed it to me. "Here, sweetheart."

"Thank you." I said.

"Oh, don't mention it," she replied as grandma retreated into her room and closed the door. "I started leaving bottles of water in the closet when Wes and Francine were teenagers. They were constantly getting up in the night and going downstairs for water. I figured it would be easier to keep bottles of water up here and never lost the habit after they moved out."

She leaned forward and kissed my cheek before stroking my damp hair. "You're such a lovely girl, Daisy. We're so glad you're dating our Frannie."

Guilt trickled through me and I clutched the water bottle before giving her a weak smile. "Thank you, Patricia. I really like your family."

"We like you too, sweetheart. Now, hurry back to Frannie. I'm sure she misses you."

"Goodnight, Patricia."

"Goodnight, Daisy."

I headed back toward Frannie's bedroom, pausing with my door on the handle. Thankfully, Patricia had already returned to her bedroom and shut the door. I leaned against the door but when I heard Owen make a low moan, I straightened and hurried away toward Wes' room.

I stared at his door for a moment before cursing under my breath and opening it. I slipped into his room and shut the door behind me. His room was on the smaller side and the twin bed was tucked against the far wall under the window. Moonlight spilled across his bed and I stared at his big body lying in the bed as he sat up on his elbows.

"Went with the old 'I'm getting a drink of water' excuse, huh? Rookie mistake."

"How was I supposed to know your mother kept bottles of water in the linen closet!" I said. "No one does that. You could have warned me."

"I could have, but where's the fun in that?"

I avoided looking at his naked chest as I crossed the room and set the water down on his nightstand. "Move over."

"Nope, I sleep on the outside, flower girl."

"I hate sleeping on the inside," I huffed. "It's too crowded and…oh God."

Wes had pulled back the covers and I stared at his big, naked body and tried not to drool.

"Y-you're naked," I stuttered.

"I always sleep naked," he said with a wicked grin. "Don't you?"

His gaze dropped to my breasts and I could feel my nipples hardening in response. His grin widened and I crossed my arms over my chest as his cock turned fully erect.

"Behave," I said before carefully crawling over his shins and lying on the bed next to him. It was crowded, Wes was a big man and the bed was on the small side. I shifted to my side to face him as he tucked his hands under his head and stared at the ceiling. The way his dick was tenting the sheets didn't seem to embarrass him at all.

"Nice room," I said. "So, did you have a crush on Anne Hathaway as a teenager?"

"How can you tell?" He laughed.

"Maybe it's the hundreds of Anne Hathaway posters

plastered on your walls?"

He laughed again. "She's hot. What teenage boy didn't have a crush on her?"

I sat up a little and squinted in the darkness at the shelf on the far wall. "What are all those trophies for?"

"Football," he said.

"Do you find it weird to come back home and have everything the same in your bedroom?" I asked.

"No, not really. Mom has said more than once that she's turning my room into a craft room and Frannie's room into an exercise room, but it hasn't happened yet.

I settled onto my side again and stared at his profile in the moonlight. God, he was handsome. "Your family is great."

"They are," he said. "My mom can be a bit overbearing sometimes but it comes from a good place."

"I don't mind. It's kind of nice to have someone 'mothering' me again."

"I'm really sorry for your loss."

"Thank you. So, where did you learn to be so merciless at Monopoly?"

He laughed. "My grandpa. He was ruthless at board games. Even when we were kids, he showed no mercy. I don't think I ever beat him at checkers. Once I was complaining to my mom about the fact that grandpa never let me win and he came thumping into the kitchen and said, 'Son, it don't mean nothin' if I let you win. Now stop your whining and come help me mow the lawn.'"

"I think I would have liked your grandpa," I said.

"He would have really liked you," Wes said. "In fact, my entire family seems to really like you. They're going to be awfully disappointed when you and Frannie break up."

I didn't say anything. I could feel the heat of his body and it was taking everything in me not to curl up against him.

"How did your waxing appointment go?" He suddenly asked.

"Fine." I couldn't resist rubbing my leg against his. "Nice and smooth now."

He groaned and shifted to his side to face me before cupping my face and stroking his thumb across my mouth.

"Wes," I said unsteadily as he shifted closer until his body was touching mine. "This is a bad idea."

"I like bad ideas," he whispered before kissing me.

I returned his kiss immediately, throwing my arm around him and rubbing his broad back as he cupped my thigh and draped it over his hip before stroking my leg.

"Better?" I asked.

"Very smooth," he said, "but I like the Sasquatch version of Daisy too."

I smacked him on the back and he laughed before pressing his cock against me. We were separated only by the thin material of my pajama shorts and I made another soft moan when he cupped my breast.

"Daisy," now his voice was unsteady, "if you don't want me to fuck you, tell me now so I can get out of the damn bed and sleep on the floor."

"You don't have to sleep on the floor," I whispered.

"Thank fucking God," he muttered before kissing me hard. I sucked on his tongue and he groaned then rolled me onto my back and pressed one thigh between mine. I rubbed against him as he lifted his upper body and I helped him pull my shirt off.

"I've missed your beautiful tits," he said in a low voice before dipping his head and capturing one hard nipple in his mouth. He sucked with firm pressure and I moaned in pleasure as I clutched at his head.

After only a moment or two, he raised his head and kissed my collarbone. "Daisy?"

"Yeah?"

"What did you mean in the truck when you said that had never happened before?"

Feeling a little stupid, I said, "I always have to touch myself or, you know, help the guy touch me, to have an orgasm. That's the first time I didn't have to."

He gave me a self-satisfied smile. "So, points for Gryffindor then?"

"Like hell you're Gryffindor," I said. "You have Hufflepuff written all over you."

He nuzzled my neck and I stroked the muscles in his back as he licked a slow path up my throat to my ear. "I liked making you come," he whispered.

"I liked it too," I said.

"I really want to taste your pussy."

I shivered all over and couldn't help rubbing my pussy against his thigh.

"Do you want that?"

"Yes, please," I said.

He grinned at me. "Can you be quiet while I'm eating your pussy? The walls are thin."

"Yes," I said.

"If you're too loud, I'll stop," he warned.

"I'll be quiet," I said even though I didn't know if that was true or not.

He brushed his mouth across mine before tracing my stomach with his fingers. I shivered and twitched and tried not to plead as he made small circles over each of my hipbones. When his hand finally dipped under the waistband of my shorts, my legs were already spread shamefully wide. He touched my pussy and I giggled at the look of surprise on his face.

The surprise turned to delight as he touched the soft curls. "You didn't wax."

"I couldn't," I said. I tried to sound disapproving. "It's not like I could let someone near my personal bits after you made me come all over your hand ten minutes earlier."

"If I told you that was my brilliant plan all along, would you believe me?" He asked.

"Nope."

"Fair enough. I just wanted to touch you again. I can't seem to get enough of you, flower girl." Wes touched my curls again before moving his hand to the waistband of my shorts. "Let's get these off."

"Yes, let's," I said eagerly. I helped him drag my shorts down my legs and he tossed them on the floor before scooting down the bed and settling his big body between my legs. His shoulders pushed at my thighs and I ran my fingers through his thick hair as he smiled up at me.

"Remember to be quiet, darlin'."

"I will," I whispered.

His warm, firm lips pressed against my pussy and I bit back my instant moan of pleasure. He licked down my slit and I gasped and arched immediately. His hot tongue probed against my entrance then slipped inside. I moaned loudly and he stopped and lifted his head.

"Daisy," he warned in a low voice. "Quiet."

"Don't stop," I whispered.

"I haven't even touched your clit and you're already being too loud," he replied. "Maybe this isn't a good idea, little flower."

"No, it's a good idea!" I whispered frantically. "It's a *great* idea. I'll be quiet!"

"Will you?"

"Yes!" I tried to push his face back into my pussy. "Wes, please."

He buried his face between my legs again and when his tongue swept across my swollen clit, I turned my head and shoved my face into his pillow. Wes flicked his tongue across my clit, licked away the moisture from my swollen lips and then licked my clit with broad, flat sweeps before sucking on my lips. I bucked against his mouth and pressed my face deeper into his pillow. Holy fuck, Wes was a champion pussy eater.

His tongue slicked back and forth over that throbbing bundle of nerves and I moaned into the pillow and pumped my pelvis shamelessly against his face. I almost screamed when he rubbed my clit roughly with his thumb and then licked it again. He alternated between the rough strokes with his thumb and the soft, wet licks of his tongue until I lifted my face from the pillow, sucked in a much-needed breath of air and pleaded mindlessly.

"Shh, little flower," he said before delving back into my pussy.

After only touching me twice before, Wes had already learned what I needed to make me come. Pretty fucking impressive considering Richard hadn't figured it out in two goddamn years.

Wes pinched my clit and I made a muffled scream into the pillow. I was so close, just one rougher pinch would push me into sweet release. Instead of pinching me again, he gave my clit a hard nip. I shrieked into the pillow and climaxed with a dizzying mix of pleasure and pain. Vaguely, I was aware of Wes licking my clit to soothe away the sting before sitting up and reaching into the nightstand drawer for a condom. My body shook as I slowly came down from the high of my orgasm. My stomach muscles were jumping and trembling like live wires and little aftershocks of pleasure still tingled in my pussy. When Wes pulled the pillow away from my face, I stared blearily up at him. He was already kneeling between my legs and I widened them automatically as he leaned down and pressed a kiss against my mouth.

"Okay, little flower?"

"So okay," I breathed as I reached between us. My

fingers stroked his cock and he groaned as I helped guide him in.

"Shh," I said. "Thin walls, remember?"

"Fuck, I remember," he muttered as he sheathed himself deep inside my pussy.

I moaned and he propped himself up on his hands before staring at my breasts. I pulled on my hard nipples and he groaned and made two hard thrusts. I gasped and arched up against him before wrapping my legs around his waist.

"So good," he moaned before thrusting in a hard and rough rhythm that made my toes curl. I met each of his strokes, squeezing around his cock with every pump of his hips. He was panting and his moans were growing progressively louder. I clapped my hand over his mouth as he moved harder and faster. He drove deep one final time and shuddered all over as he climaxed. I could feel the vibration of his low moans against my hand and I pressed soft kisses on his throat as he shook and thrust back and forth. I moved my hand from his mouth and he grinned at me before kissing me.

"I really like fucking you, Daisy."

"I really like fucking you, Wes."

He nuzzled my neck affectionately before moving off of me. I turned on my side and watched as he removed the condom and tied it off before tossing it into the trash can near his bed.

"You need to remember to empty the trash can in the morning," I said. "If your mother was cleaning and found that she'd…"

"What? Ground me?" Wes said as he eased back into the bed next to me. He rested on his back and I curled against his side, running my hand over the hair on his chest as he rubbed lazy circles across my back with his warm hand.

"She'll be suspicious," I said.

"Yep, but not suspicious that it was my sister's girlfriend," Wes said with a low laugh. "Mostly, she'll drive herself crazy trying to figure out how I snuck a girl past her."

"Your mother has crazy good hearing," I said. "Were you ever able to sneak out when you were younger?"

"Once," Wes said.

"Impressive."

"Not really. I was supposed to be sneaking out to meet my friends at the quarry. I made it out of the house but not to the quarry."

"Why not?" I asked.

"I had the brilliant idea to tie my sheets together and climb out the window. Unfortunately, I never did get my "knots tying" badge from Boy Scouts."

"Uh oh," I said with a giggle.

"Yeah. The knot came undone at the top and I fell like a rock."

"Holy shit!"

"Luckily, Dad had planted some rose bushes along the side of the house. They broke my fall, but I still fractured my ankle and got all scratched up from the thorns. I crawled out of the bushes and had to drag my sorry ass to the front door and ring the doorbell."

"You should have gone out Frannie's window and used the tree," I said.

Wes laughed. "Frannie would have ratted me out in a heartbeat if I had. I was your typical pain-in-the-ass big brother to her. Anyway, Mom and Dad drove me to the hospital, Dad giving me hell the entire way for destroying his rose bushes, and I spent the rest of the summer in a cast and hobbling around on crutches. It was my one and only time I was successful at sneaking out."

"You call falling out your window and breaking your ankle, successful?" I said.

"Hey, I got out of the house without them knowing, didn't I?" Wes said. "That counts as successfully sneaking out."

"Fair enough." I rubbed my hand across Wes' chest. "Thanks for letting me crash in your room, Wes. I really appreciate it."

"It's my pleasure," he said. His cock was starting to harden and I gave him a look of surprise.

"What?" He asked.

"Already?"

He grinned at me. "Impressive, right?"

I shrugged. "It's okay, I guess."

"Okay?" Wes growled playfully before rolling on top of me and pinning me to the bed. He nipped at my neck and then my earlobe. "I guess I need to show you exactly how impressive my dick can be, flower girl."

"Yes, I guess you do, Wesley."

He laughed. "Prepare to be impressed, little flower."

Chapter Six

Daisy

"It looks lovely, Daisy. Red is your colour," Frannie's mom said approvingly.

I touched the soft scarf she had wrapped around my neck and said, "Thank you so much for making this for me, Patricia. I really love it."

I swallowed past the lump in my throat and blinked back the tears. I really did appreciate her thoughtfulness and for a moment I felt a surge of anger at Frannie for making me lie to her mom. She was wonderful and so motherly that it made me miss my own mother with a deep-seated ache that took my breath away.

"Dearest? What's wrong?" Patricia asked.

"Nothing," I said. "I..."

I trailed off and Patricia said, "You just need a mom hug."

Before I could protest, Patricia had wrapped me in her arms. I hesitated only briefly before returning her hug. God, it felt good to be hugged by a mom again, even if it wasn't my mom. This time I couldn't stop the tears from dripping down my face. Patricia leaned back and studied me silently before wiping the tears away with her thumbs.

"Frannie told me what happened to your parents," she said. "I'm very sorry, Daisy. The holidays must be a particularly difficult time for you."

"A little," I admitted.

"Well," Patricia cleared her throat briskly and wiped at her own eyes, "anytime you need a mom hug you just ask. Okay?"

"Yeah, okay." I was still crying and Patricia handed me a tissue as Wes stepped into the living room.

"Dad says if we don't leave in the next five minutes, he's driving to Walmart and buying a fake tree," Wes said.

"He makes that threat every year," Patricia said with a laugh. "He's - "

"Daisy? What's wrong? Why are you crying?" Wes walked toward me. When he reached for me, I gave him a wide-eyed look of warning. He dropped his arms, his face flushing a dull red as he glanced at his mom before stepping back.

Patricia gave us both a considering look that made me very nervous before saying, "Nothing's wrong, honey. Daisy was just saying thank you for the scarf."

"Right. Uh, well, we should get going," Wes said. "There isn't enough room in the truck for all of us. Dad said he'd drive the car with you and grandma and Frannie and Daisy can go in the truck with me."

"Why don't you let Frannie and Daisy go with Dad," Patricia said. "It'll give your father a chance to get to know Frannie's girlfriend better."

She put a slight emphasis on Frannie's girlfriend and my insides churned with guilt and nerves as Wes said, "Sure. I don't care either way."

He sounded convincing enough to me, but his mother gave him another assessing look before smiling at me. "Ready to go chop down a Christmas tree, Daisy?"

"As long as I'm not the one chopping," I said.

Patricia laughed. "No, dearest. We'll leave that job to Wes."

❧ ❧

"Wait, so you really are allowed to just walk into the woods and cut down a tree?" I asked in confusion.

Frannie's dad nodded. "Yes. It's a tree farm. There are about 200 acres of trees. You can harvest your own or you can head over to the barn and purchase a pre-cut one."

He pointed to a large red barn that had a steady flow of people coming in and out of it. I wrapped my new scarf more snugly around my neck as Frannie took my hand and squeezed it. "Daisy's a city girl, Dad. She didn't even know tree farms existed. Did you?"

I shook my head as Wes and his mother and grandmother joined us at the edge of the woods. Patricia smiled at her husband. "Okay, so Jim says the price is seventy dollars this year and - "

"Seventy!" Frannie's dad said. "It's gone up twenty bucks."

"Hush now, Gregory," Patricia said. "You know Jim has to provide for his family. They had a third boy three months ago."

Gregory rolled his eyes. "You got the saw, Wes? Hey, earth to Wes!"

Wes dragged his gaze from my and Frannie's clasped hands. "Yes, you see it in my hand, don't you?"

"Don't get smart with me, Wesley," Gregory said with a grin.

"Sorry, Sir," Wes replied.

Frannie's hand tightened painfully onto mine and I grimaced before whispering, "Frannie, not so tight."

"Well, isn't this an unexpected surprise."

73

Gregory stiffened and spun around, glaring at the smaller man standing behind him. "What are you doing here, Brenner?"

"Getting a Christmas tree, of course. What else would I be doing here?" the man said with a sardonic grin.

Gregory flushed all over as Patricia hurried over and put her hand on his arm. "We should get going, dearest."

"Hello, Patricia. You're looking lovely," the man said.

"Thank you, Ryan," Patricia replied.

"Dad? I checked out the trees in the barn and I think we should... whoa."

Frannie made a low gasp of delight as Owen jogged up to the group.

"Hello, Owen," Patricia said. "How are you?"

"Good, thanks, Mrs. McKinley. How about yourself?" Owen asked. His gaze drifted to Frannie and an -admittedly adorable - look of adoration came over his face.

"Fine," Patricia said. Neither Frannie nor Owen noticed the way she watched as Owen approached us.

"Uh, hi. It's Francine, right?" Owen said before holding out his hand.

Frannie, her face a lovely shade of pink, shook Owen's hand. "Frannie, actually."

I discreetly elbowed Frannie in the side when she continued to hold Owen's hand. She stared blankly at me as her mother said, "Frannie, dearest, aren't you going to introduce Daisy to the Brenners?"

"Right, of course," Frannie said as she dropped Owen's hand. "Uh, Owen and Mr. Brenner, this is Daisy."

"Nice to meetcha," Owen said. He grinned at me and I shook his hand before smiling at his father.

"Hello, Mr. Brenner. It's nice to meet you."

"Likewise," he said.

"Daisy is Frannie's lesbian lover," Frannie's grandmother said. "They have sex together."

"Grandma!"

"Mother Francine!"

Frannie and Patricia made identical shrieks of horror as Wes and Owen burst into laughter. I wondered if my face was as red as Gregory and Mr. Brenner's and decided it probably was.

"What?" Her grandmother said. "I heard them having sex last night when I got up to use the bathroom. Frannie's a moaner."

"Grandma, be quiet!" Frannie said.

"Nothing to be ashamed of," her grandmother said.

"Yeah, Frannie, it's nothing to be ashamed of," Wes said teasingly.

His grandmother arched one badly-drawn eyebrow at him. "You're one to talk, Wesley. I heard you last night grunting and groaning too, you know. You got a girlfriend we don't know about?"

Wes' mouth dropped open and I wondered if I should just confess everything right then and there. I wasn't cut out for a life of lying or lesbianism.

"I – grandma, I wasn't – I mean…there was no one in my room last night," Wes said.

"So, you were pullin' your own pickle then, were you?" His grandmother said.

"Mother, please," Gregory said. "I am begging you to stop talking."

"Why don't we all go to the canteen and we'll grab a nice cup of hot chocolate to drink while we're searching for our tree," Patricia said.

"Good idea," Gregory muttered. "If we're drinking, we're not talking."

"Can you grab ours, Mom?" Frannie asked. She was

staring at Owen again. "Daisy and I want to check out the gift shop in the barn."

"Sure, but don't be long, dearest," Patricia replied.

"We won't." Frannie was still staring at Owen and I took her hand and squeezed it in warning. She gave me a distracted smile as Patricia watched the two of us.

"Owen, where's your mother?" Mr. Brenner asked.

"Over by the gate talking to Mrs. Parten," Owen said. He stayed where he was when his father started toward the gate.

"Owen? Let's go."

"Um, I think I'm going to check out the gift shop too," Owen said. "There's a snow globe I'm thinking of buying."

His father sighed irritably. "A snow globe? Since when do you care about snow globes?"

Owen shrugged. "I like snow globes, Dad. Don't make a big deal about it."

"Fine, but don't be long," his father retorted.

"Yeah, okay. Uh, do you ladies mind if I walk over there with you?" Owen asked.

"Not at all," Frannie said. Her voice was too bright and eager and I squeezed her hand again. She gave me a quick glance before pulling me toward the barn.

"Meet back here in ten minutes," Patricia called after us.

"You bet!" Frannie shouted over her shoulder.

I wondered if Wes was staring at my ass as we walked away and had to resist the urge to turn and check. Hoping he was looking at my ass was stupid. His mother was way too perceptive for her own good, and she'd undoubtedly notice if her kid was checking out his sister's girlfriend's butt.

The minute we were out of earshot, Owen said, "Babe, I miss you so bad."

"I miss you too, baby," Frannie said. "It's killing me

not to be with you."

"Uh, weren't you just together last night?" I said. "It's been like six hours."

"Yeah, but six hours is like six months in Owen and Frannie time," Owen said solemnly.

I rolled my eyes as Frannie grinned like a maniac at Owen. "Can you get away for a bit after this?"

"Probably," Owen said. "I drove my own car here because Mom and Dad are stopping at the Lestons' place."

"Let's meet at the bookstore over on Robinson Street. It'll be quiet there and they have that little nook near the back. No one will see us."

"Frannie!" I hissed at her. "You cannot have sex with Owen in a bookstore."

"We're not going to," Frannie said.

"We're not?" Owen said.

"No, baby, we're not," Frannie said. "But we can have some alone time together."

"You had alone time last night," I said.

Frannie ignored me. "What do you say, baby?"

"Of course," Owen replied. "You know I can't resist my lady."

"Oh good!" Frannie said. "So, we should be done here around two. Let's meet at the bookstore at two thirty. I'll have Wes drive me to the bookstore. I'll tell him I'm buying a last-minute gift for Daisy to explain why he has to drive her home instead of dropping her off with me."

"It's a date," Owen said as we approached the open doors of the barn.

"Excuse me," I said, "but are you seriously going to ditch me with your family for the afternoon?"

"My family loves you, Daisy," Frannie said. "Besides, it'll be like an hour or two at the most. Please? I really need time with Owen."

I opened my mouth to tell her absolutely not when I realized something. If Frannie had Wes take us to the bookstore and drop her off, I'd be alone with Wes on the way home. Sure, it wouldn't be for very long but I'd take what I could get.

"Fine," I said. "But you're being a really bad girlfriend, Frannie."

She laughed and gave me a one-armed hug. "I totally am."

෬ ෬

"Why do you want to drive back with Wes?" Patricia asked.

"Because he's my brother and I love him and I don't get to see him all that often?" Frannie said.

Patricia gave her a skeptical look. "Since when do you and Wes even get along?"

"Hey, that's hurtful." Wes' deep voice spoke beside me and I tried not to look at the way his biceps bulged against his long-sleeve shirt. He had just finished tying down the tree in the back of the truck. Staring at the muscles in his back and arms while he wrestled the tree onto the truck bed had made me shamefully hot. "Frannie and I get along great, Mom."

"No, you don't," Patricia said. "I love you both, but you drive me crazy with your fighting."

"We've turned over a new leaf," Wes said. "I'm making up for all the rotten things I did to Frannie when we were kids and trying to be a good brother. I would be happy to give Frannie and Daisy a ride home."

I could see Frannie giving Wes an odd look and I wondered if she would question him about his sudden enthusiasm for sibling bonding.

"Yes, you do seem to be rather eager to be alone with them," Patricia said.

My stomach dropped but Wes just grinned at her before giving her a loud kiss on the cheek. "Like I said, I've got some making up to do."

"That's for sure," Frannie said. "Okay, it's settled. We'll see you at home!"

She grabbed my hand and pulled me toward the truck before her parents and grandmother could argue. "You sit in the middle, Daisy."

She didn't have to ask me twice. I was reaching for the door frame to try and haul myself up, when Wes' big hands cupped my hips. He lifted me into the truck as butterflies swarmed to life in my stomach. I mumbled a thank you and moved to the middle. Wes helped Frannie into the truck before sliding behind the driver's seat.

"Ready?" He turned the key and the truck rumbled to life.

"Yes," Frannie said. She glanced at her cell phone. "Hurry up, would you, Wes?"

"Do you have somewhere to be?" He asked.

"Actually," Frannie gave him a look that would melt butter, "would you mind dropping me off at the Books For All bookstore?"

"What for?"

"I have a last-minute gift I need to pick up for my girl," Frannie replied. She put her hand on my knee and squeezed. "It's like fifteen minutes out of your way, Wes. Drop me off and I'll catch an Uber home."

"All right," Wes said.

Frannie twitched on the seat next to me. I knew she'd been gearing up for Wes to balk at her request, and I had to bite back my giggle at the look of astonishment on her face.

"Really?" She said. "Just like that?"

"Yes," Wes replied.

"Huh, I thought you were screwing with Mom when

you said all that crap about being a better brother."

"Maybe you could try being a better sister," Wes said with a grin. "Meet me halfway."

"Sorry, Wesley, not gonna happen," Frannie replied. "Your face bugs me too much."

Wes and I both burst into laughter and, after a moment, Frannie joined in.

ॐ ॐ

Wes

The minute Frannie had disappeared into the bookstore, I patted the seat beside me. "Slide back over here, Daisy."

She had moved to the passenger seat when Frannie hopped out of the truck and I missed her soft warmth. She hesitated and glanced at the street. "What if someone sees us?"

"They won't. Come sit next to me, darlin'," I coaxed.

She slid over until her thigh was pressed against mine. I pulled out onto the street and then took her hand, linking our fingers as I drove.

"So, is Frannie actually buying you a gift or is she meeting Owen?" I asked.

"She's meeting Owen," Daisy replied. "They came up with the idea at the tree farm."

"Did they plan that meeting too?"

"Nope, that was a happy coincidence." She shivered against me when I rubbed my thumb across the palm of her hand. "I almost died when your grandma said she heard you last night."

I laughed. "You and me both. I think I covered pretty well."

"Um, you definitely didn't," she said. "Your mom knows something weird is going on."

"She doesn't. Don't worry, Daisy. Besides, we'll just have to be quieter next time."

She didn't reply and I cursed inwardly. Making the assumption that there would be a next time was stupid of me. For all I knew, Daisy was done with me. The thought made the hot chocolate in my stomach curdle. God, I was falling for this girl and falling fast. I needed to slow things down before I made a complete fool of myself. We lived in different cities and she was Frannie's roommate. Frannie would lose her shit if Daisy and I started dating. Not to mention how confusing it would be for the rest of the family.

I cleared my throat as Daisy peered out the windshield. "Where are we?"

"I thought I would take the scenic route home," I said.

Her smile made my pulse speed up. "The scenic route, huh?"

"Yes." I let go of her hand and placed mine on her thigh instead. I rubbed her leg through her jeans as she studied my hand. I wondered if she was remembering the last time we were alone in the truck together.

"Thinking about being inappropriate, Mr. McKinley?" She said.

"Do you want me to be inappropriate?" I asked as I tried to move my hand between her thighs.

"Hey, eyes on the road, both hands on the wheel," she admonished.

I did what she asked. My disappointment turned to red hot need the minute I felt her hand rest on my crotch. My cock immediately hardened and she made her adorable little laugh before giving me a squeeze. "You're insatiable, Wes."

"You do that to me," I rasped.

When she unbuttoned and unzipped my jeans and stuck her hand down my briefs, I made a low groan and thrust against her soft hand. Her warm fingers curled around my cock and stroked back and forth. I tried desperately to concentrate on the road, thankful that there was hardly any traffic.

"Do you know what I want, Wes?" Daisy leaned against me and I groaned when her warm tongue traced my ear.

"What?" I gasped as she rubbed her thumb over the head of my aching cock.

"I want to taste you," she breathed into my ear.

"Fuck, yes," I said.

Daisy made a soft shriek when I abruptly turned the truck left and she was thrown against me. Her hand tightened on my dick and dammit if I didn't almost come all over her hand right there. I held onto my self-control with grim determination as I drove down the side street.

"Where are we going?" Daisy asked.

"You'll see." I pulled her hand out of my pants and smiled at her when she pouted.

"Trust me, darlin', if I don't do this, we'll get in a car accident. I don't relish the idea of explaining to my mother why the paramedics found us with your hand in my pants."

She laughed and leaned her head against my shoulder. "All right. I'll stop teasing you."

I drove another ten minutes until we were at the old warehouse on the edge of town. It had been abandoned for years and Daisy leaned forward and peered out the windshield. Most of the windows were broken and graffiti was painted across the building.

"It's kind of creepy out here," Daisy said.

"It isn't," I replied. "It's nice and private, and I need privacy for what I'm going to do to you."

"What are you going to do to me?" She asked with a sweet smile.

I cupped the back of her neck and pulled her toward

me. We kissed, our tongues touching and tasting until we were both panting. I cupped her breast through her heavy jacket, growling when I couldn't feel her nipple.

"Take off your jacket," I demanded.

She shrugged out of it as I pulled mine off as well. We tossed them on the seat beside her and she moaned when I cupped her breast again. I teased her nipple through her bra and t-shirt as we kissed repeatedly.

"You taste so good, little flower," I said.

"You too," she panted. "Like chocolate."

I grinned at her, but it dropped like a stone a few seconds later. "Shit."

"What's wrong?" She asked. She was starting to work her hand into my jeans again.

"I don't have a condom with me."

She laughed. "This is about you, anyway."

"What do you mean?" God, I hoped she meant what I thought she did.

She slipped her hand back into my briefs and rubbed my still-hard cock. "You know what I mean."

"Fuck!" My breath escaped in a low moan when she pushed the front of my briefs down. I watched her tiny hand rub my cock as she smiled at me.

"Have you ever had a blow job in the car before, Wes?"

"No," I groaned.

Her hand slowed to a stop and I gave her a pleading look. "Fuck, Daisy. Don't stop."

"You've seriously never had a girlfriend give you road head?" She asked.

"No. I never had one offer and I didn't want to ask. It seemed," I searched for the appropriate word, "disrespectful."

"Oh my God, you're adorable," she said with a soft laugh.

"Are women waiting for men to ask them to blow

them in the car?" I said. "Because I am more than happy to beg - I mean - ask if you - "

"Shut up, Wes," she said before leaning over and sucking my dick into her mouth.

"Fuck, yes!" I hissed. My hands tangled in her soft hair as she bobbed her head up and down my dick. Her mouth was hot and wet, and I groaned in sheer delight when she used her tongue to trace circles around the head. Pre-cum was already leaking out of my dick and I watched as she licked it away before smiling up at me.

"Yummy."

I twitched and pushed her mouth over my dick again. "Suck, darlin'."

I let my head drop back against the seat, closing my eyes as she went to town on my dick. Daisy was a fucking goddess at sucking dick and I thrust into her mouth as she sucked and licked and drove me crazy. I had no idea how much time passed, my focus was narrowed down to the feel of Daisy's hot mouth and tongue. Her hand was stroking the base of my cock as she made slow and almost lazy licks along the shaft.

"Please," I rasped. "Oh, please, darlin'."

She slid her mouth over my cock and made a humming sound. It vibrated against my flesh and I pulled her off my dick in a hurry.

"What's wrong?" She asked.

"I'm close. You're so fucking good at this," I moaned.

"Oh honey, you haven't seen anything yet."

"Wh-what do you – oh fucking hell!" I made a hoarse bellow of pleasure as Daisy slid her mouth down over my dick until her lips touched my pubic hair. I'd never once been deepthroated before and as Daisy pulled back, took a deep breath and then deepthroated me again, I climaxed explosively. Her throat worked as she swallowed, and I pumped my cock repeatedly into her mouth as she swallowed every drop of my come. When she finally sat up and wiped her mouth with the heel of her hand, I was shaking and weak as a kitten.

"You okay?" She asked.

"Marry me," I said hoarsely.

Her laughter filled me with warmth and I wanted to pull her into my lap and hug her, but the steering wheel was in the way and I could barely lift my damn arms. I settled for patting her weakly on the leg.

She laughed again before lifting my arm and snuggling under it. I stroked her hip and side as she rested her head on my shoulder. After I caught my breath, I said, "That was hands down the best blow job of my life, Daisy."

"Good," she said.

"I'm sorry I didn't warn you," I said. "I, uh, didn't know I was going to come."

"It's fine," she said. "Nice girls always swallow anyway."

"You're the perfect woman," I said.

She giggled and patted my chest. "Aren't you sweet."

It was obvious she thought I was being flippant. I wanted to tell her I meant every word of it but hell, what if I really was just on a post-orgasmic high? Besides, I had more important matters to take care of. Like making Daisy come all over my fingers.

"Daisy?"

She lifted her head and I kissed her. I could taste myself on her tongue and fuck if it didn't make me horny again. "Your turn," I whispered against her mouth.

"You don't have to," she said.

"I want to," I replied. I stuck my hand under her shirt but before I could cup her breast, my cell phone rang. I muttered a curse. It was my mother's ring tone.

"Wes?" Daisy said when I pulled my phone out of my pocket.

"I have to answer it," I said. "It's Mom."

"Right," she said. She rested her head against my chest again as I answered the call.

"Hey, Mom."

"Wes? Where are you?"

"On our way home, why?"

"I thought you'd been in an accident. Do you have any idea what time it is?" My mom said.

I glanced at my watch. Fuck, we'd been parked at the old warehouse for nearly forty minutes.

"Oh, uh, sorry. Frannie asked me to drop her off at Books For All so she could pick up a gift for Daisy."

"Are you waiting for her?" Mom asked.

"No, she said she'd be awhile and she'd find her own way home," I said without thinking.

"Then where the heck are you? We've been waiting for you for nearly an hour."

"Um…"

Daisy sat up and made a "think of something" motion with her hand.

"We, uh…" Fuck, my mind was a complete blank. I was pretty sure Daisy had sucked most of my brain cells right out of me.

"Wesley? Where have you been?" My mother said impatiently.

"Um, I'm driving, Mom, so I'd better go," I said. "We'll be home soon."

I hit the end button before she could reply and stared at Daisy.

"That was not so smooth," she said.

"I panicked. My mind went blank!" I said. "I'm lucky I didn't blurt out the truth."

"Oh God," Daisy said with a laugh. "That would have been a nightmare."

"Yep," I said before reaching for the button on her jeans.

She slapped my hand away. "What are you doing?"

"I'm going to make you come and then we're going to leave," I said.

"Like hell you are! Wes, we need to get to your house now."

I scowled at her. "I'm not in the habit of leaving my woman unsatisfied, Daisy."

A weird look crossed her face and I said, "What?"

"Nothing," she said. "I appreciate the thought, but we have to go, right now. Is there a coffee shop on the way home?"

"Yes," I said as I buttoned and zipped my jeans. "Why?"

"Because I have an idea. Let's go."

I could see how impatient she was, but I took a moment to kiss her anyway. "Thank you, Daisy. You're incredible."

She gave me a pleased smile. "Thanks, Wes. Now drive!"

Chapter Seven

Wes

"Daisy, it was so sweet of you to stop and get us all coffees," My mother said as she opened a large plastic tub with "Christmas" written across the top of it.

"It was my pleasure, Patricia," Daisy said. "I'm sorry it made you worry. I wanted to surprise you, but it was so busy at the coffee shop we should have texted you and told you we'd be delayed."

"Oh, it's fine," Mom said. "Although, I can't believe Frannie still isn't back."

"She texted me ten minutes ago," Daisy said. "She ran into a friend and is having a coffee with her."

"Which friend?" My grandmother asked. She was sitting on the couch drinking her coffee and watching as Dad and I strung the lights around the tree.

"She didn't say," Daisy replied. "Patricia, does this tub have ornaments as well?"

"Yes, dearest," my mother replied. "Go ahead and open that one. Love, are you almost finished with the lights?"

"We are," my father replied. "Wes, crawl under the tree and plug the lights in, would you?"

I did what he asked and then crawled back out, dusting the pine needles off the knees of my jeans. Daisy was bent over the plastic tub in front of her as she sorted through it and I stared appreciatively at her ass. God, she had amazing tits and a nice firm ass. I needed to get her alone so I could give her an orgasm. It was killing me that I'd had one and she didn't.

"Oh shoot, we should add some water to the tree before we start decorating," my mother said. "Wes, can you get some water please?"

I tore my gaze from Daisy's ass. "Sure."

My grandmother was staring at me and I groaned inwardly. No doubt she'd seen me leering at Daisy's ass. Fuck, I needed to have better self-control. I headed toward the kitchen, determined to do a better job at keeping my eyes to myself and my distance from Daisy when my family was around.

ॐॐ

Frannie returned just before dinner and Daisy must have texted her the cover story because she didn't hesitate when Mom asked her who she'd run into.

"Leslie Warburger," she said. "We went to high school together."

"I know who she is," Mom said. "Did you have a nice visit?"

"We did," Frannie said as she sat down at the island next to Daisy. She had a small bag in her hand and she set it on the top of the island. "When are we decorating the tree?"

"We already did," I said.

"You didn't wait for me?" She gave mom a hurt look.

"Why would she when her favourite kid was there to help," I said. "That's what happens when you ditch us for Leslie Warburger."

"Shut up, Wesley," she retorted. "Mom, you should have waited."

My mother shrugged. "I didn't think you would mind that much. Sorry, honey. I'm making my famous gingerbread cookies tomorrow. You can help me with that."

"Okay, but only me," Frannie said.

"And Daisy," my mother replied.

"What?" Frannie gave her a blank look.

"Your girlfriend, dearest. You don't want to exclude her, do you?"

Frannie flushed before putting her arm around Daisy and giving her a brief kiss on the mouth. "Of course not. Daisy knows I want her there. It's Wes I don't want around."

She stuck her tongue out at me as I glared at her. Jealousy was niggling at my spine and I tried to ignore it. Even though I knew it was an act, it bugged me when Frannie touched Daisy.

"Like I want to be hang around my bratty little sister, anyway," I replied.

"At least my birth certificate isn't an apology letter from a condom company," Frannie said.

Daisy started laughing and I couldn't help but join in. Frannie had always been better than me at insults.

"I see the 'turning over a new leaf' is going well," my mother said as she sliced tomatoes for the salad.

I kissed her cheek and stole a slice of tomato. "Your favourite child will be in the living room with Dad if you need him."

– –

My resolve to keep my distance from Daisy lasted until after dinner. All of us were sitting in the living room watching a movie when Daisy excused herself. I waited a couple of minutes and, when it was obvious that the rest of my family was engrossed in the movie, silently slipped out of the living room.

I found Daisy in the kitchen, pouring herself a glass of water. Before she could say anything, I took her hand and pulled her into the walk-in pantry. I shut the door and flicked on the light before pushing her back against the built-in shelves.

"Wes? What are you doing?" She said before eyeing the door nervously. "Your family's in the living room."

"I know," I said. "So, you'll have to be quiet."

"Quiet about what?"

I grinned at her. She had changed into yoga pants and a t-shirt after dinner and the elastic waistband made it simple for me to push my hand past her pants and under her panties. I was cupping her warm pussy, my fingers stroking her clit before her hand had even wrapped around my forearm.

"Wes!" She said as her nails dug into my skin. "Stop that!"

"Stop what? This?" I rubbed her clit with the hard strokes I knew would make her hot, and was rewarded with a soft moan.

"Shh," I said before kissing her. She returned my kiss eagerly but when I released her mouth, she gave me a nervous look.

"We shouldn't do this right now."

I rubbed her clit again. "Yes, we should. I won't be able to sleep tonight if I don't make sure you're satisfied, little flower."

"Oh!" She gasped. She was growing steadily wetter and I used some of her moisture to help ease my finger into her tight pussy. She clenched around me and my dick hardened. I pressed it against her hip.

"Fuck, I love it when you squeeze like that," I

whispered into her ear. "Lift your shirt, darlin'."

"Wes, we shouldn't," she moaned.

"Lift your shirt and show me your beautiful tits," I repeated.

She lifted her shirt and I admired her pink lacy bra before prompting her, "Daisy, show me."

She glanced at the door to the pantry before unhooking the front clasp of her bra and peeling back the cups.

"Beautiful," I whispered before bending my head. Her nipples were already hard and I sucked on the right one as I pushed a second finger into her. I finger fucked her with slow strokes until she pulled on my hair and made a pleading sound.

I could have teased her all night, but my family would eventually notice we were both gone. Still fucking her with my fingers, I angled my thumb over her clit and rubbed hard as I placed my mouth to her ear.

"You're so tight around my fingers. I wish it was my cock you were squeezing."

"Oh God," she moaned. "I – maybe we could have a quickie."

I shook my head and traced her ear with my tongue. "Not enough time, darlin'."

"Please, Wes," she pleaded as I used my left hand to pull and pinch at her nipples.

"No, little flower. But the next time we fuck, I'll give you my cock for as long as you need it."

"Do you promise?" She whimpered. She ground her pussy against my hand with desperate need.

"I promise," I said. "I'm going to put you on your hands and knees and fuck you until you come all over my cock."

"Oh my God," she whispered as she rose onto her tiptoes before grinding against me again. "Oh God, I'm so close."

"Good," I said.

"You're so good at touching me," she moaned. "God, I love it when you touch me."

"I love it too, darlin'. Now show me how pretty you look when you're coming all over my fingers." I pulled my fingers out of her and pulled on her clit with a short, hard tug as I covered her mouth with mine.

I swallowed her moan of pleasure, stroking my tongue against hers as she climaxed against my fingers. I could feel her nipples pressing against my chest through my shirt and I rubbed my dick along her hip as she shuddered before collapsing against me.

I held her up and pressed kisses along her jaw and over her temple as I rubbed her back with my left hand and eased my other hand out of her pants.

"Oh my God," she whispered. "That was so good."

I nuzzled her throat then helped her back into her bra before smoothing down her shirt. "Better get back to the living room before they notice we're both gone."

"Right," she said.

I kissed her again and she squeezed my ass before walking a bit unsteadily to the door of the pantry and opening it. As she stepped into the kitchen, my grandmother's voice immediately made me lose my erection.

"Daisy? Why were you in the pantry?"

"Mrs. McKinley!" Daisy's voice was high-pitched and anxious. "Hi."

"You can call me grandma," my grandmother said. "What were you doing in the pantry?"

"Oh, I was um…." Daisy's voice trailed off and I grabbed a bag of chips from the top shelf and headed toward the door.

"Daisy? I found the chips. You don't have to ask mom – oh, hey, Grandma."

"What are you doing in the pantry with Daisy?" My

grandmother asked.

"Looking for chips?" I held them up. "Did you want some too?"

She studied us for a moment. Daisy's cheeks were flushed and I wondered if grandma could see the way her body was quivering. God, I hoped not.

"No, thank you," my grandmother finally said. "I wanted a cup of tea."

"Okay." I tossed the bag of chips to Daisy who fumbled it and nearly dropped the bag. "I'm going to use the bathroom. Can you take these to the living room for me?"

"Sure," Daisy said. She left the kitchen without looking at us.

I was about to follow her when grandma called my name.

"What's up, Grannie Frannie?" I said.

She ignored my childhood nickname for her. "I know you and your sister don't always get along, but you love her. Don't you, Wesley?"

"Of course I do," I said.

"Then don't do anything that will break her heart."

"I won't."

Grandma stepped closer and I tucked my hands behind my back as she reached up and patted me on the cheek. "You've always been a good boy, Wesley. Stay that way."

"Yes, ma'am," I said.

Daisy

I supposed I shouldn't have been surprised when I walked into Frannie's bedroom and found her making out with Owen on the bed. I shut the door as they sat up and Frannie gave me a guilty look.

"Do you mind if Owen spends the night with me again?"

I cheered inwardly as I arranged a scowl on my face. "Seriously, Frannie? You just saw him today."

"But we didn't get to bone," Owen said.

I rolled my eyes as Frannie said, "I miss him, Daisy."

"Fine," I sighed. "I'll sleep in the basement. But be quieter this time."

"I will!" Frannie said happily. "Thanks, honey. You're the best!"

I nodded and grabbed my cell phone before heading out into the hallway. It was quiet and dark and I tiptoed my way down the hall to Wes' room. Afraid his parents would hear if I knocked, I opened the door and slipped inside.

The sky was clouded over tonight so no moonlight shone into his room. It was pitch black and I closed the door with a quiet click. I could hear Wes groaning softly and I whispered, "Wes?"

"Shit!" I could hear him fumbling for the light next to his bed and I blinked and squinted when he clicked it on.

"Daisy?" He said in a harsh whisper. "You scared the hell out of me!"

"Sorry," I said. "I didn't want to knock in case your parents heard." My gaze drifted down his naked chest to where the covers concealed his crotch. His erection was obvious and I flushed a little before saying, "Were you masturbating?"

"Yes," he said shamelessly.

"Oh my God," I replied. "Wes!"

He shrugged. "I started thinking about how hot you looked when you came all over my hand in the pantry."

"We were almost caught by your grandmother!" I said.

"Keep talking about my grandma and I'm gonna lose

my erection," he said.

I tried not to giggle as I gave him a disapproving look. "That was a very dangerous idea."

"Like I told you before, I don't like leaving my woman unsatisfied."

A thrill went through me. That was the second time that Wes had referred to me as his woman. It probably didn't mean anything but damn, did I like hearing it. More than I should have.

"So, uh, Owen is in Frannie's room again and I need a place to sleep," I said.

He threw back the covers. "Climb in, darlin'. But I should warn you now – you won't be sleeping."

My stomach quivered with anticipation as I crawled over his legs and sat next to him. "Is that a fact?"

"Yes, ma'am," Wes said. He waited patiently as I set the alarm on my phone for six-thirty. He placed my phone on the nightstand and then reached for my nightdress. I let him pull it over my head without protest.

He cupped my breasts and teased my nipples as we kissed. When I was panting and moaning, he pulled back and smiled at me. "You're beautiful, Daisy."

"Thank you. So are you."

His fingers were tracing my appendectomy scar and I moaned again when he pushed his hand into my panties and tugged on the curls.

"I really do love your sweet little pussy," he said as his fingers found my clit. He rubbed me until I was wet and swollen - shamefully it didn't take very long – watching my face as I bit at my lip and tried to keep my voice down.

"Oh God, that's so good."

I wasn't lying to him. After years of always having to make myself climax, Wes' skill at touching me was a drug I couldn't resist. He gave my clit a hard pinch that sent electricity zapping down my spine.

"Wes?" I whispered.

"Yeah?" He was kissing the top of my shoulder with his warm mouth.

"Can I ask you a question?"

It probably wasn't the best time to ask but I needed to know. He was the only guy who'd figured out that I needed a rough, sometimes downright hard, touch to orgasm and I was afraid he might think I was a freak.

"Mm-hmm," he replied as his tasted the hollow of my throat.

"Do you think I'm a freak because I like to be, um, touched kind of rough?" I said it in a fast whisper, trying not to panic when his fingers slowed on my clit.

He raised his head and my anxiety eased when he said, "No. Not at all."

"Okay, good," I said.

"You're perfectly normal, Daisy," he said.

"Am I?" I asked. "You're the first guy I've been with who can make me come. That isn't normal."

"You're normal," he insisted. "The other men you've slept with were terrible at fucking."

"You don't know that," I laughed.

"They didn't make you come," he said. "They're terrible at fucking."

"I think it freaked them out when I kept asking for," I hesitated, "a rougher touch."

He rolled his eyes. "Darlin', you could ask me to spank you and I still wouldn't think you were a freak."

"Have you spanked a woman before?" I asked.

"No, have you?"

I laughed so hard that Wes pressed his hand over my mouth until my laughter subsided. "No, I've never spanked a woman or a man before. For the record – I'm pretty positive I don't want to be spanked so don't be getting any ideas. But I will spank you, if you ask nicely."

"Sweet," Wes said. "I'm a lucky man."

That made me laugh again and this time Wes stopped the laughter by kissing me. I reached under the covers and stroked his cock until he groaned into my mouth. He stopped rubbing my clit and I made a whimper of protest. He ignored it as he pulled my panties down my legs and tossed them on the floor.

"On your hands and knees," he said.

My pussy quivered and I moved onto my hands and knees as Wes rolled a condom onto his cock. He kneeled behind me and I arched my back when he ran his warm hand over my butt.

"You've got a really great ass," he said in a low voice.

"Thank you," I moaned.

He traced the backs of my thighs with his fingertips, sending little shivers up and down my spine. "Spread your legs wide, little flower."

I did what he asked, holding my breath with anticipation as he moved closer. He grasped my hips and rearranged me – God, I loved how strong he was – before pressing the head of his cock against my entrance.

Without saying anything, he pushed into me until I felt his pelvis press against my ass. I bit back my moan as I stretched around his thick cock. His big hand rubbed my lower back and he waited patiently for me to adjust.

"Good?" He asked.

"Yes," I said.

I tried not to moan too loudly when Wes began a slow, steady rhythm. He pressed on my upper back and I rested my chest against the bed and buried my face in his pillow to muffle my cries of pleasure.

Wes was moving harder now, rocking me into the bed with every thrust as he bottomed out then pulled back until just the head of his cock was inside of me. He thrust again and I squeezed around his dick, pulling a moan of delight from his throat.

"Fuck, darlin', you have no idea how tight you are," he murmured.

He leaned forward and wound one hand in my hair, pulling until I moved back to my hands. He pulled again, making my back arch and holding me steady as he pounded into me. I wouldn't be able to come this way but I didn't care. I felt powerful and beautiful as Wes moaned and his hand tightened in my hair. He was close, I could already recognize his signs. I thrust back against him with frenzied enthusiasm as he dropped his hand to my shoulder and held me in a firm grip. I almost squealed out loud when I felt his other hand cup my pussy and rub my clit.

He touched me exactly the way I needed it and I buried my face in my upper arm to dampen my moans as he pushed me closer to climax. The sound of our bodies slapping together was too loud, but I barely noticed. I needed to come, I needed Wes to fuck me hard until I was screaming his name. Nothing else mattered but my orgasm. I closed my eyes, rocking my pelvis hard against Wes' big body as my climax exploded inside of me and I screamed into my arm. Dimly, I could hear Wes' low groan as both of his hands clamped around my hips and he held me still. His body arched and we shook and moaned in unison until my arms gave out and I collapsed face-first into the mattress.

Wes pulled out and rolled onto his side beside me. His chest heaved as he gasped for air. "You…okay?"

I gave him a weak thumbs-up before curling onto my side. Wes fumbled to remove the condom as I closed my eyes and listened to my pulse pounding in my ears. When he spooned me, cupping my breast with his warm hand and kissing the back of my shoulder, I sighed happily.

"That was really good, little flower," he mumbled against my skin.

"Mm, hmm," I whispered. "Night, Wes."

"Night, Daisy."

Chapter Eight

Daisy

"Frannie, dearest, try and slice the cheese a bit straighter, please," Patricia said as she stirred the gravy bubbling in a pot on the stove.

"It's the Bakers having dinner with us, not the Pope," Frannie replied. She popped a piece of cheese into her mouth before turning and throwing a slice at me. I was standing at the island arranging raw veggies on a platter. I caught the cheese and ate a bite from the slice as Frannie turned back to the cheese sitting on the counter. "They're not going to care if the cheese slices are crooked."

"It's Christmas Eve dinner and I want everything to look perfect," Patricia said as Wes entered the kitchen.

My pulse immediately sped up and I could feel my cheeks flushing. Owen had shown up in Frannie's room for the last three nights and each time I had feigned annoyance before skipping off to Wes' room. I was addicted to his touch and the way it felt when we had sex.

Just the sex? Or are you addicted to Wes in general?
I ignored my inner voice as Wes stood next to me.

He plucked the rest of the cheese from my hand and ate it, grinning at me when I gave him a mock scowl, before leaning against the island. The island was high enough that my lower body was hidden behind it. I almost fell over when I felt Wes' left hand slip under the bottom of my dress and grab my ass. He caressed it gently as he took a piece of carrot from the platter in front of me.

I froze in fear when Patricia turned from the stove. Wes stopped rubbing my ass but continued to cup it as Patricia said, "Hi, honey. Where's your dad?"

"Down in the basement. Supper smells good."

"Thank you. I'm making your favourite – roast beef."

"Why are you making his favourite?" Frannie said.

"Because I'm her favourite," Wes answered. "How many times do I have to tell you that Frannie-pants."

"Don't call me that," Frannie said with a scowl.

She was still slicing up cheese, but she turned to stare at me when her mother said, "Daisy, are you feeling all right? You look flushed."

"I'm fine," I said as Wes squeezed my ass.

"Maybe it's because Wes is practically standing on top of her," Frannie said. "God, Wes, give my girl a little space, would you? She doesn't need you looming over her like that."

Wes squeezed my ass a final time before stepping away. "Sorry, Daisy. I didn't mean to invade your personal space." He gave me an adorable grin. "I really love my vegetables."

"Since when?" Frannie scoffed.

"Since always." Wes grabbed a celery stick and crunched it down.

"Why did you invite the Bakers for dinner tonight?" Frannie asked her mom. "You and Dad aren't friends with them."

"Of course we are," Patricia said. "They sit in the

same row as us in church."

"That doesn't make you friends," Frannie said.

"Well, it's nice to make new friends," Patricia replied. She was clearly flustered as she wiped her hands on her apron. "Daisy, if you're done with the veggie platter, can you take it to the dining room? You can put it on the table and, if you wouldn't mind, grab the china from the cabinet and start setting the table."

"No problem," I said.

"I'll carry the platter," Wes said. "It looks heavy."

"Daisy doesn't need your help carrying a vegetable platter," Frannie said. "She's not a weakling."

"It's called being a gentleman," Wes replied as he picked up the platter. "After you, Daisy."

"Thank you, honey," Patricia said as Wes followed me out of the kitchen. "Set the table for nine please."

"Nine?" I heard Frannie say. "Why nine? Mr. and Mrs. Baker make eight."

I didn't hear Patricia's reply. Wes was right behind me and I was distracted by the smell of his aftershave. God, he smelled good.

The dining room was next to the living room. Wes set the vegetable platter on the table as I crossed the room to the china cabinet. I had just opened the doors when Wes' arm slipped around my waist and he pulled me back against him. He nuzzled my neck and cupped my breast, kneading it lightly.

"Wes, behave!" I whispered.

"You look very pretty in your dress, little flower," he said.

"Thank you," I replied.

"Wear it to my room tonight so I can take it off you."

"One – Frannie would be suspicious if I went to bed wearing my dress and two – Owen won't be sneaking into her room tonight," I said. "It's Christmas Eve, remember?"

103

His hand stilled on my breast and I heard the disappointment in his voice when he said, "Yeah, I guess that makes sense."

"I'm sorry," I said.

"Me too."

He turned me around and slipped both his arms around my waist before kissing me. I returned his kiss even though I knew it was stupid and dangerous. Any one of Frannie's family could come walking in, but I couldn't resist. Knowing that I wouldn't be in Wes' bed tonight was bumming me out. I'd grown used to sleeping against his warm, hard body.

Wes pulled back and cupped my face, rubbing his thumb along my swollen bottom lip. "I should have given you your Christmas present last night."

"You got me a present? I didn't get you anything," I said.

"You didn't have to," he replied. "but now I don't know when I'll give it to you. You and Frannie leave the 26th, right?"

I nodded. "Yeah. Maybe Owen will sneak over tomorrow night."

"Let's hope," Wes said.

He was bending his head to kiss me again when we heard Frannie's voice drifting down the hall. "I told you, Mom, your pumpkin pie is amazing and everyone loves it. Don't worry about it."

Wes pulled away from me and I quickly turned and grabbed some plates from the cabinet. I handed them to Wes as Frannie walked into the room.

"Daisy, do you know – you still haven't set the table?"

She joined us at the china cabinet and gave Wes a friendly shove. "Get your ass moving, Wes. The Bakers will be here any minute and you still need to change."

Wes studied his t-shirt and jeans. "Why do I need to

change?"

"Because you look like a homeless person," Frannie said. "Go put on a different shirt, for God's sake."

She suddenly stopped and sniffed at me before glaring at Wes. "Jesus, Wes, how close were you standing to Daisy? I can smell your aftershave all over her."

I immediately blushed but Wes was saved from coming up with an excuse by Patricia entering the dining room. She stared at the three of us crowded around the china cabinet before studying the empty table.

"Do you think that with the three of you, the table might get set before dinner starts?" She asked.

"Sorry, Patricia," I said. "We were, uh, talking."

"It's fine, dearest," she said. "Wes, go and change your shirt please. Put on one with a collar."

"Not you too," Wes said. "What's wrong with my shirt?"

"Just do as I say, please and don't argue," Patricia said. "The Bakers will be here any minute."

"Fine," Wes said. He set the stack of plates on the table before leaving the room.

Frannie opened the drawer to the cabinet and began to pick out the silverware. "Wes is gonna be pissed, Mom. Cheryl isn't his type."

"Oh hush, he won't be. Besides, Cheryl has changed a lot since high school. You'll see," Patricia said before hurrying out of the room.

"Who's Cheryl?" I asked.

Frannie laughed. "She's the Baker's daughter. She went to high school with Wes and she's still single. It's why Mom's invited them tonight for dinner – she's doing her matchmaking thing."

My stomach dropped, and I abruptly turned and started setting the plates at the table. "Do you think Wes will like her?" I asked.

"God, no," Frannie said. "Cheryl isn't what you would call blessed in the looks department, you know? Not that Wes is shallow about looks – you should have seen his last girlfriend, God, did that girl have a nose on her – but Cheryl was always kind of a bitch."

"Oh yeah?" I wondered if Frannie could hear the relief in my voice."

"Yep. Normally ugly girls are super sweet because they can't use their looks to get what they want, but not Cheryl," Frannie said with casual cruelty. "I can't wait to see the look on Wes' face when she shows up here tonight. She had a crush on Wes when we were kids."

She suddenly rolled her eyes. "Of course, who didn't have a crush on Wes when we were growing up. It was so gross to watch all my friends go gaga over him. He's not even that good looking. It's because he was always nice to my friends when other boys his age wouldn't give them the time of day."

"Your brother is a good guy," I said.

Frannie nodded. "Yep, he is. He drives me crazy and sometimes I want to punch him in the face, but I love him. When push comes to shove, he always has my back."

She started to place the silverware next to the plate and gave me an evil grin. "Want to make a bet with me on how long it takes Wes to figure out Mom's trying to set him up with Cheryl? The guy is completely obtuse about shit like that. I say he doesn't figure it out until after dessert. What's your guess?"

Still feeling a little sick to my stomach, I shrugged. "I don't know your brother well enough to make it a fair bet."

Frannie gave me a curious look. "You okay, honey? You look pale."

"I'm fine," I said with a forced smile. "It's all good, Frannie."

"Okay," she said. She stopped what she was doing and pulled me into her embrace for a hug. "Thank you again for doing this, honey. I know it's been a real pain in the butt for you, especially sneaking down to the basement every night, but I so appreciate it. I love you lots, Oopsie."

"I love you too, Frannie," I said.

She leaned back and pushed a strand of hair back from my face. "You won't have to sneak to the basement tonight. I promise."

"That's great," I replied. Frannie returned to the silverware and I looked out the window as disappointment flooded through me. I was pretty sure Owen wouldn't be in Frannie's room tonight but now I had confirmation of it. I hadn't realized until this moment how strongly I'd been holding out hope that I'd have an excuse to go to Wes tonight.

I sighed and moved to the cabinet to get the glasses. It was only one night. Owen was too much of a horndog to go two nights in a row without Frannie. Maybe I wouldn't see Wes tonight, but I'd be back in his bed by tomorrow night.

Yeah, and then you're leaving for home. What then? Even if Frannie eventually comes clean to her parents about dating Owen, if you think she won't be pissed that you're dating her brother, you're fooling yourself. Besides, how would you explain it to the rest of the family?

I rubbed at my temples before grabbing a couple of wine glasses. I didn't want to think about any of that. All I wanted to think about was how good I felt when I was in Wes' arms. If we got the chance to be together tomorrow night, I'd talk to him and see if he was interested in dating. If he wasn't, then none of the other issues mattered.

❧ ❧

Wes

I should have known my mother was up to something the minute she told me to change my shirt. But I was wrapped up in trying to think of a way to convince Daisy to come to my room tonight anyway. It was stupid, but the thought of sleeping without her next to me was driving me crazy.

Stupidly, I didn't even clue in when the Bakers first arrived. When mom ushered them into the living room, I was staring at Daisy's legs and thinking about how it felt when I was deep inside of her with those long legs wrapped around my waist.

"Wes!" My mother said in a sharp voice.

I dragged my mind out of the gutter and stood up, giving her an apologetic look before reaching to shake Mr. Baker's hand. "Hello, Mr. and Mrs. Baker. It's nice to see you again."

The older man laughed and gave my hand a hard shake. "I think you're old enough to call us Ralph and Josie now, Wesley."

I nodded and shook Mrs. Baker's hand as my mother said, "You remember their daughter Cheryl. Don't you, Wes?"

A woman stepped out from behind Mr. Baker and my jaw dropped. "Cheryl?"

"Hello, Wes." Her voice was the same, a low purr designed to make men forget everything but what it would be like to be in her bed, and her eyes were still a shocking bright blue. But everything else was completely different. She looked nothing like the Cheryl I remembered.

I twitched in surprise when I reached to shake her hand and she brushed past it and hugged me instead.

She'd been on the thin side in high school with small breasts and no ass to speak of. Now, her breasts were at least a triple D and they looked almost obscene on her small frame.

"It's been a long time," she said. "You look really good," she said.

She was still pressed against me and I hastily took a step back.

"Thanks, Cheryl. You do as well."

She pouted at me and I studied her mouth. Were her lips always that big?

"That's it?" She said teasingly. "All I get is a 'you look good'?"

"Uh, you look…different," I said.

Cheryl's face twitched and her eyes squinted up. After a moment, I realized she was trying to frown but the skin on her forehead remained stubbornly smooth. I watched in fascination as she scrunched her face more but nothing happened.

"Cheryl, would you be a dear and help Wes get the wine from the kitchen?" My mother said.

"I'd love to," Cheryl replied. Her weird mouth turned up in a smile as she slipped her hand into the crook of my elbow. I stared at her hand for a moment before glancing at Daisy. She was staring at us and unlike Cheryl, I could clearly see the scowl on her face. I wanted to smooth away the cute little lines between her eyes with a kiss, like I was some sort of love-sick jackass in a romantic comedy.

"Wes?" My mother prompted. "The wine please."

"Right, sorry." Cheryl still clinging to my arm, I left the room.

Once we were in the kitchen, I gave Cheryl a polite smile and eased my arm out of her grip. Before I could open the fridge, she was standing in front of it.

"Uh, I need to get the wine."

"In a minute," she said as she smoothed her now blonde hair with one pale hand. "So, how have you been, Wes?"

"Good," I said.

"I hear you're an engineer now."

"Yes," I said.

She stared expectantly at me and I said, "How about you? What are you doing?"

"Real estate agent. So, when you're ready to move back home, I'm the girl you can call to find your house." She laughed and crossed both arms over her torso. Her oversized boobs nearly spilled out of her low neckline and I hastily averted my eyes.

"Oh, I'm not moving back," I said.

"That's a shame," she replied. "There are lots of good things about our little town. Did you know when we were kids that I had a huge crush on you?"

I cleared my throat. "Uh, no, I didn't know that."

"I did. Most girls at our high-school did. Golden boy Wes, right?"

"Um…" I had no idea what to say. "It was a long time ago."

"Yes, it was," she said. "Some crushes last a long time though."

"I have a girlfriend," I said. "Back home."

"That's funny, your mom said you were single and had been for quite some time. She told my mother she was really worried about you."

I didn't reply and Cheryl smiled at me again. Jesus, her teeth were so white. How the hell did she get them that white?

"We could be good together, you know. Why don't we have coffee on Boxing Day. We can get caught up. Afterwards, you could come back to my place and maybe we can learn some new things about each other."

My jaw dropped. "I'm sorry, are you asking me

to…."

I trailed off and Cheryl laughed. "We're both adults here, Wes. Yes, I'm asking you to come back to my house so we can have sex. I'm very attracted to you and I know that you're attracted to me."

I stared at her in stunned silence and Cheryl laughed again.

"I know I sound full of myself, but all men are attracted to me now. I have a lot of guys asking me out, Wes. I'm giving you an opportunity here that not many men get. You should take advantage of it while I'm - "

She broke off as Daisy stomped into the room. She looked supremely pissed off and she glared at me before giving Cheryl a brittle smile. "They're waiting for the wine."

"I'm sorry, who are you?" Cheryl asked.

"She's my girlfriend," Frannie said as she strolled into the kitchen. She put her arm around Daisy's waist and kissed her on the mouth. "Cheryl, meet Daisy Morrison. Daisy, this is an old school friend, Cheryl."

"Girlfriend?" Cheryl said. She eyed Daisy and Frannie for a minute before shrugging. "Not surprised. I always suspected you were a lesbo."

Frannie scowled. "Why does everyone keep saying that?"

"You and Linda Rice were kissing in the art room in eleventh grade," Cheryl replied.

Daisy glanced at Frannie who shrugged before stepping forward and poking Cheryl in the arm. "Move it, Cheryl. We need the wine."

"Your brother and I are having a private conversation," Cheryl said.

"Yeah, yeah, we heard. You want to bone him on Boxing Day," Frannie replied. "Do me a favour and figure out when the two of you are going to bang when I'm not in hearing range."

She gave Cheryl a little push on the hip and the woman frowned at her before moving so that Frannie could open the fridge. She pulled out the wine and handed it to Cheryl. "Take this to the dining room, would you?"

Cheryl took the wine before sliding her hand around my arm and leaning against me. "Will you show me where the dining room is, Wesley?"

"Third door on the left," Frannie said.

"Please, Wesley," Cheryl said.

"I'll show you," Daisy said abruptly.

Cheryl glanced at me before sighing. "Fine."

She followed Daisy out of the room as Frannie rolled her eyes and leaned against the counter.

"Holy shit," I said when they were out of earshot. "Does Cheryl look different to you?"

"Yes, you idiot," Frannie laughed. "She's had a shit ton of plastic surgery. I don't think anything on her is real anymore."

"She got a boob job, right?" I said.

"Yeah, and ass implants, a nose job, a chin job, and lip augmentation. Plus, she's got so much Botox in her forehead, she won't be able to frown for at least a decade."

"Thanks for the rescue."

Frannie shrugged. "Wasn't my idea. I think it's hilarious that mom is trying to set you up with Cheryl, but Daisy insisted on finding out what was taking so long to get the wine. It's her you need to thank."

I would, I thought fervently. The minute I had Daisy alone, she'd know exactly how grateful I was to her for saving me from Cheryl.

❧ ❦

I felt like a creepy stalker as I followed Daisy down

the hallway, but I was desperate to talk to her alone for a moment. She'd been acting weird since the moment the Bakers arrived. It was bad enough that Mom put me beside Cheryl at dinner, but the clear waves of anger radiating from Daisy were much worse.

She was just walking into the bathroom when I caught up to her. I caught the door before she could shut it and her startled look turned into a scowl. "Excuse me, I need privacy."

"Daisy, we need to talk."

"Do we?" She said.

"Yes." I stepped into the bathroom and shut the door behind me as she glared at me.

"What are you doing in here? Your entire family and the Bakers are down the hallway," she said in a low voice.

"I don't care," I said.

"Well, I do. Get out of the bathroom," she retorted.

I ignored her anger and pulled her into my arms.

"Hey, let go!"

"Not until you tell me what's wrong," I said. "Why are you angry with me?"

"I'm not angry with you."

"Be truthful, little flower," I said.

She looked away. "So, have you made your plans with Cheryl?"

"What plans?" I asked in confusion.

"Don't be obtuse, Wesley," she said.

"I'm not. I don't have plans with Cheryl."

"Boxing Day," she suddenly snapped. "You're stopping by Cheryl's place for sex. Remember?"

She was jealous. A grin crossed my face. Daisy was jealous of me and Cheryl. She didn't have anything to be jealous about but holy shit, did it make me feel good that she was.

"Something funny?" She said.

"You're jealous."

"No, I'm not."

"Yes, you are."

The little angry lines were back between her eyes and I leaned down and kissed them. "You have nothing to be jealous about, little flower. I'm not interested in Cheryl."

"I leave on Boxing Day," she said.

"I remember."

"Cheryl's very pretty and it's obvious that she wants you."

"I don't want her. I'm not going to go for coffee with her, let alone go to her house and let her have her dirty way with me."

She stared up at me as relief crossed her face. "Really?"

"Yes," I said. "The only woman who gets to have her dirty way with me is you."

She smiled and I leaned down and kissed her. She returned my kiss and I squeezed her ass. "You could have your dirty way with me right now, if you want."

She giggled and shook her head. "We absolutely can't do that and you know it. In fact," she gave me a gentle push toward the door, "you need to go before we get caught."

I lifted her hand to my mouth and kissed her knuckles. "Sure. Oh, and don't be embarrassed that you're so jealous." I lifted my shirt so she could see my six-pack. The girls always go crazy over me. You'll get used to it after a while."

She rolled her eyes and gave my stomach a hard poke. "Take your ego and go, smartass."

"Yes, ma'am," I said. I gave her one final kiss and left the bathroom. Thankfully, the hallway was still empty and I headed back to the living room.

Chapter Nine

Daisy

I stared at the ceiling of the bedroom and listened to Frannie's soft snoring beside me. It was just after midnight and I was restless and wide awake. I wanted to be with Wes so much it was almost a physical ache. I rolled to my side and stared at the alarm clock, watching as the numbers changed from 12:14 to 12:15.

Well, it was Christmas. The third one without my parents. A wave of homesickness and depression washed over me, and I abruptly slid out of the bed and grabbed my cell phone. Frannie didn't move and I walked quietly to the door and eased it open before stepping into the hallway. There was a soft glow coming from under Wes' bedroom door but the rest of the rooms were dark. I held my breath and listened. The house was completely quiet and I shut Frannie's door and tiptoed to Wes' room. I opened the door and slipped inside.

Wes was sitting up in bed reading a book and a look of happiness spread across his face. "Hello, gorgeous."

"Why are you still awake?" I asked as I walked across the room.

"Couldn't sleep." He threw back the covers and I set my phone on the nightstand and crawled into the bed beside him.

"Merry Christmas, Wesley," I said.

"Merry Christmas, little flower." He kissed me but when I tried to deepen it, he pulled back. "Hold on."

He reached into the nightstand and brought out a small wrapped box. He placed it in my lap and I smiled at him. "You really didn't have to get me a present."

"I know. Open it."

I untied the ribbon and carefully unwrapped the gift to reveal a plain white box. I opened the lid and gasped in delight. "Oh, Wes. It's beautiful."

I picked up the silk scarf and let it drape over my arm. It was a myriad of different shades of red and absolutely stunning.

"Do you like it?" Wes asked.

"I love it," I said. "Thank you so much."

"You're welcome."

I carefully placed the scarf back into the box and Wes set it on the floor next to the bed. Wes laid on his back and I curled on my side next to him. I rested my head against his chest and traced my fingers through the hair as he tugged on my nightdress.

"Take this off."

I sat up and pulled it over my head, then wiggled out of my panties. I ditched them over the side of the bed, blushing a little as Wes' hot gaze roamed over my body.

"Your body is perfect," he said hoarsely.

"Thank you. So is yours." I traced his six-pack as he cupped my breast and teased my nipple into an aching hardness. I leaned over him and we kissed. Slow, deep kisses that made my pulse race and my body tingle.

"You are the best kisser," I panted against his mouth.

He sucked on my bottom lip as his hand pushed between my thighs and cupped my pussy. I pressed my breasts against his chest, as he rubbed my clit. I reached down and wrapped my fingers around his cock, stroking him back and forth as he massaged my clit.

"Fuck, that feels good," he muttered.

I was surprised when he reached down and pulled my hand away from his dick. "What's wrong?"

Can I ask you a question?" He said.

"Yes."

"Have you ever given yourself a g-spot orgasm?" His fingers had started up their slow caress of my clit again and I was finding it difficult to concentrate.

"I tried," I said. "I looked for it a few times, but it remains elusive. I probably don't have one."

Wes grinned at me. "Why don't we find out?"

I glanced at his closed bedroom door. "I've heard they can be pretty intense. What if you do find it and your family hears me…"

I trailed off and Wes wiggled his eyebrows at me. "You'll have to hold in your 'Wes is a sex god' screams."

I laughed and he kissed my collarbone. "I really want to do this for you, Daisy."

"Okay," I replied.

"Lie on your back," he said.

I relaxed on my back as Wes rolled on a condom before lying on his side next to me. I moaned when he leaned over and sucked my nipple into his mouth. He gave it a sharp little nip and I jerked against him before moaning again. His tongue was already laving away the sting. I wound my fingers in his hair as he sucked and nibbled both my nipples. His fingers were back on my clit and I moved my hips in slow, tight circles against them.

"Let's see if I can find it this way first," he murmured.

His fingers pushed into me as he lifted his head and

stared at my face. He curled his fingers and made a 'come here' motion. Feeling a little self-conscious, I said, "I tried that. It didn't really work so I don't know if – oh God!"

Wes' fingers had pressed against a spot that made me feel like I was going to pee. He continued to press firmly and I was reaching for his hand to stop him when the need to pee changed.

"Oh," I whispered. Pleasure was flooding my nervous system and as Wes pressed and released, I clutched at his arms and gave him a desperate look. "Oh my God, that – that feels so…"

I trailed off, mere words couldn't describe how it felt. My body was beginning to shake against Wes and I spread my legs shamelessly wide. The pleasure was growing more intense and I panted and moaned and made soft pleading noises.

When Wes stopped abruptly, a whine of displeasure exploded from my throat. I clawed at his chest and said, "Don't you dare fucking stop, Wesley!"

"Shh, little flower," he said as he kneeled between my legs. "I want to try something."

"No," I said frantically as he lifted my legs and draped them over his shoulders. "No, I don't want to try something. I want you to keep doing that."

He didn't even flinch when I smacked him in the stomach. "Be nice, Daisy."

"You be nice!" I said in a harsh whisper as he pressed his cock against my opening. "You be nice or I'll…ohhh."

Wes had entered me with one hard thrust and I clenched around him. It felt good, it really did, but I wanted more than his dick. I'd been so close to the most amazing orgasm of my life and I was irrationally angry at Wes for taking it away from me.

"Wes! Please!"

"Shh," he whispered again. He adjusted my legs and then pushed into me again. This time, the head of his cock pressed against the same magical spot as his fingers. I barely had time to clamp my hand over my mouth to muffle my shriek of pleasure.

"Good," Wes said. He held my thighs and thrust in and out with hard pumps of his hips. Each stroke put delicious pressure on my g-spot and it took less than thirty seconds before the pleasure crested and I was screaming into my hand and writhing under Wes. My climax rolled through me like nothing I'd ever felt before. Wave after wave of intense pleasure washed over me and I squeezed my inner walls around Wes' dick as my orgasm went on and on. Wes made a muffled groan and pushed in so deep that I felt the strain in my thigh muscles. He muttered my name as he climaxed, pumping his hips back and forth as the last of my own climax shuddered through me. He pulled out and grabbed my legs when they slipped off of his shoulders. I was quivering and shaking and he rubbed my flat stomach before disposing of the condom and lying on his side next to me.

He rubbed the trembling muscles in my stomach again. "You okay?"

"Marry me," I gasped out.

He laughed and kissed my damp shoulder. "That good, huh?"

"Wes, it was incredible," I whispered. "You – you have no idea. My orgasm went on and on. I've never felt anything like it before."

"Good, little flower," he said. He rested his head on the pillow beside my head and linked our fingers together.

"Was it okay for you?" I asked.

"Amazing," he said. "Your pussy squeezes me like a vice when you're having a g-spot orgasm. I wanted to last longer but I didn't stand a chance."

I giggled and he kissed my cheek before falling silent. I stared at the way our fingers were interlocked, and when my pulse finally slowed to a normal rate, I said, "I feel guilty."

Wes' hand squeezed mine. "About sleeping with me?"

"God no," I said. "But I feel guilty about lying to your family. They're all really nice and so accepting of me and I'm lying to them."

Wes pulled me into his embrace and I rested my head on his chest as he rubbed my back. "It was Frannie's idea."

"Yeah, but I agreed to it," I said. "I wish she would tell your family about Owen. Then maybe you and I could - "

I stopped before I could really freak Wes out. As much as I liked Wes, I suddenly had a bad case of cold feet. Just because we were good in bed together didn't mean that we should date. I knew hardly anything about him.

Yeah, it's why you date a person, you idiot.

Good point.

"We could what?" Wes asked.

"Uh, nothing," I said.

He laughed and pulled me a little tighter against his warm body. "Have you ever tried long distance dating?"

I squinted at him. It was too dark in his room to see his face clearly. I said, "No. Have you?"

"Yes. It kind of sucks but can be worth it for the right person."

I tried to sound casual. "Oh yeah?"

"Yeah," he said. "I think we could make it work. Do you?"

Holy shit. Was he serious? My pulse was pounding in my ears and excitement zinged along my veins.

"Sorry," Wes said suddenly. "Forget I said that. I was reading the room wrong."

I threw my arm around his waist and squeezed him hard. "You're not reading the room wrong. I was a little surprised that's all. I want to date you, Wes."

"Good," he said.

He kissed me and I rubbed my naked breasts against his chest. He groaned and reached down to cup my ass, kneading it as we kissed with slow brushes of our lips and tongues.

When he pulled back, I rubbed his hip and said, "I'm unemployed."

"I like to play Dungeons and Dragons," Wes said as he cupped my breast.

I blinked at him. "What?"

"Are we not playing a game of 'say the least sexy thing in bed you can think of and see if the other one is still turned on'?" Wes said. "Just so you know, I still think you're hot even without a job."

I laughed so hard that Wes pulled the covers over my head to muffle the sound. I poked my head out and gave him a mock scowl. "I'm not playing a sex game with you, Wesley. I was only pointing out that I'm unemployed, single and not particularly attached to the city I currently live in."

Wes' hand squeezed my hip. "Would you seriously consider moving to my city?"

I nodded. "Yes. If I found a job there."

"That's fucking fantastic!"

"Shh!" I said with a nervous look at the door. "Keep your voice down."

"Right, sorry," he said. "Listen, don't feel pressured to move. I mean, I want you to consider it but I don't want you to feel like you have to."

"I don't," I said. "I would move because I want to. I'd like to get the chance to know you better."

"So, this means your vow of celibacy is officially over, yeah?" Wes said with a small grin.

"I don't know," I said. "That Dungeons and Dragons revelation has me seriously considering a life of celibacy again."

"Hey, Dungeons and Dragons is sexy."

"Is it, though?"

"No," Wes said sadly. "No, it really isn't."

I laughed and threw my thigh over his before tracing my fingers over his flat abdomen. "I bet another orgasm would help me to forget you're a role-playing game nerd. Why don't you show me what else those fingers can do besides rolling some dice?"

"Yes, ma'am," Wes said with a wicked grin.

Wes

"Wesley? Time to get up!"

I sat up, my heart pounding when the door opened and my mother walked into my room. I could still feel Daisy's soft warmth behind me and I prayed feverishly that she would stay where she was. It went unanswered. She sat up and stared sleepily at me. "Wes? What's wrong?"

"Oh, Wesley," my mother said.

Daisy made a small shriek and yanked the covers to her chest as my mother pressed her lips together. "Oh, Wesley. What have you done?"

"It's my fault," Daisy said immediately. "Patricia, all of this is my fault and I can explain."

"Why would you do this to Frannie?" Mom said.

"Do what?" My grandmother wandered into the room and I groaned as her eyes nearly bulged out of her head. "Holy shit! Wesley, are you having sex with your sister's lesbian girlfriend?"

"What is Wesley doing?" My father yelled down the hallway.

"He's having sex with his sister's lesbian lover!" My grandmother shouted back.

"He's what?"

"He's having sex with Daisy! She must be bisexual!" My grandmother hollered.

My father appeared in the doorway. "She's what?"

"Bisexual," my grandmother said. "It means she likes to screw men and women."

"I know what it means, Mother!" My father retorted. "Wes, you should be ashamed of yourself."

"Everybody out of my room," I said. "Let us get dressed and we'll explain - "

"What's going on?" Her hair sticking up and rubbing her eyes, Frannie appeared in the doorway next to my father. She yawned. "Why is everyone yelling?"

"Frannie, honey, I'm so sorry," my mother said.

"Sorry about what? Why are we all standing in Wes' room... what the hell?" Frannie's eyes got wide and she stared at Daisy and me. "Daisy? You're – you're sleeping with Wes?"

"Frannie, I…" Daisy trailed off and gave me a look of misery.

I took her hand and squeezed it before staring at my sister. "Tell them the truth, Frannie."

Frannie's face paled and she glanced at my parents.

"What is he talking about?" Dad asked.

"Tell them, Frannie," I said.

Frannie took a deep breath and I scowled when big crocodile tears dripped down her face. "I can't believe my own brother would betray me like this! I was in love with her, you asshole!"

She burst into wailing sobs and ran from the room. My father and grandmother both went after her as Mom stared silently at us.

"Mom, she's faking," I said. "She's not in love with Daisy. She's in love with - "

"Stop it, Wesley," my mom said. "I am so disappointed in you." Her gaze moved to Daisy. "Disappointed in both of you. Shame on the both of you for breaking Frannie's heart."

Daisy made a low sobbing gasp as my mother left the room and shut the door behind her.

"It's okay, darlin'," I said.

"It isn't," she sobbed. "This is all my fault. I forgot to set my alarm on my phone last night. If I hadn't, we wouldn't have slept in."

"It'll be fine," I said. "Frannie will tell them the truth."

"No, she won't," Daisy said as tears ran down her face. "You know she won't, Wes. She's terrified your father will find out and be angry with her."

"Then we'll tell them."

"Like they'll believe us," Daisy whispered.

I cursed under my breath. "Get dressed, Daisy. I'll meet you downstairs, okay?"

She nodded and I kissed her before wiping at the tears on her cheeks. "Don't cry. I'm going to fix this, I promise."

ೲ ✺

Daisy

I took longer than normal to get dressed. My stomach was churning, and I kept seeing the look on Patricia's face when she said she was disappointed in me. I had ruined their Christmas and despite what Wes said, I knew Frannie would never admit to dating Owen.

I took a deep breath and started downstairs. I had heard Wes go downstairs five minutes ago and it wasn't fair of me to leave him alone to deal with his family. I could hear Frannie crying in the living room and, my legs trembling, I walked into the room.

Wes was nowhere in sight and my stomach dropped as Frannie's parents stared at me. Frannie was still crying steadily on the couch between them and her mother rubbed her back. "There, there, Frannie. It'll be all right, dearest."

"Frannie," I said. "You need to tell them the truth."

I had no idea why Wes had abandoned me to face his family alone, but I couldn't really blame him.

"You're one to talk about telling the truth," Gregory snapped. "I think you need to leave."

"Dad! No! You are not kicking Daisy out!" Frannie gave him a horrified look.

"Greg, it's Christmas Day," Patricia said.

"I don't care," Gregory replied. "She needs to leave my house right now."

"Mom, Dad, listen to me," Frannie said urgently. "There's something you need to know. There's this boy and…"

She trailed off and then said. "Oh God, this is so hard to tell you."

"What are you talking about?" Patricia said as the front door opened.

"You cannot drag my son out of our home on Christmas morning! Let him go right now, or I swear I will call the police!" The angry voice of Ryan Brenner bellowed through the house.

Gregory jumped up from the couch as Wes marched into the living room. He had Owen by the arm and Mr. and Mrs. Brenner were right behind them.

"What the hell are you doing in my house, Brenner?" Gregory snarled.

"Ask your son!" Ryan shouted. "He's the one who dragged Owen over here. He's gone insane and I'm charging him with assault!"

"Dad, chill out," Owen said. "God, dude, you are going to have a stroke. You've really gotta…"

He trailed off as he caught sight of Frannie sitting on the couch. "Babe! Oh my God! Babe, what's wrong? Why are you crying?"

He shook loose of Wes and ran across the room to kneel at Frannie's feet. He cupped her face and pressed his mouth against hers. "Babe, tell me why you're sad."

"I'm sorry, baby," Frannie cried. "We have to tell them. They're going to kick Daisy out of the house!"

"It's fine, Frannie," Owen said. He sat beside Frannie and put his arm around her shoulders. "I love you and I want them to know."

Patricia stood and walked over to Gregory as Wes put his arm around my waist and pulled me up against him. Gregory was staring at Frannie and Owen and when Patricia put her arm around him, he said, "Patty? Why is our lesbian daughter kissing Owen Brenner in our living room?"

"Love, sit down. You're pale," Patricia said.

Gregory shook his head. Two spots of red were appearing in his cheeks. "No, I want to know what's going on."

"Isn't it obvious?" Frannie's grandmother said. "Your daughter is bisexual. She's screwing Owen and Daisy, and Daisy is screwing Frannie and Wes. It's like a damn soap opera."

The old woman smiled gleefully at everyone. "This is the best Christmas ever."

"I'm not bisexual, Grandma," Frannie said, "and neither is Daisy. Owen and I have been dating for over a year, but I was too afraid to tell Dad, so I asked Daisy to pretend to be my girlfriend. I didn't want you guys to try and set me up with other men during the entire holiday. None of this is Daisy's fault. She was doing me a favour."

"Oh, Frannie. You should have told us the truth," Patricia said. "We don't care who you date, we just want you to be happy. Isn't that right, Gregory?"

He didn't reply and Patricia elbowed him sharply. "Gregory! Isn't that right?"

"Yes," Gregory sighed.

"Well, we're not okay with it," Owen's father said. "No son of ours is going to date Gregory McKinley's daughter! Owen, you get your ass off that couch and away from that girl right now. You're too good for her."

"Ryan," Mrs. Brenner said. "Stop speaking for me. I don't - "

"Too good for my daughter? That's rich, coming from a guy whose son works at a Best Buy," Gregory snapped.

"He's a manager!" Ryan shouted. "At least my son doesn't lie to my face like your daughter!"

"'You watch your mouth, Brenner! She only lied because she knew what an asshole you are!" Gregory said.

"I'm the asshole? You know, I've had just about enough of you and your family. You've always thought you're better than us and - "

"I don't think I'm better than you! I know I'm better than you!"

"All these years and you still think that you're - "
"ENOUGH!"

Patricia's voice shouted above the voices of the arguing men. I was so shocked to hear the soft-spoken Patricia yelling that I jerked against Wes and gave him a look of alarm. He returned my look before taking a step back, pulling me with him, as Patricia stalked by us.

"Both of you need to quit acting like immature assholes," Patricia said as she glared at Gregory and Ryan. "This stupid feud of yours has gone on long enough. For God's sakes, Joy and I have been friends for over twenty years!"

Ryan turned to his wife. "Joy?"

"It's true," Mrs. Brenner said. "We are."

"Wha- how?" Gregory sputtered.

"We live right next door to each other and we were both stay-at-home mom's," Patricia said. "We became friends when the kids were little. You know my monthly Friday night bridge game?"

Gregory nodded slowly and Patricia grinned at Joy. "It's actually my movie night with Joy. We have dinner and go to a movie and talk about how ridiculous our husbands' feud is."

"We text every day," Joy said.

"This can't be happening," Ryan said.

He staggered on his feet and Owen jumped up and crossed the room to take his arm. "Sit down, Dad."

"It's happening, Ryan," Joy said when he was sitting in the armchair. "Patricia and I are friends and now our children are dating. Get used to it."

"I don't want to," Ryan said.

"I don't care," Joy replied. "In fact," she glanced at Patricia, "Patty, why don't we all have Christmas dinner together this year."

"No!" Ryan and Gregory said at the same time.

"I think that's a wonderful idea," Patricia said. "I'm sure Owen and Frannie want to spend Christmas together. Why don't you come back around three? We're eating at four."

"We'll be here," Joy said. "I'll bring over our turkey as well. It's already in the oven."

"Perfect," Patricia replied. "Owen, honey, you're welcome to stay while we open up presents, if you'd like."

"Nah, that's okay," Owen said. "You do your family thing. I'll see my lady in a few hours."

He pressed another kiss against Frannie's mouth.

"See you soon."

"I love you, Owen," Frannie said.

"Love you too, babe," Owen said.

Gregory grimaced and Ryan made a sound of disgust but they both kept their mouths shut as Owen stood and ambled toward the doorway. After a moment, Mr. and Mrs. Brenner followed him. When the front door shut, Wes pressed a kiss against my forehead.

"You okay, little flower?"

"Yes," I whispered, "are you?"

He nodded before bending his head and kissing me on the mouth.

"Gross."

He pulled back and glared at his sister. "Shut up, Frannie."

"How long have you two been banging?" She asked.

"Francine," Patricia said. "Don't be rude."

"Sorry, Mom," Frannie said.

Patricia approached us and gave us both a rueful smile. "I'm sorry for what I said."

I shook my head. "No, it's fine. You didn't know, and I know how bad it looked when you found me in Wes' bed. But I want you to know that Frannie is my best friend and I would never purposely hurt her, and I really like your son."

She smiled at me before reaching up to pat Wes' cheek. "He really likes you too, I can tell."

"I knew it," Frannie's grandmother said to us. "I knew you two were going at it like bunnies."

"Mother, please," Gregory said wearily. "Not now, okay?"

"Coffee. Let's make some coffee and then we'll open presents," Patricia said briskly. "Gregory, Mother Francine, come with me, please."

As they left the living room, we heard Gregory say, "Are you really friends with Brenner's wife?"

Wes laughed. "I think Dad's more upset that Mom is friends with Mrs. Brenner than he is about Frannie dating Owen."

Frannie stood up from the couch. "So, how long have you been banging?"

Wes rolled his eyes. "None of your business."

His sister suddenly froze before giving me a suspicious look. "Oh my God. Was Wes your one-night stand, our first night here?"

My cheeks turned red and I nodded. "Yeah, I didn't know he was your brother, Frannie. I swear. I met him at the bar and we didn't exchange last names or anything. Then when he walked into the kitchen the next day..."

I trailed off as Frannie made a retching noise. "Oh God, now I have a mental image of you two having sex. That's so gross."

"Not gross at all," Wes said cheerfully.

"Why were you in Wes' room last night?" She asked.

"She's been in my room every night," Wes said, "because you kicked her out so you could have sex with Owen."

"I told her to go to the basement bedroom!" Frannie said.

"Like she could make it past Mom," Wes said. "Honestly, you're the reason we're dating."

"You're dating?" Frannie said in surprise. "You don't even live in the same city."

Wes glanced at me and Frannie said, "Oh goddammit, Wes! You convinced her to move, didn't you?"

"No," I said. "I brought up the idea of moving."

Frannie sighed. "Well, I'm grossed out that you're sleeping with my brother and sad that you're leaving me, but I guess whatever makes you happy and shit."

I laughed. "I love you too, Frannie."

She gave us an apologetic look. "I'm sorry that I pretended to be the jilted lover."

"That was a dick move," I said.

"I panicked but I should have confessed immediately," Frannie replied.

"I'll forgive you, but the next time our ruse of fake lesbianism is discovered, you have to tell the truth immediately."

"There isn't going to be a next time," Wes said. "From now on, I'm the only one who kisses you, Daisy."

"God, Wes. Possessive much?" Frannie said before hugging me. "Love you, honey. I'm gonna grab some coffee."

She left the living room and Wes tugged me back into his embrace. "See, I told you it would be fine, little flower."

I smiled at him. "So, now that your family knows about us, does this mean I should officially start looking for a job in your city, Mr. McKinley?"

"I think that's a very smart idea, Ms. Morrison," Wes said.

He pressed a kiss against my mouth. "Merry Christmas, Daisy."

"Merry Christmas, Wes."

Epilogue

Two years later

Daisy

"Daisy! Hello, dearest. Come in out of the cold!" Patricia pulled me into the house and hugged me. "Where's Wes?"

"Grabbing the suitcases from the car," I said. I took off my jacket and hung it up before following Patricia into the kitchen. "Are Frannie and Owen here yet?"

"They are but they're at the Brenners. I swear this might be the Christmas that starts up Gregory and Ryan's feud again," she said. "Although, fighting over who gets to hold their new granddaughter is a perfectly legitimate reason to bring it back to life."

I laughed as Wes walked into the kitchen. He gave his mom a hug and she kissed his cheek. "Hi, dearest. How was the trip?"

"Fine. A bit of trouble with the car rental place at the airport, but we got it sorted out. Where's Dad?"

"In the basement. Why?"

Wes wiggled his eyebrows at her before leaving the kitchen. I heard him yelling for his Dad as his grandmother walked into the kitchen.

"Hello, Daisy."

"Hello, Grandma Francine. How are you?" I stood and hugged the fragile old woman.

"Can't complain," she said. She suddenly blinked and grabbed my left hand. She stared at the ring on my finger as Patricia pulled a pan of cookies from the stove.

"I swear, this is the warmest Christmas we've had in years. We won't need our winter jackets when we get the tree tomorrow."

I put my finger to my lips and winked at Wes' grandmother. Her wrinkled face lit up and she made a zipping motion across her mouth before sitting down next to me. "Where's my great grandbaby?"

"They're still at Joy and Ryan's," Patricia said. "They should be here any minute though."

"Mom?" The front door slammed as Frannie's voice carried down the hall. "We're back."

"In the kitchen, dearest," Patricia shouted.

I turned in anticipation as Frannie and Owen walked into the kitchen. Owen was holding the car seat and he set it on the floor in front of me before kissing my cheek. "Hey, Daisy."

"Hi, Owen." I was already reaching into the car seat and I unbuckled the tiny baby before lifting her into my arms. "Hello, sweetheart. Your Aunt Daisy misses you so much."

"She misses you too. One quick visit when she was born isn't enough," Frannie said. She sat down beside me and watched as I placed the baby on my shoulder and rubbed her back. "In fact, she misses you so much that she insists you do the nighttime feedings."

I laughed. "I'm more than happy to help, Frannie."

"God, I love you. Are you sure you don't want to move back and live with me and Owen?"

"So, she can be your unpaid nanny?" Wes said as he

walked into the room. His dad was with him and I grinned when Gregory's face lit up and he hurried over. I handed the baby to him and he kissed her forehead.

Frannie scowled at Wes. "Better than living with you. She figured out you wear your underwear more than once, yet?"

"Hey, I quit doing that when I turned fifteen," Wes said as I made a face.

He laughed and kissed my forehead. "So, did you tell Frannie already?"

"No," I said.

"Tell me what?" Frannie asked.

Wes pulled me to my feet and put his arm around me. "I asked Daisy to marry me and she said yes."

"What?" Frannie shrieked. She stood up and grabbed my hand, staring wide-eyed at the ring as Patricia clapped excitedly and hugged Wes.

Frannie studied my ring for a moment before pulling me into her embrace. "Congratulations, Oopsie. I'm so happy for you!"

"Thank you, Frannie," I replied.

She stepped back as the other members of Wes' family crowded around me to say congratulations and look at the ring.

"What a wonderful surprise," Patricia said. She wiped at the tears on her face before hugging me hard. "I'm so glad you're a part of our family, dearest."

"I am too," I said. I returned her hug and then hugged Gregory and Owen and Wes' grandmother. The baby made a sharp cry and I laughed when everyone hurried to Gregory and began to fuss over her.

Wes put his arm around me and kissed my neck. "Well, we had five minutes of glory before my niece stole the show again."

"I don't mind," I said. "I love you, Wes."

"I love you too, little flower."

About the Author

Elizabeth Kelly was born and raised in Ontario, Canada. She moved west as a teenager and now lives in Alberta with her husband and a menagerie of pets. She firmly believes that a human can survive solely on sushi and coffee, and only her husband's mad cooking skills stops her from proving that theory.

If you would like more information about Elizabeth, please visit her at:

www.elizabethkelly.ca

Books by Elizabeth Kelly

Individual Books

The Necessary Engagement
Amelia's Touch
The Rancher's Daughter
Healing Gabriel
The Contract
A Home for Lily
Saving Charlotte
The Christmas Wife
Shameless
The Fairy Tales Collection
Broken
An Unlikely Seduction

Tempted Series

Tempted
Twice Tempted
Tempted 3
Breathless

Red Moon Series

Red Moon
Red Moon Rising
Dark Moon
Alpha Moon
Pale Moon

The Recruit Series

The Recruit (Book One)
The Recruit (Book Two)
The Recruit (Book Three)
The Recruit (Book Four)

The Shifters Series

Willow and the Wolf (Book One)
Ava and the Bear (Book Two)
Katarina and the Bird (Book Three)
Porter's Mate (Book Four)
Bria and the Tiger (Book Five)

Harmony Falls Series

Sweet Harmony (Book One)

Draax Series

Reign (Book One)

Dirty Intentions

Aubrey Bondurant

Chapter One

Daniella

I took a deep breath and smoothed down my wig, thinking the bright pink hair actually made my blue eyes stand out more than did my natural auburn locks. The shimmering silver, barely-covering-my-ass dress and my thigh-high, black suede boots completed the look. Although not quite. Because I was feeling festive and maybe because I needed some metaphoric balls tonight, I put on a pair of ornament earrings.

After all, I was heading to a Christmas party, one being held three days before the holiday. And I wanted to look my absolute best when busting my fiancé for cheating on me.

Yeah, nothing said Merry Christmas quite like sticking your dick in some other chick right before coming home to your loving fiancée for the holidays.

Stuck in the city working on an unfortunate project until tomorrow morning, my ass.

God, how many times over the last year had I fallen for Eric's lines about working late? Too many.

Though we shared a rented townhouse in New Jersey, I'd always been supportive of him keeping an apartment in Manhattan. I'd felt terrible about him having to schlep all the way home after a late night at work. But now I knew better. Too bad I'd already wasted two years with him, but I was determined not to squander one more day.

Of course, I could've waited to confront him at home, but I knew he'd deny it. I'd also lose the advantage of having evidence. So I was going to a party tonight that I knew he'd be attending in order to gather the undeniable proof.

Club Travesty didn't boast a flashy entrance. Matter of fact, it was damn tough to find. I imagined it would be even harder to gain entry into tonight's Christmas party. Which is why I'd cloned Eric's membership card. I'd found it in his inside jacket pocket late one evening when he'd forgotten to take it out. That had been his second misstep. The first was leaving a brochure in his glove compartment which had started my suspicions about this club he belonged to. Then, of course, he'd clearly underestimated me. He had no clue I'd be able to access his online credit card account, discover where the card had been used, and utilize parking stubs to figure out the address of the place. At which point, I'd hacked into his email to see the invitation.

Now that I was taking the fake membership card out of my purse, I fought the nerves. I was good with a computer and details—hell, I'd managed fake ID's in college for me and all my friends—but there was always a chance I'd be caught at the door. Guess Plan B would have to consist of Eric coming home to find I'd moved out all of my things earlier today.

Smiling at the large man in the black suit with the closely cropped hair at the door, I handed him my card. I watched him scan it while trying to steady my heartbeat. The idea of catching Eric in the act made me anxious. But even more did I worry about entering a sex club holiday party for God only knows what. I wondered if I'd thought this through. I mean what if everyone attending was part of an orgy? Or all of a sudden, I became a submissive for a man in a mask with a whip while "Rudolph the Red-Nosed Reindeer" blasted in the background?

Considering how boring my sex life with Eric had been, I'd be lying if I said either thought didn't turn me on a little. Matter of fact, disguised as I was and about to be very single, I found myself eager to see what was inside the club.

Coming out of my weird, holiday-themed, sex-deprived thoughts, I saw the green light flash and smiled at the bouncer who'd allowed me entry. Whew. I'd made it in. But now what?

Now to look like I belonged here. I wasn't sure what I'd expected, but classy chandeliers, posh carpets, and a beautiful Christmas tree front and center hadn't been it. I stepped past the entrance and deeper inside by way of a short hallway. I found myself in the middle of a party. Waitresses in barely-there tuxedo one-piece rompers served champagne while soft holiday music played in the background. So much for a raunchy sex dungeon. I adjusted my mask. My simple black one was nothing compared to some of the more ornate masks I could see around the room.

For a moment, I started to think I might have been mistaken about what type of party this was. Then I noticed the people congregating near the glass on the far side of the room.

Stepping closer to the window, I sucked in a breath. Rooms with glass from floor to ceiling had people on display in various sex acts. The one in front of me boasted two gorgeous women, one of whom was on her back while the other devoured her between her thighs.

Walking down a few feet, I saw the next room featured two men and one woman. She had one cock in her mouth and the other pumping deep inside of her from behind, fast and furious. I was fascinated and hard-pressed to move on from the threesome. But I had to remember I was here for a purpose and tore my eyes away to step down to the next room. I wasn't a prude by any stretch, despite the boring sex I'd been having with my fiancé, but the next scene shocked my senses. In this room a man plowed into a woman missionary-style while another man went to town, thrusting into the first man's ass.

I was about to move on when my gaze locked on the eyes of the man in the middle. The mask made it hard to determine for sure, but the unmistakable birth mark on his left pec absolutely identified him. Holy shit. Eric was not only cheating on me, but he was also bisexual?

I slid out my flash-drive-sized camera and tried to get the right angle. I wanted to get Eric's masked face along with the unmistakable birth mark: tangible evidence. I'd need it since there wasn't exactly a way I could confront him at the moment. Not unless I wanted to bang against the glass and whip off my mask. Although tempting, I would rather show him the proof with the photo. This ought to get his cooperation in returning the money he owed me, my true priority.

I'd given him seventy-five thousand dollars out of my savings to go towards a down payment on the house we planned to buy together. Hindsight made me feel stupid for having trusted him, but when you think you'll spend the rest of your life with someone, what was transferring your savings for your dream home? Unfortunately, my sleuthing revealed he'd spent the money instead of putting it in his nonexistent savings. Evidently, he was a cheater all the way around.

Tucking the camera in my purse and giving one last glance toward Eric, I was about to turn and make my way out when a hand clamped on my elbow and a low voice came in my ear.

"Miss, please follow me."

The man's grip wasn't leaving me much of a choice. A tank in a suit, he was careful, however, make it look as though he was merely guiding me through the crowd. But when he led me into a cleverly hidden elevator near the bar, I had a moment of panic.

"Where are you taking me?"

"To see the boss, ma'am."

"Um, why is that?"

"Don't know, but I reckon you'll find out soon enough."

His Southern voice might be soothing, but his words weren't. Crap. Had they figured out my ID was fake? Or had they spotted the camera? Either way, I was pretty sure I was fucked. And not in a good, sex-club kind of way.

Chapter Two

Shane

Finances didn't wait, not even for Christmas week. This was why, instead of enjoying the party downstairs, I was up in my office crunching numbers, frustrated with our part-time accountant's work or lack thereof. The IRS year-end deadline was looming, but instead of making my profit-and-loss statement his priority tonight, he was downstairs partaking in the festivities. Which is probably what I should have been doing. But ironically, as one of the owners of Club Travesty, I had very little time to indulge in the club's activities.

"Hey, Boss, you coming down?" Heather, my bar manager and long-time loyal employee, came up the stairs. The open loft-like space held both my desk and my best friend's, in addition to a round table and chairs I used for meetings.

I held my head, wanting the break but not in the mood for celebration. Looking up, I tried not to let the stress show. "Not yet. Everything going all right?"

She nodded. "Yep. Good crowd tonight. Sex rooms are hot. Matter of fact, I might be up for something later if, uh, you are."

I forced myself to scan Heather, with her bustier lifting her fake boobs and cinching her tiny waist, and tight leather pants encasing her toned legs. Her hair was long and blond, both of which weren't natural, but it did make her look younger than her thirty-eight birthdays. We'd done acts together over the years, but it had been a while. Mainly because I'd been worried she'd started to catch feelings after the last time. I didn't do feelings with sex.

Regardless, my cock should have stirred. It didn't. I blamed the numbers in front of me. "Maybe some other time, honey." The last thing I wanted to do was hurt her feelings.

"Always happy to take a raincheck. Don't work too hard now."

Right. I'd owned the club with my best friend, Max, for nearly ten years, and I did remember when it used to be fun. Of course, what two red-blooded males wouldn't love the idea of running a sex club? But lately it was literally all work and no play. Rubbing my eyes and knowing I still had a long night ahead of me, I stood up from my desk and went through the secure door on my right. There my security team monitored the rooms and the guests on the dozen screens in front of them.

"How's it going, Ron?" I addressed the head of security and the best man I had on the job.

"Nothing out of the ordinary, Mr. Nelson." His scrutinizing gaze never left the screens, scanning for any type of breach in either the sex rooms or the party crowd. Anonymity was the most important thing at Club Travesty, something I took very seriously and the reason I had top security.

"Is Max on the bar?"

"Yes, sir. Any chance he gets."

Not only was Max my best friend from childhood, but he was also my business partner. Whereas I preferred the back office, he enjoyed being in the mix, dealing with personnel and schmoozing. He was the people person. I was not.

Typically, we had a much smaller crowd. But during the holidays, we did two big VIP parties, one to celebrate Christmas and another on New Year's Eve. This was in addition to the many other services we offered. Private sex rooms for couples who wanted to come in and spice things up, kinky BDSM rooms in the basement, and a newer service I'd added a few years ago which focused on the woman. This included everything from sexual confidence counselors to the "boyfriend experience," where lonely women could come in to gain mojo.

I was just about to step out and back to the books when Ron honed in on something.

"Focus in on camera four," he instructed Alan, his junior security guy.

I wasn't sure what he was looking at until I spotted her. Pink hair that was obviously fake, tight petite body in a silver, curve-hugging dress, and thigh-high boots that were sexy as hell. "What's she holding?"

"Shit. I think it's a camera." He spoke into the intercom, reaching every security guard via their inconspicuous earpieces. "I've got a possible breach. Pink hair, silver dress, black boots. In front of room number four."

Photos were a definite violation of club policy. "Run her credentials," I instructed.

"Yes, sir. You want us to confiscate the device and escort her out?"

That would be the easiest thing to do. But I wanted answers first. "No, bring her up here. Proceed discreetly."

Chapter Three

Daniella

The elevator doors opened to a large floor space. Two desks sat in the middle of the room and a bay of one-way mirrors appeared to look down over the main floor. My anxiety was already high, but then I saw him. It went up a whole other level.

Dressed all in black in a well-tailored suit, he walked towards me with a masculine confidence which left no doubt he was in charge. He was gorgeous in a dangerous way with chiseled features, midnight black hair and a scruff that made me wonder what it would feel like between my thighs. Jesus, where had that thought come from? I blamed the sex God in front of me along with the visual from the rooms still on my mind.

He stopped a foot in front me and held out his hand. "May I see your ID card?"

Damn. His husky voice was as sexy as he was.

I swallowed hard before fishing it from my clutch and handing it over. My voice escaped me, though I didn't know whether it was from his presence or from my nerves over the fake ID.

"Scan this." He held it out for Tank Man.

"Yes, sir."

After taking the card, Tank Man opened a door off to the side, offering me a glimpse of monitors.

The moment the door closed, I felt very aware we were alone. The floor may have been spacious, but at that moment it felt anything but. "What, uh, what is this about?" I'd finally found my voice.

"It's about the camera, and the pictures you were taking."

He didn't seem like a man who would appreciate a false runaround, so I didn't bother to deny it. "I'm guessing it's against club rules?"

"You'd guess right. And if you turn it over, I won't press charges."

"You won't press charges against me for taking pictures in a sex club?" As if he would call the cops here. I might be shaking in my boots, but I wasn't stupid.

His smile didn't reach his eyes. "Take off your mask, please."

I swallowed hard but removed it as instructed. Perhaps if I cooperated, he'd be more willing to let me keep the photos.

"I've never seen you here before. What's your name?"

I looked beyond him to where the big man who'd taken my ID was coming out of the door. "I'm sure your human tank can tell you."

His lips twitched, but he simply turned towards his man with a quirked brow.

"Beth Jones, sir. But the membership code belongs to Eric Patterson."

Note to self. When lying and going undercover, wear shoes I could actually run in. These four-inch boots were definitely not fitting the bill if I wanted to make a break for it.

"Go back to your station downstairs, Chad. Send up

Lance, please."

"He so didn't look like a Chad," I commented once the door was closed. Hey, even if I was screwed, I could still be sarcastic.

Shane

I was the type of man accustomed to having people nervous upon meeting me. I might not be big like the "Tank" she'd referred to, but at six foot one, two hundred pounds, I'd been known to intimidate the people I wanted to. But this woman was cracking jokes. She was challenging me about the police, despite her hands shaking when she'd handed over the ID card and taken off her mask. I appreciated that she hadn't bothered to lie or play dumb.

"Who is Eric Patterson to you?" I hadn't missed the way she'd involuntarily flinched when his name had been mentioned.

She lifted her chin. "My soon-to-be-former fiancé."

"I'm guessing he doesn't know you're here?"

"You'd guess correctly."

She had spunk; I'd give her that. "What are the pictures for?"

"Well, nothing says insurance better than a photo of your former fiancé fucking another woman while getting it in the ass at the same time by a dude."

If this wasn't so serious, then I might have grinned at her choice of words. "Insurance against what? You're a woman who came in tonight to get proof your fiancé was cheating. So now go home, throw his clothes out, and do whatever you women do to get your revenge, but leave my club out of it."

She gritted her teeth. "I have something that could be useful to you."

I raised a brow, slowly scanning up from her fuck-me, thigh-high boots to the short dress that gave me a glimpse of skin. Her breasts, although not large, were certainly real. And despite the fact she was wearing a lot of makeup, I could see that under it she was beautiful. For a moment, I wanted nothing better than to rip off her wig to see the color of her hair. But the murderous glare she was shooting me gave me pause, not to mention amusement.

"Jesus. Are all men pigs? I meant your damn security system. Obviously, I'm not throwing myself at the owner of a sex club. I'm not that pathetic."

Normally I didn't give a shit what people thought about me, having perfected such an art form years ago. But this particular woman's audacity to think herself too good for me snapped my temper. "I can assure you I'd rather jerk off than fuck someone vanilla like you."

I immediately saw the hurt flash in her eyes and instantly regretted my words. I'd made this personal when it was only business.

"I'm sure my fiancé had the same thought. And the insurance I speak of is because he took my money, and I want it back." She dug in her clutch and handed over a small camera. "I'll be going now unless you have any other insults you'd prefer to hurl before I do."

Unbelievable. "As if implying you'd never stoop so low as to sleep with me wasn't starting it."

Her pretty face showed confusion. "What the hell are you talking about? You know what? It doesn't matter. I need to go."

I was about to let her. Getting the camera should have been enough, but I needed to address one more thing. How had she gotten in tonight?

My gaze landed on Lance coming out of the elevator. He'd been on the door when Ms. Beth Jones—which couldn't be her real name—had come through.

"Wait one moment. Lance, do you remember letting this woman in the door earlier tonight?"

Lance assessed her quickly but shook his head. "Sorry, sir. I don't remember her. There were a lot of women dressed similarly tonight."

"Yes, but this one gave you a fake ID. It might have looked authentic, but it was cloned from the card of a male member, which she is definitely not. That you should've caught. Clear out your things. You're fired."

She gasped. "What? No. You can't fire him."

৵ ৵

Daniella

The arrogant asshole had the nerve to arch a brow at me.

"I'm the owner. I can do whatever I like."

"Yes, sir. Sorry, sir." Lance spoke up, ready to leave.

Could I help it if my guilt was heavy? I'd come to expose a cheater, not make some poor guy lose his job. "No, wait. I'll show you how I cloned the cards. That's what I was offering before. But if I show you, then you have to let, uh, Lance keep his job. You have a serious security breach with the way your cards are designed."

I watched him contemplate. "Are you a computer hacker?"

"No, just really good with them."

"And how are you with accounting? Because if I dismiss Eric from the club, I'm going to be without an accountant."

My eyes widened. "You let Eric handle your books? Are you a client of his firm?"

"No. He did this on the side to compensate for his, uh, membership fee. He is an accountant, is he not?"

"Yeah, one who stole money and doesn't have the accumulated wealth he boasts about." I used air quotes to highlight the last few words.

Although his face said nothing, the set of his jaw told me everything. "Lance, go downstairs and bring Mr. Patterson up here. I have some questions for him."

"Does that mean Lance isn't fired?"

"It would seem so. For now."

Tank Two simply nodded. "Yes, sir. I'll bring Mr. Patterson up."

"How did you find out he was stealing?"

"I gave him seventy-five thousand dollars to go with his supposed two hundred thousand for a down payment on a house. None of it is in his bank accounts. Matter of fact, the statements show he's exclusively been withdrawing money for months."

"Excuse me?"

"When I hacked into his bank accounts, none of my money was there. But I did see it used to be, along with a couple hundred thousand, but it's all been withdrawn. That's why I need the pictures from tonight, as insurance he'll give my money back."

"I take it he wouldn't want people finding out he was in a threesome with another man?"

"He'd freak out if I let the pictures go to all of his buddies or coworkers."

"Are you sure you want to see him? I could just as easily do this without you here. The last thing I want is for you to start crying or get hysterical."

Seriously? "The answer to your insulting question would be no, I won't start freaking out."

Matter of fact, I was more than ready to confront Eric.

Chapter Four

Shane

I watched Eric come off the elevator doors. He took off the mask and gave me a smile before his gaze flicked over to my guest.

"Daniella. That's not you, is it?"

She ripped the pink wig off her head, letting auburn locks flow down her back and making it clear she was the person he'd guessed.

She was even prettier without the wig, with her natural dark red hair cascading down her back in waves, but it was the fire in her eyes which made her stunning. Although I'd hauled him up here wanting answers about his alleged stealing—he was acting as my accountant, after all—like a sick voyeur, I was riveted to the spot. I wanted to find out what would happen once she confronted him over the cheating.

"What the hell are you doing here?" Eric asked, still clearly in shock.

"Shouldn't that be my question for you?"

She was calm. I'd give her that.

"I, uh, I mean some people from the office—we were working late and—"

"Oh, my God. Even now you lie. After I saw you getting fucked in the ass by some guy ten minutes ago."

Eric went pale at her remark, and I have to say it made me happy. I'd never really liked the guy on a personal level and wasn't surprised to find he was a cheater. The question was whether he was a thief. If he was, I was going to break his face.

"What do you expect? You're boring as hell in the bedroom. No boobs, no adventure—"

"No cock," she supplied, arching a brow.

At least she wasn't about to let him insult her. There was no way it couldn't have stung, though, especially after my earlier comment.

"As enlightening as it would be to hear you two go back and forth all night, I don't have the time. But I do have a vested interest in bringing you up here, Eric."

His gaze shifted to me, and I could see it. The nervousness. "Uh, what's that?"

"Are you stealing from me?"

"No. No way, Shane."

I raised a brow at his familiarity.

"I mean Mr. Nelson, sir."

"Did you steal from her?"

His eyes got big, and he turned red. "No. She's my fiancée."

"Not any more I'm not."

She took off the ring and tossed it onto a nearby table. If she'd been smart, she would've used it for leverage to ensure he returned her money first, but I stayed quiet. And in fact, before he could step over to grab the considerably sized diamond ring, she snatched it up.

"Return my money, and you can have it back."

"What? That ring is worth over ten grand. All precedents say the man gets the ring back if an engagement is broken."

Dumbass. But then again, this was the most amusement I'd had in weeks.

"I'm aware of what legal precedents says. However, if the man owes her seventy-five thousand dollars, the ring can be held as collateral. I want it all returned."

"It was to go towards a house, so good luck proving anything."

I'd had enough of this asshole. It bothered me that he wasn't apologizing or appeared to show any remorse. She'd trusted him, and he'd betrayed her trust: not only by cheating, but also by taking her money. Neither of which was sitting well with me. "What do you think the guys at the office or your buddies would think of your little threesome downstairs tonight, Eric?"

His face started to turn a deep red. Although he was a handsome guy, if you preferred the Wall Street type, he certainly didn't look it now. Matter of fact, he looked like he was about to puke. Which meant I had his number.

"You can't threaten me with that. Anonymity is rule one with the club."

I shrugged. "I can't, but she can. She has pictures."

His eyes darted back and forth between us. "But that's against club rules."

"Well, see, that's a predicament. She's not actually a club member. In fact, you're in violation for allowing her to use your card tonight to get in."

"I didn't. She must've copied it."

"Which means she had access to it, which ultimately constitutes carelessness on your part."

"What do you want from me?"

"The truth. Are you stealing from me?"

"No. Definitely not."

Considering he didn't have access to my actual bank accounts but only to the reports, I chose to believe him. "Fine, but if I find one penny gone, those pictures go viral at your firm. Also, you'll return all the money to Ms.—"

"Trivioli," she supplied.

Daniella Trivioli. The name rolled around in my mind.

"Okay. Fine," he readily agreed.

"And do not come back here. Your membership has been revoked."

Now he looked like he was on the verge of crying. He certainly hadn't been as upset to lose his supposed future life partner. "Please, don't do that."

"I don't tolerate thieves or liars, Eric. Now, I suggest you leave without a scene before I make one and have you tossed out."

He turned, but not without walking in front of Daniella and mumbling something which made her go completely pale.

"What did you just say to her?"

"Nothing." Eric appeared in a hurry to be going.

I moved closer to step in front of her. "What did he say to you?" I might be a dick, but the last thing I'd allow was the victim in this situation to be made to feel worse. This woman, in particular, was pulling out a protective side I hadn't felt in years.

"He said 'have a nice life, you frigid orgasmless cunt.'"

I raised a brow. "He's never given you an orgasm?" Why the fuck did women stay with men who couldn't get them off? Monogamy was a foreign concept to me, especially if, at the very least, the sex wasn't good.

She swallowed hard. Tears glistened in her prideful gaze. "Not often."

Eric scoffed. "Because you take too long."

There was a reason my club offered sexual confidence classes. Because men like Eric systematically shredded a woman's self-assurance by being selfish in bed. I stepped closer to Daniella. My arm went around her waist, pulling her to my side. I'd be lying if I said her warmth didn't affect me. Her soft curves could be felt under the flimsy excuse for a dress she was wearing.

"I find it funny you'd automatically assume the problem is her." I let my hand wander down her side slowly, seductively, while I told myself I was helping her save face. "Because your ex-fiancée is a beautiful, sexy woman." I stepped behind her then, my one hand still splayed on her hip, the other inching up her skirt in the back.

How far would she be willing to let this go? Any moment I expected her to step away. At the same time, I hoped she wouldn't.

"But she's clearly been sexually deprived for a long time. But don't worry, Eric. She's come to the right place to remedy that." Before I could think about the ramifications or the fact that Daniella wasn't the typical guest at Club Travesty, my hand went up her skirt and between her legs.

❧ ❧

Daniella

I was absolutely frozen—no pun intended with the frigid comment. I could feel Shane's breath on the back of my neck, his hand burning into my skin despite the layer of dress material between them, and now his other hand creeping up the back of my skirt. And I was doing absolutely nothing to stop it.

"As far as her cunt is concerned..."

Oh, God. His finger lightly ghosted between my legs at the wet silk thong. I found myself closing my eyes and gripping his arm, wanting - no, needing - more.

"It's hot and wet."

His whisper, meant only for my ears, caused

goosebumps. "Tell me if you want me to stop now. Otherwise, I'm going to put my fingers inside you and make you come."

Even if I could've formed the words, there was no way I was speaking at the moment. In addition to being wildly turned on by the man since the moment I'd laid eyes on him, curiosity had me wondering if, in fact, the problem all along hadn't been me. I'd beaten myself up plenty for not being able to have a proper orgasm. So, with the hot guy offering, why the hell not? And although this was very un-Daniella of me, I suddenly felt uninhibited about having this sexy stranger behind me, giving me the pleasure I'd never experienced with the man who supposedly loved me.

My eyes flew open the moment he inserted a finger. Despite being a complete stranger, he was unapologetic with his tutorial in front of our audience of Eric and the bouncer. I might be covered by my dress in front, but I don't think it would've mattered if I hadn't been. Because I was lost in sensation. A breath left me when he wasted no time in inserting two and then curled them up deep inside of me where he started to move them against a spot that made my knees weak.

"You see, Eric, I could've gone for the easy target of her clit. Given her a nice climax by rubbing her there. But I think after the lack of orgasms she's received from you for—how long was it?"

Jesus, was he actually asking me a question?

"Two years," I offered on a whisper, digging my nails into his arm around my waist. I hoped he was fully prepared to take the majority of my weight as I could feel my legs start to shake.

"After two years, she deserves a G-spot orgasm which will rip through her body and have her coming like a porn star."

He wasn't too far off. The moment he started

pressing his two fingers up against a spot I hadn't known existed, a moan escaped my throat.

"Get out," Shane grunted.

I flicked my gaze towards Eric's face just in time to see it heat with humiliation before he was escorted out. I didn't care because my climax slammed into me with full force, taking both my breath and my ability to remember it was a stranger's fingers doing this to me.

"That's it. Ride it out."

His breath came in my ear, the huskiness of his voice causing an involuntary shiver. My body bucked against his hand, leaving me completely spent in the aftermath. Calming my breath, both hands gripping his forearm, I heard myself whimper when he withdrew his fingers.

"Are you okay to stand?"

I nodded, still unable to form words. Fortunately, the desk was next to me so I could use my hand to brace my legs, which remained shaking.

"So, I guess, thanks for that." What else do you say when a stranger finger-fucks you to the best orgasm of your life?

He chuckled. "You're welcome. Now, what?"

My gaze met his, and I felt my face heat. Something about meeting the man in the eyes after he'd had his fingers inside of me was disconcerting. Gone was the wild girl who'd wanted to be someone else tonight, and back was the reality of the jilted fiancée who'd come here for proof. This whole night was past the point of surreal. "Um, I should leave."

He frowned. "Where will you go?"

"I have my stuff in my car and need to get a hotel room."

"It's three days before Christmas, so that's not happening in Manhattan."

I hadn't thought much past busting Eric. Now that the adrenaline was fading, thanks in part to the whole orgasm thing, I was bone weary, in need of a warm shower and a comfortable bed. "I guess I'll head back towards Jersey, then. I don't know."

"I thought you were going to show me how you cloned the ID."

"Now?"

"You want Lance to keep his job, right?"

My temper suddenly flared at his use of power. But I wasn't angry enough to take a chance on him firing the unfortunate guy who'd let me in tonight. "Fine. Get your computer guy in here, and give me an hour. But that's it. If he can't keep up, it's not my problem."

He grinned. "My computer guy is out until the day after Christmas. So how about you show me instead? And rest assured I'll have no problem keeping up."

I swallowed hard at the innuendo. For some reason, I couldn't bring myself to tell him I was too tired or too emotionally exhausted. He was challenging me, and I couldn't back down. Fine. Game on, Mr. Magic Fingers.

Chapter Five

Shane

She was smart. And running on empty by the look of her. But pride had been pushing her through the last twenty minutes as she walked me through her cloning process. Part of me felt guilty, but the other part knew that once she left here, I'd never see her again. I reasoned that I pushed her into staying because I needed to figure out how she'd cloned the card.

Truth was, I wouldn't have fired Lance for more than the five minutes it would've taken to make my point. He'd made a mistake, and I was annoyed. More interesting was how she'd reacted to it. Not many people gave a shit about people they didn't know. But she'd been outraged enough to stay and show me the security breach.

I listened raptly while she explained the flaw in our card chipping. Damn if she wasn't right. It was a design flaw. Frankly, a more sophisticated hacker, one who hadn't simply wanted photos of her ex engaging in group sex, could've exploited it a lot worse.

"And that's it. With the updated chip technology, you should be fine."

"But you're not a computer programmer?"

She blushed, probably not liking such a personal question. People got weird about protecting their identity in a place like Club Travesty. "No, but working with computers has always been my hobby."

"Is that what you call hacking these days?"

She smiled. "Gotta learn how to develop before you can hack code. I'm just good at guessing passwords. Most people aren't very smart with what they use."

"Meaning Eric?"

She sighed. "Yeah. His password was his favorite sports team. Your chip is simply outdated technology. No hacking involved, actually."

She stood up, stifling a yawn. It was after midnight, and considering the kind of night she'd had, I imagined she was exhausted.

"I have an extra bed in the back if you want to crash. At this hour, you're not going to find a hotel room."

"Really?" She looked relieved.

I wasn't sure why the hell I was offering her my bed, especially when I'd had every intention of jerking off there to the smell of her on my fingers. Which was stupid considering I had an abundance of pussy to choose from downstairs. Perhaps taking advantage of that was what I needed to do to get this woman out of my head.

She bit her lip, looking uncertain. "I don't want to impose."

"I wouldn't offer if it was an imposition. There's a private bathroom, and nobody will bother you."

"I, um—That would be great. I'll go get my suitcase from my car in the garage."

I shook my head, the protective vein tapped again. "Not dressed like that by yourself. Give me the keys, and I'll have one of the tanks do it."

She smiled, clearly liking my newly adopted

nicknames for the two giant bouncers. "I'm not taking your bed, am I?"

"I have plans downstairs, so no." I didn't miss the way disappointment flashed in her expression. But the last thing I needed was her thinking the bed meant anything. In an effort to be clear, I said, "And this is simply a favor for showing me the faulty chip design. By morning, I expect you gone."

Fire shone in her eyes and straightened her spine. "You know, I can resolve that issue right now. Goodbye."

Shit. I'd gone too far. "Wait. Look, you're dead on your feet. And I'm an asshole. Okay?"

She quirked a brow. "Yes, but one of those things will be better by tomorrow. Although I appreciate your half-ass attempt at an apology, the answer is no. Good night, Mr. Nelson, and, uh, take care."

Without a glance back, she walked out.

෧෴

After calling one of my tanks to ensure he followed at a respectable distance to see her safely to her car, I decided to do some research. Then I had to enter the craziness of the party. It was approaching the witching hour for fights, drunks, and anything else that might come up.

I typed her name into a search engine. Holy shit. According to LinkedIn, Daniella Trivioli was a tax attorney. I went to the law firm's website and searched out her bio. No picture, which was disappointing. But the site did tell me she'd attended NYU and was licensed to practice in both New York and New Jersey. Considering the New York bar was nothing to sneeze at, she had to be as smart as I'd sensed.

This could be the answer to my issues with the IRS.

Although I could've hired any number of professionals to help me with my accounting problems, I decided to hire myself this particular tax attorney. I told myself it was because fate had brought her here tonight when I had an issue with the IRS. I only hoped she'd believe the lie better than I did.

Chapter Six

Daniella

"Asshole," I muttered under my breath as I went down the stairs from his office. Unfortunately, I wasn't looking where I was walking and knocked right into a handsome man coming up.

"Whoa, there. Sorry. You okay?" The tall man with light brown hair and an easy smile steadied me.

"Yeah. Sorry. I wasn't watching where I was going. Excuse me." I attempted to move past him, but he stepped in front of me.

"It's okay. So who's the asshole?" His gaze, filled with humor, flicked up the stairs.

"Judging by the look on your face, you already know. Sorry, I really must be leaving."

His grin widened. "You're the one they caught taking pictures, aren't you?"

My face heated. "I, uh—yeah. And I really need to go." I started to feel uncomfortable. This was a sex club, and I had no idea what this guy was thinking by not allowing me to pass.

As if reading my mind, he said, "Relax. I'm one of the owners. The name is Max. And I take it you met the

27

other half?"

I let out a breath. "Yes. And everything is set now. He has the camera."

"You sure it's set? You look a little pissed."

"Considering Mr. Nelson is your partner, I don't think you're surprised he has that effect on people. Now, then, I have a hotel room to find."

"Won't be easy three days before Christmas."

It irked me that everyone seemed to think of this but me. "So I've heard. Good night, Max."

He stepped aside. "Good night, uh - "

"Daniella." I provided my real name before I could think about it. Oh, well. Wasn't like I was coming back here anyhow.

"Good night, Daniella."

❧ ❦

Waking up the next morning in my hotel bed, I tried to tell myself today was just another day. So what if it was Christmas Eve tomorrow and most people were traveling to be with their families? So what if I'd had to drive back over to Jersey City in order to find a room for the night? So what if everything I owned was either in my car or in the small storage unit I'd rented until I could get my money back and find a new place?

It was tempting to call in sick to work today, but with nothing but a pity party in front of me, I decided not to. I might not emphatically enjoy my job—come on, it was taxes; how much fun could that possibly be?—it wasn't like me to shirk my responsibility, either. Especially with my savings gone and the need to get another apartment soon. Although it wasn't busy yet for tax season, most of it picking up after the end of the year, I had a few cleanup tasks which could keep me busy.

Too bad my parents had already left on their

Caribbean cruise. I'd had no interest in going with them initially, happy to have the excuse to stay home because Eric was working. But now the thought of spending the holiday alone seemed even worse than spending it with my difficult parents. Of course, if my mother found out about the breakup, I would've been jumping overboard to get away from her disappointment. When she did find out there would be no wedding to plan, she was going to be devastated.

She would be the only one. As I took stock of my feelings after rolling out of bed, I realized I wasn't.

Instead I felt a tremendous relief. So then, why hadn't I ended things sooner? The question stuck with me while I was in the shower and through a big room-service breakfast. Unfortunately, I didn't like the answer. I'd been going through the motions, checking off the boxes in life, instead of being in love with him.

When my cell phone on the desk rang, I shoved the thoughts to the side. It was Eric. And I knew I had to get this over with sooner or later.

"Hello."

"It's about damn time. I've been calling you all night."

I had absolutely no patience for him. "What do you want?"

"Where are you?"

"None of your business."

"Come on, Daniella. This isn't you. Be reasonable. We can work things out."

"Seriously? Because I think after finding out you stole money from me, are bisexual and cheating on me, and then had the audacity to call me a frigid cunt last night, that reconciling is the last thing on my mind."

"I'm sorry. I wasn't myself. And Shane putting his hands on you. What the hell was that about?"

It was reckless, freeing, and completely without

regret. "It was about finding one more reason never to see you again. In two minutes he gave me what you've never been able to. Now listen up. You owe me seventy-five thousand dollars. I want it, or I go to the authorities and things get messy."

"That's blackmail."

"No, that's giving you a chance before you lose your job over me filing embezzlement charges. Blackmail would be if I threatened to show those pictures of you taking it up the ass by the blond-haired fellow to everyone we know, including your boss."

My implication held heavy on the line until he finally spoke.

"I— Shit. Okay. I can only get you half right now. But I promise the other half will be coming."

"You have two days to wire half and two weeks to come up with the rest."

"Then will you return the ring? It belonged to my grandmother."

A reminder to get him to sign a receipt of return because he'd probably hock it and then tell his mother I kept it. "Of course. I want to hold onto it about as much as I want to hold onto our relationship. And if I get tested and find out I have something, the gloves are completely off. I hope you realize that."

"I'm clean. I swear. I always used condoms. And since we used condoms, too, we should be good."

"Hope so. Two days, and I want half the money. I'll text you the account information."

"I have it already, don't I?"

I laughed without humor. "As if I wouldn't have changed my bank accounts after learning you stole from me. Goodbye, Eric."

I sat there humming with adrenaline but still no tears. Two years gone with that man, and I was more pissed at being duped than upset at losing him.

Chapter Seven

Shane

I wasn't a man who enjoyed waiting. So I'd had a conversation with Daniella's boss in the morning and expected her any minute.

"You look smug. You finally give the numbers a rest and get laid?" Perched on the side of my desk, Max thumbed through the mail.

I glanced up from my computer. "I'm not smug. Just waiting."

He cocked a brow. "For what?"

My gaze traveled towards the elevator doors where Chad appeared with my guest. She didn't look too happy to see me.

"What in the hell are you doing calling my firm and requesting me?" Daniella's eyes were fiery while her tone was frosty.

I lifted a brow, allowing myself the pleasure of eye-fucking her from head to toe and enjoying the hell out of the way she was blushing at the scrutiny. She was dressed like an office fantasy. Her petite figure was encased in a long black pencil skirt that accented her hips. A dark blue, collared shirt showed off a tease of skin at the column of her throat. Pearls in both her ears and around her neck set off the professional image. But it was the black stilettos which gave me pause. Made me fantasize about them digging into my back as I pounded into her on my desk.

"I need a tax attorney." It was a shit answer to rile her up even further. I wasn't disappointed.

She huffed. "Then you could've discussed it with me rather than call my boss and demand I be on site this morning."

"You mean last night when you told me that you were a tax attorney?" It still annoyed me she hadn't revealed this.

"Sir, do you need me for anything else?" Chad looked awkward about witnessing our exchange.

"No, thank you. Max, you can go, too."

I couldn't explain it, but I didn't like the way he was looking at her. Suddenly, I wanted us to be alone.

"Are you kidding me? I'm enjoying the hell out of this. And I'm Max, by the way, the more charming of the owners."

Much to my amusement, Daniella didn't so much as give him a glance. "We met last night."

"Holy shit. Daniella from the stairs?"

What the hell? When had he met her, and how did he know her name?

"I must say the dress last night was fantastic, but you look more beautiful now." Max stepped in front of her, extending his hand. Doing what he did best, he kissed it.

But instead of smiling shyly or giggling like most women did when Max was romantic, she merely lifted a brow and retracted her hand.

Max glanced over at me and spoke in perfect Italian. "Wow, she really has eyes only for you, my friend. Although whether they are the kind that want you to fuck her or the kind that want you dead, I'm not sure."

My gaze didn't waver from Daniella's.

She didn't miss a beat, replying in equally perfect Italian. "The latter one definitely. And don't you know it's rude to switch to another language in front of someone?"

Turning uncharacteristically pink, he apologized in English. "I'm sorry. You're right. It was rude. How do you know Italian?"

"My name is Daniella Maria Trivioli." The 'duh' was implied by her very Italian name.

He laughed out loud. "Should've guessed as you've certainly got the temper for it. But the blue eyes and red hair don't exactly announce the fact."

"I was adopted by Italian parents; my DNA says I'm mostly Irish."

"Good thing an Irish temper is only a legend," he chuckled, causing her to smile.

The fact that she was offering up these tidbits of her life him was starting to grind on me. "Max, if there isn't anything else, Ms. Trivioli and I have business."

Laughter came from his chest. "I bet. I'll leave you two. And Daniella, if he's an asshole to you again, you can always find me at the bar."

She waited until he went down the stairs to speak again. "What do you want from me, Shane?"

It was a good thing I was sitting down because hearing her call me by my first name had my cock instantly hard. "I need a good accountant, one especially expert at taxes. The IRS is up our ass, and your boss assures me you're one of the best."

"I'm a tax attorney, not an accountant."

"You have a CPA, do you not?"

"I don't work in Manhattan. I work in New Jersey."

"But you're licensed to work in New York, too. I checked. I'll pay for your accommodation in the hotel next door as soon as they have rooms available. In the meantime, you can take the bedroom here or commute from wherever you're staying. I'll need you for at least the next week. I've made it very lucrative for your firm, assuring your boss I'll pay double time for the short notice."

I knew she was caught between a rock and a hard place.

"It's Christmas Eve tomorrow, so I can come back the day after Christmas to get started."

"This is time sensitive."

She was incredulous. "Meaning you want me to work through the holiday?"

"Did you have other plans?" It was a dick question considering those plans had most likely been with her ex-fiancé. But I wasn't exaggerating when I said it was urgent. If I didn't get my numbers fixed by the first of the year, we could be screwed at tax time.

"Fine. I'll stay here until the hotel opens up. But my things are at a hotel in Jersey City."

"I'll have Chad go fetch them." And bring them to the bedroom where I slept when I didn't make it home, which was a lot these days. The idea of her using my bed made it all the more appealing to fuck her. But I wasn't giving in to the temptation.

Although I might picture pounding into Ms. Daniella Trivioli until she screamed my name, there were three things keeping me from acting.

One, she was rebounding from her douche bag ex-fiancé. Although I was an asshole in my own right, I wasn't the type who tried to be one on purpose or who wanted to deal with the fallout of a rebound.

Two, I desperately needed to get the mess of accounting in front of me fixed before it screwed over this club on account of both taxes and losses.

And lastly, she wasn't the type of girl up for a quick fuck. She had strings written all over her. I'd learned to be crystal clear in my intentions.

"Hand over your key and jot down the hotel name and room number. I'll have everything transferred here."

"Actually, I have an appointment first, but I can come back after."

I narrowed my eyes. She could be trying to find a way to get back to her office and out of the assignment. "What appointment?"

I didn't expect the answer she gave me.

"I need to get tested. Despite Eric insisting he used condoms elsewhere, I don't want to take any chances." Her neck turned red with her admission.

My voice showed my sympathy for her situation. "I have an in-house person who can do that for you here. We insist on the staff getting tested monthly. It would be done discreetly, and you'd have the results by tomorrow."

"Thank you. That would be better than the humiliation of going to my gynecologist hoping they have a walk-in available."

"I'll set it up while you get started here and have her come up when she's ready." I slid a notepad and pen to her.

She wrote down the name of her hotel, the Doubletree in Jersey City, along with the room number. "My car is there, too, as I took the train into the city."

"I'll have it brought over, as well." I watched her now write down the description of the gray Honda Accord. Practical, just like her.

She handed over her keycard and the car keys. "Fine. Thank you."

I stood up, offering her my seat.

She took out a small laptop and notepad before fixing her stunning blue eyes on me. "Of all the tax attorneys and high-powered accountants in the city who could take on a business like yours, why do you want me here?"

Good fucking question. One I'd never admit had something to do with the mysterious effect she had on me.

"I'm not a trusting person, Ms. Trivioli."

She arched a brow. "I clone your membership card, sneak in, take pictures against club policy, and suddenly you trust me?"

"No, but you didn't lie about it once you got caught. Obviously, you have a sense of justice. Otherwise, you wouldn't have wanted to confront your ex. Nor would you have stayed to show me the way you cloned the card to ensure Lance kept his job. I don't tolerate liars."

Her shoulders relaxed, and I was afforded a wry smile. "That'll be a refreshing change. Anything else I should know?"

I leaned in closer towards her. I couldn't help myself. "Yes. I expect loyalty and discretion from my employees. I've already run your background check and will give you a pass for the employee entrance." I handed her the key card from my pocket and watched her take it in her hand.

The scent of a soft musky fragrance made me want to inhale deeply. This close, I could make out the dusting of freckles across the bridge of her nose. She practically shouted innocence. But once again, it was the fire in her eyes which intrigued me.

"First off, I'm not your employee. As far as discretion is concerned, I think we both have enough of a vested interest to ensure that happens. But my loyalty is something earned. So for now, let's agree that I'll work hard for you and keep the club secrets. Deal?"

My lips twitched at her spunk. "Deal."

"Now, let's start with what the problem is."

I laid out the facts. Our numbers weren't adding up. We were experiencing losses even while revenue was increasing. If I didn't have a good reason to report a loss to the IRS, they'd be up my ass.

"I put everything in a spreadsheet on the computer in front of you. I'll get a nondisclosure agreement, then give you whatever else you need for backup."

I watched, fascinated, for the better part of a half hour while Daniella examined my tax returns from the last five years and my computer ledger. I finally left her to it after a few pointed glares told me to leave her be. Plus, I wanted to give her privacy when Shelly came up to take her blood for the test.

When I came back up for lunch, I was surprised to see Daniella had already obtained the folder of receipts for the past year and dumped them all over my desk.

Daniella

Luckily, Shelly was completely professional in taking my blood ten minutes after Shane had left me. I wasn't sure what he'd told her, but the woman smiled and told me she'd provide the results tomorrow. I really was grateful to get this out of the way.

About two hours after I'd taken a seat, Chad returned with my things, as promised. Although staying here was unorthodox, it helped me out. With the holidays, it would be nearly impossible to find a new apartment right now. After New Year's, the search would hopefully be easier. And since Eric had wiped out my savings, I was grateful to avoid wasting money on hotel rooms at holiday prices.

After another hour, Shane returned. I could tell in one glance he was none too happy to find me going through all the backup detail. But what did he expect? I was on the clock. Although I didn't know why he'd asked me here, I'd be damned if I wouldn't give this job my best. Which meant being thorough. Plus, if I was being honest, I was intrigued by a business such as this.

But at the moment, I was starving. Judging from the smell of whatever he was carrying, he'd at least brought lunch.

"Great. You brought food. I'm hungry."

"What are you doing? How did you get these?" He strode over, set the paper bag on the desk, and scanned my notes.

"I'm doing what you're paying me for."

"You haven't signed a disclosure yet. You can't look at all of this."

I slid the signed document in front of him. "Here. Max came up and gave it to me when he brought the receipts." Whereas Shane was closed off and hard to read, Max was friendly and helpful.

His gaze didn't leave mine. Irritation reflected in his eyes, most likely because I'd taken control by starting on the books without his permission. Oh, well, time to get the fuck over it.

"I didn't give the green light—"

I held up my hand. "No, you didn't. But looking at a trial balance and tax returns is not enough. I need the details in order to do a proper audit. Anyhow, if you want to eat lunch with me, you can tell me why it is you're losing revenue and could trigger an IRS audit if you report a loss. I'm all ears."

I hadn't set out to piss him off with my words, but the vision of the vein throbbing on the side of his head was pretty hot. So was his barely contained temper. I wasn't typically one to play with fire, but somehow Shane pushed all my buttons, including those I hadn't realized I owned.

"If I knew, I wouldn't have you here. The numbers can't be correct because our membership rates are up."

I lifted a brow, trying to ignore the masculine scent of him. A mixture of mint, body wash, and pure, virile male. "I'll focus on your costs, then. Maybe they've grown. How long has Eric done your books?" Although my ex was not trustworthy, I'd never known him to be a sloppy accountant.

He shook his head. "The last two years. I did them before that."

"Explain how the business works, according to the IRS. I mean, obviously, they don't know you're a sex club."

He sighed but took a seat while digging out the contents from the bag and handing over a cheesesteak. "Club Travesty is a bar and membership-only club. We operate as such."

"Then how do members pay for sex?"

He shook his head. "Careful, that would be illegal. Members do not pay for sex. They pay for a membership, which allows them certain perks. The sort of perks depends on the level of membership. We have everything from the basic level, which has been very popular over the last few years and is essentially sexual counseling, to what we call our boyfriend package, and on to the hard-core, dominant-submissive type of play."

"What is the boyfriend package?" Rather than wanting to know for tax purposes, I found myself fascinated.

"It's where women can take sexual lessons. Gain back their confidence or learn - "

"To have a proper orgasm?"

Suddenly I realized my interest was much more than just gaining a working knowledge of the club.

Chapter Eight

Shane

Her question wasn't glib; it was genuinely curious. It was a good thing I was seated as her simply mentioning an orgasm got me hard. "Yes."

She smiled. "You're like Robin Hood, then. Only instead of gold and coins to the poor and unfortunate, you're giving orgasms."

I threw my head back and laughed. "And I make a profit from it."

She frowned, and I realized I'd inadvertently implied she should've paid for it. I was about to clarify, but she lobbed her next question.

"Mostly women sign up for these services?"

"Yes. But we have other services which are nonsexual."

"Like what?"

"Sexual confidence counseling. We started it at Max's suggestion, and it's been really popular. However, we did have to fire the manager recently."

"For what?"

"Pushing some of the guys who only did counseling into more physical aspects. Unfortunately, we lost a couple good employees. Some women need a place to go to ask questions and discover or regain their mojo. It should be up to the two of them whether to make it physical or not."

"Is that why you did what you did in front of Eric? To help me regain my mojo?"

I swallowed hard, not wanting to analyze my motives or have her do so. "It pisses me off to have any woman told the problem is her. I especially didn't like the way he did it."

Our gazes locked until she finally looked away.

"I'll look to see if losing some employees and their clientele could be some explanation for the loss of revenue." She made a note. "And last night. The Christmas party. Is that a common thing to do?"

I was happy for the change in subject. "It was one of our VIP parties. On a typical night, we allow our VIPs to reserve those rooms for group play activities. These can range from private settings to the more public type that you witnessed."

"People enjoy having sex while others watch?"

A smile curved my lips as I thought about Ms. Proper in front of a crowd. "Absolutely. Others enjoy finding new partners or adding a plus one. You'd be surprised how many couples come in looking for a third party, simply to spice things up."

"Do you partake in these, uh, demonstrations?"

Although her question wasn't meant to be judgmental, I found myself defensive. "Upon occasion, yes."

But it wasn't judgment in her eyes; it was a heavy dose of lust. Interesting. I'd long ago learned the signs of a woman aroused, and Ms. Daniella Trivioli was just that.

"What types of things do you do?"

My gaze laser focused on hers. "The dirty kind. I

need to get back downstairs. Let me know if you have any questions on the receipts you're going through."

I abruptly got up. Daniella might not know it, but she was dangerous. She represented everything I didn't want. Strings, rebound, vanilla. Those were only a few of the terms I bounced around in my head as I took the stairs down to the main level. Besides, she was here to do a job, which didn't include fucking me—no matter how her eyes lit up at the possibility of me performing.

As I passed the bar, I motioned for Heather to follow me. Once we were alone, I made my request. "Tomorrow night. Eight o'clock, the large play room. Grab one of the other girls, too."

Her face showed surprise, but I could tell she was excited. Too bad my enthusiasm was less about Heather and the other girl and more about fucking the thought of Ms. Pencil Skirt from my mind.

Chapter Nine

Daniella

My neck and back were killing me. I'd spent the last ten hours combing through Club Travesty's tax returns and looking at the books. The man kept meticulous notes; I'd give him that. But the sound of my stomach growling had me checking the time. Shit. It was past six o'clock. Where the hell was Shane? After his abrupt exit, he hadn't come back.

Just as well. Once I got into numbers, it was tough for me to get out. But I felt like I had a firm start. Tomorrow I'd start to lay out my questions for him. Since I hadn't found anything obvious missing from his returns, I would need to audit his expenditures. Auditing was normally something I'd have an on-staff auditor do. But considering the nature of this club and maybe something I didn't want to admit—me wanting to spend more time with Shane—I wasn't about to pass off the assignment to someone else.

After rolling my neck, I grudgingly put on my heels again. About five hours ago, I'd kicked them off. In search of Shane or food or maybe both, I took the front stairs down into the club.

"Wait, Miss." Lance, the man whose job I'd saved, intercepted me once I was on the main floor. Taking my arm, he led me behind the bar.

"You can't go out onto the main floor or into the bar without a mask. Unless you want to chance being recognized."

Huh. It hadn't even crossed my mind. Grateful for his quick thinking, I smiled. "Thank you. I don't suppose someone has one I could borrow."

He looked awkward. "Uh, it would be easier if you went out the back towards the employee entrance."

"Oh. I was hoping you could tell me a good place to eat around here?"

"The bar has great food. Most of the staff eats from their menu. Let me show you to the employee break room where you can place an order."

Because he was here and I felt bad I'd almost gotten him fired, I decided to say something. "By the way. I'm sorry about the other night. I never meant—"

He cut me off with a rare smile. "It's already forgotten, Ms. Trivioli."

👁️ 👁️

I waited on my chef salad, trying my best not to gawk at the other people in the room. Most of them were gorgeous. The women, especially, were all made up and wore very little by way of clothing. Two of them were seated to my left, and I couldn't help overhearing.

"You're so lucky you're performing with Shane tomorrow night."

The blonde sighed. "More like he's performing with Heather, and I'm just along for the ride. But I'm hoping he'll let me suck that big cock of his."

I could feel my neck getting red. Jealousy wasn't an emotion with which I was familiar. Not even watching my fiancé last night have sex with other people had elicited such a response. Yet the thought of Shane with another woman was provoking a completely irrational dose of it. I shook off the crazy thought, grabbed my salad, and started to walk back upstairs. But not before snagging a menu of services.

I told myself I wanted to study the club's menu in order to follow the revenue streams more easily, but I found myself completely enthralled with the descriptions of the services offered.

As I ate my dinner, I realized I had never felt lonelier. Or more sexually frustrated. Not a great combination. Maybe it was time for a change.

Shane

I'd stayed away from Daniella yesterday evening. Pure self-preservation. The quick answer to my problem would be to fuck her brains out and get her out of my system. But there was no way I was crossing that line. Women like her belonged in the suburbs with a white picket fence, minivan, and Pinterest habit. Not in a sex club. So why had I ensured she came back?

The question wouldn't leave my mind as I walked into my spacious loft office early the next morning. She was already at my desk, working. I immediately noticed the dark circles under her eyes and wondered about the cause.

"Good morning. Merry Christmas Eve," she greeted casually.

"'Morning. And, uh, Merry Christmas. How did you sleep?"

She appeared startled by my question but sighed when she lifted her gaze to mine. "Not great, honestly."

"Was the bed not comfortable?"

"No, it wasn't that. Maybe it's the holidays. Do you have plans with family?"

I didn't like the reminder. "No. We'll be open tonight and tomorrow. But you're welcome to take tomorrow off if you want to spend the day with yours."

"My parents are on a cruise. But they'll probably call later."

"We could, uh, do dinner later if you want?" Shit. Where had that thought come from? I didn't do holidays, family, or dinner dates.

She looked pleasantly surprised and then confused. "Uh, I thought you were performing tonight."

"Not until eight. We could eat beforehand. Or not. It doesn't matter." I disliked being put on the spot and that she was privy to my plans.

"Sure, dinner before would be nice. Is your performance up for people to watch?"

"Yes, for members. That does not include you." I added the last part in case she got any ideas.

I could feel her eyes on me as I kept mine averted.

"Why not?"

"Because I said so."

A smile curved her lips. "Funny. I haven't heard such a lame excuse since I was a child and my Dad couldn't come up with a good reason to forbid something. Do you have an issue with me watching you perform?"

I spared a glance and shouldn't have. The twinkle in her eyes was disarming. "Don't cross me on this, Daniella. You're not sneaking down there tonight."

"Give me a good reason, and maybe I won't."

"Tell me what it is you want from going down on that floor to watch."

I witnessed the color stain her cheeks while her gaze reluctantly met mine. "I don't know. Maybe just to feel something similar to the other night when you touched me."

Although she wasn't trying to seduce me, I could feel an instant pull toward her. "You're rebounding."

She blew out a frustrated breath. "Can I be brutally honest with you?"

"Of course."

"I'm not. Not rebounding, that is. And the fact that I'm more upset about being duped over the money than about losing my fiancé is disconcerting."

Her candor was disarming. "I'm gonna ask the obvious. Did you love him?"

"I hate to admit I might not have. I think I loved the idea of him. We both worked long hours, we liked the same restaurants, we ran in the same circles. It was safe and easy. But the bottom line is that when I went searching for proof about the money and cheating, I hoped I would find it."

"You wanted a way out?"

"Yeah, and how fucked up is it that I didn't simply say so? But it was in my gut. It's like I knew I wasn't destined for him."

"Not for me to judge."

"You ever been in love?"

"Nope." It was the truth. I'd been in lust a time or two, but love I didn't have time for.

"Not even when you were younger?"

I shook my head. "I never wanted the commitment."

"Anyone ever fall in love with you?"

My face flinched, and I knew she saw it. "She was young and didn't know what love was."

"Wish I could use that excuse with Eric. How about just being old and stupid?"

"You're twenty-seven. Hardly old."

"How do you know how old I am?"

"Ran your background check. I also know you've never gotten a speeding ticket, broken a law, or had bad credit."

Instead of looking annoyed, like I expected, she laughed. "Great. I'm even more boring on paper."

She stood up, coming within a breath of me. "How old are you?"

I dipped my head, whispering in her ear and enjoying the way goosebumps appeared on her flesh. "Thirty-two."

Her face was upturned when I pulled back, eyes half closed with lust. She looked as though she expected me to crash my lips to hers. When I didn't, she blinked rapidly but didn't move away. "Are you thinking about kissing me?"

"I don't kiss."

"Too personal or too boring?"

"Probably both." Kissing was what people did who had feelings for one another. The last time I'd kissed a woman, she'd misconstrued the meaning. Never again. Now when I fucked women, there wasn't a lot of time for kissing. "And in your own words, you're not looking to slum it with a sex club owner."

She crinkled her adorable brow before stepping back, breaking the moment. "That's the second time you've implied I insulted you. How? When?"

She couldn't be serious. "You said clearly you weren't so pathetic as to throw yourself at the owner of a sex club."

Her mind looked like it was rewinding and then the light of recognition dawned in her eyes. "Right, I did. Because you could have any girl you wanted. So why would I throw myself at someone like that? Meaning I'd be pathetic if I did so. Jesus. You actually thought I'd be that self-righteous?"

"You wouldn't be the first."

Her expression softened. "I'm sorry if it came across that way. My intent was self-deprecation, not to insult you."

Damn. Now I felt like shit. "I apologize for the retort about you being vanilla."

"I believe you said I was too vanilla for you ever to be interested. Whereas my comment was a misunderstanding, I believe yours was the truth."

I pulled her close, watching as her eyes widened and her breath caught. "It wasn't the truth." I let her feel my cock hard against her in order to drive my point home. God, it would be so easy. So satisfying to sink deep inside of her. Which made it that much harder to say my next words.

"But this isn't your world, Daniella. What you need is a nice man who'll treat you well and give you two point five kids."

She pulled out of my embrace, smiling sadly before grabbing her purse. "What I need are less people thinking they know what I need. I think I'll pass on dinner tonight."

❧ ❧

I threw back the tumbler of whiskey and checked my watch. It was nearing my performance time, but I didn't feel the least bit into the thought of Heather and the other blonde—what was her name? Brandi. Damn, since when did the thought of two women leave me uninspired?

I was a complete and utter hypocrite. Even though I'd told Daniella that Club Travesty wasn't her world, I was the one who'd dragged her back into it. My reasons were purely selfish, and not entirely truthful that it had only been to do the club's books.

According to my security team, she'd returned an hour after departing and had been working upstairs. She'd probably been crying. Most likely embarrassed about having admitted she wanted to feel something more.

While walking upstairs, I tried to remind myself why I couldn't pull her into the bedroom and fuck her out of my system. That's really all it would take. One night, and I could stop obsessing about how her pussy had climaxed around my fingers. But doing so wouldn't be fair to her.

It wasn't as though I was averse to having regular sex in a bed. Ironically, the last time I'd had sex in an actual bed, I'd been twenty-two, in college, and fucking some coed who would've freaked if I'd suggested anything other than vanilla. Now I was contemplating the flavor because it had been so long I'd forgotten the taste.

God knew, I'd been involved in some kinky shit over the years. It all started when Max and I found Gloria at a bar while on vacation right after college. She was in her forties and beautiful, not in the classic sense like Daniella, but in the self-confident, sexual kind of way. And she'd introduced us to her club. Finally, we'd both felt free. Free from what society dictated, free from drunk, giggling girls at frat parties and stupid boys who didn't know how to get a woman off properly. Gloria had made sure learning to give women pleasure had been the first of her many lessons.

But now, ten years later and with the club consuming so much of my time, I found myself bored. Now that I'd been there and done most everything, I found my appetite changing. Unfortunately, it seemed to center around a certain feisty, redhead with gorgeous skin and blazing blue eyes.

When I saw she was no longer at the desk, I knocked on the bedroom door. Silence greeted me. I opened the door to find the room empty. Where the hell was she?

I turned to find Max coming off the elevator, smirking.

"Where's Daniella?"

"Not crying over your ass, that's for sure."

"What the hell is that supposed to mean?"

"It means she isn't the girl from your old neighborhood who flipped out on you and your mom because you took her out a couple of times."

I hated the reminder of Tina. She was a girl I'd met while visiting home. Though she had a rocking body, she'd gotten way too attached after a couple dates and a single night together. That mess was the reason I was now adamant about keeping things completely black and white with my partners.

"Where is she?"

"Partaking in some club activities."

Adrenaline coursed through me. I had to fight the urge to tear through each of the rooms looking for her. What the hell? This wasn't her.

"Relax, dude. She's doing the boyfriend experience with Javier. Although I was tempted to ask if she wanted it with me, I knew you'd flip out."

So much for being worried she'd get attached to me if we slept together. Obviously, that wasn't the case if she'd entertain sex with a stranger. I gritted my teeth. "What room?"

He quirked a brow. "Number five in about ten minutes. But what about your show tonight?"

Chapter Ten

Daniella

I'd be damned if I'd spend the night above a sex club, frustrated and feeling sorry for myself. Especially while Shane was downstairs partaking in a jolly Christmas Eve threesome. No, thank you. There was at least one bright spot, though. The test results revealed I was clean. Eric hadn't given me anything.

Although my little confession to Shane earlier about wanting to feel something hadn't embarrassed me, what I did hate was that he saw me the same boring way I saw myself. Practical, safe and completely uninspired. But the night he'd touched me, something had changed; a craving I hadn't known existed was now unleashed. I refused to put it back into a box. So it was with a mix of anxiety and excitement that I looked forward to the 'boyfriend experience.'

"Hi, honey, how you feeling?" Cindy, one of the girls who worked at the club, walked me down the corridor. She was beautiful, with long black hair and legs for miles. A stunning tattoo winding down one of her arms had me staring. I didn't mean to, but in my dull, corporate world, I didn't see women like her.

"Okay."

"You like the ink?"

"It's beautiful. Is it a serpent?"

"It is. And on this side is a mermaid." She showed me the underside of her arm, revealing a raven-haired mermaid with a gorgeous tail.

"Now, then, this will be your room. Javier is wonderful, so you'll be in good hands."

I took a deep breath. "I hope so."

She led me into a space which surprised me. It was a beautifully decorated room with a bed in the center and a gorgeous chandelier overhead. Opulent carpet had my shoes sinking into it. In addition to the bed, there was a small sofa next to a table with refreshments.

"Are you nervous?"

She seemed pure and honest, making me truthful in my reply. "Yes. Very."

"It's understandable, but I promise Javier will ease your worries. He's very easy to talk to." She suddenly grabbed her earpiece. "Sorry, hold on."

I watched curiously as she flicked her headset. "I'm on my way." To me, she added, "I'll be right back. Have some champagne and relax."

Sure. Easy for her to say. As soon as the door closed, I had to fight the urge to flee. I also was nervous Shane would find out about this and put a stop to it. But then again, he had a performance tonight. Most likely, he wouldn't notice where I was.

What in the hell was I doing? My subconscious answered, "Having long overdue, great sex." She was hard to argue with.

Cindy came back in with an apologetic smile. "Sorry about that. Javier requested I get you ready for him."

"Ready how?"

"You should disrobe. You mentioned you wanted something kinky in the profile sheet, so I'll use silk straps to tie you to the bed and a blindfold if that's okay."

I gulped. I had said I wanted something other than plain vanilla sex. But now the thought had me nervous. "Sure. But, um, but can you make sure I can get my hands out if I need to? I'm a bit apprehensive about that part."

She nodded. "Of course. It'll be our secret."

Once I stripped out of my dress and undergarments, I found Cindy appraising me with frank interest. "You're incredibly sexy."

"Um, thank you." I climbed on the bed and once again fought my nerves.

"Here, take this. It'll help." She held out the shot glass.

I sniffed the contents, immediately identifying tequila. Bottoms up.

"Good girl."

My body started to shake against my will as Cindy fastened the silken ties above my head. I was happy she did as promised, keeping them loose enough to get out.

"Relax," she cajoled. "I'm going to rub some oil on you. It's pleasure-point heating oil."

After she poured something from a small vial, I gasped when she rubbed her hands gently over my breasts, centering on my nipples. She next held it up over my pubic area.

"Just a gentle touch. You into girls, Daniella?"

I blushed. "No. I mean you're very beautiful, but no."

She swiped her finger over my clit, teased my lips, and then went down my slit before inserting that finger into her mouth. "Too bad because you taste amazing."

Holy shit. I might not be into women, but my body definitely responded to her sexy display.

"Now with the blindfold. Remember to lie back and relax. And don't be shy with what you want. This is your fantasy, after all."

Yes. Yes, it was. But with the wrong guy. I had to fight the urge to change my mind about this entire thing. It was now or never. By next week, I wouldn't have this opportunity.

"He's here."

I could hear the door open and shut. In that moment, I was very aware of being blindfolded.

"Okay. Um, I guess hi, Javier."

His gruff whisper came closer to me as did soft footsteps. "Hello, beautiful." It was strange how his voice seemed somewhat familiar despite the slight accent.

"Hi." My heart was pounding in my ears. "Sorry, I already said that. I'm nervous. This is the first time I've ever done something like this."

"I plan on taking good care of you."

There it was again. The eerie sensation that instead of the Spanish accent being slight, it was exaggerated. But turning to more pressing thoughts, I wondered what he thought of me on display for him. I wasn't a bombshell or anything and not very tall, but my cup size was decent, and I worked out and stayed in shape.

The oil started to heat. First I felt my nipples tingle, making them ache for someone to touch them. Then my center started pounding as if my heartbeat had replaced its location. "What is this stuff Cindy used on me?"

"It's made to stimulate your body. Now tell me, what is your fantasy?"

Shane. Thankfully, the thought stayed internal.

My mind must have been messing with me because suddenly I had a whiff of him. "Um. Something that isn't boring. Something that takes me out of my head."

"Do you have a man you're picturing?"

Was I that transparent? "Does it matter?"

"It does very much. This is where the blindfold

comes in. With it, you can pretend anything you want. Now then, I'll never touch you without permission. For every touch, I will ask you beforehand. Do you want to try masturbating first? I can untie your hand."

"No. I don't have much luck with that." And something about touching myself in front of a stranger didn't turn me on.

"I'm going to massage your foot. Is that okay?"

Nope, because all of a sudden I had the skin-prickling sensation of his voice being off. I'd not yet met Javier, but that rasp belonged to only one man.

"Actually, can you start with rubbing my temples? Just to relax my mind as it's working overtime." And I hoped the nearness would give me confirmation.

"Uh. Sure."

He moved closer and suddenly was in back of me, reaching over and massaging my head gently. The familiar scent of him filled my senses. But what if Javier used the same body wash or cologne as Shane?

"Talk to me," I requested, needing more.

"You're very beautiful like this, Daniella."

Click. The way he said my name upped the likelihood of it being Shane. I was half tempted to whip off my mask to confirm, but I wanted something first, so I decided to keep the ruse.

I sucked in a breath when his warm hands traveled down to my neck and arms.

"In case you aren't enjoying something I do, beautiful, I want you to think of a safe word."

Wow. I never thought someone in this lifetime would be asking me that particular question. "Um, how about Jingle Bells?" As soon as I'd blurted it out, I cringed. Could I be any lamer with my safe words?

"Why that?"

Of course he would ask. "I don't know. Maybe because it's Christmas Eve. I can come up with another one."

"No. Jingle Bells it is. I'm going to move down to your legs. As I get closer to your pussy, I want you to tell me green, yellow, or red. Use your safe word if you have to, which means the same thing as red."

Somehow, I thought shouting, 'Green, Green, Green' might be an instant giveaway, so I simply said, "Okay." I forced myself to relax as his hands worked up to my calves and then concentrated on my knees. But when he stroked my thighs, I shivered, anxious for more.

"Do you want me to taste you?"

"Yes, but kiss me first." I could sense his hesitation. This had to be Shane.

"On the lips?"

"Mm-hm. It's part of my fantasy."

He moved, and I could sense him above me. His lips took mine tentatively at first.

Since I could no longer help myself, I wiggled the one hand out of my restraint and wove it into his hair, pulling him deeper. The moment his tongue entered my mouth, I sucked on it, enjoying the groan emanating from his chest.

Our tongues mated, his teeth nipped, and then his mouth traveled south. He lavished attention on each breast before kissing down my stomach, hips, and then to where I practically ached for him.

I could feel his weight shift to the bed before he pushed my heels back so my legs were spread at bended knee. While he kissed my inner thighs, my legs started to shake with anticipation. His scruff running along my tender flesh had me wanting badly to flip off the mask and see his face.

At the first swipe of his tongue over my clit, I about bucked off the bed. "Jesus."

"I've been waiting to taste you."

And just like that, he dove in. Not in a way which

said, hey, I'm getting to know your body, or maybe I'll tease you a bit first. But in the way that demonstrated a carnal appetite, not to mention a clear adeptness at the task. Lips, tongue, and teeth all worked together on my center of nerves to have blood roaring to my ears and then send me over the edge in seconds.

"Again," he murmured before I could recover. By adding his fingers curled up inside of me to the knuckle, he took me to the next level, one I hadn't known existed.

The one where he began fucking me with his tongue while his thumb focused on my pleasure point.

It was almost too much, this tension coiled through my body that wasn't getting a break. My mind scrambled as I was obliterated with such force that a half scream tore from my throat.

"Fuck. You come spectacularly."

The fake Javier had forgotten his accent that time.

"Must be you, Javier." I couldn't help but mess with him, wondering if he planned on giving up his disguise. I wasn't disappointed.

He climbed on the bed, his erection at my entrance, and whipped off my mask.

Time stood still and the air sizzled between us with his eyes locked on mine. A smirk came over my face while irritation took over his.

"How long did you know?"

"Long enough."

"Before the kiss?"

"Hey, you hijacked my fantasy, which included kissing. You're lucky I'm not pissed you're not Javier."

"You're lucky it wasn't him. What the hell were you thinking?"

Seriously, he was lecturing me with him on the precipice of penetration? I shifted my hips to remind him of exactly where we were. "Green, Shane."

"Fuck." He thrust into me deep on one stroke, filling

me completely and holding himself still.

"Kiss me again." I leaned up, pausing a millimeter away from his lips, pleasantly amazed when he framed my face.

"Last one."

Could I help the moment of triumph? "Guess you'd better make it good, then."

He possessed my mouth while I released my second hand allowing me to move both down to grip his ass, pulling him deeper inside of me.

His tongue warred with mine. I became uninhibited in what I was taking or past the point of caring if he had set a time limit to this final kiss.

He wasn't gentle, but he wasn't overly harsh. Instead, he wavered between the two. A bite, a soft suck to soothe. And I was lost. Lost in this exquisite torture as he pumped in and out of me.

"Oh, God." I could feel it building. I closed my eyes, overwhelmed with desire.

"Open them," he demanded.

"I'm going to come."

"Look at me when you do. Don't you dare close them."

Considering he was a man who didn't want the intimacy of a kiss, having an orgasm while staring deeply into his eyes wasn't exactly impersonal. In fact, I'd never experienced anything more personal.

"Fuck," he muttered, shifting his hands to lift up my lower body. This primed it for his delicious assault of stroking my G-spot over and over until he ground out his own climax.

Shane

Fuck was right. As in I was royally fucked that I'd let

go of my boundaries with this woman. And yet I hadn't been able to help myself. The sweet taste of her lips and the surprising talent of her tongue were like a drug. If I wasn't careful, I'd become addicted.

I told myself this was only to give her the 'fantasy.' That it was a one-time thing. But as her tight cunt squeezed my cock with her orgasm, I knew one time wouldn't nearly be enough.

"You okay?" I was slick with sweat and not nearly done with her.

She unclasped her sexy legs from around my waist, allowing me to pull out.

After standing up, I disposed of the condom in the cleverly hidden trash receptacle beside the bed. I then found her eyes traveling up and down my body.

"You're gorgeous," she blurted as though unable to help herself.

"I'm glad you like what you see. Now turn over."

She raised a brow. Just when I thought she'd have a saucy reply, she instead flipped over onto her stomach, allowing me a perfect view of her heart-shaped ass.

"By the way, what happened to Javier?"

I laughed that she was just now asking. "I intercepted him and told him about the change of plans."

"I thought you had a show to do tonight."

"Max is happily filling in." I didn't want to go into why I didn't want Javier to see her like this. Touch her. Be with her. I realized the double standard as I'd been about to perform with other women.

My hands massaged her cheeks first. I enjoyed the moan of ecstasy I got when I moved the pressure to her lower back. Trailing my hand down, I played with her pussy, enjoying the slick view of it from this angle. "I wonder how far you'd have let Javier get."

"Mm, guess we'll never know."

"I think he was put out when I told him I was keeping

you all to myself."

She turned so she could look at me and asked the question I was dreading. "Ah, but for how long?"

"I don't want you getting attached." It was important to me to be very clear. I didn't want a relationship. Even more critical was her comprehension of that.

Fire erupted in her eyes as I knew it would. "Maybe it's you who will get attached. Why do you assume it would be—? Oh—Oh—God, wh-what are you doing?"

I'd trailed my finger up, circling her back entrance before dipping it inside, using some of her own arousal to ease the entry. Christ, I was getting hard for her all over again.

"Has anyone had you here before?"

"No. But you're deflecting from—Wow."

I slid the fingers from my other hand into her slick heat, filling her both ways and working her gently where she'd never been touched.

"Do you like me playing with your ass, Daniella?" I added a finger, stretching her tight hole and feeling her legs start to quake. When was the last time I'd had someone innocent enough to be completely unguarded in their reaction?

"Yes."

"Say it."

She mumbled a curse before finally finding the words. "I like you—playing with my ass."

"Come for me you, dirty girl. Come hard." After curling my fingers up into her pussy while pumping her ass, I was rewarded with a gush that even took me off guard. Holy shit, my girl could come.

Now where the fuck had that dangerous thought come from? But before I could analyze it, she'd sat up. She slid so she was on the edge of the bed, legs spread around the outside of my thighs and face flushed from the orgasm I'd given her.

"What else is your fantasy for one night?" I murmured the words, wanting to give her the best time of her life.

"You. Everywhere. In my mouth, in my pussy, and in my ass."

I froze. How did a girl go from not getting a proper orgasm to wanting me to fuck her in every possible place? "Jesus."

She nipped at my ear. "Don't tell me I've shocked you?"

"A little surprised, that's all. But I'd hurt you if I had your ass tonight. You need to be prepped properly for your first time." I might not be an overly sensitive lover, but I wasn't completely without regard for my partner and her well-being.

She slid down off the table and onto her knees, taking a hold of my length. "Then just the other two."

Holy fuck. Who was this insatiable creature in front of me?

Chapter Eleven

Daniella

I'm not sure what had come over me, but I was suddenly a woman starved at a time-limited, all-you can-eat buffet. And I was getting my money's worth. Which was a really shitty metaphor since it made Shane a hooker. I guessed he wouldn't appreciate that, but I simply couldn't get enough.

I concentrated on the fully erect—Wowsers, that was a great cock in front of me. Thick, long, hard, and standing at attention as though he hadn't fucked me senseless just moments ago. And the body it belonged to. Holy hell. Like a sinful dream, he was cut and corded in muscles in all the right places.

He looked a bit taken aback that I'd dropped to my knees. I enjoyed putting that look on his face. The look which said *holy shit what is this woman doing to me*. Yes, indeed. I planned for him to wear that expression the rest of the evening.

After licking the pre-cum from the tip, I teased it for a moment before swallowing him whole to the back of my throat. I might not have a lot of talent or experience in the bedroom, but I'd discovered something when going down on my first guy in college. I'd been blessed by the blow job gods with no gag reflex.

"Christ, Daniella."

It was music to my ears to hear a man like Shane say those words as if he couldn't help himself. "Mmm," I hummed, using my tongue to lubricate him while I gripped his base and then eased to the tip before swallowing him down again.

"Fuuuuuuuuuuck."

Sucking the tip, I gave him a few pumps with my hand. "Am I doing something you don't like?"

He grinned and looked down, appearing half stunned and half amused. "Not even close, sweetheart. But here I thought I'd have to give you tips or something. I was very wrong."

After teasing the crown and mouthing the head, I took him back down, forcing myself to breathe through my nose and relaxing my throat all the way. Gripping his impressively muscled ass, I bobbed on his length for a moment before realizing he was hesitating.

"Fuck my mouth, Shane." Which kind of came out garbled because, you know—dick in my mouth and all. But he'd understood it enough to grip my hair and start to thrust.

"You're gonna make me come. Tap me now if you don't want it deep."

The fact he was considerate enough to warn me made me want him even more. And when the first drop of salty cum hit my tongue, I found myself greedy for the taste. Greedy to swallow it all down. I capped it off with a slow lick from his base to the tip to ensure I got every last drop.

I looked up to see his shocked face.

"Where did you learn to do that?"

Smirking, I rose to my feet with a hand from him and then shrugged. "No gag reflex wasn't really learned, but it does seem to get the boys excited."

It was meant as a joke, but given the way his eyes darkened and the scowl etched on his face, I knew he wasn't taking it as such. Then it was his turn to shock me when he gripped my hair and put his fingers back inside of me.

"You shouldn't be thinking about anyone but me," he growled in my ear and proceeded to kiss down the column of my neck.

His possessive tone surprised me but not as much as it turned me on. "Then make sure I don't."

〜 〜

Shane

As a rule, I didn't sleep with a woman. As in fall asleep, cuddle, or stay until morning. Which is why it felt foreign to wake up with Daniella curled up next to me, her head on my chest, hair splayed over my shoulder, and legs entwined with mine. I told myself it was out of consideration that I didn't wake her right away. In truth, I knew the moment I left this bed, whatever magic had started last night and bled into the wee hours would be gone.

One night. It's what I'd been willing to give, and what she'd been willing to settle for. So then, why was I hesitating in getting up?

Extricating myself slowly, I moved from the bed and stood at the side looking down at her. She was stunning, with her flawless skin and beautiful lashes which framed the prettiest blue eyes I'd ever seen. And her entirely fuckable naked body was doing nothing for the little bit of resolve I still had to keep things at one night. I wanted more than anything to slide into her warmth and bring her to climax all over again.

I pulled on my slacks before I could give in to the

temptation, telling myself I was doing the right thing. Since the cleaning crew would be coming in bright and early, I couldn't leave her in one of the sex rooms to wake up. So I slipped on my shirt and shoes, gathered her things, and settled on simply wrapping her in a sheet.

There probably wouldn't be anyone about this time of morning, especially on Christmas Day, but I didn't want to take any chances.

She hardly stirred in my arms when I gathered her to me and lifted her off the bed. Earlier, she'd practically passed out after I'd fucked her into so many orgasms I'd lost count. God, this girl could come. Her body was a treasure chest of ways to make her climax.

I carried her out the door and down the hall to the elevator, not passing a single person yet knowing it was all on the security cam. Not that my guys would ever let on. Discretion was our business.

After taking her up to the bed, I set her gently in the middle of it, sighing with regret at letting her go. She stirred slightly but then curled up under the warmth of the blankets.

I had to fight the physical temptation to join her. The only thing that kept me from doing so was the fear that I'd send the wrong message—in neon.

മ ഏ

I slept a couple of hours at my loft apartment a few blocks away before returning to the club. Luckily, I didn't need a lot of sleep to operate. Just some coffee, of which I grabbed a cup for Daniella, too. I was hoping to cut the awkwardness I was sure would be present this morning when I first saw her.

Scenarios floated through my head about how it would go, but ultimately, I knew if she brought up wanting another night, I'd have to let her down easy.

But when I went up the stairs, instead of finding her alone and waiting on me, I saw she had her suitcase in hand and was smiling up at Max.

Chapter Twelve

Daniella

I woke up in bed wondering how the hell I'd gotten there. At least it was still on the early side. If the lack of clothing didn't tip me off that my night with Shane had been real, then the fact I was sore pretty much everywhere confirmed it.

I got up, showered, and pulled myself together. I couldn't help grinning at the way my night had turned out. But then reality set in. At least a week's worth of work remained where I had to be around the man. Taking a deep breath, I resolved not to be weird or clingy. I'd had a night I'd never forget. In fact, I wondered if any other man would be able to measure up to the experience. But the time to dwell on that fear would be later, once I was out of Shane's world and didn't have to see him every day.

Since I was hoping there would be availability in the hotel next door, I called and was happy to snag an open room. So the first order of business was to pack my things and get my own space. As I lugged my suitcase out to the office, I felt lucky to find Max there, sipping coffee at his desk.

"Where ya going?"

"Next door to the hotel."

He arched a brow. "Shane know?"

My face scrunched up, expressing my confusion as to why it would matter. "It was the plan all along."

He relaxed some and got to his feet, giving me his trademark grin. "All right. Let me help you."

"What in the hell is going on here?"

Shane's tone and appearance had me at a loss for words.

Luckily, Max didn't have the same trouble. "Daniella is moving next door to the hotel. Why don't I go get you checked in and, uh, give you two some privacy?"

Shane simply stood there staring at me until Max disappeared into the elevator heading down. "Why are you moving out?"

"We agreed. The hotel had an opening today. And I thought to give you your room back."

He moved closer, stopping only a breath away from me. "And it has nothing to do with last night?"

"No, why would it?" I hated the fact my voice went down to an involuntary whisper.

"Not very convincing." His voice was husky, his eyes intense.

I took a deep breath, far too affected by his presence for my health. This only emphasized why I needed my own space. "It was the original plan, and after last night, I think it might be better to have a separation."

He lifted a brow. "Are you still okay with working here?"

"Of course."

My conviction must've rung true as he stepped back. "Okay. Good. How's it going so far?"

I tried not to take it personally that he might be anxious to be rid of me. "All right. I plan on working every day until the New Year except for Sunday. I have a wedding to attend."

The wedding was for my cousin, who happened to be marrying Eric's former roommate. Although the last thing I wanted was to see Eric in a social setting, I'd already sent an RSVP and felt an obligation to go. Wasn't like it was their fault my ex-fiancé was a douche bag.

Shane and I both turned when Heather came up the stairs, calling out. It was a simple reminder that we were never alone in this space.

"Hey, Shane. Oh, hi. You're not alone. I can come back."

He frowned. "No, it's fine. You've met Daniella, right?"

She gave me a half-assed smile. Upon meeting me yesterday, she hadn't been overly friendly. Obviously, that didn't change even in her boss's presence.

"Yep, we met. You have a minute?"

Damn. I was being dismissed. "Uh, I can come back."

"No, stay. We'll go." He moved towards Heather.

I heard her ask in a voice that was unmistakably meant to be overheard, "Do we have a raincheck for tonight, lover?"

Damn. Perhaps it was time to work extra hours to get done with this job because, now that we'd been together, the thought of Shane with anyone else made my stomach turn.

❧ ❧

It was after nine o'clock at night on Christmas Day, but still I worked. I was determined to get through my first two years of an audit that would go back a total of five. The good news was it was all reconciling. The bad news was that I wasn't sure my work was the only reason I was here so late. Sure, I was known to work long hours, but I admitted to myself I was still here tonight out of morbid curiosity. I wanted to see if Shane would be partaking in the night's show.

I hadn't seen him during the remainder of the day. Although Max had long ago given me the key to my hotel room next door, I hadn't moved from my spot at the desk. The exception was a late lunch, when I couldn't ignore the hunger pains any longer and had taken a break to grab a burger from the bar.

Unable to stand the uncertainty of whether or not Shane was down below in one of the playrooms, I shut my laptop down and put everything in my bag. This way if I did see him, I could leave quickly. Taking a deep breath, I went over to the door that I assumed led to the viewing room where one could see down below. I don't know if I was relieved or not when the handle turned, allowing me access.

A quick glance showed me the room was empty. The couch and two chairs made it the perfect 'box suite' to watch all of the action below. I stepped close to the glass and glanced down. There were quite a few people, although nothing close to how many had attended the Christmas party.

My breath caught at the sight of a very well-muscled man standing naked in the center of the room. There were two women placed on their knees: one in front of him, her hand wrapped around his massive erection and one in back, kneading and kissing his firm buttocks. Surely she wasn't going to— Holy shit. She was. Both women literally dove into their front and back door tasks while the man threw back his head in complete ecstasy.

"Do you like to watch, Daniella?"

Jesus. I nearly jumped out of my skin at the sound of Shane's voice. When I attempted to turn, he wasn't having it.

"Face forward and tell me."

I licked my lips. "I find myself fascinated with it all."

His breath came at my neck, and I had to resist the urge to turn around and throw myself on him.

"Why did you come in here tonight?"

I didn't bother to lie. "I wondered if you would be down there."

"If I had been, would you have stayed to watch me?"

"No."

His fingers undid my bun, letting my hair fall down my back. "Does this turn you on, to watch the man down there with two women on their knees pleasuring him?"

"With you here, yes."

"Put your hands up against the glass."

"What?" I attempted to turn around, only to have his hard body crowd my space.

"I said, place your hands on the glass. And spread your legs."

My shaking hands took purchase on the window while I widened my stance slightly, wondering what in the hell he had planned. Unable to help myself, I asked, "What are you doing?"

A shudder ran through my body when his hands cupped my backside.

"Admiring your black dress and the way it hugs your curves."

"I thought the agreement was only last night." Not that I was complaining, but my mind struggled to keep up with both my body's agenda and now his.

"What if we said twenty-four hours instead?" His fingers had slipped between my legs and under the crotch of my panties.

"Yes. Twenty-four hours." Although, technically, it was past that. I cursed my stupid brain for numbers and told it to shut the hell up.

"You're so wet. Were you this way while watching

Philip below?"

"No. Only once I heard your voice."

"Good girl."

A sharp tug and the sound of material ripping meant I was rid of my thong.

"I want you to watch the show while I fuck you."

My eyes, which had been closed, focused back on the scene in front of me. The players had now moved to the bed where Philip had one woman riding him while the other literally sat on his face. "Shane." I moaned his name when fingers entered me. I could hear the sound of a package being ripped open and soon after was practically lifted up when he entered me on one stroke.

"You're tight. You're not too sore, are you?" He hesitated, clearly waiting to thrust again.

Although I was a little tender, there was no way I was stopping now. "That ship has sailed. Fuck me."

He gripped my hair and pulled out only to slam back in. "Like this? Tell me if this is too rough."

"No, it's not. God." He set a furious pace and, as I started to build, he reached around to rub my clit. The orgasm hit me like a freight train. A string of unintelligible words ripped from my throat as the rush started at my toes and didn't seem to be stopping. Because neither was Shane.

"I can't," I mumbled, losing any strength I'd had in bracing myself against the glass. Boneless, I allowed him to turn me around, lift me up, and push my entire back flush with the wall before entering me again. My hands gripped his powerful shoulders while my legs wrapped around him. If I'd had a brain cell to spare, I would've marveled at the fact he could hold me up as though I was nothing. But I was too lost in the pleasure to think.

"Yes. Right there." He'd found the spot and increased the pace until I was coming spectacularly, raking my nails over his back while he buried himself deep and growled in my ear.

"Your pussy is like a vice grip demanding I come with you."

"Mm. I quite like that."

He walked me over to the couch and, after pulling out, let me down easy. I watched while he expertly removed the condom and tied it off. He put it into a small trash can over by the bar area to one side.

"You're welcome to spend the night in your room here."

"Are you spending it with me?" The question was part curious, part challenge.

He came over and helped me up, his arm banding around my waist, eyes on mine. "It wouldn't be a good idea."

"No. I suppose not. Good night, then."

"Good night."

And yet he didn't move. Neither did I. The temptation to lean in to kiss him was so strong I swore he could actually read my mind because he stepped back. "I'll walk you out."

The gesture surprised me, but I was grateful he led the way down the stairs and out the employee entrance to the hotel lobby next door.

"What room are you in?"

I fished the card from my bag with the number on it. "It's on the eleventh floor. Eleven fifteen."

He didn't hesitate to put his hand at the small of my back and lead me into the elevator, pressing my floor. I turned to him once the doors closed. "You don't have to see me up."

"I know." His handsome poker face gave nothing away.

We walked down the hall in silence until we reached my number. I swiped my key and opened the door to a beautiful junior suite with my suitcase in the quaint seating area.

He came in and glanced around. "I hope everything is to your liking."

I nodded. "It's nice, although you didn't have to spring for a suite."

"It wasn't me; it was Max."

"Oh." Awkward.

"So, uh, I'll see you in the morning." Suddenly, he appeared anxious to leave.

"Yep. I finished two years' worth today and will start again tomorrow." I wasn't sure why I felt this was the moment to tell him what my work plan was, but it came out before I could help myself. Perhaps it was to serve as a reminder of why I was really here.

He moved towards the door. "Great. Uh. Merry Christmas."

Yeah. Merry Christmas. It had certainly been a strange one.

Chapter Thirteen

Shane

I don't know what I'd been thinking tonight except I that had to have her. Had to possess her the moment I saw her at the window looking down at the scene with wide eyes. Then it had gotten awkward, with me taking her up to her hotel room only to say goodnight.

There'd been something about her curiosity regarding what was happening in the rooms and then her honesty about being turned on the moment I'd stepped behind her. But I was flirting with a dangerous line. Hell, using the excuse of twenty-four hours had been a flimsy one. As a result, instead of quelling my desire for her, I'd kicked it up another notch.

But tomorrow was a new day and a new resolve. I was a man of discipline, so keeping Daniella at arm's length shouldn't be a problem.

Until I walked in the next morning to see her in a fire-engine red dress, librarian glasses, and an infuriatingly sexy updo that made me want to rip it out and run my fingers through it.

She looked up smiling. "Oh, good. You're here. I need to ask you some questions about the bar inventory.

I don't have all of the receipts."

"You can talk to Heather about anything you need regarding the bar." I regretted my gruff tone the minute her smile disappeared.

"Okay. Will do." She went back to the laptop, ready to ignore me.

"How many more days do you think you'll be here?"

She glared at me before standing up, clear annoyance in her body language. "I'm working as fast as I can, twelve-hour days. I estimate I'll be done by the beginning of next week, although if you're thinking I'm not working fast enough, then by all means, I'll pack my shit and go."

That fire was the undoing of everything I'd convinced myself last night should hold true. "I wasn't criticizing your work ethic."

"Then what?"

Chad the bouncer's voice broke the moment. He'd apparently come up the stairs behind me. "Boss, we have a situation with one of the deliveries out back."

"I'll be there in a minute." I heard his retreating footsteps and closed the gap between Daniella and me in two strides. I cupped her face. "We'll talk later."

"About what?"

I smirked, a litany of dirty thoughts running through my head. "About you taking off your panties and working here all morning while I think about your bare pussy under your dress and prepare to take a long lunch when I can fuck you."

Her breath caught, and I could see the arousal reflected in her expression. So her words took me off guard. "Twenty-four hours is up."

I stroked her face. "Guess we'll have to negotiate something else, then."

⋘ ⋙

Daniella

It was nearly two hours after Shane had said he wanted to negotiate something else, and I sat at my desk staring unseeingly at my computer screen. I didn't know whether his arrogance was a turn-on or an irritation. If I was being honest with myself, it was a bit of both. The moment he'd walked in this morning, my body, the traitor it was becoming, had reacted to him. Then he'd been a dick, but instead of turning me off, it had only upped the ante.

Even I wasn't fool enough not to recognize I was out of my depth with a man like Shane. This was why I was adamant I not become anxious for his affection. I had more self-respect than that. Not to mention that as good as it felt to be with him, I couldn't help challenging him.

But then he'd gone and thrown me for a loop by saying we would be negotiating something else. Why? It was the first question that came to mind. In a world where he could go downstairs and have any woman he wanted, women with far more experience and who were far more sexy, why did he want me? I wasn't the insecure type, but I was logical in asking the obvious question.

Annoyed at myself at losing time over the distraction and the anticipation of Shane's return, I jumped when Max's question brought me out of my thoughts.

"How's it going, Daniella?"

"Good. Although I need to go talk to Heather about the bar inventory, unless you think you can help." I was hopeful he could assist me with avoiding her.

He grinned. "Afraid not. But Heather is pretty on top of things. She should be able to answer all your questions."

"I'll go down there in a bit."

"Psyching yourself up for it?"

I had to laugh. "She doesn't care for me, and I have no clue why, so, yeah."

He quirked a brow. "You don't know why?"

"And you do?"

He chuckled. "Let's just say Heather has long had a thing for Shane even though she's tried to hide that it's anything more than physical. And him standing her up the other night in order to be with you didn't win you any favors."

Ah. "Wait, but she was with you. Isn't that, uh, offensive?"

Now he was really grinning. "I don't take offense at much."

He must not.

"And good luck with Heather."

◈ ◈

I decided not to put off inquiring about the receipts any longer. I went downstairs to find the long-time bar manager. She was doing inventory in the back with two other guys who were helping her move some things.

"Hey, Heather," I said from the doorway.

She turned at the sound of my voice and then went back to her task without so much as a smile or a welcome.

"Shane said you would have the detailed bar records from the last few years."

That got her attention and earned me a glare. "What of it?"

"As you're probably aware, I'm doing an audit of the last five years. In order to do that, I need to go through the ledger and all the receipts."

"I keep meticulous records."

"Great. If you could give me the last five years, I'll be able to complete the audit on the bar."

Her eyes raked over me from head to toe, a less-than-nice smirk on her face. "You do realize you're only a fad to him, right?"

I checked my temper and tried not to look around at the two guys who were obviously watching our exchange. "I'm only here speaking with you about the receipts, not asking for unsolicited advice."

"It wasn't advice, honey. It's a warning. Shane doesn't get attached. You're just a new piece of ass for a short time before he goes back to what he knows."

Implying her. "Then think of it as incentive to get me the receipts quickly. Because the quicker I have them, the faster I finish and the faster I'm gone."

With those parting words, I turned on my heel.

Chapter Fourteen

Shane

In a place like this, the rumor mill runs rampant. That's why I waited until later that evening to approach Daniella. Somehow I knew I wouldn't find her in the best of moods after the exchange with Heather I'd heard about. What I found most impressive was how Daniella had kept her cool with Heather.

I found her poring over her notebook, an adorable little frown on her face as she crunched the numbers with a pen between her lips.

"You trying to get out of here sooner by working late nights?"

She glanced up and then back toward her book. "Considering how often people keep asking when I'm leaving, I'd say it's in everyone's interest to get this done quickly."

"Not everyone. Did you lose the panties?" If I was a betting man, I'd say she absolutely hadn't.

"What do you think?" She finally put down her pen, stood up, and focused fully on me.

I walked towards her, stopping a breath away from her. "I think if I were to reach up under your dress, I'd find cotton."

She smirked. "Satin, but yes."

"Ah, but the question is would it be wet?"

"What are we doing, Shane?"

This wasn't a question I was familiar with hearing, let alone answering. But then again, Daniella was the type of woman I was normally avoided. Yet here I was, about to step into dangerous territory. "Redefining our timeframe." I brushed my fingertips down the column of her neck, feeling her shiver at my touch.

"To what end?"

This was the part about which I needed to be absolutely clear. Not only did I want to ensure things didn't get messy, but I also wasn't a complete asshole and didn't want to give her the wrong impression. I'd made that mistake when I was younger and hurt someone who'd fancied herself in love with me. "The same end it would have been if this was still yesterday morning."

She sucked in a breath when my hand moved up her dress, stroking her inner thigh. "I think I'm having déjà vu from our first time."

I smiled in remembrance, brushing my knuckle over the soaked material. "I do believe I was behind you, loving the way your ass fit perfectly against me."

She leaned in. "Does this new arrangement include kissing?"

I shook my head, partly regretful because she was a great kisser.

"Too intimate?"

"I don't want any misunderstandings. This isn't a relationship, a start of one, or anything resembling one."

"Thank fuck, because the last thing I want is another one right now."

I threw my head back and laughed at her unexpected words. Then I got serious, cupping her chin. "What do you want, then?"

She smiled. "You. And although I'm okay with the no kissing, I'm not okay with sharing."

"Monogamy without kissing. That's a new one."

Her gasp was like music to my ears when I moved her thong to the side and plunged a finger deep inside of her.

"Think of it as short-term exclusivity. I realize in your position that might make things difficult, but oh—oh, God."

I didn't let her finish her thought, instead curling my fingers up and bringing her to orgasm, loving the rush of wetness coating my fingers and running down her thighs.

"Now, what were you saying?"

"I—Jesus. I can't even remember my own name at the moment."

A satisfied smile curved my lips. "I'll agree to only you and me for the short term. Considering everything I have planned, neither of us would have time for anyone else."

"Mm, 'kay."

I grinned at her post-orgasmic answer, walked her into the bedroom, and made quick work of having her naked and writhing beneath me under the tutelage of my fingers. But I wasn't done by a mile, choosing to go south and stay there for the next thirty minutes until I brought her orgasm count to five.

"I can't. I can't possibly have any more," she panted.

I swiped at her clit again with my tongue before relenting and kissing up her flat stomach, marveling at how soft her skin was.

"I bet you can because I'm not even close to being done."

❧ ❦

Daniella

The next morning I awoke naked and alone with one thought.

Jesus, the man had stamina.

Not to mention a very sophisticated skill set regarding bringing a woman to orgasm. When he'd said he wasn't close to being done, it turned out he was a man of his word. Even after fucking me doggy style until I collapsed into a heap on the bed, unable to support myself any longer, he hadn't been finished. He'd then positioned me on top of him, my back to his front, and strummed me like a cello while he continued to thrust into me from below. Although I normally had a head for numbers, I couldn't keep track of the tally of orgasms he'd given me over the hours.

Yes. Hours. That much I'd learned from looking at the clock once I'd collapsed, completely spent. As much as I knew it would be most prudent to return to my hotel room to sleep, I could hardly move and had fallen asleep where I lay.

Without another choice now that it was morning, I donned the dress I'd worn yesterday. I slipped out to find Max eating cereal at his desk.

He looked up with a smirk. "Walk of shame?"

I quirked a brow. "I have nothing to feel ashamed about, so no."

He grinned. "Atta girl. You want some Lucky Charms?"

I laughed. "No, thank you. Uh, I guess have a good night."

"More like morning. It's five o'clock."

I yawned as if on cue. "Damn. Guess I'll see you in a couple hours."

"See ya then."

Shit. I'd overslept. Was it any wonder, though? I slipped out of bed sore yet at the same time very satisfied. I took a quick shower, put my hair up in a high ponytail, and settled for a simple blue shift dress.

Since I was already running late, I took an extra ten minutes to grab coffee before walking next door. It wasn't like I had an actual start time, although pushing ten o'clock in the morning seemed late for any work day.

I had just sat down at Shane's desk when I heard the footsteps on the stairs. I looked up to see him looking absolutely drool worthy in a dark gray suit with a black tie on a crisp white shirt.

"You're late."

I took a sip of coffee, defiance emanating in my slow drink. "I was unaware we set a start time."

He moved closer, stopping on the other side of the desk and leaning in so I could smell him. Damn. I already craved him again. His suit wasn't helping. I wanted to rip it off.

"Why are you late?"

I wasn't about to let him have the satisfaction of telling him he'd worn me out last night. "Long line at Starbucks."

He grinned and then straightened, taking something out of his pocket. "Stand up and bend over the desk."

"Pardon?" He couldn't mean here and now, could he?

"I'm pretty sure you heard me, Dani. If you expect me to take your ass, we need to work you in."

Shane

Despite the shock evident on her beautiful face with her wide eyes and parted lips, I could spot the tell-tale

85

signs of arousal my blunt words had produced by the pink on her cheeks and her quickened breath.

Considering I'd left her with reluctance in the wee hours, I was now unable to resist touching her a moment longer. I moved behind her and coaxed her to a standing position. Banding my arm around her waist, I breathed in her ear and enjoyed the shiver caused by my words.

"Put your hands on the desk and bend over."

"But anyone could come up here." Her protest came at the same time as her compliance.

"Then we need to be quick." My hand snaked up her dress, only to come in contact with her thong. "From now on, no panties while you're working here. Every morning and every lunch hour, I'm going to bend you over and ah— You're so fucking wet for me, aren't you?"

Her breath caught at the sweet intrusion of my fingers. I would never tire of the way she responded to me. Like it was the first time every time.

"You do seem to have that effect on me."

I trailed the pad of my thumb over her most sensitive spot, so very tempted to give her what her body craved, but she was right. Anyone could come up at any time, and I knew Daniella would be mortified if we were caught. Which meant I had limited time. I took the cylinder butt plug out of my pocket and loved the fact I wouldn't need the lube. Instead, I slid it into her heat.

"Holy shit. What is that?"

I pulled it out of her pussy and slid it backward, setting it in place in her pucker and gently pushing it in. "It's the smallest size plug. You'll wear it until this afternoon and then I'll take it out. Tomorrow, we'll do it with one that's larger."

"It feels strange. How am I supposed to sit down?"

I chuckled, removing my hand. "You'll manage."

She straightened up and turned with temper written

all over her expression. "That's it? You're just going to tease me and leave me with this?"

"Indeed I am. And don't even think about touching yourself."

She rolled her eyes. "As if that's ever worked."

Damn. As if I wasn't hard enough, a vision sprang to mind of her playing with herself while I watched and taught her how to give herself an orgasm.

Her gaze wandered down and a smirk came to rest on her perfect lips. "I see I'm not the only one affected. I'm assuming the same rules apply?"

Actually, I'd planned on jerking off. "You positive you're prepared if I abide by the same rule? Might be better for me to take the edge off."

She lifted a brow. "Challenge accepted."

I chuckled, framing her face, and not quite knowing what the hell I was doing. If it wasn't for Heather's voice, I might have kissed her perfect, pouty lips.

"Shane, are you ready to go?"

I didn't miss the way Daniella's body stiffened at the interruption. "Yeah. I'll meet you downstairs."

I didn't break contact until Heather's footsteps retreated, and then I dropped my hands from Daniella's face.

She surprised me by reaching up to straighten my tie. It was an intimate gesture which suddenly had me in a hurry to put some space between us.

"I dig the suit, by the way."

"You would. Sort of gives the impression I'm an actual business man."

She sighed as she tightened the knot, not letting me go. "Whatever you need to tell yourself so you can keep your barriers up. Maybe when you're with your bar manager on the way to the meeting, you can tell her to get me her receipts. Without them, one has to wonder if you've found your problem for missing revenue right there."

I disliked her implication regarding either statement. "Don't let your jealousy cloud your judgment. Heather has been a hell of an employee for ten years."

Her eyes blazed, but she simply stepped back and took her seat. "Then providing the receipts should be an easy task for her."

Chapter Fifteen

Shane

I didn't like that she'd called me on my shit about keeping my barriers up. There was only one person who made a habit of doing so. Max. I also didn't care for her tone about Heather. But considering that once Heather got into my car to drive to Jersey for our meeting, she tried to dive into my lap, I could see where the jealousy stemmed from.

"Not today, honey." I tried to let her down easy, but she wasn't taking no for an answer.

Using a tone which instantly grated on my nerves, she whined, "But it's been forever, and then you stuck me with Max the other night. Are you not attracted to me anymore?"

This was the shit I tried to avoid with females. There was no right answer aside from the words she was looking for, which was to allow her to suck me off in the car. What I was about to say would make my life a whole lot more complicated, but it was the truth.

"I've got something going on with Daniella."

As predicted, this went over like a cum shot in the eye. "So, what? Now, all of a sudden, you do relationships?"

"Enough. My personal business is just that. We've always maintained a professional working friendship, Heather, and I would hate for this to come between us."

She stewed on my warning for a few seconds.

Because I was tired of the shit she was giving Daniella in doing her job, I made myself clear. "Also, give her the receipts she requested."

Heather glanced my way, about to open her mouth, but the look I gave her stifled whatever she was about to say.

It was good to know I hadn't lost my touch on most women, making them recognize when I meant business.

"Fine."

ॐ ॐ

I'd avoided Daniella until later than planned. I could tell myself it wasn't because she had my number about my defense mechanisms or it wasn't because I was pissed the entire bar now knew I was in some sort of relationship with her—thanks to Heather's big mouth. But the truth was that all of it had me feeling out of sorts. And I didn't do out of sorts. I did control. And I did it well. Until recently, that is.

If I'd been a wise man, I would've marched up my steps to my office and told her this arrangement was off. Instead, I stood there watching her type away on her laptop, poring over the receipts Heather must've finally provided.

Sensing my presence, she glanced up briefly but then went back to work.

Huh. Not being a man who typically garnered this type of reaction from a woman, I wasn't sure what to do. "I take it you got the receipts from Heather."

She lifted her eyes, slid off her glasses, and met my

gaze as I walked towards her. "Indeed. I'm guessing the thanks should go to you?"

Her tone was cool, professional even, but her eyes were anything but. They reflected her temper.

"None necessary. It should've been done sooner."

"Right. Glad you could discuss that—and our arrangement—in the car ride with her."

Ah. So that was the irritation. "It was either tell her we had a thing going on or let her suck my dick along the way."

Although I wasn't known for my filter, now would've probably been the time to exercise one. She was up and gathering her stuff, turning off the desk lamp and clearly ready to leave. "Good night, Shane."

Fuck. "Wait. Look, don't be mad. She made a move, and I shut her down. I don't get why it would piss you off."

"What pisses me off is I've had this plug up my ass all day with a promise of this afternoon, which you conveniently forgot about. I'm not well versed in the rules of anal etiquette, but that just seems straight-up rude."

My brows shot sky high. "You still have it in?"

She threw up her hands. "Seriously? What the hell was I supposed to do with it?"

No wonder she was cranky. I had to bite my lip to keep from laughing or else she'd give me a well-deserved punch in the face.

"I'm sorry. You should've taken it out. Just a couple hours a day, not eight hours."

Her face was beet red, and I found it adorable.

"Great. Now I'm going to have a big gaping you know what."

The fact she couldn't say asshole had uncontrollable laughter bubbling up from inside of me. This, of course, only served to turn her a brighter shade of red and piss her off.

"Come here." I pulled in her close to me, wrapping her up in my arms and breathing in her signature scent of something light and floral. "I'm sorry. It may not seem this way, but I'm not laughing at you. I'm only completely and totally enthralled by the combination of your humor and innocence." I leaned back and tucked her hair behind her ear. "It makes me want to know what you're thinking all the time."

"Right now I'm thinking I'm a butt plug failure."

We both erupted into a fit of laughter together.

Max interrupted, looking completely amused to find us both giggling like starry-eyed lovers in an embrace.

"Uh, sorry to intrude, but, uh, we have a situation down in room four I need your help with."

Shit. "I need to—"

"Go on. It'll give me time to, uh, take care of things."

I chuckled, wishing like hell I could help.

❧ ❧

Daniella

I took care of business by way of removing the plug. For the record, this wasn't as sexy as when Shane had put it in. Then I took a shower, hoping he would join me any minute. Then, because he hadn't, I went into the viewing room. I hoped I could see what might be going on with room four. But other than two couples having group sex, I didn't see anything out of the ordinary. Since when did four people having group sex become normal? Evidently, the club and Shane had changed my expectations.

"Whatcha doing in here?"

I spun around to see the object of my thoughts. Despite looking hot as ever, his eyes were tired. It seemed he was never "off" of work.

"Looking for you. What happened?"

He sighed. "Someone got too rough. It doesn't occur often, but unfortunately, it does happen. It gets tricky because oftentimes an untrained submissive doesn't recognize their limit. Even worse, an untrained dominant doesn't always know how to use some of the devices."

My jaw about dropped. I'd obviously guessed kinky stuff happened here, but I hadn't thought about it from that perspective. "Any liability for your club?"

He shook his head. "There's always a possibility, but we do make them sign waivers. Plus, we asked if she wanted to press charges and ensured she did not. Matter of fact, they left together, so I'm assuming they'll work out whatever happened."

Not for the first time, I wondered if I was barely scratching the surface of sexually satisfying a man like Shane. "Are you into that sort of stuff?"

He smirked. "Why? You thinking you might want to try to be submissive?"

I scrunched up my nose. "I don't think I'd make a very good one. Most likely, you bossing me around would piss me off within minutes."

He moved closer, grasping my waist with his hands. "You enjoy me being bossy."

A smile curved my lips. "True. But I'm not really into pain for pleasure."

"Says the girl who had a plug up her ass most of the day."

I grinned. "I was told the end result would be worth it."

He stepped into me, dipping his lips to my ear. "Oh, it will be. You'll come so hard you'll nearly pass out from it."

Yes, please. "Mm, and when is this happening?"

"Sunday night. You'll wear a bigger one tomorrow in preparation."

I sighed. "I won't be here. I have a wedding to go to."

"What wedding?"

"The one I told you about the other day. It's my cousin, which means I can't back out."

He didn't mince words. "Sounds dreadful."

At least I had a sexy dress to wear. In fact, I looked pretty damn good in the black strapless Vera Wang dress. "It will be, especially if Eric shows up which, knowing him, he probably will."

"Did he pay you half the money?"

I nodded. "Yep. Wired as directed. He has two more weeks for the other half. You know, I don't even know if our friends have heard we broke up."

That was weird. I mean, normally, didn't a woman, upon realizing her fiancé was cheating, call her friends, have a girls' night, and cry on their shoulders? I could say I hadn't wanted to bother anyone during the holidays—which is why we'd done the whole shower and bachelorette party weeks ago. But the truth was that I'd been enveloped in the club and Shane so quickly that the whole tragedy had sort of slipped my mind.

He quirked a brow. "You didn't tell anyone about the breakup?"

"Um, I guess I forgot." Was it any wonder? Since Eric's betrayal, I'd been absolutely consumed with either the man in front of me or his taxes. "My parents were out of town. Matter of fact, I think they returned today from their cruise."

Crap. I guess I should call them since we'd only traded voicemails on Christmas. I dreaded having to do so. My mom would make my breakup with Eric a reflection of my inability to make a good wife. She'd then bring up the whole not-wanting-to-have-kids thing again. Evidently in her mind, my lack of desire to procreate made me somehow less worthy of love and marriage.

"Huh."

I frowned. "What do you mean 'huh'?"

"Sometimes people don't tell others about a breakup because they hope to maybe work things out."

I couldn't help laughing. There was no part of me wanting to work it out with Eric. "That is not happening. Not only is he a thief, but also a cheater. Normally people are upset by a breakup instead of feeling freed, so maybe that's why I haven't told anyone. Because I realize it was a mistake to be engaged to him in the first place. Any chance you want to come with me?"

I realized my mistake the moment the words left my lips. Shit. Shane wasn't the type of guy you brought to a wedding. He was intense and antisocial, for one thing. For another, we were merely having sex, not crossing all sorts of bridges into relationship land. "Sorry, forget I asked."

"Why? Don't want people knowing you're with the owner of a sex club?"

Not for the first time, I sensed some vulnerability around the subject, so I decided to put the topic to rest. "Honestly, I don't really care. Hell, I think half the people there would probably high-five me and the other half—Well, let's just say it's about time I stop caring about their opinion. After all, they thought Eric was a good guy, so what do they know?" I meant every word. My newfound resolution was to avoid trying to please others. From here on out, I was pleasing myself.

"Okay, I'll go."

"What?" I couldn't be more shocked. "Seriously?"

He shrugged. "Sure. Why not."

"You must really want butt sex."

He grinned. The expression, though rare, looked good on him. "You have no idea."

Chapter Sixteen

Shane

"What the fuck was I thinking?" I said these words aloud to my best friend while getting ready to go pick up Daniella on Sunday afternoon. I couldn't believe I was going to a wedding—and with a date with whom I'd supposedly established boundaries.

"Beats me. You gonna try to catch the garter?"

Leave it to Max to fuck with me.

"Ha. And no. Maybe I should tell her I've changed my mind."

His eyes narrowed. "Dude. The girl calls and gets a plus one, thus able to save face in front of her ex by bringing a new date—and you want to bail? Even for you, that would be shitty."

I scrunched my face. "What the hell does *even for me* mean?"

"It means you aren't exactly into social graces. But if you'd wanted to back out, then fifteen minutes before you go pick her up is not the time. Man up. She's not like Tina, so I don't think you need to worry about her taking tonight the wrong way."

I hated it when he knew exactly what I was thinking.

Then again, I often returned the favor. "You're right. Unless you think you'll need help tonight?"

He shook his head. "New Year's Eve is the day after tomorrow. That's the party. Tonight will be the same old shit with the same old people. You should go and enjoy a rare Sunday evening off."

Rare was right. Seldom did I take a night completely off. If I did, it was typically a weekday, not on the weekend when things were busy. But I did plan on enjoying tonight. Hell, just the thought of having Daniella's ass made me hard. We'd been moving up the size of her plugs. I wasn't an anal virgin, but knowing she was had me all sorts of giddy.

Yes. Giddy. Like a fucking teenager.

Damn. I couldn't explain this hold she had over me, but the fact that even my dick had fallen suit was really getting to me. "Daniella indicated she should be done with the audit by Wednesday."

"So she said. In fact, I need to help her on Monday or Tuesday to reconcile some of the bar receipts. Heather is being less than obliging."

"Yeah. She's jealous of the attention I'm giving Daniella." I closed down the computer screen I'd been looking at and stood up. I was already dressed in a charcoal gray suit with a proper white, starched shirt and a blue tie. "Call me if you have any trouble."

Max laughed. "Sorry, buddy. No lifelines for you tonight."

Any reservation I had about attending a wedding quickly went out the window once Daniella opened her hotel room door. She was wearing a black strapless dress and her hair piled on top of her head in a curled coif.

"You look, uh, nice."

She rolled her saucy blue eyes. "Your compliments outside of the bedroom need work."

I watched while she grabbed her clutch and a small duffel bag. "Is that all you're bringing?"

She quirked her head to the side. "I don't plan on wearing a whole lot once I get out of this dress tonight."

I smiled, stepping closer so I could breathe in her scent. As I dropped a kiss to the curve of her neck, I loved how her breath caught at the simple action. "Lucky me, then. You look sexy."

Because my thoughts were turning carnal in a hurry, I retreated and offered my arm. We'd best go before I got the notion to fuck her on every available surface in her hotel room.

⤞ ⤝

Daniella's smile grew big when she spotted my Viper. What can I say? I loved a beautiful sports car. Of course it was black because that was my signature color. Maybe I liked things to match the color of my soul.

She slipped into the passenger seat after I held the door open for her, allowing me a tempting view of her toned legs. As soon as I was behind the wheel and started the car, I glanced over.

"Are you wearing panties?"

She smirked. "Only one way to find out."

I didn't hesitate to reach over. When my fingers met no barrier, coming into contact with her hot, wet heat, I smiled. Since she wasn't the type of girl who'd normally go commando, knowing she did it for me was even more of a turn-on.

I withdrew my hand, much to her frustration. But my options were limited while driving a stick shift. Plus, it wasn't a long drive over to Jersey City.

Daniella blew out a breath, but then was distracted by her buzzing phone, which she answered. "Hey, Mom. No, we're on the way. We're not late. We're on time. Okay, fine. See you at the church."

She shut the phone with a big sigh. "I already can't wait to get to the reception and leave early."

I fought down the panic starting to well up. "Your mother is going to be there?"

She flipped down the visor and touched up her lipstick, either choosing to ignore the anxiety in my question or not recognizing it. "Yeah. Both her and my dad."

"You didn't mention that." Did she?

She flipped up the visor and capped her lipstick before glancing over. "I said it was for my cousin. I think that implies my family would be there."

"I don't do family." It was too much.

"What does that mean exactly?"

"It means I don't appreciate the blindside. I told you from the beginning this isn't a relationship."

Instead of looking upset, like I thought she would, she laughed. "I asked you if you wanted to come to my cousin's wedding. You said yes. Implying I sprang my family on you is complete crap. But you know what? Drop me off at the church. You're off the hook. The last thing I need is you thinking I somehow snared you into tonight."

Fuck. The guilt was already sinking in. "Look, it's nothing—"

She held up her hand. "Not trying to be rude here, but you don't owe me an explanation. I should've known better than to ask."

She was pissed, and I didn't blame her. It should've clicked when she'd said 'cousin's wedding' that it would include her family. But something didn't make sense. "Why would Eric be attending if it's your cousin's wedding?"

"Because the groom was his college roommate. They met at a happy hour for his firm that I dragged her to."

"Maybe I can go for a moment. That way Eric sees us and then—"

"Un—fucking—believable. I didn't invite you so I could save face. Whether I walk in there with you or by myself, my head is high. First, I did nothing wrong. Second, I don't care if he thinks I'm with someone or not."

Huh. Proving yet again that Daniella wasn't like most of the other women I knew. Any of them would've wanted to make their ex jealous. "I didn't mean to make it sound that way."

She was looking out the window, and I wasn't sure what else to say. Ten minutes later she directed me to the front of the church. I'd barely come to a stop before she was out of the car and shutting my door. I had to lower the window to shout out to her.

"Am I meeting you at the hotel later?"

She stopped for a moment, turned, and walked back to the car with purpose. There, she leaned down to the open window. "You know, for a smart man, that was a really dumb question. Especially when I'm sure you already can guess the answer."

I was a dick. And I'd screwed up. Big time. Knowing this only fueled my anger. My character and crappy judgment was why a guy like me did not belong even in a simple sex arrangement, let alone a relationship. Our argument was clearly a sign. But no-showing to a wedding after she'd called to bring a plus one was shitty. And it wasn't as though Daniella had given me any sign she was becoming attached or clingy. But meeting her parents... They would certainly have expectations about me, especially when Daniella was coming off her engagement.

Shit. It took me five minutes to make up my mind about what I needed to do.

Chapter Seventeen

Daniella

I should've known better than to ask him. Although it was an asshole move on his part to freak out at the last minute, it served as a reminder. I'd stepped out of the box into which we'd put our whatever-the hell-you-would-call-it, temporary, monogamous, non-kissing thing. But I'd meant what I said. I wasn't bringing him to save face. On the other hand, I had wanted him to be there as an ally. Someone who would be on my side, a person who represented unapologetic choices.

As I walked into the church, I kept my head high and gazed straight ahead. The last thing I wanted to do was mingle with anyone I didn't have to. Namely, Eric or any of his friends. My mother had already told me we'd be in the fourth row on the left side. I smiled at the usher, took the program, and allowed him to escort me down.

My mother, with her olive skin and big brown eyes, looked up smiling. She quickly dropped the expression for a frown. I already knew what was coming.

"Where is this date you insisted on bringing?"

"Unfortunately, something came up at work."

I took my seat and smiled at my dad. He was a big man with the trademark Italian accent. "Hi, Dad. Looking good from the trip."

They were both sporting a glow from the Caribbean sun. "Hi, honey. Nice to see you."

But my mom wasn't done. "What do you mean he had to work? What does he do?"

"He manages a club in Manhattan. Something came up."

"Your cousin paid one hundred fifty per person."

I smiled tightly. "I'll send her a check and an apology."

"I swear, with your luck in men, Daniella, you're never going to settle down."

"Maybe I don't want to." I could tell from the intake of her breath she hadn't expected my retort.

She'd always preached that unless you had a ring on your finger and bun in the oven, you were not doing your part for society as a woman. "I saw Eric here, and he didn't bring a date. I'm certain if you guys talked things out, you could salvage the relationship."

"As I told you on the phone, he not only cheated on me, but he also stole from me. Is that who you really want as part of the family?"

My father wasn't helping. "You said he's paying you back. As for the other, maybe he just needed to get it out of his system."

Who were these people? If ever I wondered why I'd stayed longer than I should've in the relationship with Eric, these were certainly the influences. It made me even more grateful I'd gotten out. At least I didn't have to go home with them tonight and be surrounded by their disappointment like I would've had to do in my youth. Then again, when I was younger, I actually had done everything I could in order to please them. It had never been enough.

"I'm not discussing this here." I was done trying to please them.

The ceremony was about to start, and I already had a headache. I was quickly thinking perhaps Shane had been right to bail. The thought slammed home when Eric stepped into our pew, much to my mother's delight.

"Here, dear, I saved a place for you."

His smile made me want to flee. With him now sitting between my mother and me, I seriously contemplated it. Only the onset of the wedding music stopped me.

"How are you?" he whispered.

"Shh. It's starting."

∿ ∿

The moment the bride and groom made it to the back of the church, I bolted. It was only four blocks to the hotel where the reception was being held. I hoofed it rather than spend a moment longer in Eric's company. God, he'd been staring at me as my cousin and her new husband had been saying their vows like I would turn to him and say, 'let's get married.' If anything, the ceremony only reaffirmed my decision never to settle again.

Upon arriving at the hotel, I realized I'd beaten most guests there. Probably because they were doing some pictures after the ceremony, and people were mingling. At least this gave me time to go check in. Only one problem. My duffle bag was in Shane's car.

Not that I had a lot in there, but the contents did include my makeup bag, toiletries, and a change of clothes for tomorrow. Now, I had nothing but my purse and the hotel-provided items I'd find in the room. I sighed, thinking this was bad luck until it got worse.

"Can we talk for a minute?" Eric's voice came from

behind me.

I accepted my key from the hotel clerk and turned around. "I have nothing to say to you unless the words out of your mouth are 'here's the rest of your money.'"

He winced. "Please keep your voice down. Look, there's no way I can get the rest of the money in two weeks."

I walked towards the elevators, already done with this conversation. "Then you'd best sell your car, condo, or a kidney."

"Come on, Daniella. I was talking to your mom, and she agrees we'd still be good together."

I lifted a brow. "Now that you don't have the money, you want to get back together. Unbelievable."

"What? She said you were showing up with some date, and you didn't."

"Says who?"

Shane's husky words came from behind me, but before I could turn to see him, he'd put his arm around my waist, intimately pinning my back to his front. Considering we'd been in much the same position the last time Eric had seen us together, I blushed.

"He's your date?" Eric stammered.

I'd be lying if I said I didn't get a lot of satisfaction from the look on his face. "It would seem so."

"You heading up to the room before the reception?" Shane whispered in my ear.

"Yes." I turned and saw he was holding my duffle along with his. "Thanks for bringing my bag."

He smirked. "Not a problem. Shall we?"

I gave one last glance toward Eric as Shane ushered me to the elevator, but my date wasn't done.

"Money to Dani in two weeks, Eric. Don't make her wait for it."

In epic, usually-only-see-it-in-the-movies fashion, the doors closed after his words, making Eric's face turn bright red.

I had goosebumps from Shane's don't-fuck-with-me tone. But it wasn't enough to override my annoyance from earlier.

I took a step to the side, but he wasn't having it. Instead he pulled me close, dipping his face into the crook of my neck and kissing the top of my shoulder.

"I'm sorry."

I pulled back to look at his face, shocked those words had come from him.

"Don't look so astounded. I do manage those words every once in a while. I came back for the ceremony, but it had already started, so I stood in the back. Then you all but bolted, so I couldn't catch up with you until now. It was a dick move to back out."

"It was, but I should've been clearer about the family element. To tell you the truth, after five minutes talking with my mother, I really can't blame you. I don't know what I was thinking."

"Why were you sitting by Eric in the church?"

The elevator stopped on my floor, and he followed me out. "My mother seems to think I should let bygones be bygones and trade in his pedigree for my self-worth."

"She wants you married with kids in the burbs."

I smiled sadly. "More than she wants my happiness."

He turned me, pinning me up against our room door. "And what do you want, Daniella?"

His gaze was burning into mine, and I found the breath catching in my chest. It was as though I had no choice but to utter my next words. "To feel free from the burden of being responsible for everyone else's happiness. Instead, I'd like to be responsible for just my own for once."

He cupped my face, running his thumb over my bottom lip in an intimate gesture. For a suspended moment in time, I was convinced he would kiss me. It could have been my imagination, but in his eyes, I saw the indecision. Then it was gone.

"What do you want, Shane?"

"To taste you before we go back downstairs."

The old me would've argued we didn't have time and worried about being late. The new me was already wet with anticipation.

But if I'd thought it would be as expected, I should've known better. Shane had other ideas. Once the hotel room door opened, he backed me into the first available surface, which happened to be the desk, and dove under my dress.

"Hold up the bottom so I can see your face when you come for me."

"Oh, Good Lord." At this rate, we wouldn't be late at all. I was about to combust simply from the vibration of his words against my cleft.

"You taste amazing." His finger entered me and curled up. "Ah, and so wet."

He sucked on my clit while his finger moved in a rhythm that had me climaxing in a matter of minutes. But when he reached back, he froze.

"I wanted to surprise you." I'd put in one of the jeweled butt plugs. Not only was it a delicious type of foreplay, anticipating when he'd have me there, but I knew it would turn him on.

"Jesus, Dani. I'm rock hard for you. And I can't wait to be deep inside your ass."

He tugged on the plug, sending a zing straight to my center.

"How about now?" I was desperate for it and not above begging.

He stood up, his lips an inch from mine and still glistening from my wetness.

I couldn't help myself; I kissed him, groaning at the taste of myself on his lips until he pulled away.

"Sorry." But I wasn't because, for a moment, he'd returned my kiss.

He smiled. "I don't believe you. But because you're a naughty girl, you'll have to wait for me to have your ass. Now get on your knees and put your lips to good use."

It was the humor reflected in his eyes and the fact I was turned on which had me ignoring his bossy tone. Instead, I hopped down and unbuckled him, marveling at how hard he was. He lay heavy in my hand while I licked him from tip to base and enjoyed the way he sucked in his breath with the action.

Because I wanted to take him completely off guard, I swallowed him to the back of my throat in one motion, pulling back only to use my tongue to lubricate him and also my pinky finger.

"Jesus."

Music to my ears. I set a rhythm, bobbing on his cock like it was my mission in life to make him come as quickly as possible. And because I wasn't done with surprises and was curious about how Shane would react, I moved my pinky back and penetrated his backside with the coated little finger.

"Mother fucking—fuck."

He jerked his hips but then relaxed, allowing me to move it in further before he came spectacularly in my mouth.

❧ ❦

Shane

To say Daniella had just rocked my world was an understatement. She'd fucking annihilated it.

"Where did that trick come from?"

We'd finished cleaning up in the bathroom, where she was now reapplying her lipstick.

She shrugged. "I figured someone should at least get

some ass play before we return for the reception."

I chuckled, loving her wit.

"I've never done it before. Did you like it?"

Although I wasn't normally into having my ass played with, her innocence and fearless way of trying new things was the biggest turn-on. I stepped into her, dropping my lips to her ear and grabbing her ass with both hands. "You have no idea. Now let's get downstairs before I fuck you on this vanity. Because you really don't know what you've started."

The slow, satisfied smile on her face let me know she was sorely tempted to find out and skip the reception. But if I was to make up for earlier, then I needed to ensure I escorted her downstairs.

By the time we walked into the ballroom, most people were seated and eating dinner. I hadn't been to many weddings in my lifetime, but it was clear, from the flowers to the china, that no expense had been spared on this one.

As we made our way towards our table, I swallowed hard, fighting the panic about meeting her parents. But she gave me a reprieve by leading us to the bar first.

"Figured you might want a whiskey first."

"You figured right. Uh, I—" I decided just to put the disclaimer out there while we were alone. "Look, I don't want to cause you any judgment from these people."

She straightened my tie, giving me a smile. "Let them judge away. I'm through caring. And think of it this way. You'll never have to see any of them again after tonight."

Right. The thought should've comforted me. But instead, for reasons I didn't want to examine, it annoyed me.

After we gathered our drinks and me my nerve, we made our way over to the table. A woman who had to be Daniella's mother sat beside a man who had to be her father.

The urge to flee was strong, but not as strong as my feelings for the woman beside me. Shit. Where had that thought come from? But I didn't have the time to examine it because introductions were happening.

I smiled tightly, taking my seat next to Daniella after I'd pulled out hers like a gentleman. The entire table went around introducing themselves: her aunt, uncle, a couple cousins and, last but not least, her parents.

"Why are you so late? And why did you take off after the ceremony? We were looking for you for family pictures," her mother started in.

My annoyance immediately flared, but I noticed my date simply took a sip of her martini and replied, her lips twitching. "I found out Shane was able to make it and was waiting at the hotel."

"Yes, well, at least it's not wasted money with an empty place setting."

I gritted my teeth, thinking it was no wonder Daniella wanted company if this was her family.

She turned and gave me an apologetic smile.

We ate quickly, but not quickly enough. Her father leveled his eyes to mine. "So, Shane, what is it you do?"

I dabbed my mouth with my napkin. "I own a bar in Manhattan."

"What kind of bar?"

Before the wedding, I would have answered that question with the blunt truth. Absolutely, no question about it. But I couldn't do that to Daniella. I didn't want the disapproval at the table to be directed in the slightest towards her. "It's geared towards singles and requires a club membership."

Daniella about choked on her drink, obviously not expecting me to lie.

"Is it successful?" her mother asked.

"Mother, really?" Dani gave her a glare.

I waved a hand, used to this sort of interrogation from people. Although I was tempted to blurt out something equally tacky, like: *does clearing forty million over the last decade satisfy you*? But I managed not to. "Depends on your perspective. We've been in business ten years and operated in the black for nine. Matter of fact, I met your daughter when she started doing our taxes."

They got to stew on that tidbit while the toasts were made and the first dance started. When the other couples were invited out, I took Daniella's hand. "May I have this dance?"

She smirked and let me lead her out to the floor.

"What's with the smug look?"

"I was thinking you must really want anal tonight to put up with this and then ask me to dance."

I laughed, moving my hands down to inappropriately cop a feel on the subject matter. "I have no issue with dancing, and your mother's questions aren't unlike other judgments I've received over the last decade. And to think, she's made all these negative conclusions without even knowing it's a sex club."

She leaned back, studying my eyes. I swore she could see through all my defenses. "Did your mom judge you?"

"Yeah." But I didn't want to get into it here. "So back to the anal. When do you think we can get out of here?"

She leaned in, tightening her arms around me. "Mm. Maybe after a couple of dances. I'm kind of enjoying this. You look very handsome, by the way."

I was thankful she'd dropped the subject. "You look sexy, too, but I can't wait to see you in nothing but your plug."

৵ ৻

We waited until the cake was cut, allowing Daniella

111

to speak with her cousin, the bride, and get a couple photos before we went upstairs, drinks in hand. Neither of us had seen any sign of Eric at the reception. Most likely, he'd gone home. Just as well. I wasn't sure my capacity for civil behavior would hold out if he'd come around again.

As we entered the room, we laughed about how her great-aunt Mary had patted my ass after one too many cocktails.

I sipped my whiskey, watching while she slipped out of her heels and let her hair down. "You're beautiful." The words slipped out easily because it's what this woman was. Effortless beauty and class.

"Thank you. And thanks for coming back. I'm sorry my mom was so unpleasant."

I framed her face. "Don't ever apologize for someone else's actions, Dani. She is who she is."

She blew out a breath. "You're right. And I'm becoming less tolerant of it. Do you know, when I was little, I convinced myself that if I wasn't the perfect little girl, they'd send me back to where they'd adopted me?"

The thought made my stomach roll. "They said that to you?"

She shook her head. "No, no. But it's how I felt. Like they'd adopted me, and therefore I needed to be the daughter they wanted. Almost like I was obligated. But I don't feel that anymore. Instead, I feel like I'm done being that person."

"I'm a big fan of the way you are." I untied my tie and undid two of the shirt buttons. The vibe immediately changed. "Strip for me?"

She looked unsure for half a second, but then gave me one of her saucy smiles.

After slipping off my shoes, I got comfortable on the bed with the pillows behind my head at the top so I could watch. What I did in the club was normally rushed to the point where sex occurred. I didn't mind it because that was the ultimate goal. However, right now I wanted to savor. I wanted to appreciate. And then I wanted her ass.

৵ ৵

Daniella

I unzipped my dress, trying to keep from being nervous. Wasn't as though this man hadn't already seen me naked. Besides, baring my innermost thoughts to him made me more vulnerable than the physical. But doing this deliberately was a little disconcerting. Especially with him watching me like a predator eyes its prey. Yet his frank appraisal brought me confidence. Somehow, I already knew tonight would be epic. Of course, that would only make it that much harder to think about leaving in three days' time. But for now, well, I was seizing the moment.

Once I was down to merely my lacy bra, his husky voice broke me out of my thoughts. "Turn around. And after you lose the bra, bend over and let me see that plug."

Damn. I'd started this game, however, and I was determined to give him the show he craved.

I could hear his muttered curse when I did what he asked, but was unprepared for his next request.

"Come here and sit on my face."

Huh. I'd kind of thought we'd get right to it, but clearly he had other plans. Never having assumed this position, I wasn't sure how to accomplish it. But he took control once I approached the bed, lifting me up by the waist and having me straddle his shoulders.

"Grab the headboard for leverage."

"Oh, fuck."

He hadn't hesitated, instead devouring me from this

113

angle, pressing my pussy into his face by gripping my ass. "Ride it like you want it, baby."

I was digging the term of endearment, but not as much as the newfound sensation of him having all access. One of his fingers was pushing the plug while others were up inside of me, working together with his mouth to have me exploding on his face in no time. But he wasn't done. Instead, he replaced his fingers with his tongue.

"Ohhhhhhh." I was pretty sure my words were only a jumble as my eyes rolled back, and all that was present was white light in the climax which washed over me.

I didn't know how he managed it, but the next thing I registered was being on my back. I opened my eyes to see him shedding his clothing in record time and then rolling on the condom. He was between my thighs and thrusting deep inside of me before my aftershocks had stopped.

"Christ, I love it when your cunt grips me, and I can still feel your orgasm."

My nails raked down his back, and I reveled in the feel of his skin.

Suddenly, he pulled out. "Get on your knees, gorgeous."

As I did so, he crossed the room and came back with a bag in hand.

"What's that?"

"Toys. Now be a good girl and put those pillows under your stomach to help support you."

I could hear the sound of lube before I felt him take the plug out. He replaced it with his readied fingers. "You're fucking perfect. And because I want to give you ultimate pleasure, I'm putting this in your pussy."

I gasped at the sensation of the large dildo being placed inside of me and then moaned when it started to vibrate.

"This is only the head of my cock. To work you in. We'll go slow."

I burned a little despite being readied, and I was even more thankful he'd been courteous enough to work me in over the last two days. I appreciated that he was talking me through it.

"Just an inch. That's it. Relax and let me in."

I sucked in my breath as he made it past the ring of muscle, deeper inside of me.

"Christ, your ass is tight. I can't wait to bottom out in you, Daniella, and fuck you hard. You want that, don't you?" He slipped in another inch.

"Yes. Oh, God." I was quickly becoming overwhelmed by what was happening to my body. My legs were shaking while my desire was at a precipice it had never been. If his stuttered breaths were any indication, Shane was having a hard time with control.

"I'm almost there. You okay?"

"Uh-huh. Shane, I—" Whatever I'd been thinking to say evaporated. Rooted, he'd started moving while working the dildo in tandem. It was as though all my brain synapses exploded in the tidal wave of the climax washing over me. My body was on autopilot, bucking against his thrusts and seemingly going from one orgasm into another. As I was about to black out, I heard him grunt his own climax with a string of curses following. Then it went black.

Shane

Making a woman come like Daniella had should be the crowning achievement of manhood. I washed her intimately, smiling as she hardly moved, merely murmuring a thanks and something about being boneless. Then I put the blanket up around her, unsure what to do next.

I didn't spend the night with a woman. Ever. Yet the last thing I wanted to do was ditch her to find her own way back to New York in the morning, especially after my epic screwup earlier. Fuck. I really hadn't thought this whole hotel night thing out. So I took a long hot shower. Then I slipped into the bed, naked and already hard again. I'd decided to take care of things myself when she shocked me by speaking.

"You're not wasting a hard-on with me in the bed naked next to you?"

I froze mid-stroke. "You were kind of passed out."

"I needed a few minutes. You pretty much rocked my world."

She scooted over to me, and I tensed. I was not accustomed to naked cuddling or the skin on skin contact. Hell, it would be too easy to slide right into her about now. And her kisses down my neck were doing nothing to halt the temptation to do just that. I was on the brink of sinking into her heat without anything between us.

"Did the test results come back clean?" I couldn't believe I was asking this question. I'd never been bareback with any woman.

"Yes."

"I can show you my test results."

"I'm not on the pill."

"I got a vasectomy, so I won't get you pregnant."

She popped up, her expression full of surprise. I wondered if I'd managed to slam shut any hope she might have about a future with me. I told myself it was for the best. But instead, she smiled.

"Good, because I don't want children."

I hardly had time to analyze her statement before she hit me with her next words. "But don't you think it would be odd to go bare and not kiss?"

She was right. And I was crazy to have suggested it. "You're right. It was a stupid thought. Hold tight." I jumped out of bed and retrieved a condom, putting it on in record time while avoiding her eyes. I didn't want to see the disappointment that I'd been about to fuck her bare but didn't want the intimacy of a kiss.

"Shane, are you upset?"

I plastered a smile on my face and forced myself to lose the tension. "Only at myself for losing my head for a moment. Now spread those legs and let me in."

Chapter Eighteen

Daniella

The man had fucked me into a coma. That's why, when the light came on and Shane's voice woke me, I could hardly manage an acknowledgement.

"Come on, sleepyhead. I need to get back."

I ran my hands over my face and winced at the soreness all over my body. "Do I have time for a shower?" I definitely needed one, not only to clean up, but also to get my wits about me.

"Just enough if you get up now."

I opened my eyes slowly and realized he was already dressed, looking ready to go. I slid naked from the bed, not missing the appreciation in his expression when I did so.

"You want to join me?"

"Can't. I, uh, have a call. Be quick, and I'll get the car brought around."

Well, if that wasn't a dismissal, I didn't know what was. Sighing, I realized something had changed since last night. He'd retreated. Maybe it was the line he had suggested we cross last night by using no protection. Or maybe he wasn't comfortable waking up with a woman.

For whatever reason, he was definitely acting strange.

When I got into the car fifteen minutes later, he occupied himself with anything but conversing with me.

"Everything okay?" I refused to sit there getting the silent treatment.

"Yeah, fine. But tomorrow is New Year's Eve, the busiest night of the year."

"Oh. I didn't realize. Anything I can help with?"

"Nope. Matter of fact, if you want to take off today, I'm sure things can wait."

In other words, he didn't want me around. "I'd prefer to get some things done today so I can possibly finish up by tomorrow."

"Suit yourself."

Evidently, I would.

❧ ❧

I worked until four o'clock that afternoon, frustrated that Heather's bar receipts weren't adding up. Either she was keeping some stuff from me in order to torture me or make me look inept, or she was hiding something. I rubbed my temples, wondering if I should leave this to fresh eyes in the morning.

That's when Max came up. "Hey, you planning to attend the New Year's Eve party tomorrow night?"

"Uh, I'm not sure. What does it entail?"

He chuckled. "Not a gang bang. At least, not including you. It'll be like the Christmas party, only more festive because of the countdown. Make sure you stick to the main floor, though. Don't go into the basement."

"There's a basement?"

"No. No. And no," came Shane's words from the elevator doors, which had just opened to reveal him.

"There isn't a basement?" I played coy, enjoying that

119

it instantly irritated him. Considering he'd ignored me all day, I wasn't sorry.

"There is, but you're not going to the main floor, let alone the basement, which Max shouldn't have mentioned to you. I'll have enough on my mind without worrying about you in that crowd."

"Yes, well, I'm not your responsibility, Shane."

"You're working here, so yes, you are."

I turned towards Max, who was looking amused at our exchange. "You know, I'll have to see how this job goes with my pain-in-the-ass, temporary boss. Suddenly, I have the urge to work longer hours to get this assignment done." I gathered the rest of my stuff and turned off the desk lamp. "Good night, gentleman."

As I lay in my bed later that night waiting for the knock which never came, I realized I needed to heed my own words. It was time to be done with whatever I'd had with Shane. Although I'd told myself it was only sex, my wounded feelings were calling me a liar.

❧ ❦

Shane

If we'd been in a relationship, which we weren't, I would have chased after her. Knocked on her door and fucked her into understanding I didn't want her around the sometimes rowdy crowd that attended New Year's Eve. But we weren't, which is why I was nursing my whiskey, hard and alone, in my condo a couple blocks away. I looked out the windows over the city and tried not to wonder what Daniella would think of the view. Then I cursed myself for the thought. I realized the best thing for both of us would be for her to finish the job and move on.

The next morning I was at the club at the crack of dawn. I loved this hour because there weren't a lot of people about. The chef, a couple security guys, but no patrons since we didn't open the doors until three o'clock. Even then, it never got busy before nine.

After I climbed the stairs to my office, I was shocked to see Daniella already at my desk, poring over receipts and typing into her spreadsheet. I took a moment, drinking her in, hating that after one night without her, I'd missed her.

"Good morning."

She looked up but didn't smile. "'Morning."

"You're here early."

"I was hoping a fresh start would help fill in the holes in the information Heather provided me. It hasn't."

I sighed, thinking Heather would go ballistic if Daniella questioned her. "What's missing?"

She frowned. "I don't know."

I walked towards her and looked over her shoulder at a spreadsheet that would make my eyes cross. "If you don't know, then how can you accuse—?"

"Whoa, I'm not accusing. I'm simply stating that something doesn't add up. Considering she wasn't exactly forthcoming with all of the requested information, it could be a matter of that, or it could be my lack of understanding. Maybe I need a tutorial on the inventory."

"Aside from Heather, Max is the most familiar with the bar area. I'm sure when he comes in, he can give you one."

I wasn't trying to blow her off. It was just fact. Max loved to man the bar from time to time as his roots were in bartending. My expertise was more on the financials and security. But Daniella's face betrayed she wasn't buying it.

"Okay, I'll speak to Max, then."

"Look, it isn't personal. He really does know the bar better than I do."

She took off her glasses and leveled me with her gaze. "Some of the girls mentioned you normally perform on New Year's Eve. If you want out of our agreement for that, then I'd understand."

Would she, now? The thought instantly pissed me off. "Oh, yeah? You're okay with the thought of me fucking another woman?"

She flinched, and I knew I'd gone too far. "Maybe I wouldn't care."

My brows went high. If it weren't for her blush or the fact she couldn't meet my gaze, I might've believed her. I pulled her up for her chair, and framed her face with my hands. "You wouldn't care, huh?"

She lifted her chin while defiance showed in her eyes.

"You wouldn't care if it's not your mouth on me, not your pussy or your ass that I'm fucking?" I was pushing her, recognizing the last thing I wanted was for her not to care. Because the very thought of her with another man made me feel like I was going to lose my shit. Which is one of the reasons I didn't want her down on the floor. It was also why I was trying, unsuccessfully, to wean myself off of her.

"I wouldn't want to," she finally relented, maybe not expecting the same feelings I was warring with.

"Me, either. Come on." I led her into the bedroom next door and quickly lost my jacket and tie.

"What are you doing?"

"What I should've been doing last night. Fucking you senseless."

"The wedding and morning after freaked you out, didn't it?"

Clearly, she needed an explanation before anything would happen. Not exactly the order I would've preferred, but I got it. "Yes. I didn't know what to do. That isn't my world, and this isn't yours. And this thing between us is more than I expected." There, I'd manned up and said it.

"For me, too. But there's something more. A reason you won't kiss me. A reason you freaked about family and then spending the night. What is it?"

I didn't want to get into this. But perhaps telling her would make her understand. "There was a girl I met when I was visiting my mom for the holidays about ten years ago. She was home from college. We went out twice. I'd just purchased the club and took her here for our second date when she'd indicated she wanted to have sex. We had fun. But then she developed feelings. I had to break it to her that I didn't feel the same. She accused me of leading her on. And hell, maybe I had."

"By doing what?"

"Kissing. Holding hands. Taking her on dates. It all screams relationship."

"Not after two times."

"That's what Max said. What's worse is she told my mother, about me owning a sex club."

She sucked in a breath. "Crap. What ended up happening?"

"My mom, who is very conservative and worried about everyone else's opinion told me to choose between the family or the club."

"And she never came around?"

"Not even on her deathbed. She didn't even want to see me. She died just as disappointed in me as she'd been the day I begged her not to make me choose. Since the fiasco with Tina, I've tried to be very clear about my intentions and that I don't want a relationship. And I've become unapologetic with those who judge me regarding the choices I've made."

She put her arms around me. "No wonder a wedding with family freaked you out. Your mother never should've made you choose. But as for my intentions, I mean what I say, Shane. This may be more than I bargained for, but I know what it is. And more importantly, what it isn't."

I'd expected to be relieved. But shockingly, I wasn't. "When you talked before about wanting to feel free, Daniella, I know what you're craving." What I didn't say was that sometimes there was a cost to it all. Disappointment in those you love didn't come cheap.

Her hand stroked my face. And now it was time to get back to even ground.

"Turn around. Face the wall and put your hands up to brace yourself. We don't have much time, so I'm going to fuck you fast. Then this afternoon before things get busy, I'm taking you into one of the rooms downstairs before it gets busy. And we're playing."

She swallowed hard before turning around to put her hands on the wall and then spreading her feet.

I grabbed her ass, enjoying how her burgundy fitted dress hugged her curves, matched her hair, and showed off her assets. Assets that, for the time being, were all mine to do with as I pleased.

I ran my hand up the inside of her thighs and came into contact with her thong. "Tsk, tsk, you didn't follow instructions, Daniella." My hand smacked her backside with enough of a sting to make her squeal.

"Oh."

Rubbing the area, I whispered in her ear. "Did you enjoy that?"

She pushed her ass back toward my ever-growing erection. "I didn't think I would, but I like it when you do it."

"God, how I wish I had more time. Later, we'll play."

I found the foil packet in my wallet and slipped the condom on, afterward wasting no time sinking into her heat and thrusting up. Reaching around, I strummed her clit and enjoyed how quickly I could make her come. I was quick to follow, grinding out my orgasm deep inside of her while my hands tangled with hers against the wall.

Stepping back, I quickly tied off the condom and tucked myself back into my pants. "I'll see you at three o'clock. Room forty-two."

Chapter Nineteen

Daniella

After my quickie with Shane, I went over the bar inventory with Max, trying to focus even though I was distracted by the events of the morning.

I'd wanted to argue with Shane when he'd said that was my world and this was his. Tell him we could possibly find some sort of middle ground. But then I realized I'd be going against everything I'd agreed to. At least he'd acknowledged this was more intense than either of us could've guessed it would be. And he'd confided in me about where his trust issues came from. But all the information did was confirm the fact he'd never had or ever wanted a relationship. I knew from experience that monogamy could never compete with what he had here at the club.

All of this told me I was better off recognizing this was ending on Wednesday. But if I was to make that happen, I needed to understand what Max was telling me.

"So the liquor arrives from the distributor in boxes?"

He nodded. "Yes. Normally in four, six, or ten packs."

"And how can I tell what arrives in what?"

He frowned. "It should tell you on each packing slip."

I held one out for him.

He looked perplexed after scanning it. "Weird. There's a total, and the box number, but not how many units per package."

"Exactly. That's my problem. From the prices, I can determine they weren't singles, but unless I know the count, I can't figure out if they're correct."

"We should be able to get you the boxes. I don't get why the number of units aren't printed on there. I seem to remember seeing they were in the past. But maybe since Heather knows the counts, she hasn't questioned it."

Or maybe she was stealing. I didn't want to believe it simply because Max and Shane would be devastated, but things weren't adding up. Literally.

"When does the next inventory come in?"

"Later this afternoon in prep for the party. I'm sure Heather could—"

I was already shaking my head. "That's not gonna work." Heather was not about to do me any favors, and I was now very suspicious of her.

He chuckled. "Yeah, she's pretty pissy since finding out about you and Shane."

"Why, though? In a couple days it'll be over, and I'll be gone."

He quirked his head to the side. "Is that what you want?"

He appeared sincere in his question, and for a moment I thought about being truthful. But this was Shane's best friend. I chose to stay neutral and not reveal too much. "It's what we agreed to."

"Agreements can be amended."

One of the guys stepped in, calling for Max.

"It's okay. I know you're busy. But later this afternoon after the order comes in, can you show me what a typical one looks like? It'll only take a few minutes."

"Uh, sure. But I'll have to figure out something to tell Heather. Inventory is kind of her baby, and she gets territorial over it."

I bet.

꙳ ꙳

I walked into room forty-two right on time and found Shane waiting in a high wingback chair. Unlike the last time I'd been in one of these rooms, I wasn't nervous. Instead, I was full of delicious anticipation for what he had in store.

Smiling, I walked towards him, my gaze on his.

"Stop there and strip."

Whereas this morning had been quick and hurried, I could tell he would now take his time. I started with my boots and then shimmied out of my thong. After that, I removed my stockings and, finally, my dress and bra.

He leaned forward, eyes simmering with lust. "I've been fantasizing about something since the first time I met you."

I swallowed hard. "What's that?"

"You touching yourself in front me. Making yourself come."

My sigh was audible. "I've never—"

But he wasn't having it. "You've never had me talking you through it. Try. For me?"

How could I possibly say no?

"Take a seat on this chair and spread your legs."

I did as he requested, watching in stunned silence when he knelt in front of me and put his hands on my thighs.

"I want to be up close and personal while I watch you. Spread your lips; show me that pretty pussy."

My fingers from one hand dipped down and spread myself open. I was very aware of how close he was. The fingers from my other hand found my clit and rubbed circles.

"Damn, that's sexy. Do you have any idea how much I want to dive in and taste you? How I plan to put you on the bed and pleasure you with toys and my cock? I'm going to fuck you in your mouth first. I have dreams about how well you suck me off. Then I'm putting a long dildo in your ass while I fuck your pussy at the same time. And finally, I'm going to come all over your luscious body. Mark you with it."

"Oh, Jesus." I was rubbing faster and faster with his dirty words, wanting all of it and more.

"That's it, Dani. Make yourself come, and I'll lick up your mess."

"Fuck." I was there. I was coming under my own hand. I let my head fall back as the climax washed over me. But before I could come down from the rush, Shane was there, pulling my hips into his face and eating me with such abandon it seemed like mere seconds before I was coming again, calling out his name.

"That was the hottest thing I've ever seen." His face was still shiny with my wetness as he traveled up to suck on my nipple, giving it a tug with his teeth before doing the same with the other one. "Stay here."

As I watched with appreciation while he stripped out of his clothes, I found my hand making it's way back between my legs. I was so very hot for him.

"Christ. I can hear how wet you are. Use this. Make yourself come again."

He produced a dildo from a package, handing it over already vibrating. I inserted it, letting my eyes flutter closed with the sensation. But they snapped open when he pulled me onto the edge and put my feet on a stool, allowing me to be completely bared for him. I felt a pressure at my backside and realized he was pushing something hard and lubricated inside. I sucked in a shuddered breath at the sensation.

"You have no idea how sexy you are. Play with yourself and come again while I have your mouth."

He positioned himself at my head, feeding me his cock one glorious inch at a time. I was anxious for the taste of him, but finding it hard to concentrate as I didn't have the use of my hands. "Allow me."

He took over for the dildo, pumping it deep inside me while I took a hold of his length and went to work.

"Come with me, baby. I want to feel it while you swallow it down."

My body erupted, and as a result, his did too. Although an orgasm made it tough to remember to swallow, I managed to get most of it in my mouth. The rest spilled onto my chest, which served to turn him on even more.

"Christ, I love the sight of my cum on your tits. But I'm not done with you."

I was grateful when he scooped me up and lay me on the bed because I wasn't sure I had the strength to do it under my own power. I'd lost the vibrator, but he'd kept the dildo in my ass. He was now moving that slowly.

"Are you sore?"

"A little, but not bad."

"Good."

He quickly put on a condom and was on top of me in minutes. "Wrap your legs around me, gorgeous, and hold on. I'm going to pound you hard."

Although I'd just had three intense orgasms, my body was greedy for more. So when he entered me, I tightened my intimate muscles around him, liking the way I'd taken him off guard.

"Jesus."

The only thing missing, however, was the way he buried his face in my neck instead of taking my lips. But I didn't have time to dwell on the disappointment because he was giving me another orgasm, followed by flipping me over and taking me hard from behind. The primal sound of flesh smacking flesh filled the room. He insisted on another and then another, stealing them from my body as if in a challenge. Then he did as he'd promised, losing the condom and coming all over my ass.

"Let's take a shower, and then I need to get prepared for the party."

Right. The party. Where did this man get his energy?

Chapter Twenty

Daniella

New York City was absolutely nuts for New Year's Eve, which is why I'd spent most of my life avoiding the place on that night. But tonight I was in the absolute heart of it, in a sex club, of all places. Ironically, I was doing the books, the most nonsexual activity possible.

Since it was the bar that was giving me trouble, I went down to the stock room, hoping to see the newly delivered boxes in order to get my brain wrapped around what was missing.

"What? Are you checking up on me now?" Heather appeared in the doorway.

"I'm doing an audit, which means I'm checking up on everything, not everyone."

"Look, just because I fucked Shane before you got here and certainly will fuck him again after you leave, doesn't give you the right to single me out."

"That's absurd. I'm simply trying to understand the invoices so I can make sense of them."

"Then why are you down here? Shouldn't you be at your computer if it's a matter of you not understanding the invoices?"

I bristled at her tone but kept my face neutral. "Actually, I'm meeting Max."

He came into the stock room, obviously having received my text message that I was ready to meet. He looked from me to Heather. "Hey, ladies. Uh, where is the delivery?"

"I already unloaded everything. What, now you're in on this investigation, too, Max?"

I found it an interesting choice of words but stood quiet.

He sighed. "Look, I don't have time for this. She's doing a job, Heather. That's all. And sorry, Daniella. At the next delivery, I'll walk you through the process."

Heather bristled. "The hell you will. And the next delivery isn't until Wednesday. Shane indicated she'd be gone by then. After all, he has his scheduled performance on Friday night."

A slap in the face would've felt better. The satisfied look on Heather's face told me she knew it.

I watched her walk out and gave a fake smile to Max. Then something occurred to me. "Where would the emptied boxes be taken?"

"There's a dumpster out back. They should be there. You want me to help you look?"

I shook my head, knowing he and Shane were insanely busy trying to get things ready. "No, no. I'm fine on my own. Thanks."

I purposefully made a show out of going up the front stairs back to the office so Heather would see me. Then I grabbed my winter coat, because it was absolutely freezing outside, and went down the back stairs. I wasn't surprised that I didn't find any of the boxes in the two dumpsters. What in the hell was she hiding? I couldn't explain my determination except that I was certain I was onto something.

After stomping back up to the office, I found Shane

at my desk.

"Hey, where were you?"

"Trying to get a sense of inventory, but Heather had already unloaded and stocked up."

He didn't seem bothered by it. "It's a busy night. She probably did it early to get ahead."

"The next delivery isn't until Wednesday morning."

I didn't miss the way his shoulders tensed. "Is it that important? If you're still struggling with the inventory numbers and don't want to talk to Heather about it, then write down your questions for me or for Max. We'll try to get you the answers."

In other words, he didn't want me staying. In other words, he thought the problem was my lack of understanding. And of course, there was the performance he was already moving on to once I left. "Right. Well, I guess I'll figure out what I can. Um, how many boxes do you get during a normal delivery, by the way?"

"Not sure. Sometimes a hundred or so. I'm sure today's was extra large. We get deliveries twice a week. I've gotta go, but I'll, um, talk to you later, okay?"

I nodded. Then I realized I wanted to go back outside. A hundred boxes couldn't have gone far. And maybe I had something to prove to Shane: that my hunch wasn't unfounded.

&⁊ ⹓

An hour later, my fingers were absolutely frozen. I'd tromped around to all the businesses in the area, looking inside of their dumpsters. I had nothing to show for it. Since neither the recycling nor trash trucks had come through on New Year's Eve to empty the dumpsters, Heather had to be hiding something.

"Where the hell have you been?"

Shane looked like he'd been waiting for me when I

returned to the office, but I didn't appreciate his tone. "I went outside and walked around a bit."

He stepped closer, taking my hands in his to warm them. "Jesus. Without gloves? I told you I don't want to have to worry about you tonight. How about you go back to the hotel?"

"Why? What is this really about?"

He sighed. "I have a big shot coming in tonight who'll be using the viewing room up here. He does this every year. He's obnoxious, rich, and believes he can buy anything with money. If he sees you, he'll assume you're one of the girls here."

"So I tell him I'm not."

Shane shook his head. "He isn't someone you say no to. The last thing I want is to have to step in and piss him off. Even worse, I'd come unglued if I saw him paw at you."

I occurred to me that in a normal relationship, Shane would simply tell the guy I was with him. But this wasn't such a thing. Besides, it wasn't like we'd be kissing at midnight. "Sure, I can work from my room at the hotel. Will I see you later?"

"I'll be lucky if I'm out of here before four in the morning. But we have one last night tomorrow night. Okay?"

Yep. Emphasis on last. "Sure. I guess Happy New Year."

He smiled, already looking tired. "Yeah, Happy New Year."

᠅ ᠅

As soon as I arrived at my hotel room, I went to work with my sleuthing skills. I needed to get box counts. If I could get a quote for the same types of liquor, it would give me an idea for the number of bottles in a box. So I called the distributor, but as I should have expected this late on New Year's Eve, I got no one. When I went to the website, I discovered I wouldn't be able to get anyone until the day after tomorrow.

Shit. I couldn't wait until Thursday. I'd be gone by then. I'd even made vacation plans to make sure I wouldn't wallow here after my last day. And although I had good computer skills, I wasn't advanced enough to hack into the distributor's client accounts. And, yes, I tried.

Frustrated, I was about to give up, but then I came up with an idea. Club Travesty couldn't be the only place around serviced by this distributor. However, the chances of anyone answering the phone this late were slim. Which meant I'd be going out for New Year's Eve.

My first stop was downstairs at the hotel bar, but I wasn't in luck. They used a smaller scale supplier than Club Travesty's. But they did tip me off that the sports bar around the corner most likely used the same distributor as the club. So, two blocks down, I went amongst the growing number of people and into the bar.

It was just my luck the place was packed. When I asked to see the manager, the snippy hostess appeared completely put out. Shit, maybe I should've waited until tomorrow.

When the large man, sporting tattoos on his rippling biceps, came to the front, looking none to happy to be bothered, I almost bolted. Only the adrenaline from the chase gave me the courage to stay put.

"What's the problem?"

"No problem. Um, I'm Daniella, and my client is currently using a distributor named Wicked Liquor. I was wondering if you use them?"

"Yeah, what of it?"

"Well, I'm doing the books and found the box counts are missing from my receipts. I wondered if Wicked

Liquor is doing the same with other clients."

"Call them to ask."

Oh, boy. "I would, but it's New Year's Eve."

"No shit. This place is a zoo, and I have you asking me about suppliers on the busiest night of the year. What club are you at?"

"You're right, and I'm sorry. I'm with Club Travesty."

"You know Max?"

"Yes, Max and Shane."

"Why didn't you say so? What do you need?"

"Uh, just your last order. You can redact the amounts; I'm only interested in the box counts for each type of liquor."

"Sure. You want to come back with me to the office?"

Nope. Not even a little. "If you don't mind, I'll wait out here."

"No problem."

He was back in ten minutes with papers in his hands and an apologetic look on his face. "Uh, spoke with Shane. Hope you don't mind me verifying you're with the club. He said to give these to you, but he was pissed you were here. Told me to tell you to get your ass back to your hotel room."

I bristled. Not because the bar manager had called the club. I should've expected that. But because Shane was treating me as though I was under curfew. "Thanks for the paperwork, uh—Sorry, I didn't catch your name."

"Joe, and you're welcome. And you're not going back, are you?"

I smirked. "Nope. Suddenly I feel like a drink."

Chapter Twenty-One

Shane

After hanging up the phone with Joe, I had one thought.

I was going to kill her. I'd asked for one simple thing. For Daniella to stay in her hotel room. But evidently, that was too much. And what the hell was she doing asking for Joe's inventory forms? It occurred to me that I could've told him not to give her the paperwork, but I was too curious about why she wanted it to do that.

As if the night wasn't already off to a busy start, I'd already had to have two people escorted out for being intoxicated and had been obliged to break up a cat fight. Added to that, Mr. Moneybags was in rare form, causing my staff to kiss his ass and that of his entourage. I had to remind myself he'd paid a hundred thousand dollars for the box suite and he tipped the girls, some of whom were quite happy to service him.

And now I had to go drag Daniella's ass back. Joe had called back to inform me she hadn't taken my advice and was now sitting at his bar. Fuck.

I walked in and noticed the place was packed, as were most bars now that it was close to midnight. Yet she stood out with her copper hair down her back and a lyrical laugh at something Joe was saying to her from behind the bar.

I wasted no time stepping up and settling my hands at her waist.

She instantly tensed, but then must've realized it was me.

Joe gave me a nod. "What's up, Shane?"

"Busy night. You?"

"Same."

"You ready?" I whispered in her ear.

"Actually, no. I think this beats spending New Year's Eve by myself in my room."

"How many has she had?"

Joe chuckled. "Only one, my friend. I think perhaps you met your match."

"Indeed. Let's go, Dani." I used a tone which didn't leave room for argument, and yet she was able to ignore it.

She spun around. "And if I'm not ready to go?"

"Then I can get you ready." I let the implication settle and was relieved to see her smile.

"Well, then. In that case." She turned saying goodbye to the bar manager. "Nice to meet you, Joe."

I led her outside and down the sidewalk at breakneck speed, already hard at the thought of sneaking in a quickie with her before returning to the club. It was crazy to think this would be our third time today and yet I still hadn't had enough.

"I'm going to sit in your hotel chair where you'll ride me reverse cowgirl while I play with your ass. But after that, I need to get back to work."

"You don't have to do me any favors, you know. And you're not my keeper. I went to bars by myself before I met you. You don't get to tell me what to do."

I backed her up against the cold brick wall of the

nearest building and let her feel my erection through the layers of clothing between us. "Point taken. Now am I taking you to your hotel room or leaving you here?"

My phone interrupted. "What?" I answered tersely.

"Moneybags is asking for you. Where are you?" Max's voice came over.

"Shit. Give me two minutes." I hung up, looking at Daniella and already feeling regret. "I need to get back to work."

We both looked around when people started counting down. It only got louder as they got closer. "Five, four, three, two, one. Happy New Year."

Our eyes locked. I didn't miss the disappointment which flashed in hers when I pulled away, not even willing to give her a kiss when it hit midnight.

We walked in silence back to the hotel entrance where she gave me a small wave and went into the lobby.

For the first time, I felt torn between the club and a woman.

۾ 潔

It wasn't until four o'clock in the morning that we cleared every room. I was on my second Red Bull and Max had gone straight for black coffee. Even Heather was uncharacteristically quiet while she wiped down the bar and put the last few things away.

Housekeeping had started their impossible task of cleaning up every room, and my security detail was due to change over in another hour. In all, it had been a good party, but I was over the holiday season and all its festivities. Thankfully, we wouldn't have another one until summer. Tomorrow would be a fairly quiet day, and I looked forward to spending the night with Daniella. Knowing it would be our last night was leaving me restless. I reasoned it was because it was time to start getting back to normal. Put the holidays behind me and get back into the routine of things.

Speaking of which, I had a show on Friday night with a performer by the name of Donna Starr who'd be in town one night. I'd been with her before. She was spectacular at putting on a show, and I should be looking forward to it. The woman could suck a penny through a fifty-foot hose. Yet the thought of someone other than Daniella on her knees in front of me left me uninspired.

Crap. What was with this girl? Luckily, I had one more night to fuck her out of my system. Then she'd be back to her life, and I'd be back to mine. All I needed was some separation to get her off my mind.

I sent Max home to get some sleep while I prepared to make it an all-nighter. I'd catch a nap later if I got too tired.

※ ※

Daniella

I brought coffee in for Max, Shane, and myself. They had to be even more exhausted than I was this morning. Knowing Shane, he probably hadn't slept at all.

I'd stayed up late looking at the delivery sheets from Joe's bar, attempting to match up the liquor types with quantities. Unfortunately, the amounts told a confusing story. It seemed Travesty was not getting the better deal. It might have made sense if Joe's bar had more inventory. Then it would be understandable they'd be getting a better discount than the club. But judging from the slips and what had arrived at the club earlier today, we should have been the ones getting the bigger discount. Furthermore, numbers weren't adding up. One case of Patron, for example, should contain four bottles. Yet it appeared we were being charged for ten. Same with the Grey Goose. And that was just on the stuff we had in common with Joe's place. I knew for a fact that Travesty stocked some premium Scotch at four hundred dollars a bottle and some champagne worth the same. The sports bar wouldn't. By the time I was done estimating, I calculated an approximate discrepancy of between three to five thousand dollars per delivery. If I multiplied that times twice a week, it could be like sixty thousand a month, if not more. The numbers corresponded with the loss I'd been looking for, but unfortunately, I had no absolute proof. Just a hunch to dig further for it.

If I stayed for Thursday's order, that would provide the proof. And what was one more day, really? I was sure when I explained this to Shane and Max they'd be just as anxious as I to see if Heather was stealing.

I was right about Shane pulling an all-nighter. This was evident when he came up the stairs a few minutes after I'd arrived. "You look tired."

"I am. And you look like you've been busy."

I had paperwork spread out all over the desk, attempting to paint the picture I wanted to share with both him and Max. "I am. Here, I got you coffee. One for Max, too."

"He's catching a few hours but will be back soon. I'm sure he'll appreciate it."

"Everything okay from last night?"

"Yeah. Just busy. I'll be glad to get back to normal."

I had to bite my lip, wondering if part of the 'abnormal' had to do with me. "Definitely. Uh. So I think I've found your discrepancy, but I'd rather wait for Max to be here in order to discuss it."

"Did I hear my name?" A bleary-eyed Max came out the elevator doors.

I smiled and handed over a coffee. "You did. Here."

"You're a saint, Daniella. Thanks."

"Is, uh, Heather around?" The last thing I wanted to do was have this conversation if she could walk up or overhear it.

"Nope," Max remarked. "She's off today. Will be in Thursday morning, though. Why?"

"Well, actually, one of the things I wanted to talk to you about is coming in on Thursday for the delivery. I'd like for both of you to be there, too."

"Why?" Shane asked sharply.

"Because Thursday would show—"

"You said tomorrow was your last day. Whatever you have today is what we've got. And what does it have to do with Heather?"

I tried to fight the hurt that he didn't want me here even for one extra day. "The invoice slips from Joe at Libations Bar and Grill, coming from the same distributor you use, showed what I've been missing from our invoices: the quantity per box. Now obviously, their pricing can be different, depending on the deal. For instance, a box of Patron normally comes in a box of four, but you're being charged for a box of ten if I'm doing an average wholesale price per bottle."

"What the hell are you saying, Daniella?"

I took a deep breath. "I'm saying I think Heather is stealing from you. And she has someone in the distributor's office or on the delivery truck helping her."

His expression turned angry. "You can't be serious. What proof do you have?"

"I have enough that you should want to look at the inventory on Thursday to see for yourself. If you don't want me here, fine. It's not like I'm trying to overstay my welcome, just attempting to do my job."

"Which includes accusing a long-time employee of theft. One who you profess not to care for and have had issues with."

I stood up, my temper snapping. "You hired me to

find out why your numbers weren't adding up."

"Clearly, you're looking in the wrong place."

"You've had a loss every month for the last two years. At first it was hundreds, easily written off. But now it appears to be at least twenty thousand a week. You want to know why you're numbers aren't making sense and why it'll trigger an audit for the IRS. It's because you're losing inventory."

Since Shane looked so pissed off, my eyes shifted towards Max. He was running a hand through his hair but had stood quiet. Gathering my documents that showed the trend, I handed them to him. "You're welcome to look for yourself. And don't worry. My last day will be today."

"Fuck," Max cursed, looking over my notes.

"You don't actually believe her, do you?" Shane asked.

Forget fighting the hurt. I was hurt. And pissed. I knew the man had trust issues, but the fact he'd put me in that camp stung. "Believe whatever the fuck you want to. I'll be in touch next month with your tax return, but I won't need to be on site for it."

I intended to gather my shit and leave, but Max's voice stopped me cold.

"Six months ago, I was here for stocking. I noticed a missing box of champagne and questioned Heather."

Shane's furious gaze settled on his friend. "What did she say?"

"She said she had partied and admitted to taking it home."

"What the hell, man? And you didn't tell me."

"She made me promise not to, afraid you'd be furious. She gave me five hundred dollars later that day, saying she'd always intended to pay it back. I believed her. She's been here the entire time we have and has always been a loyal, trusted employee. It would be no different than if you'd done the same."

"Fuck. I'm going over to see her at her place. She'll tell me the truth."

"Do you want me to come with?"

Shane shook his head. "No."

Without so much as a backward glance, he strode out, evidently on his way to wake Heather up.

I stood there in shock until Max's voice broke through. "He's running on adrenaline, honey. Try not to take it personally."

I gave a humorless laugh. "Yeah, like he didn't accuse me of making it personal with Heather. Anyways..." I made myself smile and not get emotional. Never could I have imagined things ending this way. But maybe it was for the best. Maybe leaving Shane and this club should be easy because I was pissed instead of sad. "It was a pleasure, Max."

"I'm sorry it had to end the way it did. What are your plans?"

"A nice nap and a flight leaving tomorrow afternoon."

He looked surprised. "New client?"

I shook my head. "Long overdue vacation." I'd requested the time off last week, using the excuse I'd had to work during the holidays.

"Some place warm, I hope."

I smiled. "Jamaica, at an all-inclusive resort where all I want to do is lie in the sun, read a book, and eat good food."

"Sounds amazing. And if there is anything you need: a recommendation, help with your move—"

I'd enjoyed the rush of forensic accounting and had started to think I might have found my niche. It certainly beat the hell out of boring taxes. And if other clubs could trust my discretion, then I might be able to quickly build a client base. "I may take you up on that recommendation for other clubs such as this."

"New client for your firm?"

"Actually, I've been thinking about doing some freelancing. Maybe I have a thing for sex clubs now."

He chuckled. "Please, please make sure you run them past me. Not all of them are reputable."

"Deal. Take care, Max." I gave him a hug, gathered my computer bag, and took one last look before leaving.

Chapter Twenty-Two

Shane

It took exactly five minutes for Heather to break down and give up the name of her partner in crime. What I hadn't expected, and should have, was that Eric, Daniella's ex, had also been involved. He'd helped hide the money over the last couple of years for a cut. Sure, that fucker hadn't technically stolen from me, but he'd helped cover up for someone who was and had made a tidy profit from it.

The worst part was Heather's reasoning. It wasn't for a sick family member or because she owed money to someone. Nope, it was because she wanted to live in Tribeca and needed the money so she could pay for her condo. One, I might add, that was nicer than my own. Simply put, she somehow had convinced herself she was owed a lifestyle she couldn't afford.

I couldn't believe that after confessing, she even had the audacity to ask to keep her job. Not only was she fired, but she was also lucky we weren't pressing charges. Of course, I needed to discuss it with Max, but the last thing we needed was either the scrutiny or embarrassment. As it was, it would be hard to explain the situation to the other employees. And after I made a call to the distributer later, Heather wouldn't be the only one out of a job. As for Eric, I hadn't decided what his fate would be, but I planned to give him a call to ensure he returned Daniella's money by the end of the week. Otherwise, his big secret would be public in a hurry.

Daniella. Fuck. I'd hurt her. In my defense, I'd been operating on no sleep, and her bombshell had caught me completely off guard.

I walked up the steps to my office slowly and deliberately. There I met the eyes of Max, who was anxiously waiting.

Based on my grim expression, he knew instantly how it had turned out.

"Did she at least give a reason?"

I poured a whiskey and sighed. "Her condo overlooking the city. Her plastic surgery. A lifestyle she feels entitled to."

"I was really hoping for a better excuse, like a sick relative."

"Me, too. She gave up the name of the distributer."

"Fucker. I take it you'll call the supplier and get him fired tomorrow?"

"Chances are she's already called him, and he's taken off. And for a cut, Eric helped shift around money to hide it from being obvious."

He cursed again. "Will you have the pics go viral?"

"I haven't decided. Heather actually had the nerve to ask if she could remain working here."

"She's lucky we won't press charges. We aren't, right?"

I shook my head. "Not worth it. Where's Daniella?"

He leveled me with a look. "Dude. Where do you think she is? She took off after you basically accused her of being jealous of Heather. I believe you also implied that her wanting to stay another morning to give you proof was because she wasn't ready to let you go."

"I didn't mean—shit."

He held up a hand. "If that's your excuse, then it's probably best you don't see her again."

"I don't want that. Is she back at the hotel?"

He shrugged. "Not sure, but I do know she's not coming back here. Matter of fact, she has a flight out tomorrow, leaving on vacation."

This was news. Although come tomorrow, was it really my business? I didn't like the answer.

"I fucked up." I had. Although I hadn't known Daniella that long, I should've handled what she was saying better and not made it personal.

"Guess you could start with that."

Here's hoping it would work.

Daniella

Even after packing everything up and taking a shower, I was restless. I told myself I didn't care that he hadn't knocked. But it was a lie. I cared. Too much.

As evidence, I realized I'd wanted too badly to prove myself in his eyes. Earn his impossible trust by finding the damn boxes in the frigid cold and figuring out the mystery of his lost revenue. But my quest had left me cold, both literally and figuratively. I wasn't any closer to earning his trust. And I was a fool for not realizing my motivation ran deeper than simply doing my job and an even bigger one for allowing myself to be hurt by it.

That alone made me glad I was leaving tomorrow. I needed to get Shane out of my system.

The knock at the door instantly caused butterflies. I opened it to the object of my thoughts.

He stepped inside, cupping my face. "I'm sorry. So sorry for doubting you. My only defense is I was exhausted, and I didn't want to believe someone who has been with Max and me from the beginning could do such a thing. I fucked up, Dani."

I swallowed hard. "You hurt me by assuming I'd made it personal towards her."

"I know. And I'm sorry. You were right. She'd been stealing with the help of the distributor who kept the box counts off the receipts. And Eric had been helping her to hide the numbers, making it harder for me to see it."

Of all the things he could've said, Eric's involvement shouldn't have shocked me, but it did. "I'm sorry."

He shook his head. "For what? If it wasn't for you, who knows if we ever would've found out the truth? I not only owe you an apology, but a big thank you, too."

Before I could respond, his lips descended to mine, the kiss so unexpected that I pulled back in shock, meeting his eyes.

"I've never wanted this more than I do right now."

A mix of vulnerability and sincerity were reflected in his gaze. If this was our last night, who was I to deny something I'd longed for every time we were together? I didn't hesitate to pull his mouth back to mine, aware he was moving me into the room and letting the door shut behind him.

His tongue tangled with mine, making me desperate for this intimate contact to continue. One taste wasn't enough. Instead, it felt like I'd been starved for it and was finally getting my fix. He must've felt the same as he didn't break contact, instead deepening the kiss and throwing everything in his arsenal at it with lips, tongue, and teeth. His hand tangled in my hair while the other went straight for my pussy.

"So fucking perfect every time," he whispered, moving his kisses to my ear and throat. "I want nothing between us."

"God. Yes." Meanwhile, the logical part of my brain

thought, why? Why on the last day? But it was overruled by lust. Yep, now I knew how after-school specials were made. And I couldn't even say my intentions were good. Because they were, oh, so dirty instead. Which is why, when he buried himself deep inside of me, skin on skin, coming deep inside of me, I reveled in our last time together.

After falling asleep in his arms, I awoke with a start the next morning. Checking my phone, I breathed a sigh of relief at the time reflected. I had a plane to catch in four hours. Glancing over, I saw Shane still fast asleep. Considering he'd pulled an all-nighter and then had marathon sex with me, I couldn't say I was surprised.

Even after I'd showered and dressed, he was still passed out. I was tempted to wake him, but for what? A sad goodbye? A stupid hope that he'd want me to stay? I thought about a note, but the same problem persisted. What would I say? It was fun?

Turns out it had been a hell of a lot more than that.

Chapter Twenty-Three

Shane

I woke up slowly, taking a moment to remember where in the hell I was. Then I smiled and reached for Daniella, only to find her side of the bed empty. And cold. I sat up, rubbing the sleep from my eyes. Jesus, I'd slept like the dead.

I listened for the shower but didn't hear it. Then I realized the suitcase I'd noticed by the door last night was gone. And so was everything Daniella.

Ten minutes later, Max looked up from his desk to see me walking towards him with purpose.

"Where is Dani? Did she come by here?"

He shook his head. "No, man. Weren't you with her? When you didn't come back yesterday, I assumed you two made up."

"We did, but she left."

He checked his watch. "Probably for her flight."

Shit. I'd forgotten about the trip. "Where was she going?"

"Jamaica, mon."

I didn't even crack a smile. Instead, I ran a hand through my hair in frustration.

"Question to ask is if you're going after her?"

"To what end?"

He leveled me a look. "That's the question you need to ask yourself. But if you want my opinion, I've never seen you happier than you've been the last week with her around."

"I'd be selfish to keep her in this world."

He chuckled. "Considering she's looking at offers to freelance at other clubs, I'd say she's not in a hurry to leave it."

"The hell she is."

He stood up. "Seems to me if you want a right to weigh in on her decision, you'd better get your ass to JFK."

"And say what? That we've known each a little over a week and I might have feelings?" At this point, old insecurities surfaced, stemming from my mother's decision to disown me. How could a woman like Daniella want to tie herself to man like me? Sure, I had money. But what else could I offer her? Long work hours which included weekends and nights. A parade of women I'd been with in front of others at the club. A tendency to be a dick and to have a tough time apologizing. And what would her family and friends think if they learned the truth about me?

Max sighed. "What if I came to you and said I'd met someone who I wanted to have a relationship with? Would you tell me I wasn't worthy of it because I owned this club? Would you tell me I didn't deserve to be happy with someone I could fall in love with?"

"Of course not."

"Then stop questioning whether or not you deserve it and simply ask her. She's a big girl who can make her own decisions. Not as though she isn't aware you can be a moody son-of-a-bitch. Yet she continues to like you."

I cracked a smile and blew out a breath. "I'm not sure

I can do this."

"You act like you need to choose between this club and her. But what if you can have both? Wouldn't that be worth it? I know for me it would be."

My decision came easily. "Can you manage a few days without me?"

∂~ ~∂

Daniella

I arrived at the airport exactly one hour after leaving Shane in bed. My first thought while putting my heavy suitcase up on the scale with my muscles screaming from the effort was that I needed a massage. It would be my first order of business once I arrived at the resort. I had every intention of taking a relaxing vacation before returning and figuring out where I'd live and if I wanted to stay in my job. I wasn't sure what I was going to do, but for the first time, I did feel the freedom to choose.

Smiling at the desk agent, I handed her my passport.

"Ms. Trivioli, good news for you today. You've been upgraded to first class."

"Oh. Why?" I didn't mean to sound ungrateful, but it didn't make sense.

She shrugged. "Don't know. Could be a full flight, and your airfare made you eligible. Did you not want it?"

"No, no, I do. Thanks." Considering Eric had sent confirmation about ten minutes ago that he'd wire the rest of my money by the end of the week, perhaps everything was looking up.

After security, I made my way to the lounge where I had a cocktail—okay, maybe three—and tried not to think about Shane. How was it this last week with him was leaving me more broken-hearted than my two years with Eric? I couldn't be in love with him already, could

I? Perhaps it was simply lust. I didn't want to think about it. Instead, I got up, ready for my flight and an escape via first class.

I took the window seat in the third row. The setup was awesome with the flat screen in front of me and the additional leg room. I didn't fly much, but this was the way to do it. I couldn't wait to recline and maybe get some much-needed sleep; last night hadn't afforded me much. While the plane filled up, I flipped around the movie channels and figured I might end up with an empty seat beside me. Then he sat down.

Despite tired eyes, a dark scruff, and wearing his clothes from last night, Shane still looked devastatingly handsome.

"What are you doing here?" I posed the obvious question.

He put a small bag under the seat before turning to me. "Heading to Jamaica."

"But why? Wait. Were you the one who upgraded me?"

"Max technically did, but I asked if he could do me the favor while I was busy getting to the airport. I was happy to find out this flight wasn't completely full, and we could get seats together. I don't fly much, so the extra room is nice."

"Uh. Okay, but why are you here?"

For the first time in this little exchange, he appeared nervous.

"When I woke up, you were gone. I realized it's because I didn't give you any indication or reason to stay and—"

He was interrupted by the flight attendant asking us for our drink orders.

"To be continued once we get in the air."

I gripped his arm, impatient for his words. "What? No, say what you were going to."

But it was too late. The announcements were being made, the flight attendant was back to get our cups, and then came the safety briefing. Finally, after what seemed to take forever, we were airborne.

He quickly reclined both his seat and mine fully and then put up the privacy screen. Once we were both reclined flat, we turned towards one another, our heads propped on our hands, eye to eye.

"Hi."

I laughed at his greeting. "Hi."

"Where was I?"

"I believe you were about to answer why you're on a flight to Jamaica with me."

"Right." He exhaled a breath. "I don't want what we have to stop."

His words caused a shiver to run up my body. I was about to respond, but he wasn't done.

"I realize it's crazy to feel this way after a few days. I mean we hardly know one another. You just got out of an engagement, and I've never been in a real relationship. Tell me it's crazy."

I smiled. "It is crazy, but I'd be lying if I said I didn't feel the same way."

He scooted closer to me, pulling my hips in line with his. "I'm an owner of a sex club, and I won't give that up. I can't change my past, and I won't apologize for it. My own mother died still disowning me for my choices."

I reached out, stroking his face where pain was etched in his expression. I fought my own emotion in watching a man like him say such difficult things. "No one should have to feel judged like that."

He swallowed hard. "No, they shouldn't. But being involved with me will mean people in your life will judge. I guess what I'm saying is I don't know what to offer you, Daniella. What I can give to a relationship."

"The same could be said for me. What am I offering you? Monogamous sex that doesn't include your show room at the club and the complications of having a girlfriend."

"You sell yourself short."

"Right back at you. Now, as for what you give me. You give me honesty. Freedom to be myself." I hesitated before blurting it out. "But I've wondered if you miss the club and performing or being with other women. I know we've watched some shows together, and I enjoy it. But I wonder if you prefer to be down there. I even thought about how I'd feel performing with you. I mean I wouldn't want more than just me and you in a scene, but—"

He was already shaking his head. "Baby, there is no way I'm allowing one other person to see you naked. Your body and your orgasms are for me only. I recognize that makes me a hypocrite considering most of the club has seen me, but there's no way I want any other man watching you. And as for the other. You make me feel things I never thought I would. And I've never felt half as attracted to a woman as I am to you."

I smiled at his admission.

"Did you mean it when you said you didn't want to have kids? Because that's not something I can change either. Even if I wanted to."

"I've never wanted them. Frankly, it'll be nice to date someone I don't have to worry about pressuring me later."

He looked relieved. "I can't promise you that by the end of the month you won't be thoroughly sick of me working so many hours or being grumpy or having to apologize for getting this relationship stuff wrong. But it won't fall apart because I'd ever cheat. That I can promise. I trust you, Dani. The bottom line is I can't think of anyone I'd rather try this with than you."

"Me, neither." I appreciated that we were being logical about this. We weren't calling it insta-love or ignoring the fact we each still had a lot to learn about the another. "Would this relationship include kissing?"

He grinned in return. "So much you'll be wishing for the days I didn't."

I shook my head. "Not possible." And because I could, I leaned in and kissed him. The free license to do so had me anxious to get closer to him.

He pulled back to chuckle. "Easy, or they'll know exactly what's going on in seats three A and B."

"Mm. Don't tell me you're shy about the mile-high club?"

He arched a brow. "Are you already a card holder?"

I shook my head. "Nope. Would be my first."

He went to work unzipping my jeans. "Mine, too. Now kiss me before everyone hears your orgasm on this plane."

I didn't have time to relish being his first at something before he had me climaxing around his fingers while he swallowed down my moan. When I opened up my eyes, I watched him taste his fingers with hooded eyes.

"Unbelievable every time."

Reaching for him, I was surprised when he took my hand in his and kissed my wrist softly. "Not so fast. Next time I come, it'll be inside of you, so I can watch it drip down your inner thighs and think about how it's still inside of you when we go to dinner tonight."

"Jesus," I muttered, his dirty words doing nothing to quell my hunger for him. "Guess I know how we'll be spending a good portion of our vacation."

"Daniella Trivioli. Will you do me the honor of trying a real relationship with me?"

I grinned at his proposal. "A hundred times yes."

Epilogue

Shane

After a busy Friday night at my club, I slipped into bed a happy man. Because Daniella was already sound asleep in it.

Four months after I'd first set eyes on her, I was still just as convinced I'd never get enough. Although I still enjoyed owning and operating the club, I didn't feel truly at peace until I held her in my arms. Which wasn't happening nearly enough for my liking. Sure, we spent at least three nights together per week. But with her condo sublet near her office in Jersey City while I maintained my loft in Manhattan close to the club, that wasn't nearly enough.

When my arms went around her, she sighed in contentment, snuggling closer.

"Mm, how was your night?"

"Better now." I kissed the side of her neck, feeling emotion over this woman who made me laugh, challenged me, but best of all, made me unbelievably happy.

"Me, too."

She was gloriously naked, with her smooth skin

rubbing against mine. Although I enjoyed stripping her out of her clothing, especially when she'd come from work to the club in her pencil skirts and fuck-me heels, I loved the best this skin-on-skin connection with her in my bed in the wee hours of the morning.

After reaching around, I groaned when I found her wet and ready for me. I wasted no time pushing inside of her, gripping her hip and rubbing her centerpoint of pleasure until she was wildly bucking against me, begging me to thrust. But I waited until she was teetering on the edge before I set a rhythm, taking her over and up again to an orgasm that squeezed my cock like a vice grip.

But I wasn't done. I pulled out and put her on her back before thrusting deep inside of her again, putting my forearms next to her head and diving into her kiss. I'd often scoffed at the word intimacy, but now I knew the true meaning of it.

That's why after I'd made love to her with a second round, I lay with her entwined with my body, not wanting to sever the connection.

"Move in with me," I said in the dark, hoping she wasn't already asleep.

She popped up and looked down on me, moonlight making her look even more beautiful. "What did you say?"

"Move in with me. Or if you don't like my place, then we can find another one together. Especially after you start your new job." She'd given notice after tax time, intending to start free-lancing in the city, doing everything from accounting to fraud investigations. Clearly, she already had one loyal client in the club. She'd also earned Joe's business at the sport's bar around the corner.

"Your loft is amazing, but, uh, how did this come up tonight?"

"I've been thinking about it for a while now. Matter of fact, the guys at work mentioned I'm a real dick Monday through Thursday unless I've spent the night with you."

"So, I should move in with you because Max and your employees would appreciate it?"

Her voice was quiet and I knew immediately I'd screwed this up. Time to lay it out. "No, you should do it because I love you and don't want to spend our nights apart anymore."

She blew out a breath. "You love me?"

I started to feel a kernel of fear that she might not feel the same. "I really screwed up the order of things. Probably should've told you that part before asking you to move in or making it seem like it had been the idea of the guys at work."

I flipped her on her back so I could be eye to eye with her. "Let me start over. I love you, Daniella. More than I ever thought possible to love someone. And when I'm with you, I'm happy. When I know you're in my bed at home waiting for me, I'm anxious to get here. I wasn't sure how I'd adapt to a relationship, but the last four months have taught me the reason I didn't want one before now was because I didn't have you."

"Wow. When you do a do-over, you reach for the stars. That was—Well, it was everything. I love you, too. So much."

I hadn't realized how much I needed to hear those words until they came from her lips.

"Guess that means we're out of the trying phase?" she quipped.

"Must mean we're in a full-blown relationship now."

"Does that freak you out?"

I shook my head. "Not at all. Actually, I don't think we're done trying, after all."

"Why is that?"

I tucked her hair behind her ear, nuzzling her neck. "Because I have every intention of trying to make you happy every day."

She smiled. "I have the same intentions."

"Good. Now let's ensure at least half of them are dirty."

About the Author

Aubrey Bondurant is a working mom who loves to write, read, and travel.

She describes her writing style as: "Adult Contemporary Erotic Romantic Comedy," which is just another way of saying she likes her characters funny, her bedroom scenes hot, and her romances with a happy ending.

When Aubrey isn't working her day job or spending time with her family, she's on her laptop typing away on her next story. She only wishes there were more hours of the day! She's a former member of the US Marine Corps and passionate about veteran charities and giving back to the community. She loves a big drooly dog, a fantastic margarita, and football.

If you would like more information about Aubrey, please visit her at:

www.aubreybondurant.com

Books by Aubrey Bondurant

Something Series

Tell Me Something
Ask Me Something
Bet Me Something
Teach Me Something
Show Me Something

Filthy Appeal

Ramona Gray

Chapter One

"I'm worried about you, Libby." My mother's voice was cutting in and out, and I shifted my cell phone to my other ear. I crossed the room and drew back the drapes, staring down at the park across from me. Dusk was falling. There was a glow of green and red Christmas lights that were strung through the trees in the park, illuminating the people hurrying down the shovelled paths.

"I told you, the roads were fine. I'm at the hotel and I pick up the key for my new place tomorrow afternoon. I'm good."

"You're not good. How can you be?" My mother almost wailed into the phone.

I tried to hold in my sigh of irritation. "Because I've just landed my dream job? I'm not only the first female partner at the law firm of Martin, Clarke and Bones, I'm the youngest partner in the history of the firm, Mom."

"What good is a dream job when your heart is broken?"

"My heart is not broken."

"I know you still love him."

"No, I don't," I snapped. "He cheated on me. Repeatedly. In our bed with a twenty-two-year-old."

"Honey," my mother said, "I know that Wayne made a terrible decision and I understand how difficult it's been for you, but men have needs."

"Don't, Mom. It's been a long day and I'm tired," I warned.

"Hear me out, honey. You were working a lot of overtime and you had - "

"I was working to secure our future," I hissed into the phone. "Do you think Wayne was going to provide for us by being a short-order cook at a second-rate diner?"

"See, that's what I'm talking about," my mother said.

"I have no idea what you mean," I said.

"You were always belittling him, honey. I've had some long talks with Wayne since you broke up with him and he told me how you didn't approve of his job or his dream of one day owning his own restaurant. If you want to keep a man, you have to be supportive of their dreams. Add in the fact that you've let yourself go in the last few years and is it any wonder that Wayne was tempted to stray?"

I wished I could say I was shocked by my mother's behaviour, but I wasn't. I'd spent my entire life listening to her lecture me on all the ways I failed at – well – everything. I'd already heard this particular gem of a lecture twice before, but I suddenly couldn't stand to listen to it for a moment longer. Unfortunately, my mother was relentless.

"You did so well to lose all that weight, honey, and it's a real shame that you lost focus and gained it back."

"I didn't lose focus. I was very busy at work and I got tired of starving myself and going to the gym every night for two hours," I said. "Just because I'm fat and busy at work doesn't give Wayne the right to cheat on me, Mom."

"Of course it doesn't," my mother said. "But, honey, you know men are visual creatures. They want to be proud of their lady and you can't blame Wayne for not being proud of the fact that you've gained forty pounds in the last two years. You have such a pretty face, Libby, it's a shame that - "

"I have to go," I interrupted.

"Honey, wait! We haven't talked about Christmas. What day are you driving back?"

"We did talk about Christmas, remember? I said I wasn't going to be there."

"I didn't think you meant it," my mother said. "You're really going to leave me all alone on Christmas?"

"You won't be alone," I said. "You're going to grandma and grandpa's and the rest of your siblings will be there as well."

She carried on like she hadn't heard a word I'd said. Honestly, she probably hadn't.

"Christmas is for family, Elizabeth. Family!"

"It's a very busy time at the firm, and they needed me to start this week," I lied.

My mother sighed dramatically. "Well, my only child is abandoning me for her career. I guess I can understand where Wayne is coming from."

Anger and frustration and a healthy dose of hurt settled in my stomach and I blinked back the tears savagely. "That's not what I'm doing and you know it. I have to go. Good night, Mom. I'll call you in a few days when I'm settled."

I pushed the end button on my phone before she could reply and could barely restrain myself from throwing my phone across the room. I leaned my forehead against the window, closed my eyes, and tried not to let my mother's obvious disappointment in me change my mind about what I was going to do.

I straightened and crossed the hotel room to study myself in the full-length mirror. I was wearing my tightest pair of jeans and a shimmery blue top that hugged my breasts and had a scandalously low neckline. My push-up bra was doing a marvelous job of keeping my tits where they were supposed to be, and I studied my cleavage before pulling self-consciously at my top. I was certain that if I took too deep of a breath, my boobs would fall right out of my shirt. I glanced at my suitcase and briefly considered changing my shirt before turning to the mirror again. I needed a pep talk stat.

"Elizabeth Gertrude Brecken, you are not changing your shirt. One does not simply walk into a generic hotel bar and seduce a stranger wearing a t-shirt. Your tits are amazing and you're going to need them out front and center and working overtime."

I turned and stared at my butt. I couldn't hide the size of my ass or thickness of my thighs or my extra-large muffin top. Not in these clothes. For a moment, I mourned the loss of my thinness before I shook my head. I was being stupid. Until I walked in on Wayne banging the twenty-two-year-old like a screen door in a tornado, I'd been perfectly content with my larger body.

Always a chubby kid and teenager, I'd finally grown tired of my mother's constant nagging about my weight and started a strict regime of diet and exercise when I entered university. I'd stayed thin through starvation and exercise until the last two years. My busy career and my lack of enthusiasm for constantly monitoring what I ate, led to a slow but gradual weight gain. I still exercised on a regular basis and I ate healthy for the most part, but my body wasn't meant to be thin. I wasn't bothered by it, it was a relief to finally be myself again, and Wayne hadn't seemed upset by it either. Of course, the twenty-two-year-old he was screwing had the lithe body of a gymnast and when I'd confronted him, he had said that -

I cut off that thought immediately. Bile rose in my

throat and I swallowed it down. Best not to think about Wayne and his betrayal. Despite what my mother thought, I was supportive of his dream of owning his own restaurant. It wasn't my fault that he lacked the motivation to actually pursue his dream.

I shook off the memories of Wayne and grabbed my purse from the bed. I was starting a new job in a new city and I couldn't be happier. Christmas was a week away and yes, I would be spending it alone for the first time in my life, but even that didn't upset me. My new company was more than willing to let me start in the new year. They were a little surprised that I wanted to start so close to the holidays, but I couldn't get away from my old life fast enough. Given the choice between spending Christmas alone binge watching my favourite shows on Netflix, or spending Christmas with my mother listening to her lecture me on all my shortcomings, it wasn't hard to choose.

"Netflix," I said to my reflection in the mirror. "Definitely Netflix. Okay, girl, let's do this."

Libby, are you sure you want to do this?

I ignored my inner me. My self-esteem had taken a nosedive when I walked in on Wayne and his floozy. While I might have been happy with how my career was going, there was a stupid part of me that was desperate to find out if I could still seduce a guy into sleeping with me. It had been years since I dated, and while I wasn't interested in dating right now, I was interested in finding a man to fuck. I blushed at my dirty thoughts, but if I couldn't be truthful with myself about what I wanted, then I shouldn't be going to the damn hotel bar in the first place.

Wayne and I hadn't had sex in months, I was single, and I was in a city where no one knew me. I wanted to prove to myself that I was still attractive enough to land a man, even with a muffin top and oversize ass.

Prove it to yourself or to your mother? Inner me whispered. *We both know you're not a one-night stand kind of woman. Also, men like thin girls, not a fatty like you.*

I spun around abruptly and stalked out of the room, letting the door slam behind me. I was getting laid tonight, no matter what.

⋙ ⋘

For a Saturday night, the hotel bar was relatively empty and my prospects for having sex with a stranger seemed dismally slim. Although, it was still early, I told myself. In this particular case, maybe the early bird didn't get the worm.

Girl, you need to look for something bigger than a worm. You've spent years denying it, but Wayne's dick was small and nothing special. You need a man with a big dick who knows how to use it.

When had I become such a damn nymphomaniac? I had always liked sex but in the last month or so I'd become obsessed with it. Become obsessed with finding someone who would find me attractive and sexy at my current size. Someone who wouldn't tell me that –

Nope, I wasn't going there. Reliving the memory of Wayne telling me that my weight was crushing him – both figuratively and literally – was a terrible idea. I straightened my back before sweeping my gaze over the bar. There was a group of businessmen sitting at a table close to the entrance. They were talking loudly, and from the look of their flailing hands and red faces, they'd already had too much to drink. I crossed all of them off my mental "try and have sex with" list.

A few couples were sitting at the booths and tables scattered around the bar. A trio of women wearing jeans and t-shirts – they had the harried look of overworked mothers – were conversing quietly. The one closest to me glanced at the street entrance and I followed her gaze when her eyes widened and she nudged her friend sitting next to her.

My breath caught in my throat. The two gods who had just walked in were smiling at the hostess and even from here she looked flustered and nervous. I couldn't blame her. Both men were well over six feet tall with broad shoulders and narrow hips. The one on the left had dark hair and he was slightly taller and heavier than his friend. I could see the muscles bulging in his arms as he stuck his hands into the back pockets of his faded jeans. The motion made his t-shirt cling to his abdomen and my pussy made a weird little flutter as I stared at the ridges of muscles. His friend had a leaner build and sandy-brown coloured hair and I took a deep shuddering breath when he grinned at the hostess and two deep dimples appeared in his cheeks.

Oh God, my panties were getting wet. The two men practically screamed sex and for one moment I allowed myself the fantasy of sleeping with one of them.

One of them? You want to choose? Go for both!

I almost laughed out loud. I was barely the type of girl who had a one-night stand with one man, let alone two. Besides, men who looked like them were not interested in women who looked like me.

Of course, that didn't prevent my heart from stopping and then galloping back into beat when the dark-haired god glanced my way. I stood frozen to the spot as his gaze drifted down my body before returning to my face. Was that… lust on his face?

I could feel my cheeks burning and I sucked in my gut and looked away. I was an idiot. The denim-wearing god and his dimpled friend were way, *way* out of my league. I was wasting my time even fantasizing about them.

Forcing myself not to peek at them again, I studied the curved wooden bar. Mirrors lined the wall behind it and I studied the reflection of the lone man sitting at the bar. He had olive coloured skin and black hair that was thinning on top. He looked a little older than me and he was clean shaven and wearing a custom-made suit. He was handsome enough and he looked...safe. Like someone I could seduce.

Keeping my head high, I walked to the bar and slid onto the stool beside him. He glanced at my face and his gaze dipped briefly to my cleavage before he returned to staring at his glass of wine. Not exactly an encouraging start but I checked for a wedding band anyway. His ring finger was bare. It was time to put my plan – code name "bang a total stranger" – into motion.

I waved at the bartender. She took her sweet time walking over and gave me a polite smile. I ordered a glass of wine and when she returned with it, I fumbled my money out of my wallet. God, I was so nervous.

I took a few sips of wine for courage before clearing my throat. "Hi there. My name is Libby. What's yours?"

The man glanced at me again. "Dwayne."

I jerked wildly and nearly fell off the stool. Fuck, that was too close to Wayne for comfort. The man arched his eyebrow at me and I gave him a weak smile. "Sorry, I'm a little clumsy."

"Sure," he replied.

I held out my hand and after a moment, he shook it briefly. His hand was soft and sweaty and his nails were perfectly manicured. He tapped one finger against his wine glass as I said, "So, are you in town for business?"

He nodded but didn't offer any more information. I took another sip of wine. "What do you do?"

"Marketing," he said.

I waited for him to ask what I did and when he didn't,

said, "Do you enjoy it?"

"Yes." He drank some wine and I was encouraged when he took a quick peek at my tits. Maybe he was shy.

"That's good. Enjoying your work is important. I'm a…"

I trailed off as the dark-haired god sat down on the stool on my other side. His dimpled friend had already sat down next to him. The butterflies flickered to life in my stomach and I forgot about Dwayne from marketing as I inhaled. The dark-haired man smelled incredible and I gripped my wine glass as the bartender came hurrying over.

"Hi there. What can I get you guys?" She said. She placed her hands on the edge of the bar and bent a little at the waist, giving them both a smile and a good look down her shirt. She had nothing on me when it came to tits, but I supposed that didn't matter. She was beautiful with tanned skin and long dark hair and a slender body. She probably did yoga every day and drank organic kale smoothies. Seeing as she was the most gorgeous woman in the bar, there was no doubt in my mind that she'd be going home with one of the gods tonight.

So, wait to see which one she takes and then you take the other!

I almost scoffed out loud as they ordered beers and the bartender gave them a slow inviting smile before hurrying off to get their drinks. Just because they happened to sit next to me at the bar didn't mean I could seduce which ever one the bartender rejected. No, they weren't for me. I needed to concentrate on nice, safe Dwayne. He was probably amazing in bed. Didn't they say that the men who looked stuffy and stiff were actually animals in the sack?

Yes, I decided as the bartender returned with the beers, that's what they said. Dwayne was probably incredible in bed and, dammit, I was determined to find out for certain. I ignored the god sitting on my left side and turned back to Dwayne.

"So, Dwayne, what do you like to do for fun?"

Dwayne smiled condescendingly at me before saying, "Look, Lily, you seem like a nice lady but I'm not interested in you. I like my women a little more fit, okay?"

Hot shame flooded my cheeks as Dwayne drank the last of his wine, slid off the stool and walked away without looking back. I clenched my hand around my wine glass as I blinked back the hot tears. No doubt the hottie sitting next to me had heard every word. I was beyond humiliated. Why the fuck had I ever thought a man would find me attractive? Wayne and my mother were right. Men didn't want a fat girl, they wanted –

"You're going to break that glass, sweetheart." A big hand, warm and covered in hard calluses wrapped around mine. He tugged lightly on my fingers. "Let go of the glass."

I let go and dropped my hand into my lap. It latched onto my other one and they worried and twisted together as I stared dully at the top of the bar. Oh God, I couldn't stand the humiliation.

"You okay?" His voice was a deep rasp that sent shivers down my spine.

I nodded and croaked, "I have to go."

"He's an idiot, sweetheart."

Now the tears were slipping down my cheeks and I brushed them away. "Th-thanks. I have to go now."

"Don't go, love." A second voice, just as low as the first, spoke from my right. The dimpled god had moved to sit on Dwayne's empty stool and I groaned inwardly as he said, "Have a drink with us."

"I shouldn't," I whispered.

"You should," the dark-haired one said. He signaled

for the bartender and ordered me another glass of wine. When it arrived, he paid for it and handed it over. I took two large swallows and was about to take a third when the glass was tugged from my hand.

"Whoa, slow down, love," the dimpled god said. "We don't want you getting drunk on us."

I didn't reply. I couldn't look either of them in the eye and fresh embarrassment washed over me when the dark-haired one said, "He really is an idiot. You shouldn't listen to a word he says, Lily."

"Libby," I whispered. "My name is Libby. He-he got it wrong."

"See? Complete idiot," the dark-haired man said. "My name is Seth and this is my friend Theo."

"It's a pleasure to meet you, Libby." Theo held out his hand and after a moment I shook it. His hand had rough calluses as well that scraped across my palm. "Are you visiting our city for pleasure or business?"

"I – I just moved here. I'm staying at the hotel tonight because my, uh, place isn't ready until tomorrow."

"Welcome to Mansford," Seth said. "I assure you that not all the men here are assholes like old Dwayne."

I shrugged and Seth leaned closer. I shivered when I felt his warm breath on the side of my face. "He's wrong, Libby. You look - "

"I know what I look like," I interrupted. "Thank you for the glass of wine but I'm dying of embarrassment and I want to forget this ever happened."

I grabbed my purse but before I slid off the stool, Seth said, "Libby, wait."

The command in his voice kept me frozen to the stool. I didn't object when he tugged my purse from my hand and placed it back on the bar before taking my hand and rubbing his thumb over my palm.

I was trembling and my skin felt hot and tight. I

watched Seth's thumb rub across my palm and shamefully made a soft moan when he leaned in and brushed his lips against my cheek.

"You're beautiful, Libby and much too good for a man like him."

"I'm not," I whispered.

"You are," he insisted. "Look at me."

I dragged my gaze away from his thumb and stared into his eyes. They were the colour of dark chocolate and a shiver went down my spine when he dipped his head and pressed a feather-light kiss against my mouth.

I whimpered quietly, my body arching toward him and a ghost of a smile crossed his lips. "Beautiful and responsive. Your turn, Theo."

I blinked at him but before I could ask him what he meant, Theo was cupping the back of my neck and tugging gently on it. I turned to face him and moaned when his mouth descended on mine. The tip of his tongue traced my lower lip and I parted my lips immediately. He pulled back and smiled at me, squeezing the back of my neck before dropping his hand from my neck and picking up his beer.

He took a long drink as I said in a low and shaky voice, "What is happening?"

"Why are you in this bar tonight, Libby?" Seth's voice was right in my ear and I licked my lips as both men crowded close. The babbled conversation of the other patrons in the bar faded away and I had to work very hard not to lean against the warm bodies of either men. Their shoulders brushed mine and their heads were tilted toward me.

"I came here because I," my face flushed, "I couldn't sleep and I thought a nightcap might help."

Seth's eyebrow arched up and he glanced at Theo. "Do you believe her, Theo?"

"No," Theo said with a small grin. "Do you?"

Seth shook his head and I gasped when his big hand rested on my thigh. His fingers pushed between them and he rubbed my inner thigh as Theo put his hand on my lower back and traced tiny circles.

"I think you're lying to us, sweetheart," Seth said.

"I'm not," I whispered.

"Lying gets you a spanking," Theo said.

All the muscles in my pussy clenched in a heart-stopping spasm of pleasure and my nipples beaded into hard points. I was nearly panting now and a flush was rising up my neck. Why did the thought of being spanked by them bring a shameful amount of liquid to my pussy? Spanking wasn't my kink.

How do you know? Old stick-in-the-mud Wayne liked two positions and wouldn't know a kink if it smacked him in the face.

"Tell us why you're really here, Libby," Seth said.

His big hand squeezed my thigh and the words came tumbling out of me in a low rush. "I came home one day and my boyfriend was having sex with a much younger and thinner woman in our bed. When I asked him why he said, he-he said …"

I trailed off and swallowed past the aching burn in my throat. I couldn't say it. It was too humiliating. Seth rubbed my thigh and Theo pressed a gentle kiss against my cheek.

"How are you guys doing? Need a fresh drink?"

The bartender was back and I stared grimly at my hands in my lap as Seth said, "No thank you."

"Are you sure?" The bartender was persistent, I'd give her that. "I can bring you a menu if you're hungry."

"No thank you," Seth repeated. "We want privacy please."

"Oh, of course." The bartender sounded both surprised and deflated and my inner voice cheered loudly. Score one for the big girl.

When she was gone, Seth said, "Tell us, Libby."

I hesitated and then said, "If I don't, will you spank me?"

What the fuck?

"Yes," Theo said in a low voice. "We'll bend you over the bed, pull down your jeans and your panties and spank your lovely ass until it's covered in our handprints."

I moaned and Seth squeezed my thigh again before grinning at Theo. "I think we might have better luck if we threaten *not* to spank her."

"Oh God," I whispered. "What is wrong with me?"

"Nothing," Theo said. "Tell us what we want to know, love."

"He cheated on me because I'd gained weight."

I didn't have to tell them exactly what he said. I'd just make sure that if I did have sex with one of them, I wouldn't be on top. Easy.

I jerked when Seth made a low curse. Theo was studying me and I closed my eyes and said, "I came to the bar because I wanted to find someone to sleep with me. I wanted to convince myself that I was still attractive and desirable. I just wanted a fling, you know?"

"Why did you choose Dwayne?" Seth asked.

"Well, because he looked safe and," I paused, "attainable for someone who looked like me."

"You saw us when we first came in, didn't you?" Seth said.

I nodded and he squeezed my leg again. "You saw the way I looked at you. You knew I wanted you."

"I didn't," I lied.

"You did," he insisted.

"I – I didn't think it was real," I whispered.

His hand moved off my thigh and he turned me on

the stool to face him before kissing me again. This time there was no gentleness in the kiss. He took my mouth with a hard possessiveness that made me ache with need. His tongue pushed past my lips and flicked against mine. I forgot that we were in the bar and returned his kiss with an eagerness that surprised me. My heart was pounding in my ears and I was pressing myself against the stool in a vain attempt to ease the ache between my thighs. When Seth pulled away, I nearly fell off the stool. Only Theo's hand on my hip kept me in my seat.

"I want you, little Libby," Seth said bluntly. "I want to take you back to your hotel room, spread your legs and fuck you into the best orgasm of your life. Does that clear things up for you?"

I stared mutely at him before whispering, "You – you're not safe."

He grinned. "Is safe what you really want, sweetheart?"

"I don't know."

Theo's breath was warm on the back of my neck. "It isn't, love."

I had forgotten completely about Theo and I shivered when he pressed up against my back and kissed my neck. "Play with us tonight, Libby. I promise it'll be a night you won't forget."

"Us?" I whispered. I gave Seth a shocked look and he nodded gravely.

"We're a package deal, sweetheart."

"I – I can't take both of you to my room," I said in a low voice.

"Why not?" Seth asked.

"Well, because it isn't – I mean, what would people say if they knew that I…"

I trailed off and Seth grinned at me. "We won't say anything if you won't."

I didn't reply and Theo kissed the side of my neck

15

again. "Say yes, love. We want you very much. You want a one-night stand, let us give it to you."

"You can't tell anyone I did this," I whispered. I was being ridiculous. Seth and Theo's rough hands and the way they were dressed suggested they were laborers. The thin layer of sawdust that clung to Seth's jeans and the paint spatters on Theo's shirt meant they most likely worked in a trade. This was a large city and since my circle of friends would probably be the people I worked with, we wouldn't be in the same social circle. After tonight, I'd never see them again.

Then take them to your room and fuck them! For God's sake, you could have the time of your life tonight if you'd stop thinking about what others might say.

Inner me was right. I came to the bar looking to find a man who found me attractive and wanted to fuck me. I had found not one, but two, and suddenly I was getting cold feet? Fuck that. No, not fuck that – fuck *them*, both of them… a lot.

"We won't say a word, love," Theo said. "Cross our hearts, hope to die."

Seth made an X across his chest before winking at me.

"Yes," I said abruptly.

Chapter Two

Neither of them waited for me to say anything else. Theo urged me off the stool and Seth took my hand in a firm grip. We left the bar and although I was certain that everyone was staring at us, in reality no one gave us a second look. We rode up the elevator in complete silence. The men flanked me, Seth still holding my hand and Theo resting his on the small of my back.

At the door to my room, Seth took the card key from me and opened the door before handing it back. I tucked it into my purse as they followed me into my room.

"Nice room," Seth said as Theo crossed the room and drew the curtains shut.

"Thank you," I said. My voice was an anxious squeak and my entire body was shaking as Seth drew me into his arms.

"Don't be nervous, little Libby."

"I've never slept with two men before," I said. "So, how does this work? Are you two, um, fond of each other as well?"

Seth shook his head. "No, Theo and I are only into women."

"Okay," I whispered. "Now what?"

"Now?" Theo had come up behind me and I

twitched when he put his arms around me above Seth's arms and cupped both my breasts. "Now we get you naked and make you come repeatedly."

"I can't do multiple orgasms," I said.

"Seth and I love a good challenge," Theo said before licking the skin on my throat. I moaned and arched into his hands as Seth pulled on the hem of my shirt.

"Move for a minute, Theo."

Theo stepped away and Seth quickly pulled my shirt over my head and tossed it on the other bed.

"Fuck," he muttered as he stared at my tits. "Theo, get that fucking bra off."

The hooks on my bra were released with a quick flick of Theo's fingers and before I could think of protesting, it had joined my shirt. I reached to cover my breasts and Theo's fingers slid around my upper arms. He pulled my arms back, forcing my back to arch, and held me in a firm grip as Seth studied my breasts.

I wiggled and squirmed against Theo. His hot breath tickled my ear when he leaned down and said, "Hold still so Seth can see your tits or I'll spank your ass."

I twisted my head to stare at him and he kissed my mouth before sucking on my bottom lip. I moaned as he lifted his head. "Give us a safe word, Libby."

"Wh-what are you going to do to me?"

Seth laughed. "Nothing you won't enjoy, sweetheart, I promise. But Theo and I are dominant and we never play with a submissive unless she gives us a safe word."

"I'm not a submissive," I said.

"You still need a safe word, love," Theo said.

I hesitated as the sensible part of my brain started throwing out large neon caution signals.

"Libby," Seth said, "we promise we won't do anything you're not comfortable with. And if you are uncomfortable, say your safe word and we'll stop immediately."

"Do-do you promise?" I whispered.

"Yes," Theo said solemnly. "We promise."

"Okay, I guess, uh, red will be my safe word," I said. "Is that too cliché?"

Seth laughed and shook his head. "No, sweetheart, it's perfect."

Theo's hands tightened on my arms and I arched my back a little more.

"Good girl," Theo said.

Warmth flooded through me but before I could try and analyze why Theo's approval should make me feel so good, Seth was cupping both my breasts. He tugged on my nipples and I moaned and rubbed my ass against Theo's crotch. He pressed his erection against me as Seth said, "Her left tit is slightly bigger than her right one." He pulled on my nipples again and smiled when I gasped. "Her nipples seem to be very sensitive."

He cupped my breasts and lifted them. "Nice and heavy, just how we like them."

"Very nice," Theo said. He was looking over my shoulder and I shivered when he nipped at my collarbone. "Show me her cunt."

Seth quickly unbuttoned and unzipped my jeans and yanked them down my legs. They dragged my panties with them and I squirmed a little when the cool air washed over my pussy. Theo dropped my arms but before I could move, he'd grabbed my wrists with one hand and held them in the small of my back.

He stepped back as Seth encouraged me to lift first one foot and than the other. He removed my shoes, my jeans, and my panties, and left them on the floor before straightening. I squirmed again. I was completely naked and neither Seth or Theo had even taken off their shoes.

"Fuck, her ass is amazing," Theo groaned.

I twitched when Theo's hand smoothed over the

curve of my right ass cheek and then squeezed. "How does her cunt look?" He asked in a hoarse voice.

"Spread your legs, Libby," Seth said.

I kept my legs closed. Seth and Theo were examining my body almost like it was a piece of meat. I should have been insulted, I should have been safe wording and then telling them to get the hell out. Instead I was so turned on by the way they were treating me, I was afraid to open my legs because I was certain I'd drip all over the carpet. What was wrong with me?

I squealed when Theo slapped my ass. It hurt like hell and I turned my head and glared at him.

"Do what Seth says, love," Theo said calmly.

When I didn't spread my legs, Theo spanked my ass again. This one hurt even more and I cried out and spread my legs wide.

"That's our good girl," Theo said. His big hand rubbed my stinging ass but I barely noticed. Seth had cupped my pussy the moment I spread my legs and his rough fingers were rubbing my clit.

"She's soaking wet already and her little clit is swollen and hard," he said in a low voice.

"Oh God, please," I moaned as he brushed the tips of his fingers over my clit.

Theo's hand stroked down my ass and slid between my legs. Seth spread my pussy lips apart and Theo rubbed at my clit before making a noise of approval.

I moaned and twisted against their hands and when Theo released my wrists, I grabbed Seth's shoulders in a desperate grip.

"Please, Seth," I pleaded. "I need – oh my God!"

I rose up on my tiptoes as two of Theo's thick fingers invaded my pussy. I clenched around him in surprise at the invasion and he groaned against my back. "Fuck, her cunt is tight."

He removed his fingers and I whimpered at the loss.

He kissed the back of my shoulder as Seth cupped one heavy breast and pinched my nipple. My back arched and I squealed in surprise when I felt Theo's wet finger push against my anus.

"Hey!" I squeaked out.

Theo stopped and pressed another kiss against my shoulder. "Have you been fucked in the ass before, Libby?"

"No," I said.

A look of disappointment crossed Seth's face and I pressed my lips together. "I'm sorry." For some reason, I hated that I was disappointing him even though he was pretty much a stranger. "I'm willing to give it a try though."

Libby! You're going to let them fuck you in the ass? Sleeping with two men is one thing but do you really want to just have a go at the old DP? You haven't even seen their dicks yet – they're probably huge!

Seth smiled at me. "No, sweetheart, we can't."

"I – what? Why not?" I stuttered.

"Because you'll be too tight. You need to be stretched first before you take a cock, and that takes more than one night," Seth said.

I scowled at him. "It's my body and I'm willing to give it a try so – ouch! Goddammit! Why are you spanking me?"

Theo stopped with his hand hovering over my ass and said, "Seth told you no and you argued with him. You'll do what you're told or be punished."

"But it's my body! I can decide if I…shit!"

Theo had pulled me over to the bed. He sat on the side of it and I was sprawled face down over his lap before I knew what was happening. One hard hand splayed across my lower back, holding me down easily despite the way I was starting to wiggle. My face burned with humiliation and I squealed when Theo spanked me hard. I squirmed wildly but I was no match for his strength. As his hand painted my ass with bright red prints, I squealed again and said, "That hurts! Stop it!"

He ignored me completely, slapping each ass cheek in a hard, unforgiving rhythm as Seth quickly undressed. Even with the burning pain and humiliation of being spanked, lust tinged with a little fear coursed through me when I saw the size of his dick.

I was distracted by another hard slap across my burning ass. Tears were beginning to slide down my face and I moaned at Theo to stop and tried to squirm away again. Why wasn't he stopping? I was practically begging him.

Safe word, idiot. If you want him to stop you have to use your safe word.

Fuck, I *was* an idiot. I opened my mouth to snap 'red' at Theo, but before I could say a word, he stopped spanking me and slipped his hand between my thighs. He rubbed my clit with a firm touch and all thoughts of safe wording disappeared in an instant. I had no idea if the pain had made me extra sensitive or if Theo was amazing at touching clits, but pleasure exploded in my belly. I cried out, my ass arching up and my hands clenching into the bedcovers as Seth grinned at Theo.

"Is she wet?"

Theo laughed. "Drenched. She loves being spanked."

"No, I don't!" I said. "I don't like it – oh fuck!"

Theo was spanking me again and tears streamed down my face as I wailed. He stopped spanking me and rubbed my sore ass with a light caress.

"Are you going to keep arguing with us, love?" He asked.

"No," I whimpered. "No, I – I won't."

"Good," Theo said. His hand slipped between my

legs again and I moaned happily when he rubbed my clit. "Tell us that you're being a bad girl and deserve your spanking and we'll make you come."

I shook my head stubbornly. I wanted to come but I wasn't about to say that. It was one thing to be spanked and realize that it turned you on, but quite another to admit to being a bad girl and deserving a spanking. I was thirty-two years old, for God's sake. I wasn't going to –

"Libby," Theo's voice held a soft warning as he traced a finger over one red ass cheek, "be a good girl and do as I say."

I shook my head again and then moaned when Theo rubbed at my clit. Oh God, it felt so good. He knew the exact amount of pressure to use, the exact way to touch and –

"No!" I squealed when he stopped. I was right on the verge of my climax and I glared at him over my shoulder. "Theo, please!"

"Tell me what I want to hear," he said calmly.

I scowled at him and he laughed before giving me a quick spank to the ass. "I can deny you your orgasm all night, love."

"You wouldn't!" I gasped as he delved back between my legs and rubbed my clit again. This time he stroked too lightly to bring me to climax and I tried to rub myself against his hard thigh to find the relief I craved.

"Stop!" He said and slapped my ass again before returning to my clit.

"Oh God, oh God," I whispered. Within minutes he had me writhing and moaning and pleading for relief. I was so close to my orgasm, I just needed a little more, but Theo refused to give it to me. He was no longer a dimpled god, but the dimpled devil and I was almost irrationally angry with him.

"Seth, please," I pleaded. He was standing close to

us, stroking his cock and watching as Theo held me across his lap and tormented me. "Please tell him to make me come."

Seth laughed. "Be a good girl, sweetheart, and do what he says."

"Fuck!" I moaned. "I – I've been a bad girl and I deserve my spanking."

"That's my good girl," Theo said.

Another flush of warmth at his approval but I barely noticed it as Theo helped me stand. My legs were shaking and I was almost crying with the need for release.

"You promised!" I said. "You promised me!"

"Shh, love," Theo said as he stood next to me and kissed me on the forehead. "Seth is going to eat your sweet cunt for you."

"What? No!" I said as Theo turned me and pushed me into a sitting position on the bed. Seth moved forward and knelt next to the bed, his big hands grabbing my tightly-closed thighs and forcing them apart.

"No!" I said again. "I – I don't know you well enough to let you…"

I trailed off. Fuck, even I could hear how stupid I sounded. Seth laughed as Theo said, "You are delightful, sweet Libby."

"I think we should maybe get to know each other a little better before – oh my God!"

Seth had pulled my thighs wide and buried his face into my pussy. He licked at my swollen lips and then nibbled at them as my hands fisted in his hair. I moaned in disappointment when Seth lifted his head and grinned at Theo.

"How does she taste?" Theo was stripping off his shirt.

"Fucking delicious," Seth growled. He forced my legs over his shoulders and dived back into my wet pussy.

He reached up and cupped both of my breasts. He pulled hard on my nipples as his tongue finally found my throbbing clit. He licked it with light strokes and then sucked it into his mouth as he pinched both my nipples again.

I barely had time to throw my hand over my mouth before I was screaming with pleasure and coming all over his damn face. The orgasm tore through me, making my legs shake, my feet drum against his back and my entire body buck and heave. I had never come so hard in my life and I screamed against my palm for a second time as Seth raised his head and let my legs slip from his shoulders.

He stood up as Theo crowded in next to him. Now both men were naked and I stared at their erect cocks as Seth leaned down. "Sit up, sweetheart."

I was still shaking from my orgasm and wanted nothing more than to close my eyes and go to sleep but Seth wouldn't let me. He grasped my shoulders and helped me into a sitting position. Feeling weak and incredibly sated, I blinked up at them as Theo said, "She looks like a satisfied little kitten, doesn't she, Seth?"

He nodded and I blinked again when Theo's hand curved around the back of my skull. "Open up, little kitten."

The head of his cock pressed against my lips and I opened my mouth automatically. He slid his cock between my lips and made a harsh groan. "Suck, Libby."

I sucked on the head of his cock, sliding my tongue back and forth over the tip before tracing the ridge. He moaned and pressed forward. His cock was huge and I could feel my lips stretching as he fed me more of his dick. I made a muffled sound of protest and he petted my hair.

"I won't give you too much, Libby. Relax for me."

I did what he asked and he petted my hair again as I bobbed my head back and forth over his cock.

"Look up at me, Libby."

I stared up at him as I sucked and he nodded. "That's my good girl. Always look at me when you're sucking my dick."

"Theo," Seth said hoarsely.

"I'm being greedy, little Libby," Theo said. He pulled back and I released his cock with a soft pop and licked my already swollen lips. He turned my head to the right and I stared at Seth's cock.

This time I didn't have to be told what to do. I opened my mouth and stared obediently at Seth as I took his cock into my mouth and sucked hard. The two men were similar in length and width but Seth had a slightly saltier taste than Theo. I realized that I actually loved the way they both tasted and I licked at the head of Seth's cock as precum dripped out of the slit.

"Oh fuck," Seth groaned.

Theo's hand was still cupping the back of my skull and he held me in place as Seth pushed forward. His cock brushed against the back of my throat and I made another muffled noise of protest.

"We want to see how much you can take, sweetheart," Seth said. "Be a good girl and open wide."

I did what he asked despite my sudden real fear of choking on Seth's giant dick. He pushed forward even more, cutting off my oxygen and making my eyes water as I sucked. He pulled out and I took a deep gasping breath as Seth wiped away the moisture leaking from my eyes.

"Good girl," he said. "You're doing so well."

My head was turned back toward Theo and I accepted his cock without protest.

"Have you deep throated a guy before, Libby?" Theo asked.

I shook my head around his cock and gave him a wary look as he pushed further in. He smiled reassuringly at me. "I'm not going to force you to deepthroat me, but you are going to try very hard and take as much as you can. Aren't you, love?"

I stared up at him and he pulled out and rubbed the head of his cock against my lips. "Aren't you?"

"Yes," I whispered.

"Yes, what?"

I thought for a moment before licking my swollen lips again. "Yes, Sir."

His and Seth's smiles of approval made my clit pulse with need and I squeezed my thighs together as Seth said, "We're going to fuck your mouth, sweetheart. If it's too much and you can't safe word because you've got one of our dicks in your mouth, tap me twice on the hip. Okay?"

"Okay," I whispered.

"Good. Open up, Libby," Theo said.

I opened wide and Theo slid his cock into my mouth. I sucked and licked and tried to relax my throat as Theo groaned under his breath and pulled on my hair. After a few minutes, Seth took his place. I lost track of time as they took turns fucking my mouth. Whoever didn't have their dick in my mouth, crooned soft words of encouragement and cupped and kneaded my breasts, playing with my nipples until I was rubbing my ass and pussy against the bed in a silent plea for relief.

"She looks like she needs to come again," Seth said to Theo.

"Fuck, I need to come too," Theo muttered. "Do you want her pussy or her mouth?"

"Pussy," Seth said immediately as he watched his cock disappear into my mouth.

When he pulled out and walked away, I whined in protest. Theo lifted me to my feet and pressed a kiss against my swollen mouth. "He's getting a condom, love."

"Please fuck me," I whispered.

I couldn't believe how turned on I was. I'd always been enthusiastic about giving Wayne blowjobs – I loved a dick in my mouth as much as the next girl – but sucking Wayne's dick had never made me so wet I was dripping. Especially when I'd already had an unbelievable orgasm not half an hour earlier.

Yeah, well, Wayne's dick was nothing to write home about and it wasn't like he was all that great about returning the favour.

My inner voice had a point. Wayne loved blowjobs but wasn't as enthusiastic about giving me oral. I thought about the way Seth had eaten my pussy, how he had dived in like I was a bowl of his favourite ice cream, and my pussy pulsed with need. Liquid dripped down my thighs as Theo said, "Get on your hands and knees."

Feeling a little embarrassed, I climbed up on the bed and settled onto my hands and knees. Wayne had two positions he stuck with – missionary and me on top – and I'd been too young and shy to experiment much with boyfriends before Wayne. Still, I wasn't about to tell the two hot naked men in my hotel room that I'd never been fucked doggy style before so I tried to look like I knew what I was doing as Theo urged me to the middle of the bed.

I watched as Seth rolled on a condom before kneeling behind me on the bed. His hard hands stroked my tender ass and I winced. He pressed a kiss on my lower back.

"Is your ass sore, sweetheart?"

"Yes," I said a bit snottily.

He laughed and gave my ass a light slap. "Maybe next time you'll be quicker to obey us."

I didn't reply. There wouldn't be a next time. As much as I was enjoying this night, I couldn't sleep with two men on a regular basis. That wasn't me. I didn't do stuff like this on a regular night for God's sake.

"Libby, look at me."

I turned forward as the bed dipped. Theo was standing next to the bed in front of me and his cock was directly in front of my mouth. I leaned forward, my lips already parting as Theo gathered my hair into a loose ponytail. His other hand stroked the back of my neck and he guided my mouth over his dick. I sucked with enthusiasm, staring up at him as he held me by my hair.

I pulled my mouth away when I felt the head of Seth's dick press against my opening. I looked over my shoulder, feeling the pull against my scalp when Theo refused to release my hair.

"You're, um, bigger than I'm used to. Will you go slow?" I asked. I sounded timid and unsure even to myself. Gratitude flooded through me when both men immediately stroked my body with their warm hands and made soothing noises.

"I will," Seth said as his big hands rubbed my lower back. "Spread your legs wider, sweetheart."

I did what he asked and stared up at Theo again as he smoothed my hair back from my face before gathering it into a ponytail again. "If you can't safe word, two taps on my hip. Remember, love?"

I nodded and he leaned down and kissed my mouth. "Good girl. You're going to love this, I promise."

I expected him to push his dick into my mouth again but instead he glanced up at Seth. "Give her your dick. I want to watch her face as she takes it."

I tried not to tense when Seth pushed the head of his cock into my narrow entrance. He made a low moan as Theo studied my face intently. Seth's rough fingers trailed across my hip and I sucked in my gut when they crossed my stomach.

He made a low grunt of disapproval and I flinched

when he slapped me sharply on the ass. "Don't do that, Libby."

I licked my lips and tried to take Theo's cock into my mouth. What better way to distract myself from the giant dick about to invade my pussy than with a giant dick in my mouth, right? Unfortunately, Theo wouldn't let me and I pouted at him as Seth's hand slid underneath me.

"I want your cock in my mouth." I blushed at my boldness but Theo shook his head.

"Not yet, love. And next time add a 'Sir' to your request or you'll get another spanking."

I didn't reply. Seth's fingers were brushing my clit and I had lost all interest in Theo's dick. I squirmed on Seth's hand, panting and pleading quietly as he stroked the sensitive nub. I was close to coming when I felt Seth's dick push into my pussy. This time I pushed back eagerly. My clit was throbbing and my pussy was clenching uselessly around nothing and wanted what Seth was offering. Seth surged forward and Theo pulled my head back with a tight grip on my hair. He studied my face as Seth forced my pussy to take every inch of his dick.

My mouth dropped open and I whimpered as I struggled to take all of it. When he was completely sheathed, he stopped and rubbed my lower back. I moaned and tried to wiggle away from the invasion. My inner walls were stretching around him, but it was still more discomfort than I was used to from sex. Seth's hands cupped my hips and held me firmly as Theo smiled at me.

"How does it feel, Libby?"

"Too big," I said stupidly.

He laughed and tugged on my hair. "Open your mouth."

I opened my mouth and took Theo's cock when he

pushed it past my lips. Seth began a slow slide and retreat motion as Theo used my hair to glide my mouth back and forth over his cock. I moaned and clenched around Seth's dick when he rubbed my clit.

"Fuck!" Seth muttered. "She's goddamn tight, Theo."

"Fuck her hard," Theo suddenly demanded.

My squeal of surprise was muffled around Theo's cock as Seth immediately began to fuck me with rough thrusts. His fingers rubbed at my clit as Theo's hand pulled at my hair. The sting in my scalp, the way Seth's cock stretched my pussy, and the feel of his fingers against my sensitive clit were lighting up my nerve endings like a goddamn Christmas tree. Both men were groaning now and they were losing their smooth, natural rhythm.

As Theo shoved his cock deep into my mouth, he groaned, "Fuck, I'm gonna come. Make her come first."

Seth's fingers rubbed furiously at my clit as he pounded into my pussy. My back arched, I screamed around Theo's thick cock and came in a roaring rush of pleasure that blotted out all rational thought. Theo pulled his dick out of my mouth and yanked my head back by my hair. He made a low growl of pleasure as he pumped his dick with his hand and came all over my throat and chest. Still shaking with my climax, I cried out when Seth's hands clamped down on my hips and he shoved himself in deep. He did short and hard strokes until he made his own roar of pleasure and his big body tensed. He jerked against my ass, panting harshly as he came deep inside of me.

Theo released my hair and I wanted to fall flat on my face, but he steadied me with one hand on my shoulder. "Seth, lift her up."

He disappeared from view as Seth wrapped his arm around my waist and hauled me up until I was on my knees. He was still inside of me and made a few gentle thrusts as he cupped my breast and kissed my cheek.

"You're so beautiful, Libby," he whispered into my ear. "Beautiful and tight and so fucking submissive. Do you have any idea how badly I want to put a collar around your neck and clamps on your beautiful nipples?"

His fingers pulled at my right nipple. Surprisingly, a little shiver of need went down my spine even as my body was still shaking from my orgasm. What the hell was wrong with me?

Before I could answer my question, Theo had returned. He was carrying a towel from the bathroom and he wiped away his cum from my throat and chest before dropping the towel on the floor.

"How do you feel, love?"

"Really, really good," I mumbled. "You guys are really, really good at sex."

Seth laughed and kissed my cheek again before pulling out of me. I swayed on my knees and Theo helped me off the bed before pulling back the covers. "Climb in, Libby."

I wondered if they were going to leave. Was I supposed to ask them to stay or was that weird? I'd never had a one-night stand before. I assumed that I would find a guy, fuck him, and the guy would leave. But here I was with two men and wishing desperately they would crawl into bed and snuggle with me.

Before I could make a fool of myself and ask, Theo was crawling into the bed behind me. He curved his body around mine and cupped my pussy before kissing my neck. "This is our pussy. Say it, Libby."

"It's your pussy," I said obediently. Whether I believed it or not, didn't matter I supposed. There was no harm in saying what they wanted to hear. I'd never see either of them again after tonight.

Seth slid into the bed on my other side and I smiled at him when he rested his head on the pillow next to mine before kissing the tip of my nose. "Have I mentioned you're beautiful, Libby?"

"Thank you. So are you," I said before yawning.

He laughed and cupped my right tit, giving the nipple a little pinch. "Our sweet cunt and our tits. Right?"

"Right," I said. "All yours."

I was so sleepy, I could barely keep my eyes open. It was dangerous to fall asleep with two men I didn't know, but it didn't feel dangerous to me. It felt good and normal and...*right*. As Seth and Theo pushed in close, their hard bodies cocooning me in warmth, I closed my eyes and slept.

Chapter Three

I studied my reflection in the mirror on the back of my bedroom door. I straightened the skirt of my dark green suit and adjusted the collar before smoothing back a stray strand of hair. I had put my dark hair up in a twist, maintaining a look of competent and easy sophistication. My makeup was minimal with just a bit of blush, mascara and a tinted lip gloss. A plain silver bangle around my wrist and pearl drop earrings finished my outfit.

I grabbed my heels out of my suitcase and bent to pick up my cell phone from where it was plugged in next to the air mattress. Yesterday morning, I had picked up the key to the townhouse I rented but a storm had stranded the moving truck carrying my stuff. The representative from the moving company couldn't even give me an estimate of when my things would arrive. Her vague warning that it might not be until after Christmas had turned my blood cold.

Thankfully I had packed enough work clothes to last me the week I'd be at the office before the Christmas holidays started, so I didn't need to buy clothes. However, clothes and toiletries were the only things I had packed in my car. I had already checked out of the hotel and while I could have rented a room again, I decided to pick up a few supplies to camp out at the townhouse. I bought groceries, an air mattress, pillows and bedding and hauled it up to my townhouse, setting it up in the master bedroom on Sunday afternoon. I had an early dinner and a couple of glasses of wine. My mother had called twice and I let both calls go to voicemail. Feeling nervous and anxious about my first day, I went to bed early.

Now, I checked my reflection again and turned to glance at my ass. I smoothed my skirt over it and then winced. God, my ass was still sore. Even this morning there were visible handprints on it.

I blushed furiously and left the bedroom. I slipped into my boots and grabbed my coat from the front closet before stuffing my heels and my phone into my oversized bag. With my coffee maker stuck in a moving truck, I wanted to leave early to find a coffee shop. I locked the door and hurried down the sidewalk to my parking spot. The morning air was cold, the sky dark with grey, ominous looking clouds, and I could almost taste the snow that was going to fall.

I unlocked my car and sat down behind the wheel, wincing again when my sore ass met the seat. I would need to make a concentrated effort not to flinch when I sat at the office. I started the car and turned the heater to high, rubbing my hands together briskly. As I waited for the car to warm, I couldn't help but think about Saturday night. I had tried and failed miserably not to think about Theo and Seth yesterday. But today, I should have been concentrating on my new job, not wishing for about the fiftieth time that I hadn't thrown away Theo's cell number. I sighed, my warm breath clouding the cold air as I stared blankly out the windshield and my mind drifted back to yesterday.

Theo and Seth woke me around four in the morning

with their warm mouths and hard hands. Half asleep, I hadn't protested when they kissed and touched me into another unbelievably aching arousal. I climbed to my hands and knees again and this time sucked on Seth's cock as Theo fucked me from behind. Theo was maybe a tiny bit larger than Seth, but he had rubbed and caressed my clit until I was soaking wet and it seemed a little easier to take his dick than Seth's. Like before, I'd had a crazy intense orgasm that left me shaking and weak as a kitten. Theo and Seth tucked me back into bed and we'd slept again until Seth shook me awake at ten.

"We have to go, sweetheart," he said as he sat on the side of the bed.

I sat up and clutched the sheets to my naked chest. Seth was fully dressed and Theo was finishing dressing. He pulled his boots on and sat on the other side of me as I blinked owlishly at them.

"I – what time is it?" I asked.

"Just after ten," Theo said. He leaned forward and pressed a kiss against my bare shoulder. "We had a great time last night, Libby. Thank you."

Suddenly feeling shy, I glanced at my hands twisting in my lap. "I did too. Thank you."

Seth tipped my chin up before planting a soft kiss against my lips. "We'd like to see you again."

"What?" I stared at him in surprise and he grinned.

"We want to see you again. Will you have dinner with us this week?"

"Oh, um, I don't... I mean, I'm starting a new job and it's the holidays and I'm kind of busy," I said.

Libby! What is wrong with you? Say yes!

"Fair enough," Theo said as he pressed another kiss against my shoulder. "I've left my cell number written down on the pad of paper on the desk. Call or text me if you'd like to have dinner with us after the holidays.

Okay?"

"Uh, sure, okay," I said.

Seth smiled at me. "Good bye, Libby. It was great to meet you, I hope to see you again soon."

"Bye, Seth," I whispered.

He pressed a kiss against my mouth and stood as Theo leaned in and kissed me as well. Both men headed toward the door and hesitated for a moment, glancing at each other.

"Bye, Libby," Theo finally said.

"Bye."

They left, shutting the door behind them and I collapsed on the bed for a moment before hopping out and heading to the bathroom. I peed and then brushed my teeth and had a long hot shower before dressing. My ass hurt and my body was aching but I felt strangely satisfied and the pain in my ass almost made me proud.

I sighed and packed my suitcase before staring fixedly at the piece of paper with Theo's number written on it. Last night was amazing and I'd enjoyed it a great deal, but I couldn't see them again. It was a one-time thing, a 'get your mojo back' moment and besides, I couldn't date two men at once. Nice girls didn't do that sort of thing and if anyone at the office were to find out, I'd die of shame. I shuddered at the thought and immediately crumpled up the paper and tossed it into the trash before grabbing my suitcase and nearly running out of the room. I was a new partner at a new firm, I needed to concentrate on doing my damn job instead of having a fling with two playboy construction workers. No matter how good they made me feel.

The shrill ring of my cell phone brought me back to the present and I fumbled my phone out of my purse. Caught up in my memories of yesterday, I almost believed that it would be Theo or Seth calling me. I was being stupid. They didn't have my number and they didn't even know my last name. I checked the number and sighed before answering it.

"Hi, Mom."

"Elizabeth! I tried calling you twice last night and you didn't answer. Are you okay? I've been worried sick."

"I'm fine, Mom," I said as I put her on speaker and set my phone on the seat. I pulled out of my parking spot and turned right onto the street. "I went to bed early last night."

"I was so worried about you."

"You need to stop worrying. The city is very safe."

"Are you unpacked yet?"

I grimaced. "My stuff has been delayed because of a snowstorm."

"Oh my God! What are you doing to do?"

"I bought an air mattress and I'm camping out in my townhouse," I said. I caught glimpse of a Starbucks sign and muttered a quiet 'thank god' as I drove toward it. I turned into the parking lot and headed toward the drive-thru.

"Your Aunt Leona called yesterday. Apparently, Uncle Bert was caught with his pants down at the store with their newest employee. You remember Jolene, don't you? She's only forty-five years old but apparently, she likes older men because Leona said she and Bert were having sex in the storage room like a couple of randy teenagers! Bert is sixty-eight years old. Can you imagine it?"

"Mom," I said as I waited in line, "can we talk about Uncle Bert's sex life later? I'm on my way to my new job and I'm a little nervous."

"You should be nervous," my mother said. "Being a partner is a big responsibility and I'm not sure you're quite ready for it."

I tried not to let her words sting. "Thanks for the

vote of confidence."

"You need someone who will be truthful to you," she snapped. "Don't be angry with me because I'm trying to keep you from making a fool of yourself."

"I'm not angry," I said. "But I do have to go. I'll call you later."

"Fine," my mother huffed. "Goodbye, Elizabeth."

My cell phone beeped as she ended the call and I sighed and rubbed my forehead as I inched forward in the drive-thru line. I wished to God I had never answered her call and I tried to forget what she had said as I rolled my window down and placed my order. Today would go fine. I was a damn good lawyer and I deserved to be partner. Absolutely nothing would go wrong today.

∂∾ ∾∂

"Elizabeth!" Jeff Martin, the head partner at Martin, Clarke and Bones, strolled into my office. I stood and he shook my hand with a hard grip. "How's your first morning going?"

"Call me Libby," I said. "It's going well. IT already had my system set up and ready to go and Sandra has been a real-life saver in familiarizing me with the computer system."

"Excellent," Jeff said. "Sandra is one of our best legal assistants in the office. I had a feeling the two of you would get along which is why I assigned her to you. Now, if you have a minute, I've asked everyone in the office to come to the boardroom. There's coffee and snacks there, and we'll formally introduce you to the rest of the staff."

"Sounds good," I said. I took a deep breath and followed Jeff to the boardroom. It was crowded with people and I smiled at the other two head partners,

Emmett Clark and Mario Bones. I had met with all three partners during negotiations for partnership and liked all of them. Jeff and I joined them at the front of the room and I shook both their hands before standing next to Mario.

Jeff cleared his throat and clapped his hands. The murmur of voices quieted and Jeff said, "Is everyone here, Wanda?"

"Almost," a small chubby woman said from the back. "Seth and Theo are at a client, but they should be back any minute."

I jerked and Mario gave me a curious look. "Are you okay, Elizabeth?"

"Call me Libby," I said automatically. Wanda hadn't said Seth and Theo, of course she hadn't. I was hearing things because I was suddenly obsessed with two damn construction workers who had giant dicks and an almost magical ability to make me come.

"We'll start without them," Jeff said. "Everyone, I'd like to formally introduce you to Elizabeth Brecken, our newest associate partner. She comes to us from – ah, Seth, Theo, you made it. Come on in."

I stared at the two men who had entered the boardroom. My face paled and my stomach rolled with nausea as they gave each other identical grins of delight. I swallowed down the bile and stared straight ahead, keeping a smile on my face by sheer willpower alone. Seth and Theo, the two men who had spanked me, ate my pussy and fucked me into multiple orgasms the night before last, were goddamn lawyers at my goddamn firm.

Fuck me.

∽ ∾

An hour later, I was back at my desk and grimly staving off the panic that was gnawing at my guts. I had met almost all of my coworkers at the gathering, but I couldn't remember a single one of their names. Nor could I remember Jeff's introductory speech. I know he kept it short and simple. I know he mentioned my experience and the client I brought with me to the firm, but only because a few of the lawyers had mentioned it to me when we chatted. At least, I think they did. I'd been so busy trying to not freak the fuck out that I couldn't be sure of anything. The only thing I did know, is that Seth and Theo had slipped out of the boardroom without talking to me and I was stupidly grateful. I had no idea what to say to them and pretending that I didn't know them would have been impossible with my current level of shock.

I spun around in my chair and stared out the window at the falling snow. Okay, everything was fine. So, two guys that I fucked happened to be my new coworkers. No big deal. We were all adults, right?

They're not just coworkers, Libby, inner me moaned. *You're their boss! You fucked two subordinates! What if they blackmail you? What if they threaten to tell the other partners?*

Oh God, what the fuck was I going to do? My panic pushed to the front and feeling half-crazed, I jumped to my feet. I had to tell the other partners what happened before Seth and Theo told them. It was better coming from me, I rationalized as I crossed my office.

Libby no! You can't tell them you fucked Seth and Theo! You're the only woman partner at this firm, and if you tell them what you did, you can kiss your career goodbye! They'll never look at you the same again. You know they won't!

"I have to do something!" I hissed to the empty room. "I can't just sit here and – and…"

I trailed off as there was a knock on my door and it opened. Jeff stepped into my office and my stomach dropped when Seth and Theo followed him in.

"Hello, Elizabeth," Jeff said.

I smiled at him but said nothing. If I opened my mouth I was very certain I would throw up on his fucking shoes.

"I don't think you got the chance to meet Seth and Theo so I wanted to bring them to you. They'll be working directly with you on your client, Etco Drilling Ltd."

No! Oh fuck me, no!

I remained silent and Jeff gave me an odd look before turning to Seth and Theo. "Elizabeth, meet Seth Waters and Theo Camden."

Theo stepped toward me and held out his hand. He gave me an encouraging look and my hand trembling, I took his. He shook it quickly. "It's nice to meet you, Elizabeth."

"You too," I said in a low voice as I turned to Seth.

"Hi, Libby. Nice to meet you," he said before shaking my hand.

"How do you know she's a Libby?" Jeff asked as both men stepped away from me.

I almost moaned out loud with sheer terror but Seth simply grinned and shrugged. "She looks like a Libby. Am I right?"

"Yes," I said. My voice came out squeaky and I cleared my throat as Jeff gave me a look of concern.

"Are you all right, Elizabeth? You're very pale."

"Fine," I said. For a moment, I thought about blurting out exactly what I had done with Seth and Theo, but my common sense kicked in and I kept my mouth shut.

"All right. Well, I'll let you three get acquainted," Jeff said. "Seth, come see me after about the Moranis file."

"Of course," Seth said.

Jeff left the office and closed the door. As soon as it was shut, Theo grinned at me. "Hello again, Libby."

I didn't reply and Seth gave me a wicked little grin. "You have no idea how happy we are to see you again."

I staggered back and their flirty grins dropped away.

"Libby?" Theo was reaching for me and I tried to pull back, but my legs were shaking badly and I stumbled into him instead. He steadied me and muttered 'shit' under his breath before leading me to the small couch in the corner of my office.

I collapsed in an ungraceful heap on it and Theo glanced at Seth. "Grab some water, would you?"

"Libby, are you okay?" Theo asked as he sat next to me. Seth walked to the credenza behind my desk, grabbed a bottle of water and returned. He sat down on the couch on my other side - it was a tight fit for the three of us - and opened the bottle of water before handing it to me.

"Drink, sweetheart."

My hands were still shaking, and Theo muttered another curse before helping guide the water bottle to my mouth. I drank a few swallows and then pushed it away. I stared mutely at Theo and Seth as Theo said, "Better?"

"You're supposed to be construction workers," I said.

Seth blinked at me. "What?"

"You – your hands are so rough and your clothes were covered in paint and sawdust. You're labourers, not lawyers," I whispered.

Theo glanced at Seth. "We're doing our renovations on our house, Libby. It's why we looked the way we did Saturday night."

"Oh God, oh no," I groaned before burying my hands in my face. "What have I done?"

"It's no big deal," Seth said.

I lifted my head. "No big deal? No big fucking deal? I'm your goddamn boss, Seth! I'm your boss and I let you spank me and – and fuck me and…"

I trailed off and buried my face in my hands again. Theo rubbed my lower back. "You didn't know who we were, Libby."

"Did you know who I was?" I lifted my head again as I had a sudden thought. "Did you fucking plan this? Get the boss into our bed so we can – can blackmail her?"

"Christ, no," Seth said. "Sweetheart, how would we know who you were?"

"You knew there was a new associate partner coming in," I snapped.

"Yes," Theo said patiently. "We knew there was an associate partner named Elizabeth Brecken. But we didn't know what you looked like and you introduced yourself at the bar as Libby."

"Libby is a common nickname for Elizabeth," I retorted.

"We didn't know who you were. We swear it, love," Theo said.

"Don't call me that," I whispered. "I'm your boss."

"Sorry," Theo said immediately. "But we honestly didn't know who you were."

I studied him before nodding. "Yeah, okay, I believe you."

"Good," Theo said. "Drink some more water. You're very shaky."

I drank a couple more swallows of water before staring at my hands. "So, now what?"

Seth shrugged. "We're not going to say anything to anyone at the office, if that's what you mean. We keep our personal lives private, Libby."

"I appreciate that," I said, "but I meant more about the fact that we're supposed to work on the Etco file together. You know Jeff better than I do, would he find it strange if I asked for you both to be reassigned?"

"Why would you do that?" Theo said. "Seth and I are good at what we do and we're the only lawyers in the firm who have some experience with drilling companies."

I gaped at him. "Why – why would I do that? Have you lost your damn mind?"

"I don't think so," Theo said.

"I let you spank me!" I hissed at him. "I called you Sir and sucked your dick and you're wondering why I don't want to work with you? I've lost all credibility with you both. Can you honestly tell me that you can take orders from a woman who you put across your lap and spanked? I still have your goddam handprints on my ass!"

A small smile crossed Theo's face and I shoved him in the chest. "This is not fucking funny!"

"I apologize," Theo said. "I know it's not funny, Libby."

"Libby, listen to us," Seth said. "We're only dominant with a woman in the bedroom. We have no problem following your orders in the office, I promise. We can keep what happened in bed between us completely separate from our office lives."

"Maybe you can," I said dully, "but I don't think I can."

"You can," Theo said. "You're a bright, capable woman and from what we've heard, a damn good lawyer. Just because you're submissive in bed doesn't mean you can't do your job."

"I'm not submissive in bed," I said.

Theo and Seth glanced at each other over my head and I groaned. "Oh God, I should never have gone to the bar."

"But you did and you can't change that," Seth said. "Listen, it will look strange to Jeff if you ask for us to be reassigned without even working with us. Can you give it a try? There's no harm in that and if, after a couple of weeks, it isn't working, then you can talk to Jeff about reassigning us."

I studied both of them before straightening. I was a good lawyer and I was a natural leader when it came to work. I tried to sound like my usual authoritative self. "It has to be completely professional. At all times. If I even think you're looking at me in a way that might suggest you're remembering what I looked like naked, I'll ask Jeff to reassign you. Do you understand?"

"We do," Theo said.

"Good," I replied. I stood and moved to my desk. My legs were still trembling but I kept my back straight and gave them a polite and professional smile. "It was nice to meet you both. I look forward to working with you."

A goddamn lie but if this was going to work I had to make myself believe that I had never seen them naked, never had their dicks in my mouth and my pussy. The only way to do that was to shove those memories right out of my head and pretend that they were total strangers.

I sat down at my desk and stared at my laptop as Seth said, "This will work, Libby. I promise."

"I'm sure it will," I said with an indifference I didn't feel. "Unless you have any specific questions about Etco, you're dismissed."

I glanced up at them as they moved toward the door. They didn't seem put off by my coolness as they left my office. The second the door was closed, I slumped in my chair and rubbed at my temples.

Oh God, I was so fucking screwed.

Chapter Four

Tuesday night I was walking through the door of my townhouse when my cell phone rang. I kicked off my boots and pulled my phone out of my purse as I shrugged out of my coat.

"Hey, Sandra. What's up?"

"Hi, Libby. Are you home yet?" My legal assistant's voice was apologetic.

"I am, why?" I asked.

"You were going to work on the Henden file tonight, right?"

"Yes," I said.

"It's sitting on my desk."

"Crap," I muttered. "Okay, I'm headed back to the office now."

"Don't do that," Sandra said. "There are still a few people at the office, I'm sure I can find someone to drop it off for you on their way home."

"I don't want to put anyone out," I said. "I'll come back to the office and - "

"It's fine," Sandra replied. "Don't worry about it, Libby."

"Thanks, Sandra. I appreciate it." I ended the call and tossed my phone on the counter before dropping my workbag at my feet.

It was only my second day but I already had a full client list. Not that I minded. I needed something to take my mind off of Seth and Theo. Just the thought of them made my pussy damp, and I cursed my libido as I headed to the bedroom and changed into yoga pants and a t-shirt. I hadn't seen them at all since Monday and I told myself repeatedly that it was a good thing. The less I had to do with them, the better.

So why had I spent most of last night tossing and turning on my stupid air mattress? Why couldn't I stop thinking about what they had done to me and how it had made me feel? And why did I finally have to masturbate just to fall asleep?

Not that it helped, I thought as I headed back to the kitchen. I could barely concentrate on my new job and I was furious with myself over it. It's like I was trying to sabotage my own damn career, and for what? The possibility of getting fucked by two men at once? Since when did my need for sex override my desire to have a fulfilling career?

Why not have both? Inner me whispered slyly. *You can have your cake and eat it too, Libby.*

No, I couldn't. Especially not with two of my coworkers. It didn't matter how damn hot they were or how easily they made me come. Nothing good would come of sleeping with them, and trying to talk myself into it not being a problem, was a career ending move.

They said they can keep it separate. You can too. Simple.

"No, it isn't simple," I said to my empty kitchen. "It isn't simple at all."

You suck, my inner voice pouted.

I ignored it and pulled my laptop out of my workbag. I needed to concentrate on my career and pretend like I had no idea what Seth and Theo's dicks looked like.

Easy. Simple. Doable.

You know who else is doable?

I made a harsh groan of frustration and yanked open my laptop. I was going insane.

ᔊ ᔌ

Half an hour later, I cursed and nearly pounded my fists against my laptop. I had wasted thirty minutes looking for an answer to a question that had already been answered. I wanted to scream in anger. Never before had I questioned my abilities as a lawyer, but if I couldn't stop thinking about what it would be like to have Seth and Theo both inside of me at once, I could kiss my damn career goodbye.

I took a deep breath and rubbed my temples before taking a bite of cereal. Okay, I was overreacting. My entire career wasn't on the precipice of collapse just because I was horny. There was a simple solution to this whole damn mess. Hit up another bar this weekend and find a guy – *one guy* – to have sex with. That would help with the horniness and make me forget all about Seth and Theo. Right?

Nope. So wrong, girl. So. Very. Wrong.

I wasn't wrong. Wayne might have crushed my sexual self-esteem with one sentence but Seth and Theo had at least brought a little of it back. It was enough for me to have the courage to find someone else to have sex with. Maybe I could fuck away my memories of my two coworkers.

I rubbed my back as I shifted from foot to foot. I don't know why I didn't stay at the damn office and work on the Henden file. I'd received an email this morning from the moving company that my furniture was definitely stranded until after the New Year. I didn't even have a kitchen table or chairs which meant I was trying to work standing at the counter. I ate another bite of cereal. Tomorrow I would stay at the office until I was finished work. It made the most sense.

The doorbell rang and I crunched down another bite of cereal as I headed down the front hallway. I opened the door, the smile dropping from my face.

"What are you doing here?" I asked.

Theo held up the manila covered file folder as Seth smiled at me. "Dropping off the Henden file."

I stared silently at them and Theo said, "Sandra said you needed it and your place is close to ours."

"It is?" I ignored the dirty thoughts that immediately coursed through my head.

"Yes," Seth said. "We told Sandra we would be happy to drop off the file for you."

"You live together?" I said.

"We do," Theo replied.

"Okay, well, thanks for dropping off the file." Ignoring my mad idea to invite them in, I reached for the folder, but Theo refused to relinquish it.

"Invite us in, Libby."

"Why?" I said.

"Because I'm freezing my nutsack off standing out here and Seth has to pee."

I bit back my smile as Seth said, "It's true. I have to pee."

Knowing it was insanity, I took a step back and said, "Come in."

"Thanks, Libby," Theo said.

He and Seth stepped into the hallway and there was a moment of awkwardness before I said, "Um, the guest bathroom is down the hallway to the right."

"Perfect." Seth headed to the bathroom and I took the file from Theo.

"Thanks for bringing this by," I said. I pulled self-consciously at my t-shirt as Theo smiled at me.

"You're welcome. Hey, can I grab a glass of water from you?"

"Yeah, uh, okay."

He followed me into the kitchen. I wondered if he was staring at my ass as I opened the fridge and grabbed a bottle of water for him.

"Here you go…what's wrong?"

Theo was staring at my kitchen. "Don't take this the wrong way, Libby, but if you're a minimalist, I think you've taken it too far."

I laughed. "I'm not, I just - "

"Whoa," Seth had joined us in the kitchen. "You know most people have a table in their kitchen, right, Libs?"

"I'm aware," I said dryly. "The moving truck with all of my furniture and belongings is stranded about four hours from here. I won't get it until after the New Year."

"Jesus, that sucks," Theo said. "Why don't you rent a hotel room?"

"It's not that bad."

"Is that why you're eating cold cereal out of a Styrofoam bowl?" Seth asked. He crossed the kitchen and peered at my bowl of cereal.

"Yeah," I said. "I didn't want to buy new kitchen stuff just to cook food for a couple of weeks and eating at a restaurant alone isn't my thing."

"Do you even have a bed?" Theo asked.

I immediately blushed but he didn't seem to notice as he twisted open the cap on his water and took a drink. "I have an air mattress."

"Well that fucking sucks," he replied.

"It's not that bad," I said.

"I have a great idea," Seth said. "We live like ten minutes from here. Come back to our place and I'll cook you dinner."

"Hell, no," I said. "That is not happening."

"Why not?" Theo said.

"You know why not," I replied.

Seth shrugged. "We can keep it professional if you can."

"Of course I can!" I snapped at him.

Fuck, could I?

"Then it isn't a problem to have dinner with us."

"I have to work on the Henden file," I said.

"Bring it with you," Theo said. "We have a home office. You use the office to work while Seth cooks dinner. Come on, Libby. It's a lot easier than standing at your counter and Seth is an amazing cook. He'll make something much better than cold cereal, I guarantee it."

I couldn't say yes, no matter what my libido was screaming.

"No one from the office will find out," Seth said. "We're the only three who live in the west end of the city. No one will know you're at our house."

I couldn't go to their house. I couldn't. I took a deep breath and said, "Sure, okay."

Libby!

"Great!" Theo gave me a boyish grin that made the butterflies in my stomach start up. "Grab your jacket and we'll give you a ride over to - "

"No," I interrupted. "I'll drive myself over."

"All right," Theo said. "Let's get out of here."

৵৹ ৵ঌ

"Hey, how's it going in here?" Theo stuck his head into the office as I was closing my laptop.

"Good. I'm done."

"Perfect timing," Theo said. "Dinner is ready."

I stood and tried not to notice the way Theo's gaze

dropped to my tits. I was still wearing my t-shirt and yoga pants. I had thought about changing into something a little more flattering before berating myself internally. I shouldn't care what I looked like around Seth and Theo.

I followed him out of the office and down the hallway. They'd given me a brief tour of their house when we first arrived, pointing out the renovations they'd done. I was genuinely impressed. They had gutted and remodeled the kitchen themselves as well as their bedrooms, the office and all three of the bathrooms. They were currently working on the guest bedroom and in the spring, would start the living room.

"Have a seat, Libs," Seth said as he pointed to the large marble island. Plates and silverware were already in place and I climbed onto the stool as Theo moved to the fridge.

"Do you want wine?"

"No, just water, please," I said. There was no way in hell I was having anything to drink around these two. I was already turned on and wanting to beg them to fuck me. If I had even a drop of liquor, I was deathly afraid I'd lose the tenuous grip on my control.

I took a deep breath and drank some of the water that Theo handed me. Surprisingly, I could focus enough to get my damn work done. I had thought it would be impossible but apparently just being near the two men, soothed me enough to concentrate. Before I could think too much on that, Seth was standing next to me and adding a delicious smelling pasta concoction to my plate.

"It smells delicious," I said as I placed my napkin on my lap.

"Thanks," Seth said. "Theo, get the biscuits out of the oven, would you?"

As Theo pulled the biscuits out, I stare at Seth. "You

made your own biscuits?"

He gave me a flirty grin that made my pussy tingle. "I'm an excellent biscuit maker, Libby."

They sat down with me at the island and I took a biscuit when Theo passed them to me. The food was incredible tasting and I smiled at Seth. "Theo's right. You're an amazing cook."

"Thank you," Seth said. He took a drink of beer and I tried not to drool when he licked a drop from his bottom lip.

"So, uh, how long have you guys been friends?" I asked.

"We met in high school," Theo replied.

"That's a long time."

"It is," Seth agreed.

"Have you lived together long?"

"Since we finished high school," Theo replied. "At first it was because it was cheaper to live with roommates."

"But now?"

Seth shrugged. "We enjoy each other's company."

I ate a bite of pasta and chased it down with a sip of water. "How long have you two been, um, tag teaming women?"

Libby! What the hell?

Seth and Theo both laughed and I turned bright red. "Oh God. I'm sorry. It's none of my business and I shouldn't have asked that."

"We don't mind," Theo said. "During university, I started dating a girl named Lisa. Seth and I lived in a cheap apartment together close to campus and Lisa would spend a lot of time at our place. She was attracted to Seth, I could tell, and one night when she'd had too much to drink, she proposed a threesome."

"It was her idea?" I said.

He nodded. "Yep. Honestly, it had never crossed my

mind to fuck a girl with Seth before."

"Me either," Seth said.

"So that was the first night you tried it?"

Seth shook his head. "No, not that night. Lisa was drunk and we weren't taking advantage of that. We waited until she was sober and when she admitted that she still wanted it, we had the threesome."

"You weren't jealous?" I asked Theo.

He shook his head. "No. I thought maybe I would be and Seth and I talked about it beforehand but," he paused, "I wasn't. In fact, it felt…"

He trailed off and Seth took another swallow of beer before saying, "It felt right."

Theo finished the last of his pasta before wiping his mouth with a napkin. "We had sex separately a few more times after that but honestly, it was more fun together. We're both dominant and it's unbelievably hot to take a woman together."

His voice had lowered and he leaned closer as I swallowed heavily. "To have a woman impaled on both of our cocks at once, watch her moan and beg and plead to come while we're fucking her pussy and ass is incredible, Libby. It's even better if she lets us put a collar on her or restrain her."

I didn't say anything. My panties were flooded and my nipples were hard enough to cut glass, and I was afraid if I opened my mouth it would be to beg them to fuck me like that. To tie me up, collar me and make me plead for their cocks.

The idea of losing that control, to give in and let them make all the decisions was intoxicating. I had worked hard at my career, sacrificing time and energy and even relationships and it had paid off. I was a partner at only thirty-two years old. It was an incredible accomplishment and I was proud of it. But it had come at a cost, and the tight control I kept over my emotions was starting to wear thin. Wayne said my weight was the problem but there had to be more. I hadn't always been the best girlfriend and I knew that, but I tried to balance it out. I tried to make both Wayne and myself happy. Until the moment I walked in on him fucking another woman, I thought I was making it work.

Maybe I was wrong. Maybe it was the fact that I'd gained weight that had resulted in Wayne cheating on me. But what if it wasn't. Wayne wasn't dominant, not in the bedroom or out of it, and while our sex life was pleasant enough, it hadn't set the bed on fire or anything. I could try and deny it out of a sense of embarrassment or pride, but I needed men like Theo and Seth. Men who liked that I wanted to give up that control, wanted to have my hair pulled and my ass spanked and to – I bit at my bottom lip as my pussy throbbed – to wear a collar.

"You okay, Libby?" Theo asked in a low voice.

I nodded. "Yeah, sorry. I'm a little tired."

Theo reached out to touch my face before thinking better of it. "I suppose sleeping on an air mattress isn't the best way to get a good night's sleep."

I shrugged. "I'm not a great sleeper. At least not usually. Saturday night I slept like a damn baby."

I immediately blushed. Bringing up Saturday night wasn't a good idea. What the hell was I thinking?

Seth smiled at me. "Glad we could help, sweetheart."

"Why don't you sleep well, usually?" Theo asked.

"I have a hard time shutting off my brain," I said. "Saturday night though, I guess I was relaxed enough to sleep."

Theo eyed me silently before standing. "Excuse me."

He left the kitchen and I blinked at his abrupt exit as Seth stood and began to clear the island off.

"Here, let me help," I said.

"Sit and relax," Seth replied.

"No, I want to help," I insisted.

Working silently, we loaded the dishwasher. As Seth put the pan in the sink and added hot water and dish soap to it, I stared out the window over the sink. Their neighbours had their Christmas lights turned on and I watched them blink off and on. It was starting to snow and I sighed inwardly. I had upset Theo somehow and I felt terrible about it. It was best that I leave so why was I hesitating? I couldn't stay the night. That was madness.

"Libby? What's wrong, sweetheart?"

"I've made Theo angry," I said. I blinked back the hot tears that wanted to fall.

Seth shook his head before sliding his arm around my waist and pulling me up against his big, hard body. I knew I shouldn't have been encouraging his behaviour, but it felt so good to be in his arms again. "You haven't, sweetheart."

"He left so quickly," I said. "I know he's - "

"He left because he's not as good at controlling his dick as I am," Seth interrupted.

"I – what?"

"Odds are - he has a massive erection and he's probably in his bedroom yanking his crank as we speak."

I stared at him in shock. "He – he doesn't have an erection."

"Are you kidding me?" Seth said. "Sweetheart, both of us have had at least half a woody since we left your bed Sunday morning. It's only gotten worse since we discovered you were our new boss."

He gave me a rueful smile. "I don't know about Theo, but I've had to twice go to the bathroom at work and rub one out and it's only been one goddamn day since you started at the office. My dick will be rubbed raw by Friday if this keeps up."

A slightly hysterical and confused giggle dropped

from my mouth. "You're lying."

"I wish I was," Seth said. "You have no idea how much we want you, Libs."

"I – I want you too," I confessed.

He groaned and before I could stop him, kissed me hard on the mouth. I returned his kiss eagerly, rubbing my body against his as he cupped my breast and squeezed.

"Libby," he whispered raggedly against my mouth, "please let us fuck you again. Please, sweetheart."

I tried to pull away when Theo said, "What's going on in here?".

Seth held me firmly and grinned at his best friend who was leaning against the door jamb. "Not much. Me just begging Libby, rather pathetically I might add, to let us fuck her again."

Theo joined us and I didn't object when he pressed up against my back. His cock was hard against my ass and I ground against him as Seth cupped my tits again.

Theo bent his head and nipped my earlobe before sliding his hand down toward my pussy. "Open your legs."

I obeyed him immediately and he groaned into my ear before cupping me through my yoga pants. "Are you wet, Libby?"

"Yes," I said.

His other hand immediately spanked me hard on the ass and I squealed as his hand tightened around my pussy. "Try again, sweet Libby."

"Yes, Sir. I'm wet, Sir," I whispered.

"Good girl," Theo said. He started to slide his hand into the waistband of my pants.

"Theo, wait."

He scowled at Seth as I whimpered in protest.

"Libby, is this what you really want?" Seth said.

"Yes," I said. "This is what I want."

"Are you sure?"

"Seth, shut up, for fuck's sake," Theo said.

"Theo, it's important," Seth snapped.

I sighed and pulled away from both of them. I crossed my arms over my torso and bit at my bottom lip. "Here's the thing – I'm going to be completely honest with you. Even though I know it's a potentially career ending move, I want to have sex with both of you. Ever since Saturday night I can't stop thinking about what it would be like to take both of you at once."

"Oh, fuck yes," Theo said before reaching for me.

I held up my hand and backed away. "But, once that happens, this has to end. You know that, right? We can't keep sleeping together."

Theo and Seth glanced at each other before Theo nodded. "If that's what you want, Libby."

"It is," I said. "After tonight, after I'm uh, fucked by both of you together, we go back to being completely professional at the office and outside of it too."

"Sweetheart, we can't fuck you together tonight," Seth said.

"Why not?"

"You've never done anal before and we need to stretch you first," Theo said bluntly.

I sighed impatiently. "I told you Saturday night that it's my body and I'm willing to give it a try. I'm sure if you go slowly and - "

"No," Seth interrupted. "We won't take the risk of hurting you, Libby."

I gave him a look of frustration. "So, I have to wait?"

"Yes," Theo said.

"Until when?" I sounded like a petulant little kid but neither Theo nor Seth seemed to notice.

Seth glanced at Theo. "What do you think? By the weekend?"

"Maybe," Theo said. "If we stretch her with a plug every night."

I blinked at them. "The weekend? It's Tuesday! I can't wait that long."

Seth laughed. "It's only a few days, sweetheart."

"You'll come to our place every night after work and we'll get you ready for it," Theo said.

"I can't take that risk," I said. "What if someone from the office finds out?"

"They won't," Seth said. "We're very discreet with our personal lives, Libby."

"No one will find out," Theo said. "We'll give you a key to our house and you can park in the alley behind the house and come in through the back."

I bit at my lip as I considered what they were saying.

"It's this way or not at all, love," Theo said.

I sighed and wrinkled my nose at him. "Fine. But after the weekend, we end it. Do you understand?"

"Yes," Seth said.

"If you tell anyone at the office – hell, if you tell anyone at all – I'll cut off both of your sacks and nail them to my office wall for everyone to see. Deal?" I said cheerily.

They both gaped at me before Theo cleared his throat. "Yes, ma'am."

"And I'm only submissive to you in the bedroom," I said. "If you even try to be dominant at the office or - "

"We won't," Seth said. "Trust me, sweetheart. Your confidence and abilities at work are one of the sexiest things about you."

"I – really?"

He grinned as Theo said, "Yes, really."

"But you like submissive women."

"Only in the bedroom," Theo said. "We promise we won't try to pull any dominant bullshit over you at work."

I wasn't sure that I completely believed him, but my lust was overriding my common sense. I nodded. "Okay, good."

"But I can't promise that I won't occasionally look at you at work and remember how you look when you're naked, while you're wearing our collar with my dick in your mouth," Seth said.

My mouth dropped open and there was silence for a moment before I started to giggle. I shouldn't have found that funny, but God help me, I did. Seth laughed and pulled me back into his embrace. "Come on, gorgeous girl. Let's get you naked."

Chapter Five

Seth and Theo led me upstairs to Theo's bedroom.

"Why Theo's bedroom?" I asked.

"Bigger bed," Seth said with a grin. I didn't object when he started to strip off my clothes. Theo disappeared into the walk-in closet. By the time he returned, I was completely naked and Seth had my legs spread and was fingering my pussy while I clutched at his broad shoulders.

"God, Seth, you couldn't wait two minutes?"

"No," Seth said as he pumped his fingers in and out of my pussy. "Fuck, she's soaking wet already."

"Please, Sir," I moaned. "Please."

"Our little kitten is begging already," Theo said with a smug grin. "Seth, stop fingering her for a minute."

"No!" I protested and then squealed when Seth withdrew his fingers from my sopping pussy and slapped my ass hard.

"Lift her hair," Theo said as I rubbed at my burning ass.

Theo was now naked and I stared greedily at his erect cock as he moved closer and Seth gathered my hair into a ponytail on top of my head.

"Lift your chin, Libby," Theo instructed.

I lifted my head and stared at the black leather collar he was holding in his hands. It was thinner than I thought and I eyed the silver buckle as Theo unbuckled it.

"How many other women have worn this?" I asked.

Theo glanced at Seth and I thought I saw embarrassment flicker in his eyes.

"What?" I asked.

"No one else has worn it," Theo said. "I bought it last night specifically for you."

"But you had no idea I would…"

I trailed off as Theo gave me an adorable boyish grin. "I had high hopes we could change your mind."

"Oh," I said.

There was a moment of silence and then Theo was placing the collar around my throat. He buckled it and slipped his finger between the collar and my neck before stepping back. "It looks beautiful on you, love," he said. "Show her, Seth."

Seth walked me over to the full-length mirror in the corner of the room. I stared at the collar around my throat as Theo stood to my right and Seth stood behind me.

"It looks good," I said. I wasn't lying. I never would have thought I'd say a collar looked good on me, but looking at the way the leather pressed against my pale skin made me a little hot.

Seth cupped my tits and I watched as he pulled and tugged on my nipples. It sent pleasure straight to my pussy and I moaned with need as he kissed my neck above the collar.

"Did you get the other stuff?" Seth asked Theo.

He nodded as they led me back to the bed. Sitting on the bed was a pair of leather cuffs, a bottle of lube and – I swallowed hard – a butt plug. The plug part was silver and at the opposite end a bright red jewel caught the light from the lamp.

"Give me your hands, love," Theo said.

I held them out obediently and as Seth undressed, Theo buckled the cuffs around my wrists. They were a tight fit and I stared at the metal hoops embedded in them as Seth joined us by the bed.

"Ready?" Seth asked.

"Yes," I said.

"Safe word?"

"Red."

"Good," Theo said. "Bend over the bed, spread your legs wide and hold your ass cheeks open for me, Libby."

I stared at him as my face turned bright red. I knew I would have the butt plug inserted but I thought we would make out a little first and then one of them would discreetly insert it for me. I couldn't just bend over and – and hold myself open for it. No way, no how.

"Libby," Theo prompted.

I shook my head. "No. I know I need the butt plug but I'm not going to hold myself open. That's humiliating."

"Libby," Theo said. "Do what I say. Last chance."

I shook my head and gave him a stubborn look. "No. You can make it a bit more romantic or at the very least, help me to – oh dammit!"

Seth had grabbed my arms and without a word, he turned me and bent me over the bed until my cheek was resting against the quilt and my ass was in the air. Still silent, he spanked me in a hard, quick rhythm as I squealed and twisted. I reached back and tried to protect my burning ass with my flailing hands. Seth immediately grabbed my wrists by the leather cuffs and held them against my lower back before spanking my ass again. The pain made my legs shake and I collapsed face-down on the bed and buried my face in the quilt to muffle my cries.

Seth was merciless. He spanked me at least twenty times while I wiggled and squirmed and cursed a blue streak. When I finally collapsed against the bed in silent submission, he rubbed his hand over the curve of my burning ass before pushing it between my thighs. He rubbed my shamefully wet and swollen clit as I moaned and spread my legs wide.

"On your knees, sweetheart," Seth commanded.

I climbed to my knees, keeping my face and upper body buried in the bed, and moaned when Seth pushed my thighs wide. Cool air washed over my anus, but Seth said, "Use your hands to spread yourself open, Libby."

This time I did what he asked. Certain that my face was as red as my ass, I kept my eyes squeezed shut as I reached back and held my ass cheeks apart. I was embarrassed beyond belief but there was also a deep and painfully strong part of me that was incredibly turned on by what they were forcing me to do.

I moaned and twitched when Theo sat down on the bed beside me and ran his rough fingers over my clit. He used the moisture from my pussy and rubbed his fingers over my anus as my fingers dug into my butt cheeks.

I gasped when Seth pressed a kiss against my right ass cheek. "You look so pretty in this position, Libby."

"Yeah, right," I muttered.

I received a hard spank to my left cheek from Theo for my impertinence and I gasped and cried out, "I'm sorry, Sir."

Theo rubbed my aching ass. "Hold still, love."

The lube was cold against my ass and I tried to clench my ass shut when Theo probed at me with his slick finger.

"No," Seth said. "Don't do that, sweetheart. Relax."

"Easy for you to say," I added a hasty "Sir" before he could spank me.

I could hear the grin in Seth's voice as he said, "Take some deep breaths."

I breathed deep and tried not to moan when Theo eased his finger past the tight ring of muscle. "How does that feel?"

"Like I have a finger up my ass?" I said.

Both men laughed and my answering giggle turned to a moan of need when Seth rubbed my clit. My discomfort disappeared in an instant and I rubbed my pussy against Seth's fingers as I dropped my hands to the bed.

"Make her come first," Theo murmured.

I cried out when both men leaned over me and kissed their way up my back. The combination of their mouths and tongue, the feel of Seth's rough fingers against my swollen clit and the way Theo trailed his free hand up and down the back of my thigh, brought my climax on in an embarrassingly quick fashion. I moaned and shuddered and clawed at the quilt as Seth kissed my shoulder before brushing my hair back from my sweaty face.

"Hold your ass open again, sweetheart," he demanded.

My embarrassment gone, I did what he asked, spreading my cheeks wide as Theo removed his finger. I jerked when he added more lube and Seth kissed my back again. Thanks to my orgasm, I was more relaxed than before, but I still tensed the moment I felt the blunt end of the plug against my ass.

"Don't tense," Theo said.

"I'm not."

He slapped the back of my thigh and I grunted in pain before saying, "I'm trying not to, Sir."

My fingers squeezed my sore ass as Theo said, "Take a deep breath and push back against the plug."

I did what he said, groaning a little at the pressure as

he steadily pushed it into my ass. There was a brief eye-watering burst of pain and then nothing but a feeling of dull pressure in my butt.

"You okay?" Seth asked.

"Yes, Sir," I replied. "Is it in?"

"It is." Theo leaned over and pressed a kiss against my cheek. "You did so well, love. How do you feel?"

"Very glad that you ignored my suggestion to just stick your dick in my ass," I said.

They both laughed and I made a small noise of protest when Theo took my arms and lifted me to my knees.

"Off the bed, Libby," he said.

"What? No, why?" I didn't even want to try and walk with the plug.

"Because we want to show you how pretty your ass is," Seth said.

I tried to resist when they pulled me off the bed, but I was no match for their strength. I felt incredibly self-conscious as they walked me over to the mirror. Afraid the plug would fall out, I kept clenching my ass around it and I was shocked at the little spikes of pleasure it sent through my body.

They turned me away from the mirror and I stared at the wall as Theo said, "Turn your head and look, Libby."

"I'd rather not," I said.

He started to bend me over and I hastily turned my head. "No, wait. I'll look, Sir. I'll look!"

I stared over my shoulder at my flaming red ass and the jewel between my ass cheeks. The red of the jewel matched the skin on my butt and I twitched when Seth ran his fingers over one ass cheek.

"So pretty, sweetheart."

I moaned a little when Theo pressed on the jewelled part. He grinned at Seth and my cheeks flushed. I knew some women got pleasure from having something shoved in their ass, but I didn't think I would be one of them.

"Our little kitten looks so pretty in her collar, maybe we should get a tail for her too," Theo said thoughtfully as he stared at my ass in the mirror.

My eyes widened and I shook my head immediately. "No fucking way, Theo. I am not having a tail hanging out of my ass."

Theo grinned at Seth. "Sounds like pet play is a hard limit."

"Damn straight it is," I said. "You come anywhere near me with a tail and I'll scream red so loudly, your neighbours will hear it."

Theo leaned forward and pressed a kiss against my mouth. "Understood, love. Come back to the bed."

We returned to the bed. Seth cupped one breast and toyed with my nipple as Theo sat on the bed before reclining on his back. I was shaking my head before the words were out of his mouth.

"I'm not riding you," I snapped. I could hear the anxiety and shame in my voice.

Seth rubbed my lower back as Theo said, "I don't want you to ride me, love. I want you to sit on my face."

My jaw dropped and I pulled away from Seth. "You what?"

"I want to taste my kitten's sweet cunt," Theo said.
"No."

"It'll be fine, Libby," Seth said. He tried to guide me closer to the bed and I tore away from him. Adrenaline was rushing through my veins and Theo sat up and gave me a look of concern.

"Love, it's okay."

"It's not," I said. "I'm-I'm yellow right now and if you try and make me do this, I'll be red. Do you understand? It all stops, and I won't come back to your place."

"We understand," Seth said immediately.

"We'll do a different position," Theo said. "It's okay, love."

I stared wide-eyed at them before whispering, "I'm sorry."

"Don't be," Theo said. He crossed to me and took me into his embrace, pressing kisses against my face and my mouth. "Don't ever apologize for telling us exactly how you feel. That's why we have a safe word, right?"

"Right," I said shakily.

"Do you want to stop, sweetheart?" Seth had joined us and he gave me a solemn look.

"No," I said. "No, I don't want to stop."

Theo and Seth glanced at each other and I shook my head. "I'm good now. Just – I don't want to sit on your face."

"Okay," Theo said before giving me another gentle kiss.

He led me back to the bed and I didn't protest when he and Seth had me sit at the head of the bed with my back leaning against the headboard, my knees bent and my feet resting on the bed. There was added pressure on the plug and I shifted a bit as Theo pushed my thighs apart before stretching out between them. He kissed the patch of curls on my pussy as Seth kneeled next to me. One hard hand was stroking his cock and I stared at the bead of pre-cum at the tip of it before leaning down and licking it away.

"Fuck!" Seth muttered. He cupped the back of my head and I sucked at his cock with enthusiasm as Theo licked my inner thighs. I moaned around Seth's cock when Theo kissed the wet lips of my pussy. When his tongue wandered over my clit, I arched my hips and clutched at his head as I stared up at Seth.

He gathered up my hair and pulled roughly on it. "Suck harder, Libby."

I tried to concentrate on Seth's dick, but Theo's tongue was goddamn magic. It didn't take long before I was moaning and thrusting my hips against Theo's face. I pulled Theo's hair with one hand and stroked the base of Seth's cock with the other as he pushed his dick in and out of my mouth.

I was already close to a second orgasm. When Theo reached under me and wiggled the plug in my ass, my climax was hot and immediate and lasted incredibly long. Wave after wave of intense pleasure flooded my lower body. My scream was muffled by Seth's cock and he shoved it in deep as I writhed against Theo's tongue and lips.

Seth pulled out and I gasped in some much-needed oxygen as I pushed at Theo's head. I was shaking all over and was so weak I slumped against the headboard. I barely noticed when Theo sat up and rolled a condom onto his dick before lying on his back next to me.

Seth was urging me to my knees and I pouted and whined, "Tired, Sir."

"I know, sweetheart. Theo's going to fuck you and then you can sleep."

I smiled at the thought of being fucked as Seth pulled on my right thigh. "Come on, sweetheart. Leg over Theo, now."

Feeling almost drunk from my unbelievable orgasm, I did what he asked. It wasn't until I was straddling Theo, my knees pressed against his hips as Seth pulled my arms behind my back and held them firmly, that I realized what was happening.

Theo was beginning to press his dick against my opening and I froze as fresh adrenaline pumped through my veins.

"I can't be on top!" I shouted like an idiot. "Stop, wait, I'm going to hurt…oh fuck!"

Seth had pushed me down, impaling me on Theo's

thick cock. I moaned and wiggled and tried to ignore how good it felt to have my pussy filled to the brim with dick.

"Stop," I whispered unconvincingly. "Theo, I'm too heavy."

"You're not," he rasped as he reached up and cupped my tits. He pulled hard on the nipples and I arched my back. "Baby, your soft curves feel like heaven. I need you to fuck me right now before I go insane."

"Are you sure?" I whispered as Seth tightened his hold on my arms.

"Fuck, yes," Theo groaned. "Seth, let her go."

He released my arms and Theo tugged me down until I was bent over him with my hands resting on the bed above his shoulders. He kissed my upper chest and I rubbed my nipples against his chest as his hands cupped my tender ass. He thrust in and out and I moaned with pleasure before bouncing enthusiastically on his dick.

"Fuck," he muttered again, "the plug makes her even tighter."

"Libby, look at me."

I turned my head and automatically opened my mouth for Seth's cock. He was kneeling next to my head again and I sucked on his cock as Theo fucked me hard. His rhythm was rough and out-of-control and I cried out when one of his hands pushed on the plug in my ass and the other rubbed furiously at my clit.

Seth held tightly to my hair, guiding my mouth back and forth over his dick as Theo made another hoarse groan. "Fuck, I'm not going to... I can't..."

His body arched beneath mine and he pinched my clit hard. It should have hurt, and it did, but the pain brought on a third and completely unexpected orgasm. I forgot completely about hurting Theo and ground my pelvis against his as he grabbed my hips and came deep inside of me. Seth pulled me away from his cock and into a sitting position with a hard tug to my collar. He pumped his dick with his hand and came with a loud roar of pleasure, his cum splattering all over my breasts.

Panting harshly, Theo helped me ease off of him. I fell to the bed on my side, my entire body quivering and pulsing. Theo disposed of the condom as Seth used a towel to wipe my chest clean. I kept my eyes closed and moaned happily when both men slid into the bed on either side of me. Seth was at my back and I jerked when he touched the plug still in my ass.

"Take it out," I whispered.

"No, sweetheart," he said.

"Please, Sir?" I asked.

"No," Seth repeated.

I must have been pouting because Theo made a low chuckle before pressing a kiss against my mouth. "The longer you wear it, the sooner you can take Seth's dick in your ass."

"But it's getting late and I should go home."

"No," Seth said. "You're spending the night with us, Libby."

I should have argued. I should have gotten up, taken the plug out of my damn ass, dressed and driven home. Instead, I snuggled in closer to their hard bodies and sighed with pleasure when Theo cupped my breast and Seth kissed my back.

"Sleep now, Libby."

"Yes, Sir," I murmured.

Chapter Six

"Libby?" Mario knocked on my office door. "Why are you still here? The office closes at five thirty, or did we forget to tell you that?"

He grinned good-naturedly at me and I laughed. "I wanted to finish up a few things."

"Ah, well since you're still here, can I take a few minutes of your time?"

"Of course," I said as I leaned back in my chair. "What's up?"

"Did anyone go over the Christmas office schedule with you?" He asked as he sat in the chair across from my desk.

"Sandra sent me the email," I replied. "I told her I would be more than happy to be the partner at the office between Christmas and New Year's."

"She mentioned that," Mario said. "But I talked to Jeff and Emmett and we've made the decision to close the office completely."

"Oh," I said.

"We'll have a couple of the support staff come in for a few hours each day between the 27th and the 2nd, and Jim has offered to be on call if anything should come up."

"As the newest associate partner, shouldn't I be the one to get the 'work during the holidays' job instead of Jim?" I asked with a small smile.

Mario laughed. "We don't want to scare you into quitting your first month."

"I don't mind working," I said. I didn't. I hadn't been here long enough to make any friends so the prospect of having a week off with nothing to do wasn't exactly appealing.

Maybe you could spend it with Seth and Theo.

I ignored my inner voice. Seth and Theo would have holiday plans with their families. I wasn't asking them to spend Christmas with me. That was ridiculous. Christmas was Tuesday and after this weekend I wouldn't even be seeing them outside of work anymore.

"Libby?"

"Sorry, what was that?" I apologized.

"I asked if you were going home for the holidays?"

"No, which is why I can work."

"We're going to keep you busy enough after the holidays," Mario said with a laugh. "Enjoy your free time while you still have it. Sandra has sent out the email to our clients with our holiday office hours. I asked her to add Etco Drilling Ltd. to the email so that Charles knows.

"Perfect, thanks," I said. Not that it mattered. Charles had my personal cell number and wouldn't hesitate to call it if he couldn't get a hold of me at the office.

"You bet." Mario glanced at his watch. "It's almost seven now. You should get out of here."

"I'm about to head home," I lied.

"Good. See you tomorrow."

"Bye, Mario."

He walked out of my office and I packed up my laptop and shut off the lights to my office before heading to the elevator. I was going to Seth and Theo's place for sex, butt stretching and if I was lucky, multiple orgasms.

I shivered all over as I walked to my car. My ass was sore, more from being spanked than the plug, not to mention my thighs ached. Hell, all of my muscles ached but it wasn't stopping me from going back to them. Fucking two men I worked with was a mind-numbingly stupid idea, but I was addicted to what they did and said to me.

What happens when they blackmail you over this? When they demand better pay and bigger clients or they'll tell the other partners what you let them do to you?

I ignored my inner voice. They wouldn't blackmail me. I didn't know them very well and maybe it was stupid to go with my gut on this one, but I knew instinctively that blackmailing me or using this brief affair to get them ahead at the office wasn't their style. Trying to convince me to keep fucking them though, was an entirely different story.

I climbed into my car and threw my purse on the seat beside me. The thought of allowing Seth and Theo to convince me to keep going with our affair was intoxicating. What if I liked fucking both of them at once? It hardly seemed fair to try it and then never get to do it again.

I started my car. One, I couldn't keep fucking them and two, I was being presumptuous. Just because Seth and Theo were willing to help me live my fantasy of fucking two men at once, didn't mean they were willing to keep going once we actually fucked.

You got that right. You're too fat to keep them interested. You know that, don't you, Libby? In fact, I'm pretty sure they're throwing you a pity fuck. Men who look like them are not chubby chasers.

My stomach rolled with nausea and I forced deep

breaths of cold air into my lungs. They weren't throwing me a pity fuck. They thought I was gorgeous and sexy and they loved my curves. Just because inner me had suddenly turned into a stone-cold bitch who apparently reveled in making me feel bad, it didn't mean I had to listen to her. They didn't believe I was fat. Hell, Theo had even let me ride him and he was fine afterwards.

Are you sure? You didn't see him get up and move around, did you? He was still in bed when you left this morning. You didn't even see him at the office today. Maybe he didn't come in. Maybe he's at the hospital getting those crushed ribs checked out. You didn't even think about your goddamn weight, did you? You rode him like the world's fattest cowgirl and he had a prime viewing of every single part of you that jiggles. Of your fat rolls and the way your tits sag. I bet you crushed his need for you and his ribs in one single –

"Shut up!" I snapped out loud. "They still want me. Would they have asked me to come over tonight if they didn't?"

My inner self had nothing to say to that. I tried to will my nausea away. I had planned on stopping and grabbing a bite to eat but the nausea had driven away my appetite. Instead, I drove directly toward Seth and Theo's house. It was fine. Everything was fine. Theo and Seth wanted me. They thought I was beautiful. They wanted me, and I was going to let them have me.

❦ ❧

"Libby," Seth smiled at me when I stuck my head into the kitchen. I had used the key he gave me this morning to let myself into the back door after parking a street over and walking down the alley. "How are you?"

"Good," I said. He took my jacket and disappeared

down the front hallway. When he returned, he pressed a warm kiss against my mouth and squeezed my ass. I winced and a wicked little grin crossed his face. "Sore bottom?"

"Yes," I replied.

"I guess you'd better be a good girl tonight then," Seth said with another wicked smile.

"Sure," I said absently. I yelped when Seth gave me a hard slap to the ass.

"Misbehaving already," he said.

"I'm not!"

"You are. You're distracted and unfocused which means you're thinking about work. You don't think about work when you're here, sweetheart."

"I'm not thinking about work," I protested.

"No?" Seth raised his eyebrows. "Then what are you thinking about?"

I worried my bottom lip with my teeth. "Where's Theo?"

"He had an errand to run," Seth said. "He'll be back soon."

"Is he, I mean, does he feel okay?" I asked.

Seth gave me a puzzled look. "What do you mean?"

Oh God, he was going to make me say it. My cheeks burning, I said, "Is he sore or, ah, injured?"

"Why would he be injured?" Seth was looking at me like I had grown two heads, but I was positive he was being deliberately obtuse. Anger flared in me and I scowled at him.

"Because I'm heavy and you two assholes made me ride him last night!" My nausea grew and I felt frantic and angry and out of control. I shouted foolishly, "I told you I didn't want to be on top and now Theo probably has crushed ribs and you're being too polite to tell me!"

I yelped again when Seth turned me and pushed me over the island. He held me down with one hand in the middle of my back as his other hand shoved up my skirt. I was wearing thick tights and he yanked them down to my knees, dragging my underwear down with them.

Without saying a word, he spanked my already-sore ass with heavy slaps. It burned like fire and I immediately began to cry and plead for him to stop. He ignored me, and I slumped across the table as his rough hand kept up a steady rhythm of spanks.

Within minutes, my anger and fear had left and despite how much it hurt, a weird kind of peace consumed me. I pressed my hot cheek against the cool marble as I accepted the spanking. I floated happily in the bubble, still feeling the stinging pain of each of Seth's spanks but the pain was tinged with sweetness and pleasure.

I hadn't realized it but all day long I'd been stressed and overwhelmed. My desire to do well at my new job and prove I was worthy of partnership, my fear that I had hurt Theo, even my hard-to-shake belief that Seth and Theo weren't actually attracted to me had weighed on me. But for the first time, I wasn't worried about proving myself at my job, or stressed about my looks or even feeling shame for possibly hurting Theo. I couldn't be. Right or wrong, Seth's firm discipline of my outburst had sent me to my happy place and I felt…free.

"Spanking already?"

I was only vaguely aware of Theo's deep voice, but I whined a little when Seth stopped spanking me and ran his hand over my ass.

"She was being disrespectful and raising her voice," Seth said.

"Why?" Theo asked.

"She has this silly idea that she hurt you when you were fucking her last night." Seth's voice was dark with disapproval, but I didn't notice. I was still floating.

"Are you kidding me?" Theo forced me to straighten

up from the table. He smelled like snow and pine trees and I inhaled deeply as he studied me. "Christ, is she in subspace?"

"She can't be," Seth said as he turned me to face him. "She can't possibly trust us enough yet to…"

He trailed off and I smiled dreamily at him.

"Sweetheart, you okay?"

"Yes, Sir," I said. "Can I please come now?"

My peaceful, dreamy state was already starting to subside, and I caught the look between Theo and Seth. "What?"

"Nothing, love," Theo said. "Come to the bedroom."

He peeled off my tights and underwear as Seth pulled my skirt down over my ass. Theo took my hand and I followed him to his bedroom. I wanted to stay in that dreamy floating state forever but by the time I was standing in front of his bed, it was gone completely. The frustration was almost overwhelming, and I blinked back the hot tears. What the hell was wrong with me? I would not cry in front of Seth and Theo. I was their goddamn boss and I wouldn't fucking cry in front of them.

Are you kidding me? You let them put a collar around your neck and a plug up your ass. You call them both Sir and suck their dicks until your jaw aches, but you won't cry in front of them?

No, I fucking well wouldn't.

"You all right, sweetheart?"

"Fine," I snapped irritably at Seth. I immediately tensed and fought my urge to cover my ass with my hands. My attitude almost guaranteed a punishment.

To my utter surprise, Seth simply started to undress me while Theo went to the closet. I was naked when he returned and he buckled the collar around my neck and the leather cuffs around my wrists before Seth urged me onto the bed. I was still incredibly close to tears, my skin felt too tight and hot and that lovely feeling I had earlier was a distant memory.

Be a bad girl. They'll spank you again and you can get it back.

Now that was a very fucking good idea. I suddenly didn't care that my ass was swollen and painful or that the faint bruises I had from yesterday would become dark purple blotches by tomorrow. I needed that feeling back. I needed it and they were going to give it to me.

I moved my legs restlessly on the bed as Seth and Theo, still fully-clothed, laid down on either side of me. I glared at Theo. "Not going to get naked because you don't want me to see the bruises on your ribs?"

He arched his eyebrows at me. "Why would I have bruises?"

"Because a fat girl rode you last night?" I retorted.

Seth immediately rolled me to my side to face Theo and I could have crowed with victory even as I was tensing for that first painful slap. Instead of a spank, he kissed my upper back as Theo cupped my breast and toyed with my nipple.

"No," I whined. "No, not that."

Oh my God, what the hell was wrong with me? I was acting like a spoiled brat.

"Yes, this," Theo said.

"I'm being bad," I moaned and arched my back as Seth licked my spine and Theo pulled on my nipple. "I need to be punished."

"No, Libby," Seth said. His hands traced circles on the back of my thighs as he kissed the top of my shoulder.

"Theo, please," I whimpered. "Please spank me, Sir."

"No, you've had enough spanking for now," Theo said. He kissed me hard on the mouth, forcing my lips open so he could thrust his tongue between them. I sucked at it before fisting my hands in his shirt and clinging to him. He tasted so damn good and as desire and need burned in my belly, I could feel my frustration melting away.

Seth was lifting my leg and hooking it behind his. He was wearing jeans and the denim made my ass sting, but I rubbed my butt against the bulge of his erection anyway. As Theo trailed his fingers down across my belly, I whispered, "Please, Sir."

I realized with sudden clarity that I didn't want to be teased or tormented. If I couldn't have that floaty feeling back, I wanted an orgasm. Wanted and needed it in a way I didn't quite understand.

"Don't tease," I moaned. "Please, don't tease."

"No teasing this time, baby," Theo whispered into my ear before nipping my earlobe. "We know what you need."

As Seth reached around and cupped my breast, Theo slipped his hand between my legs. His warm fingers found my swollen clit and he rubbed it with precise strokes that had me on the edge almost immediately. I cried out when Seth pinched my nipple hard as his other hand pulled on my collar and forced my head back. I arched my body, rubbing my ass against Seth's erection as Theo stroked my clit.

I moaned – or maybe I screamed – both their names as my climax rushed over me and I collapsed in a quivering heap between them. As the high of my orgasm started to fade, I slumped against Theo and tried to bury my face in his t-shirt, but Seth tugged on my collar and forced my head back.

"Is she in subspace again?" He asked.

Theo studied my face before shaking his head. "No, but she is more relaxed now."

"Good," Seth said.

I tried to hide my surprise when both men moved in

close and cuddled me. Theo stroked my hair and Seth rubbed my thigh and hip as I stared up at Theo.

"Do you feel okay, love?"

"Yes. Why aren't you fucking me? Did I hurt you yesterday?" I asked anxiously.

He scowled and tucked my hair back behind my ear. "No, you most definitely didn't hurt me. Also, if I ever hear you refer to yourself as a fat girl again, I'll spank you until you can't sit down. Do you understand?"

I nodded, stupidly happy at the thought of being punished by Theo. "Then why aren't we fucking?"

"Later," Theo said.

I leaned my head back until it was resting against Seth's chest. He pressed a kiss against my temple. "How do you feel, Libby?"

I frowned. Why did they keep asking me that?

"Fine." I hesitated and then said, "What's subspace?"

"Subspace is a reaction to intense stimuli," Seth said. "It varies for each submissive but, generally speaking, it's an awareness change. Lots of subs refer to it as flying or floating."

I jerked against him. "That – it felt like that for me earlier when you were spanking me."

He cupped my breast and squeezed it gently as Theo said, "When a submissive goes into subspace, his or her Dom needs to be very careful."

"Why?" I asked.

"Because usually a submissive doesn't care what happens to them at that point. They're completely unaware and will let a scene go too long. They can be hurt if the Dom doesn't know what he or she is doing."

I shivered and Seth gave my breast another almost soothing squeeze. "That rarely happens, sweetheart. A submissive takes a long time to go into subspace with a new Dom. She needs to feel complete trust with her

Dom before she goes into subspace around them. By the time she does, her Dom knows her limits intimately and won't let a scene go too far, even if his sub isn't safe wording."

"Oh," I said. "But you said I was in subspace earlier and we've barely, uh, played together."

Theo and Seth glanced at each other and I groaned in sudden understanding. "Oh my God, so I'm not just a freak, I'm a super freak."

"You're not a freak," Theo scolded. "Being submissive doesn't make you a freak, Libs."

"No, but going into subspace so quickly does," I argued.

"It's a bit unusual," Seth admitted, "but you didn't go in very deep and you didn't stay in it very long."

"I was upset and frustrated when I wasn't, uh, in subspace anymore," I said. "It's why I begged you to spank me."

I turned bright red and buried my face against Theo's chest. I smelled pine trees again as I said, "I am a freak."

"You're not," Seth insisted. "There can be a low coming out of subspace – it's normal. Besides, going into subspace so quickly with me was a gift of trust and I'm glad it happened."

I sighed and said, "I was feeling stressed and worried and when you started spanking me, even though it hurt, it made all of that fade away. Maybe because it hurt and that was all I could concentrate on, you know?"

"Were you spanked in your previous relationships?" Theo asked.

"No," I said. "The thought of being spanked and of being forced to, you know, suck on a dick or even being, um, fucked when it wasn't exactly, uh…"

Oh God, how did I say this without really sounding like a freak?

"When it wasn't one hundred percent clear that you wanted to be fucked?" Seth asked.

I nodded, my cheeks burning like fire and my entire body tense. "Yeah. Anyway, those things turned me on and I knew that they did, but my previous partners weren't like you and I was shy and nervous about certain things. Sometimes when I was having sex, I would close my eyes and pretend they were forcing me to have sex with them. It always made it hotter, but I'd feel so dirty after. Like I had used them for something they would never understand and would be disgusted by if they knew."

I took a deep breath. "My ex, Wayne, he was – was not experimental at all. I had more self-confidence when I started dating him and I asked him one night to pin my arms above my head while we were having sex in missionary style. He would only do two positions – me on top and missionary. I never even tried doggy style until that night in the hotel room with the two of you."

"Christ," Theo said in a low mutter.

Libby! Stop talking! You do not have to spill every single humiliating detail.

Inner me was right but I couldn't seem to stop. There was a cathartic release in telling them.

"Anyway, he did it and it was hot to be pinned down so I asked him a few times to do that. He always would but it started to lose some of its appeal. I guess because it never truly felt real. Like I knew if I actually tried to break free, he'd let me and that wasn't what I wanted. I wanted to be...helpless. You know?"

"Yes," Seth said. He kissed the back of my shoulder as his fingers stroked across my nipple.

"I thought about asking him to restrain me to the bed with handcuffs or ropes, but I couldn't work up the nerve. But I asked him to spank me once. I'd had a couple glasses of wine and figured it wouldn't hurt to ask, right? Only, the look he gave me was so humiliating. He couldn't even hide how disgusted he was by the idea. He said no immediately, and I tried to pass it off as a joke. In the morning, he wanted to know why I would ever ask him to hurt me like that and I – I told him I had more wine than he thought and was really drunk."

Theo leaned forward and kissed my forehead. "I'm sorry, Libs."

"It's fine," I said. "It's not a big deal. But it's why I reacted the way I did when you guys threatened to spank me at the bar that night. My biggest fantasy was just handed to me on a silver platter."

"I'm glad we could help," Seth murmured into my ear. His fingers pulled on my nipple and I made a soft moan.

"Are you – are you sure that I'm not a freak for wanting to be hurt?" I asked.

"Positive," Theo said. "Why did you and Wayne break up?"

I immediately tensed and Seth kissed my shoulder again as Theo rubbed my hip. "Tell us the truth, sweetheart."

I didn't want to, but fuck I'd already spilled my pathetic sex experience to them. Why not go for the gold, right?

"When I first started dating Wayne I was thin," I said. "I had lost a lot of weight, but it took work to stay that way. I was never happy constantly watching what I ate and going to the gym for two hours a day. My career was going well and I was busy with that. Eventually I stopped counting calories and, instead, tried to eat healthy and do some exercising every day. For some people, that's enough. It isn't for me, and I gained the weight back until I was my normal size."

Theo and Seth didn't reply and I said hastily, "I'm

very healthy. My blood pressure is good and my cholesterol level is completely normal and - "

"Libs, stop," Seth said. "Your health is your own business, not ours. We're not judging you for anything."

I blinked at him in surprise before continuing. "Right. Well, anyway, Wayne didn't seem to be bothered by my weight gain. We still had sex and he never called me fat or anything. But then we started having sex less and less. I blamed it on how busy I was with building my career, and Wayne was, well, he was pretending to try and open his own restaurant. I never even thought it was because of my weight gain. Then I came home early from work one day and found Wayne banging a younger and thinner woman in our bed."

"Asshole!" Theo snapped as Seth made a sound of disgust.

"I broke it off with him, obviously, but I asked him why he cheated. I thought he would say because I spent so much time and energy on my career." I laughed bitterly. "I couldn't have been more wrong. He said it was my weight. He said that he was tired of being that guy with his friends – the guy who had a fat girlfriend and all his buddies felt sorry for him and were secretly glad it wasn't them. He also said that I…"

I trailed off and Seth rubbed my back. "Tell us, sweetheart."

"He said that I was so fat it hurt him when we had sex and I was on top," I said. "He said that he had a cracked rib from letting me ride him."

"He was lying," Theo said.

"He went to the doctor," I replied.

"I don't fucking care if he went to the doctor or if he did have a cracked rib," Theo snapped. "He didn't get it from you riding him."

"Fuck," Seth muttered, "so, that's why you freaked out about sitting on Theo's face and about being on top."

"I don't want to hurt you like I hurt Wayne," I said. "It's humiliating and - "

"He was lying," Theo repeated.

"He wasn't as big as you are," I said. "He was taller than me, but I probably weigh more than him now and - "

Theo cupped my face, his fingers digging into my cheek as he forced my head up to look him in the eye. "Look at me, Libby. You are not too heavy to ride a man's dick, and you're going to ride both Seth and me repeatedly until you believe it."

"I don't want to," I said.

Theo gave me a predatory grin that both unnerved me and lit up my nerve endings with lust. "You don't get a say in the matter, love. You belong to us and we'll fuck you however and in whatever position we want. Is that clear?"

I swallowed and licked my lips. "Theo, I don't - "

"Is that clear?" He repeated.

"Yes, Sir," I whispered.

"Good." He bent his head and sucked my right nipple into his mouth. He bit it hard and I cried out, my back arching as Seth pulled my legs apart and pushed his hand between them. He cupped my pussy, rubbing it almost angrily as Theo licked away the sting of his bite.

"Seth," he said, "I want to use the clamps on her tonight."

"Fuck, yes," Seth said. "Get her nipples nice and hard while I grab them from the - "

I blushed furiously when he was interrupted by the loud growling of my stomach.

"Sorry," I said.

"Did you eat dinner?" Seth asked with a frown.

I shook my head. "No, I worked late and then I wasn't hungry. I'll have a bigger breakfast in the morning."

"No," Seth said. "You need to eat, Libs."

"I don't," I said as I rubbed the bulge at the front of Theo's jeans. He groaned and Seth gave him a warning look.

"Hey," I said when both men pulled away from me, "I don't want to stop."

"Not your decision, remember, love?" Theo said with a wicked grin. "Besides, I should go and grab the tree. It's still strapped to the top of the car."

I gave him a blank look as Seth said, "On your hands and knees, sweetheart."

My stomach made a happy little flip of excitement. Seth had changed his mind and even though I was hungry, I wanted his dick a whole fucking lot more than food. I climbed to my hands and knees and spread my legs eagerly when Seth pushed up behind me.

"Good girl," he praised. "Spread your ass cheeks for me."

I gave him a startled look, my gaze dropping to the plug he held in his right hand. "What?"

"Spread your cheeks, sweetheart." He tapped my burning ass with the end of the plug. "We'll pop this in and then I'll make you something to eat."

"You're going to make me wear the plug while I'm eating?"

"Yes," he said. "Now, take a deep breath and try to relax. This one is a bigger size than yesterday's plug."

"Fuck," I muttered but I grabbed my ass cheeks and spread them apart as Seth spread lube over my anus and the plug.

"Ready, sweetheart?" He asked.

"Is anyone ever ready to have a plug stuck in their ass?" I asked.

He laughed and kissed my lower back. "You're my good girl, Libs. Relax, please."

I tingled with happiness when he called me his good

girl and buried my face into the quilt as Seth eased the plug into my ass.

"Oh my God," I moaned.

Theo reached under me and pinched my nipples hard. The sharp pain distracted me from the dull pain in my ass and I gasped and tried to wiggle away. He slapped my dangling breast and wound his hand in my hair, yanking my face up until I was staring at him.

"Be good, Libby," he warned as Seth pushed the plug in deeper.

"I – I am, Sir," I gasped.

"There, how does that feel?" Seth asked as he patted my ass cheek.

"Uh, good, I think," I said. He pushed on the plug at the same time Theo pulled on one nipple and I cried out like a needy cat. "Oh please, I'm not hungry. Please!"

"Liar," Seth said and gave my throbbing ass a hard slap. "Let's go to the kitchen, sweetheart."

Theo helped me off the bed but shook his head when I reached for my clothes. "You don't need them."

I balked immediately. "I can't walk around naked."

"Why not?" Seth asked. "The blinds are all closed. No one to see you but us."

"I can't," I repeated. "I don't want to safe word so please don't make me go naked."

Seth nodded and stripped off his shirt. "You can wear this but no bra or panties. Clear?"

"Yes, Sir. Thank you, Sir," I said gratefully. I tugged his t-shirt over my head. I was afraid it would be too small, but it was actually too big and fell to mid-thigh. I felt much better even though the plug in my ass made it feel weird to walk and it would be even harder to sit.

"Ready?" Seth asked.

"Yes, Sir," I replied.

He took my hand and I followed him and Theo out of

the bedroom.

Chapter Seven

"Do you have any idea how hard it is to hang balls when you're doing that?" I said.

Theo laughed and squeezed my tits again, rubbing his crotch against my ass as I stood on my tiptoes to hang the round silver ornament on one of the branches. His movement jostled the plug in my ass and I couldn't help but moan.

"Someone's getting horny," he said.

"I've been horny since I got here," I replied. "But someone made me eat dinner first and then someone else made me decorate their Christmas tree."

"Hey, it can't be sex, sex, sex all the time," Seth said as he crawled out from under the tree. "We're not just dicks for your pleasure, you filthy girl."

"Really?" I said. Theo was kissing my neck and I arched into his hands when he cupped my breasts again and played with my nipples through the fabric of Seth's t-shirt.

"Mostly," Seth said as he watched my nipples harden under Theo's ministration. "Fuck, are we done decorating this goddamn tree yet?"

"Yes," Theo said. "Did you plug the lights in?"

Seth nodded and brushed some pine needles from his

shoulders. "Yeah, turn them on."

Theo flicked the switch to turn on the lights. The Christmas lights flickered to life and Seth joined us as we stared up at the glowing tree.

"It's beautiful," I said.

"Yes, beautiful," Seth replied. He was staring at me and I gave him a sweet smile as he took my hand and kissed my knuckles.

While Seth made me dinner, Theo had set the tree up in their living room. I was secretly thrilled when they asked me to help decorate it. I knew it was stupid. I was only here to have sex with them, but even naked under Seth's shirt and wearing a plug in my ass, it had felt good to do something with them that wasn't sex related.

Be careful, Libby. You're thinking dangerous thoughts. This isn't a relationship and it all ends the minute they both get their dicks into you at the same time.

I know, I thought irritably to inner me. *I know, so give it a rest, would you?*

"Libby?"

"Sorry, what was that?" I smiled apologetically at Theo.

"I said it was getting late," he replied.

I glanced at the clock over the fireplace. It was almost ten and all of us had to work in the morning. I ignored my disappointment. Yes, I had loved decorating the tree with them and drinking hot chocolate and laughing and swapping childhood Christmas stories like we were in some kind of weird threesome relationship. But apparently, deep down, I was more interested in the sex. Pathetic, but true. I would have happily given up all of that if I'd known it meant I wouldn't get laid tonight. Ignoring how sorry I felt for myself, I smiled cheerfully at them. "Yes, it is. Thank you for dinner. I had a lovely time. Should I leave the plug in for a few more hours and then bring it, um, back to you tomorrow night?"

"What are you talking about?" Seth asked with a frown.

"The butt plug," I said patiently. "Should I take it out now and leave it here or drive home with it in and take it out in another hour or so?"

"You're not going home," Theo said. "You're marching your sweet little ass up to the bedroom so we can fuck you."

Excitement radiated through me but I said, "I know its late and we have work in the morning so - "

"Libby," Seth warned, "if you keep arguing with us, you will get spanked again."

I shut my mouth with a snap and took Theo's offered hand as Seth shut the lights off on the Christmas tree. We walked upstairs to Theo's bedroom and Seth disappeared into the closet as Theo stripped off my shirt before stepping behind me. He was rubbing my clit with one hand and wiggling the plug in my ass with the other when Seth returned. I was moaning and rubbing my pussy against Theo's hand and paid no attention to what Seth was carrying.

When he bent and sucked on my right nipple, I wound my fingers through his thick hair and held him tightly. He sucked and licked until my nipple was hard and swollen.

Theo stopped playing with the plug in my ass and said, "Put your arms behind your back, love."

I did what he asked, a little thrill going through me when he hooked his arm around both of mine and held me firmly. I was trapped against him and I arched my back, pushing more of my breast into Seth's mouth as Theo bent his head and kissed me.

The pain on my nipple had me yanking my mouth from Theo's. I hissed and stared at the small metal alligator clamp fastened to my right nipple. It had a silver chain attached to it and I moaned and tried to wiggle free when Seth adjusted the fit.

"Too tight!" I gasped.

"It isn't," Seth said.

"It hurts!"

"It's supposed to," he said with a small grin. He sucked on my left nipple and I tried to will it not to harden so he couldn't attach the clamp. Unaware of what was about to happen to it, my left nipple cheerfully rose to the occasion and I couldn't help moaning in a combination of pleasure and pain. Seth attached the second clamp and tightened it before smiling at me.

"How's that?"

"Painful," I retorted.

He tugged on the silver chain that dangled between my breasts and I moaned as it pulled on my aching nipples. "Oh God! Don't – don't do that."

"Behave and I won't have to," he said.

He turned to Theo and said, "Is she wet enough to be fucked?"

God, why did his crudeness turn me on so much? And would there always be a small part of me that believed I was sick for wanting to be treated this way?

Theo was still holding my arms behind my back. He glanced at Seth and a silent communication rippled between them. Theo pressed a kiss against my cheek before saying, "Safe word, love?"

"Red," I said.

"We'll only stop for your safe word. Nothing else," Theo said.

"I know," I said in confusion. Why was he reminding me of that?

"Is she wet enough?" Seth repeated.

Theo cupped my pussy and rubbed it roughly. "Fuck, yes. She's dripping."

"Good. Are you ready to be fucked, Libby, or have you changed your mind?" Seth asked.

I gave him a blank look. Why the hell would he think I'd changed my mind? I was practically begging them to fuck me earlier before dinner, and…

My eyes widened. Holy shit, Seth and Theo were trying to give me exactly what I wanted. Fresh excitement raced through my veins and I was suddenly so turned on, I could hardly stand it. I had never taken a single acting class, had never joined the drama club or participated in a school play but I was about to play the part in my fantasy as eagerly as a waitress trying to make it in Hollywood.

I took a deep breath and said, "I've changed my mind."

Seth arched his eyebrow at me. "What did you say?"

"I've changed my mind. I – I don't want to fuck you. I'd like to go home now, please."

"Did you hear what she said, Theo?"

"I did."

A shiver of fear and anticipation went down my spine. Theo's voice had both deepened and roughened and he sounded angry. More fear licked along my veins but beneath it was – oh god, was it anticipation?

Seth reached out and traced my bottom lip with his finger. I tried to pull back from his touch and liquid dripped out of my pussy when Theo tightened his hold on my arms. I was trapped between them and that odd but compelling combination of fear and need tingled through me again.

"We gave you what you wanted tonight. Didn't we, Libby?"

"I- I don't know," I stammered.

"You don't know?" Seth's voice was silky soft. "I spanked you and Theo gave you an orgasm. Hell, I even made you dinner. Is that right?"

"Yes," I whispered.

"We did all of that for *you*, and now you're going to leave without spreading your pretty thighs and giving us a go at your cunt? Does that seem fair?"

"I don't have to – to have sex with you just because you did those things." I tried to sound strong but there was a waver in my voice that made Seth smile.

"No, sweetheart, you don't. But do you know what they call girls like you?"

I shook my head and then moaned when Seth brushed his mouth across mine before whispering, "Cock tease."

I gasped in a combination of shock and pain when Theo tugged on the chain connecting the nipple clamps. It made my nipples throb and I whimpered when Seth leaned down and licked the swollen and tender tip of my right one. It sent pleasure straight to my pussy and I squeezed my thighs together in an attempt to ease the ache as Theo whispered in my ear.

"Are you a cock tease, Libby?"

"No," I moaned.

"Wrong answer," Theo replied before tugging again on the chain.

It sent fresh sparks of pleasure and pain radiating through me and I arched my back and stood on my tiptoes. Fuck, I was so wet I was about to drip all over the floor of the bedroom.

"Please," I cried out as Theo bit my neck and Seth nipped at my collarbone.

"Tell us what you are, Libby," Seth demanded.

"I – I'm a cock tease!" I said as Theo used his knee to push my thighs apart. He stuck his leg between mine and I rubbed against his denim-clad thigh with shameless need. "Oh, please!"

"Say it again," Seth demanded.

"I'm a cock tease," I said.

"That's right, you are. Your little cunt belongs to

both of us and we'll fuck it whenever we want.

I barely heard Seth, I was rubbing my clit against Theo's hard thigh and I was so damn close to coming. I needed a little more friction, a little more pressure and…

I howled with pain when Seth pulled hard on the chain between my breasts. It yanked me back from the exquisite edge of my orgasm and I made inarticulate pleading noises as Theo pulled his leg from between mine.

"Fuck, Seth, I can't wait another goddamn minute."

Theo's voice was as ragged as my breath and to be honest, Seth was looking like he was on the verge of losing his control as well.

"Please, Seth, oh, please," I moaned.

He hesitated and then cursed under his breath before grabbing my arm and roughly pulling me to the bed. "On your hands and knees, facing the headboard, Libby."

I obeyed him without hesitation. Part of me was sorry I had ruined my fantasy so quickly, but I felt nearly wild. If they didn't give me what I wanted, what I *needed*, I would lose my goddamn mind.

I clambered onto the bed and dropped to my hands and knees, staring at the headboard. Seth and Theo were tearing off their clothes in record time and I only made a small whimper of protest when Seth wrapped a heavy chain around the center iron spindle of the headboard and grabbed both my wrists.

"Hands up," he demanded hoarsely.

I lifted my hands, balancing myself on my knees as Seth threaded the chain through the hoops in the leather cuffs around my wrists before securing the chain to the headboard.

I squealed in surprise when Theo grabbed my hips and lifted me up enough for Seth to slide beneath me. My legs were spread wide around his hips and my back was arched from the way my hands were tied. Seth was already wearing a condom and I resisted when his hands replaced Theo's on my hips and pulled.

"Libby," he said warningly, "lower your tight pussy on my dick, right now."

"Seth," I whispered. Even as turned on as I was, my insecurities were rearing their ugly head. "Seth, don't make me do this."

"You're going to ride me, sweetheart, because if you don't, I'll tell Theo to pull that plug from your ass and replace it with his cock. What do you think, Libby? You think your ass is stretched enough to take Theo's cock?"

I stared at Seth and knew he meant every word of what he was saying. I must have hesitated too long because he pulled hard on the chain between my breasts. I cried out and quickly lowered my body until the tip of his cock brushed against my pussy. He groaned and reached between us, guiding his cock to my entrance. I pushed down and we both moaned when he entered me fully with one hard thrust.

Thanks to my hands being restrained, I had to bend over him, leaving my breasts in his face. He took advantage of it, sucking on my protruding nipples and pulling on the clamps with his teeth. I moaned and pleaded for mercy as the bed dipped and Theo kneeled between Seth's legs behind me.

I was stuffed full of Seth's cock, restrained with my nipples clamped and there was so much lust coursing through my veins, I was afraid my heart would explode from it. The deep breath I took that was meant to help calm me, turned into a wailing scream of pure pleasure. Theo was pushing and tugging on the plug in my ass while his fingers pinched my clit and that was it for me. I came with another hard scream as the pleasure rolled through me in endless tumbling waves that made my entire body shake. Dimly, I was aware of Seth thrusting into me from below, of the way his hard cock pounded into my pussy. He made a harsh roar that shook me to my core with its intensity and arched upward. There was a brief flash of pain as he thrust deep and then it was his turn to shake and moan.

"Seth, fucking move!" Theo's voice was the sound of a desperate animal.

I cried out when he yanked on my hips, pulling my body up until Seth's cock popped out of me.

"Goddammit move, Seth!" Theo said furiously.

With a low groan Seth slid out from under me, rolling to the far side of the bed and laying on his back as he gasped for air.

My thighs were pulled apart so wide that the muscles screamed in protest. I hung my head and took great gasping breaths of air and then squealed with pleasure when Theo pushed in to the hilt.

"Fuck, oh fuck," he chanted in a low moan as he pushed and retreated with hard and punishing strokes. I braced my hands against the headboard, the chain that bound me to it rattling loudly as new tingles of exquisite pleasure started up in my pussy.

"Oh God, no," I moaned. "I can't have another one. I can't have… oh God!"

Without breaking his rhythm, Theo had reached under me and was rubbing at my clit. It was too much and I tried to break free, crying out when his hand wrapped in my hair and yanked my head back.

"No," he snarled into my ear. "You come for me right now, baby. Come all over my cock with your tight pussy!"

He pulled on my clit and I screamed as I climaxed again. This one was just as intense as the first one and I shook wildly as white light exploded behind my eyelids. Theo shouted my name before driving me down into the mattress. His big body shook on top of mine and his hand pulled hard at my hair as he came deep inside of me.

His weight was making it hard to breathe and I protested my lack of oxygen. He pulled out and collapsed on the other side of me, nearly falling off the bed in the process. I pulled at the chain connecting me to the bed and Seth quickly unclasped it before tossing the chain on the floor beside the bed. He rolled me over onto my back and I stared glassy-eyed at him as he made soft crooning noises into my ear and rubbed my quivering belly and thighs.

"Such a good girl, Libby," he said. "She's our good girl, isn't she, Theo?"

"Yes," Theo said. He was removing his condom and he tossed it into the trash can next to the bed. He rolled to his side to face us and propped his head up with one trembling hand. "Fuck, that was unbelievable."

I stared mutely at them and Seth smoothed the hair away from my sweaty face. "You okay, Libs?"

"Yes," I whispered. "I'm sorry."

"Sorry for what?" Theo gave me a puzzled look.

"For – for ruining the fantasy," I said. "I tried to pretend I didn't want it for longer but…"

I trailed off and blushed when both Seth and Theo laughed.

"Baby, it was amazing. Besides, this was all for you so if you wanted to end the role playing five minutes in, that's perfectly fine."

"I really liked it," I whispered.

"Good," Seth said. "We liked it too and we can always try it again and see if we can make it past five minutes."

I didn't reply. What had happened was so intense, I couldn't imagine trying it again any time soon. I needed time to recuperate, time to reflect on what it was about me that found this type of role playing so appealing. This was my only chance to live out that fantasy and I had kind of ruined it, but I refused to feel bad about it. I couldn't feel bad about it. Even if it was short-lived, it was fucking amazing and I would masturbate to this night in my head for years to come. I was sure of it.

"Are you ready, sweetheart?" Seth asked.

"Ready for what?" I gave him a look of confusion. Oh God, they didn't want another round already did they? My legs were like noodles and my heart was still beating like a runaway freight train. I needed some recovery time.

"This is going to hurt," Theo said.

"What's going to hurt?" I asked as he released the clamp around my right nipple and Seth released the clamp on my left. For a moment there was nothing and I shifted on the bed. "It doesn't hurt. It doesn't even...oh fucking hell!"

The blood was returning to my swollen nipples and oh sweet Jesus, did it fucking hurt! Tears gushed from my eyes and I tried to clap my hands over my nipples in some misguided attempt to soothe them. Before I could touch them, both Theo and Seth took a nipple into their mouth. They soothed and licked my nipples with their warm mouths and tongues. It helped ease the pain and tingling and I moaned and bit my bottom lip as they lifted their heads.

"Sorry, sweetheart," Seth said. He wiped the moisture from my cheeks as Theo rubbed the soft skin between my breasts.

"Fuck, that hurts," I said.

"I know and we're sorry," Theo said.

"Are you?" I squinted at them in suspicion and Theo laughed before rolling me to my side. He pulled the plug from my ass and tossed it into a basket on the nightstand.

"Should I go now?" I mumbled. I didn't want to go. I was tired and warm and wanted to sleep but spending the night had never been part of the deal despite sleeping over last night

Theo curled up behind me and stroked my side and hip as Seth rubbed my upper chest. He avoided touching my nipples and I relaxed into Theo's embrace as Seth kissed my forehead.

"No, sweetheart. You're spending the night with us."

"K, cool," I mumbled again before yawning. "Night, guys."

"Goodnight, love," Theo whispered into my ear.

Chapter Eight

I stared at the whiteboard in my office before adding another note to myself at the bottom. My cell phone rang and I snagged it from where I'd tossed it on my desk. It was Thursday afternoon and I had spent most of the day in my office finishing up a file. It was the last file on my desk and if I didn't find something else, Friday and Monday morning were going to be ridiculously long. I glanced at my phone screen and smiled. The number was very familiar and I hit the answer button.

"Good afternoon, Elizabeth speaking."

"Libby!" Charles Emerson's southern drawl washed over me. "It's Charles Emerson. How the fuck are you?"

I ignored my urge to laugh. Charles was a second-generation oil driller. He was a big, tough Texan with permanently stained hands, a handlebar mustache that would make Sam Elliot jealous and a big booming voice. He bred horses in his spare time, cursed like a sailor and went to church without fail every Sunday. He also had a wife he very obviously adored and four children who were all involved in the family business.

His company, Etco Drilling Ltd., was my previous

firm's biggest client. I was assigned to the Etco file in my first year. I had a feeling that my old boss - a sexist pig of a man who only hired female lawyers because he was forced to - believed that Charles with his quick temper and hard and grizzled exterior would eat me alive. Instead, we had forged an unlikely friendship over the next eight years. When I told Charles that I was thinking of leaving my firm and pursuing a partnership opportunity, he hadn't hesitated to let me know he would follow me. I wasn't naïve or stupid enough to think that having a multi-million-dollar drilling company as a loyal client wasn't part of the reason that I got the partnership at Martin, Clarke and Bones.

"Hello, Charles. I'm good. How are you?" I said.

"Can't complain. Well I could, but ain't no one around who cares enough to listen."

There was an outraged voice in the background and Charles gave a big booming laugh. "Now I'm in trouble with my Mags. She says hello and wants you to check your mailbox. She sent your Christmas present to your new address last week."

I felt a rush of love for Charles' wife Maggie. "She did? That's so sweet. Please tell her I said thank you and ask her if she found that knitting pattern she was looking for online."

He harrumphed irritably as his short temper got the best of him. "Jesus Christ, I ain't no messenger boy, Elizabeth. Call her up once the holidays are over and ask her yourself. She's been pining for a good chinwag with ya anyway."

I laughed. "All right, I will. Now, what can I help you with?"

"Nothing work related," Charles said. His voice softened a touch. "Just wanted to check in on ya, make sure the new job is going okay and to say Merry Christmas and shit like that."

Out of the corner of my eye I saw Sandra stick her head into my office. I waved her in as I shifted my cell phone to my other ear. "It's going well."

"Good," he said. "Real fuckin' glad to hear it, Libby. You have a good Christmas, okay?"

"You too. Give my love to Maggie and tell her I'll call her in the new year."

"Will do."

Like always, he hung up without saying goodbye and I grinned at Sandra as I hit the end button on my cell phone. "Sorry, Sandra. That was Charles from Etco Drilling."

"I spoke to him this morning. He called the office while you were meeting with Mario and got a little huffy when I wouldn't interrupt you," Sandra said.

I laughed. "That sounds like Charles."

"I was actually just coming in to talk to you about Etco," Sandra said.

"All right." I walked back to my desk and sat down in my chair. I thought I did a good job of hiding my flinch, but Sandra frowned at me immediately.

"Are you hurt, Libby? This is the second time I've seen you wince when you sat down."

Shit.

"Uh, no. I did a bit too much yoga this week and strained some muscles," I lied.

Truthfully, my ass was covered in big purple bruises and it hurt like fire when I sat. Not to mention how painful my damn nipples were. Despite the pain, I didn't feel any regret for what I'd done. In fact, I was almost late for work because I kept admiring the way my bruised ass looked in the mirror. There was a bruise in the shape of a handprint on my lower left cheek. I had stared at it for over a minute, knowing that if Seth put his hand over the bruise it would be the perfect match. That thought had made me shiver with lust and even now, I could feel fresh lust trickling through me.

"Right," Sandra said.

Shit. A topic change was sorely needed. "So, what is your question about Etco?"

"No questions. Emmett asked me to mention to you that Seth and Theo aren't going to be available to help you with the file until after Christmas," Sandra said.

"Oh really?" I tried to sound casual.

"Yes. We have a high-maintenance client in Georgia and," Sandra paused and rolled her eyes, "they've had another self-proclaimed crisis and insisted that Seth and Theo fly out this afternoon."

Dismay rippled through me and Sandra gave me an odd look. "Libby? Are you okay? Is there a problem with the Etco file?"

"No, everything's fine." I made myself smile cheerfully at her. "When are they back. Do you know?"

"I booked their return flight for late Monday morning. The client wanted me to book them to come back on Wednesday. Can you believe it? Tuesday is Christmas for heaven's sake!" Sandra rolled her eyes again. "I know Jeff and Mario have been urging Emmett to drop them as clients and I think this might be the straw that breaks the camel's back. Anyway, they're coming back Monday morning, but Jeff already told them not to come into the office and to start their Christmas holidays with their families."

"Well, I'm sure it will be fine for the Etco file," I said.

"Good," Sandra said. "Are you leaving tomorrow or Saturday?"

I gave her a blank look and she frowned at me. "Aren't you driving home this weekend for Christmas?"

I shook my head. "No, I'm staying here. It's such a long drive, you know?"

"I guess," Sandra said slowly. "What are you doing

for Christmas?"

"Oh, I, uh, I'm, um…"

"You're not spending Christmas alone?" Sandra asked in horror.

"I am," I admitted.

"You can come to my house," Sandra said. "We're eating dinner at two."

"No, thank you," I said. "I'm not intruding on your family dinner and besides, I'm looking forward to having Christmas by myself this year."

It wasn't entirely true, but I couldn't tell a woman I barely knew that I was looking forward to not spending Christmas with my overbearing and disapproving mother.

"Libby, no one should spend Christmas alone," Sandra said.

I shrugged. "Honestly, I need to be alone this year, Sandra."

Sandra gave me a searching look before sighing. "Okay, well if you change your mind, it's an open invitation. I'll email you my address. Come over at any time."

"Thanks, Sandra. That's very nice of you and I appreciate it," I said.

"Well, I mean it," she replied.

"I know," I said and then to mollify her, I said, "I'll think about it, okay?"

"Okay," she said. "Are you coming in Monday morning?"

"I was going to," I replied.

"Don't bother," she said. "No one is coming in. It's going to be dead in here and most of our clients are used to us having limited staff during the holiday break. I know the other partners told you not to come in. Take their advice and stay home and sleep in."

I laughed. "All right. I won't come in on Monday."

"Good," Sandra said with a satisfied smile.

❧ ❧

Monday afternoon, I stepped out the shower and wrapped the towel around my wet body. I wiped the steam from the mirror and stared at my reflection before running a comb through my hair. There was a small pink box on the bathroom vanity and I flipped the lid off, staring at the butt plug sitting inside of it.

I'd purchased it Thursday night, walking into the adult store with a vague sense of embarrassment. I'd never been in a store like that before and I'd walked the entire store staring at the inventory with equal amounts of curiosity and shock. I'd purchased a butt plug and lube, a small part of me wondering what the store employee was thinking as she placed it in the pink box. Once I was home, I'd inserted the plug and worn it the entire evening as I ate my dinner of cold cereal, and used my laptop to watch a couple of shows on Hulu.

Now, I sighed and put the lid back on the box. I'd already worn it for a few hours this morning. I'd worn it for a few hours each day on the weekend as well. Although why I bothered, I didn't know. I hadn't heard a single word from Seth or Theo since I'd left their bed Thursday morning.

As I'd been doing all weekend, I tried to console myself. They were working, we weren't dating – hell, we weren't even friends – so why would they contact me? It didn't hurt my feelings that they hadn't texted me even once. Why would they?

Why are you still wearing that damn plug? Inner me whispered.

"Once the holidays are over, I'm sure we'll pick up where we left off. I still haven't had sex with both of them at once." I said to my reflection.

Are you sure about that? They haven't contacted you once since they left. Yeah, you're not dating them, but wouldn't it be at least polite of them to send you one text?

Fuck, inner me just didn't know when to shut the hell up.

Maybe they're tired of you. You told them what Wayne said to you – maybe they realized they don't want to be those men with the fat girlfriend either. Maybe they –

Shut up! I snarled at my inner self. *Just shut up! We're not dating and I don't care if they don't call or text me. I want one thing from them and that's it, so shut the fuck up for once!*

Mercifully, my inner self lapsed into silence. I rubbed at my forehead before leaving the bathroom and walking to my bedroom. I dressed in yoga pants and a t-shirt, not bothering with a bra or underwear, and stared at my pathetic air mattress for a moment.

I was lying to myself and didn't want to admit it. I missed Theo and Seth. More than I should have if I was only using them for sex. I sighed and stared out the window at the falling snow. The last four days had passed agonizingly slow and I was already going a little stir crazy. I missed my stuff, I missed my friends and there was a part of me that wanted to jump in my car and drive home. If I left now, I could be home before midnight. Mom would be happy to have me home. Then, at least, I wouldn't spend the next week roaming a nearly empty apartment, eating cold cereal and wishing I was doing something inappropriate like fucking my funny, sweet and stupidly hot coworkers.

I could tell myself repeatedly that it wasn't over and that we would simply pick up where we left off when the craziness of the holidays was over, but not hearing from them had rattled me badly. Thinking they would text or call just to say hello was ridiculous so why was I hurt that they hadn't?

I needed to stop thinking about them, needed to stop wondering if they would –

My cell phone rang and I snatched it up from the floor next to the air mattress. It was my mother. For the first time in forever, I was eager to talk to her. It would take my mind off Theo and Seth and maybe I would let her talk me into driving home. I hit the answer button as I walked to the kitchen.

"Hey, Mom!" I said cheerfully. "How are you?"

There was a pause and then my mother said suspiciously, "Libby? Why are you so happy?"

"Why shouldn't I be?" I asked.

She snorted. "Maybe because you've left your mother all alone at Christmas? Do you even feel bad at all, Elizabeth?"

Guilt flooded through me immediately. "Mom, of course I do. I was even thinking that maybe I would - "

"I don't think you do, Libby." My mother steamrolled right over me. "I think you're doing this as some kind of punishment, because I was honest about my disappointment over the way you treated Wayne."

"The way I treated Wayne?" I could hear the irritation in my voice and I tried to rein it in. It was Christmas and I didn't want to fight with my mother, no matter how difficult our relationship was. "Mom, Wayne cheated on me."

"Oh for God's sake, Elizabeth," my mother retorted, "when are you going to let that go?"

My jaw dropped. "Let that go? You're kidding me, right?"

"Libby, honey, I think you need to give Wayne another chance. You refuse to lose the weight and because of that, he's as good as you're going to get. Men are visual creatures, they don't want a fat girl."

My stomach clenched and I said, "Do you hear yourself, Mom? You just called your own kid fat. Does that seem like something a mother would do?"

"If she's a mother who has her child's best interest at heart, then yes."

Anger flooded through me and I welcomed it. Embraced it and let it flourish. "No, Mom. That's isn't true and I won't let you keep treating me this way."

My doorbell rang and I stalked to the front door and yanked it open without even bothering to look at who it was.

"Treating you what way?" My mother said with that tone of fake hurt that made my skin crawl. "I love you, Libby and I only want what's best for you."

I barely heard her. I was staring wide-eyed at Theo and Seth standing on my doorstep. Without saying anything, I stepped aside so they could brush past me. "Mom, I have to go."

"Of course you do," my mother snapped. "You always have to go."

"I'll call you tomorrow," I said and ended the call as Seth closed the door.

The three of us stood silently in the front hall before I stuttered, "W-what are you doing here?"

"What are you doing here?" Seth countered. "We thought you would be driving home to your family for Christmas."

I shrugged. "I'm not. If you thought I was gone, why did you stop by?"

"We stopped at the office after our flight landed," Theo said. "We overheard Sandra telling Allison that you would be alone at Christmas. Why aren't you going home?"

"It's a long story but let's just say that it's preferable to spending Christmas with my mother," I said.

There was another moment of awkward silence and I

shifted from foot to foot before saying, "Well, thanks for stopping by. Merry Christmas."

Seth scowled at me. "You're not spending Christmas alone, Libby. You're spending it with us."

I blinked at him. "I'm not spending Christmas with yours or Theo's family. I don't even know them and how would you even explain who I was? Oh hey, fam, this is my pathetic boss who doesn't have anywhere to go for Christmas."

"Theo's parents are in Europe for Christmas and mine are in Montana at my grandparents," Seth replied. "It's just the two of us for Christmas this year."

I ignored the excitement brewing in my belly. "Oh, well, I appreciate the offer but I'm looking forward to my alone time."

Theo rolled his eyes. "Eating cold cereal and sleeping on an air mattress?"

"I don't need your pity invite to spend Christmas with you!" I suddenly hissed at them.

"It's not a pity invite," Theo replied.

"Yeah, right," I muttered.

Seth gave me a thoughtful look. "We're sorry we didn't call you while we were in Georgia, Libby. We didn't mean to upset you."

I was surprised by his intuitiveness to my emotional reaction. I chewed at my bottom lip before saying, "Why would you? I didn't expect you to call me and I'm not upset that you didn't."

Seth glanced at Theo. "Do you think she's lying to us because she wants a spanking or because she thinks we want to hear that she isn't upset."

I backed away, my hands dropping to cover my ass automatically. "I'm not lying."

Seth grinned and stepped toward me before hauling me into his embrace. He nuzzled my neck and pressed a kiss against my cheek. "You are lying and you should be upset with us. We were dicks not to text or call but we were busy with an absolute bastard of a client and," he paused and glanced at Theo.

"We weren't sure if you wanted us to contact you," Theo finished. "All we have is your work cell phone number and…"

He trailed off and I found myself feeling grateful for their discretion. Work phones were the property of the office and any texts could be monitored. I didn't want anyone at work knowing what I was doing with them and they were trying to respect that.

"I'm sorry. I'm being a total bitch and I had no right to be upset that I didn't hear from you. I just missed you both," I admitted.

"We're glad you're upset," Seth said and winced when Theo punched him in the arm. "That didn't come out right. What I mean is that we're glad you missed us because holy fuck, did we miss you."

He squeezed my ass and I smiled at him even though a pang of disappointment went through me. It was fine that they had missed me because of the sex. I didn't want more from them.

Seth stepped away and Theo took his place. He cupped my breast and circled my hardening nipple with his thumb. "Pack a bag and come spend Christmas with us, Libby. Please."

"I – okay," I whispered.

"Good," Theo said. He pressed a kiss against my mouth. "Come on, love. I'll help you pack."

❧ ❧

"What's this?" I stared at the wrapped package that Seth placed in my lap. It was later that evening. After arriving at their home, I'd helped Seth cook dinner and the three of us had enjoyed the meal with a couple glasses of wine. I thought we'd go to the bedroom and have sex but instead, they'd led me into the living room. The lights in the tree gleamed as Theo turned on the TV. Explaining it was a Christmas Eve tradition, we had watched two movies – *Elf* and *A Christmas Story* – both men laughing like little kids and quoting lines as we watched.

"It's a gift for you," Seth said.

"I didn't get you guys anything," I replied.

"You weren't supposed to," Theo said. "Open it, love."

I ripped off the packaging and opened the lid of the box. Nestled in pink tissue paper was a heart-shaped jewelled anal plug. I stared at it for a moment before bursting into giggles.

"Do you like it, sweetheart?" Seth asked with a grin.

"It's the most unique Christmas gift I've ever gotten," I laughed.

"And most romantic, right?" Theo said.

I laughed even harder. "Oh, definitely."

"Theo wanted to go with the kitty cat tail one, but I talked him out of it," Seth said.

I poked Theo in the stomach. "Don't be a brat."

"What do you say we go to the bedroom and try out your new Christmas gift?" Theo said before kissing me. "If we use it for a few more days, you should be stretched enough."

"I've, uh, been using a butt plug every day since Thursday," I said. My cheeks reddened and I wished I didn't feel embarrassed by my admission.

Seth gave me a look of glee. "Seriously?"

"Yes," I said. "I bought one and have been using it daily."

"Fuck, you are the perfect fucking woman," Seth said before leaning in and kissing me hard on the mouth. "Theo, get our perfect woman to the bedroom right now while I shut off the lights.

Theo tossed the box with the plug on the couch and pulled me to my feet. I followed him to the bedroom and he undressed me and himself in record time before pushing me onto my back on the bed.

"Theo, what – oh my god!"

Theo was lying between my legs with his face buried in my pussy before I could even blink. "Theo!" I moaned when he sucked on my clit.

He raised his head. "Yes, love?"

"Wh-what are you doing?"

"It's called foreplay," he said with a teasing grin.

"Shouldn't we wait for Seth?" I whispered. My hands were already tangling in his hair and I whimpered with pleasure when Theo nipped my inner thigh.

"He'll be here soon. I've spent the last four days dreaming about your cunt and how sweet it tastes. Don't even think of denying me, Libby."

"I'm not," I said quickly.

"Good. Let's see how wet I can make your pussy before Seth shows up." He dove back into my pussy and I closed my eyes and arched my back when he licked my clit with warm strokes of his tongue. He teased and licked and nipped until I was digging my feet into the small of his back and grinding my pussy against his mouth.

My eyes popped open the moment I felt a warm mouth cover my aching nipple. Seth was lying on the bed beside me and he licked and sucked at my nipple almost lazily as Theo ate my pussy with undisguised enthusiasm.

"Are your nipples still sore, sweetheart?" Seth asked.

"No," I panted as I rocked my hips against Theo's face. "No, they – they're fine."

"I'm glad. If you're our good girl, we won't use the clamps tonight."

I didn't reply and Seth gave my nipple a hard pinch. "Libby? Are you paying attention to me?"

"Fuck, no I'm not paying attention to you!" I retorted. I glared at him and he laughed and pinched my other nipple until I cried out.

"Theo, stop for a minute," Seth said.

"No! Theo, do not stop!" I shouted.

Theo lifted his head and smiled at Seth. "What's up?"

"Goddammit!" I shouted and tried to shove Theo's head back between my thighs.

Seth grabbed my wrists and yanked them above my head, pinning them to the bed. I cried out when Theo gave my pussy two hard slaps. It stung like hell so why was I spreading my legs in a silent plea for more?

Instead of slapping me, Theo pressed a kiss against the swollen lips of my pussy as Seth nipped my collarbone. "Be our good girl, Libby."

"I am, Sir" I said.

"Say it."

"I'll be your good girl, Sir," I said.

"What do good girls do?"

I stared at him for a moment before hit with inspiration. "They suck cock, Sir."

Seth smiled and I felt an absurd tingle of pride when he said, "That's right. Open up, good girl."

I opened my mouth as Seth shifted until he was kneeling next to me. He slipped a hand under my neck and lifted my head, supporting me as I sucked his cock into my mouth.

"Fuck, that's good," he muttered as he thrust in and out of my mouth. "Suck my cock like my good girl."

Theo sucked on my clit again and I moaned around Seth's cock. The vibration made Seth groan and he thrust even harder into my mouth. I barely noticed my inability to breathe or the spit that was running down my chin as Seth pushed in and out. Theo was teasing my clit with small flicks of his tongue and I was on the verge of climaxing.

Theo nipped my clit and I screamed, the sound muffled by Seth's thick cock, as I came in a violent rush of dizzying pleasure. Theo held my lower body still with hard hands on my hips and licked and sucked at my clit as my climax rolled through me.

I screamed again and Seth's hand tightened around my neck before he abruptly pulled out. I sucked in a lungful of air and let it out in a loud moan as Theo rubbed my oversensitive clit with the pad of his thumb. I jerked away and waited for the spank, but Theo simply pressed a kiss against my quivering thigh before standing up and opening the nightstand drawer. He pulled out a bottle of lube and condoms and handed a condom and the lube to Seth. Both men rolled on their condoms as I panted and moaned and twitched on the bed.

The bed dipped as Theo reclined on his back. "Climb on, Libby."

My legs were still shaking but I sat up and straddled him. I realized I wasn't worrying one bit about hurting him and scored myself a mental victory as Theo cupped both my breasts. "You're so beautiful, Libby."

"Thank you," I whispered. "So are you. Both of you."

Theo cupped my face and tenderly stroked my cheekbone with his thumb. "If it hurts too much or you want to stop at any time, say your safe word, okay? We won't be upset."

I glanced at Seth who was opening the bottle of lube. He smiled and leaned forward to kiss me. "We won't be, sweetheart. I promise."

"Okay," I said. "So, uh what do we do first?"

"First you put my cock in that soaking wet cunt of

yours," Theo said.

I blushed a little but grasped Theo's cock at the base and guided it to my opening. He was right about being soaking wet and I sank down on his cock with ease despite his size. Theo released his breath in a low groan before urging me to lean over him.

I braced my hands on the bed on either side of his head and we kissed with slow, deep strokes of our tongues as Seth kneeled between Theo's spread legs. Theo made a few lazy thrusts into my pussy as we kissed and I moaned into his mouth. God, it felt so good to have his cock again.

Feeling a little drunk on pleasure, I whispered, "I love your cock, Theo."

He nuzzled my neck before sucking on my earlobe. "I love your hot little pussy, Libby. You're an amazing woman and fucking you is all I can think about."

I moaned when he cupped my breasts and tugged on my nipples. Behind me, Seth was rubbing lube into my anus and I took a deep breath and pushed against his fingers when he pushed them deep into my ass. He made a scissoring motion with his fingers to stretch me. I pushed my breast against Theo's mouth and he sucked obligingly on my nipple as he made gentle little thrusts with his hips.

"Are you ready, sweetheart?" Seth asked.

"Yes."

"I'll go slow, I promise. Remember to breathe and to push back against me, okay?"

I looked over my shoulder at him. "Yes."

"You're sure?"

"Positive. Fuck my ass, Seth," I said.

He groaned and a look of almost feral need crossed his face before he moved a little closer. "Theo, stop moving."

Theo held still and gave me a reassuring look as Seth

pressed the head of his dick against my anus. I took a deep breath and pushed back against the steady pressure. I groaned and bit at my lip. Fuck, even with the plugs, it was hurting more than I thought it would.

I was about to say stop and ask for more time when Theo's hand slipped between my legs and rubbed at my swollen clit.

"Oh!" I squeaked as pleasure immediately mixed with the pain. "Oh, that helps!"

"Good," Theo said. "Concentrate on my fingers touching you, love. Your little clit is so swollen and hard. You want to come again, don't you?"

"Yes," I moaned. "I really do."

"Soon," Theo said soothingly.

There was a sudden flare of pain and I groaned. Seth rubbed my ass and Theo rubbed my clit as I hung my head and took deep breaths. The pain subsided rather quickly, leaving a feeling of dull pressure that was actually a little pleasurable.

"Is it in?" I panted.

"The head is," Seth replied.

I groaned and swivelled my head to stare at him. "Just the head?"

I already felt stuffed to the brim and couldn't imagine taking any more of Seth's cock. "I don't think I can take any more."

"Yes, you can," Seth said. "Take my cock up your ass like a good girl or I'll give you a spanking."

That made me clench around both men's dicks and Theo groaned. "Jesus, Seth, stop threatening to spank her!"

"Rub her clit again," Seth ordered.

Theo rubbed my clit and I moaned and rubbed my pussy against his fingers as Seth pushed and retreated slowly until I felt his pelvis pressing against my ass and he made a satisfied grunt.

"Good girl," he said.

"Oh God," I moaned. "It's too much. I can't take it."

Seth ignored me and made a few gentle thrusts that sent lightning coursing up and down my nerve endings.

"Fuck!" I squealed. "Oh God, that's – that's good."

Both men laughed and I blushed but gave Theo a pleading look. "Please touch my clit again."

He shook his head. "No, we're going to make you come with just our dicks this time, love."

I gave him another pleading look, but he ignored it and cupped my breasts as Seth held my hips. They began a slow rhythm of one man pushing in while the other withdrew. It made my toes curl and I panted and moaned as they both fucked me.

"Feel good, little Libby?" Seth pressed on my lower back.

"Oh God, fuck, yes," I groaned. "I think – harder, please."

They moved faster and harder. My body was buzzing and twitching with pleasure and I wasn't sure if I should be happy or ashamed at how much pleasure I was deriving from a dick in my ass. Having Seth's cock in my ass made Theo's cock feel even thicker in my pussy. I squeezed around both of them experimentally and both men immediately did hard and out-of-control thrusts that made me squeal.

"Fuck! Don't squeeze like that, love," Theo begged below me as Seth panted harshly behind me.

I squeezed again and Seth slapped my ass hard. I squealed a second time and turned my head to pout at him.

"Behave," he said but there was a pleading tone to it that I'd never heard in his voice before.

I grinned and rocked my body a little. "What's wrong, Seth? Going to blow your load before you make me come?"

I received another glorious slap to the ass for my impertinence. I flushed with happiness and didn't object when both men pounded roughly into me. In fact, their roughness ratcheted up my excitement and I clutched at Theo's shoulders and made soft cries for more.

"She's so fucking tight," Theo suddenly moaned. "Seth, I can't…"

"Make her come first," Seth demanded but he sounded as frantic as Theo.

"Fuck, I'm trying," Theo panted.

To my surprise and delight, he reached beneath me and rubbed my clit in hard, rough circles. I cried out happily and rocked against his fingers. I was coming against his fingers in less than thirty seconds, my pussy and ass tightening around their cocks helplessly as I climaxed. Seth made a hoarse roar of need and then both men were pounding into me. I clung to Theo as a new and unrecognizable pleasure grew in my body.

"Oh, oh, God," I moaned. "What is that? What – oh fuck!" I was gasping and sobbing with need as both men moved harder and faster. I couldn't stop clenching around both dicks. The motion heightened my pleasure and I heard Theo groan loudly.

He arched beneath me. I barely registered that he was coming as Seth shoved his dick in and out of my ass. The only thing mattered was the orgasm that was agonizingly close. I squeezed my eyes shut and ground my pussy against Theo's dick as I reached for my climax. As Seth made a low roar and his hands dug into my hips, I shrieked with pleasure and came wildly. My body shook and I screamed again before collapsing on top of Theo.

I could feel Theo's heart beating like a drum beneath my cheek and I told myself to roll off of him before I crushed him. I made a half-hearted attempt to move before collapsing on him again. He rubbed my back and I was only vaguely aware of Seth moving away to the other side of the bed.

After a few minutes, Theo kissed the top of my head. "Okay?" He asked hoarsely.

"Yes," I mumbled. "Sorry, I'll move."

"You're fine," he said as his arms tightened around my waist. "Give it a minute."

I snuggled against him and it wasn't until his heart was beating a normal rhythm again that I eased off of him and lay weakly between the two men.

Seth had already removed his condom and as Theo removed his and tossed it in the trash, I stared at Seth. He was lying on his back, staring at the ceiling and I touched his chest tentatively.

"Seth? Was it okay for you?"

"Okay?" He rasped. "Libby, I nearly fucking passed out when I came."

I laughed and leaned against Theo when he spooned me and kissed the back of my shoulder. I squeezed his hand. "Theo? You, um, enjoyed it, right?"

"Do you really have to ask?" He said before patting my ass. "How are you? Are you sore? Do you want me to run you a hot bath?"

"I'm good," I said. I wasn't lying. My ass was a little sore, but the rest of my body felt incredible. I'd never had orgasms like that before. Hell, the last one was so good, I thought my head was going to blow off.

"It was amazing," I said suddenly. "Thank you so much. It was incredible."

"Good, we're glad," Seth said.

"I don't think I'll be able to ever have sex with just one man again," I said without thinking.

There was silence and I cleared my throat. "Uh, I didn't mean – that is, I know this is it for us. I wasn't trying to imply that the two of you had to keep fucking me."

"What if we want to keep fucking you?" Theo asked.

I stiffened and Theo sighed. "Sorry, I shouldn't have said that."

I licked my lips. "Did you want to keep having sex with me?"

"No," Seth said bluntly and my sudden hope deflated like a balloon.

"I should go," I whispered. I didn't regret what I had done with them but the knowledge that they didn't want to continue hurt way more than it should have considering we had agreed on a casual sex agreement.

Before I could squirm away from them, Theo's arm was tightening around my waist and Seth was cupping my face. "Sweetheart, we don't want to just have sex with you. We want to see if it could be something more."

I stared in shock at him. "You – you're kidding, right?"

"No," Theo said solemnly. "We're not."

"We're good together, Libs," Seth said. "You know we are. I know it's not a conventional relationship, but you said yourself that you couldn't sleep with only one man anymore. You don't have to. You have two men right here very willing to kiss, lick, suck and spank this delicious little body of yours. Let us."

"I'm your boss," I said in a low voice. "If the other partners found out…"

"We can find new jobs," Theo said.

"Are you – you can't quit your job because we enjoy fucking each other," I said. "Have you lost your minds?"

Seth laughed. "No, I don't think so. Neither of us thought we'd be at Martin, Clarke and Bones forever anyway."

"You can't quit your job for me," I whispered. "We

don't even know if this dating thing would work out."

"No, I suppose we don't," Seth said thoughtfully. "Tell you what, we'll give it a couple of months. We can keep it a secret from our coworkers if we're very careful. If we can convince you at the end of two months that this could be something more than just sex, we'll start looking for new jobs. What do you think?"

They waited patiently as I thought it over. What they were suggesting was madness, but it was incredibly tempting. I liked both of them, and getting to know them better was dangerously appealing.

"What if it doesn't work out between us?" I asked.

"We won't say anything to the other partners about what happened between us if it doesn't," Theo assured me.

I blinked at him. That thought hadn't even crossed my mind. I knew instinctively that they wouldn't use a failed relationship to blackmail me, just like they weren't using what we were doing now to blackmail me. They were good men – possibly the best men I'd ever met - and I would be a fool not to see where this would lead.

"I only meant that it will be incredibly awkward at work," I said.

"Possibly," Seth agreed. "But that's only if it didn't work out. Do you believe that it won't?"

I studied him before shaking my head. "No, I don't think that."

Theo nuzzled my neck. "So, is that a yes to dating us?"

"This is crazy as hell but yes. Let's see where this goes," I replied.

A huge smile crossed Seth's face and he pressed a kiss against my mouth as Theo kissed my neck.

"You won't regret it, sweetheart. We promise."